CHILD OF THE NIGHT

THOMAS LAIRD

Black Rose Writing | Texas

The author grants the final approval for this literary material.

First printing

This is a work of fiction. Names, characters, businesses, places, events, and incidents are either the products of the author's imagination or used in a fictitious manner. Any resemblance to actual persons, living or dead, or actual events is purely coincidental.

ISBN: 978-1-68433-900-6
PUBLISHED BY BLACK ROSE WRITING
www.blackrosewriting.com

Printed in the United States of America
Suggested Retail Price (SRP) $21.95

Child of the Night is printed in Calluna

*As a planet-friendly publisher, Black Rose Writing does its best to eliminate unnecessary waste to reduce paper usage and energy costs, while never compromising the reading experience. As a result, the final word count vs. page count may not meet common expectations.

For my wife, Marsha,
and for Kathy, Anne, Andy,
and my five grandchildren.
With love. Siempre.

CHILD OF THE NIGHT

PART ONE

CHAPTER ONE

Whitechapel, 23 April 1891

Their whistles screech like a hawk in predatory descent. They think they've trapped me, but I find the alley where I turn hard right and then I'm speeding toward the gap in the fence that I've used here five times before.

And I elude them again. I can still hear their damnable whistles, but the sound becomes progressively weak. They lose my scent in that fortunate backway where I manage to 'disappear' on them. There is an abandoned warehouse just beyond the gap, and I retreat there through a broken-out window. My bag of clothes rests inside, here in the darkness, and now I cannot hear my pursuers at all.

I am not safe, however. I know they've surrounded the entire area, here in Whitechapel. They have set a trap, you see, but I killed her, anyway, before they could spring it on me. Now they're desperate to ensnare me, but Scotland Yard's finest and all their coppers will fail once again.

They're after a Jew, a butcher, and they think I am he.

I change clothes from the bag I've left here. It wouldn't do to be seen on those fog-laden streets with the bloody garb I have on. I must have sliced a major artery with my first swipe, and the gore flew at me before I could avoid the spew. Now I'm covered in what appears to be black, here in the darkness of this burned-out warehouse.

I can't remain here, though. They'll check these ruins eventually.

I put on my clean attire, and I must say I make a very handsome copper. It took some doing to procure the uniform, but a few quid placed here and there will buy you most anything.

When I climb back out of the glassless window, I see the lights of their torches converging toward me. I flash my own light back at them.

"Nothing here!" I yell out to them.

The beams are lowered after they catch sight of my copper's trappings. They don't seem to mind that no one knows me. They're in far too big a hurry to ask for my credentials. The uniform appears genuine because it *is.*

They retreat in a hurry to check out another misted street in this toilet of a district. Whores, drunks, and filthy immigrants, most of them from eastern Europe. And most of them Jews.

I would have liked to have hailed them with my identity:

"Here I am, boys! It's Saucy Jack! Just the man you've been looking for, for all these three years!"

• • • • •

When I get home, I enter through the basement door. It's my office, but I sport no shingle. I do abortions, you see. They are illegal, of course. But my 'practice' is a bit doubtful since I never received a license. For all the world I seem to be a chemicals' salesman. During the days I peddle my wares to the local apothecaries. It's not nearly as lucrative as my 'private' practice with all the poor souls who want to be relieved of an 'inconvenience.' I do a lot of trade with very wealthy women who made unfortunate choices in becoming pregnant by their lovers instead of their spouses. Consequently, I charge them according to their ability to pay, and none of them argues the price because I am discrete and I am very good with a scalpel—as you might imagine.

But they have come damnably close to nabbing me, this time. I have been playing Russian roulette, but each time I've relieved Whitechapel of another miserable portion of flesh, I've added one more bullet into the cylinder. One's fortunes can only hold out so many times before the odds fail me.

So, I'm headed for America. I have no wife or children to hold me back, and I've saved enough to keep me happily provided for. I won't have to help out any more unfortunate brides who've strayed from their marital bonds. And I might even manage to get a license to practice in the United States. I've heard money can be quite accommodating there. You can buy anything, I've been told. We shall see.

But it would be nice to see a 'Doctor' in front of Francis S. Amjac. Wouldn't my degenerate mother and father, may they rest in eternal flames, be proud?

I'm headed for the heartland of America. New York is too over-ripe with population, so I'm on my way to Chicago. The thieves are thick, there, so I should fit right in. And should I wish to continue with the elimination of lowly creatures of the night, perhaps I might just continue my personal purge.

• • • • •

Michael Parisi, 2017

My father insists on taking me out when I receive my shield into Homicide. The promotion means a lot to me, of course, but the old man is especially proud that I rose to Homicide by the time I turned thirty-three. I worked as a patrolman when I got out of my last deployment in Afghanistan, and I rose to Robbery in just four years, and I got the new shield just a few years after Robbery. The ascension was pretty fast, from what my father tells me. I got to Homicide even faster than he did. It appears I broke his own personal record of rising to the most elite branch of Chicago Homicide.

He takes me to Sal's Pizza on the far southwest side, out on Kedzie Avenue. All the neighborhood joints he and his partner Doc Gibron used to patronize have closed or have moved southwest into the suburbs like Orland Park or Palos Hills. You can hear the sadness in his voice when he talks about Doc. I only knew him for a little while when I was a kid, but I know how close my dad was to him.

Jimmy Parisi, my patriarch, is still married to Natalie, who he calls the Redhead. She was in Homicide, too, and now they're both retired. But they won't do the retiree thing by moving to Florida or Arizona because they both love their house on the northwest side. It's the bungalow I lived in after I was born, and I left it only after I went to college and then into the Army.

My half-sisters, the twins, are now getting out of college after landing their master's. My biological sister, Mary, is an MD, now, and she has a child of her own, an eight-year-old boy named Michael—after me.

I went into the service after I received a degree from Chicago Loyola in Criminal Justice. My dad tried to talk me out of the military. He said he didn't want me to see the things he saw in Vietnam, but he didn't protest too much when I explained that I didn't feel it was right for anyone else to do the bleeding for me. He said he lost my mother Erin to cancer and he couldn't bear losing one of his own to some unnecessary war, but I felt I owed something to someone other than myself, and I enlisted.

I was accepted by the Army's Rangers, and I served three deployments in Afghanistan, as I said. I was wounded superficially three times, one for each tour, and now I can predict rain about as successfully as the TV weather people.

Sal's is a family-friendly joint, which is why my dad likes it as much as he does. And the pizza is outstanding. We sit in a booth by the back, as is my father's wont. He likes privacy, such as it is, with a back booth.

They have the standard red and white checkerboard table cloths with the equally usual poster of Marlon Brando as Don Corleone on the wall behind us.

I'm on lunch break, so we don't drink beer. I have a brew occasionally, but Jimmy Parisi was not a drinker, and neither am I.

"You beat me, kid," he smiles. "*Salud!*"

He raises his mug of Diet Coke and I clink my own with his.

The steaming sausage pie lies before us on the checkerboard tablecloth.

"I'm very proud of you, Michael."

I can only smile back as a response.

"I was proud of you when you went into the Army against my expressed wishes, but I couldn't say it, then. I don't know that I have any influence on you, Michael, but I rather like your independence. I always have admired that trait in you, so I guess I can tell you all that now."

He's aged, but not in a bad way, since I got back from the third tour. He's lost some hair on the top of his head in the back, and he's a bit more jowly than he was, back in the day. He works out by walking the neighborhood with Red. He never was a big eater, so his weight is good for a man of seventy. Red makes him eat sensible foods, he likes to tell me, but she won't deny him the occasional pizza or cheeseburger.

"You have any advice for me, Pa?"

"Yeah. Don't listen to advice. Use your instincts. I know they're good or you wouldn't be where you are...When's the last time I told you I love you, Michael?"

My eyes begin to sting in the corners. I redden a bit.

"Don't worry. I'm not going to get sentimental on your ass."

He hasn't slung an F-bomb once, so far today. There's another record for the elder Parisi. I try not to use street language when I can avoid it. It's just not me. Other people's scatology doesn't offend me. I was in the military long enough to hear every variation of profanity, so it rolls off me. Maybe my brothers in arms in the Rangers thought I was odd because I didn't talk the talk, but they didn't care about my use of English, particularly. As long as I backed them up, we were solid.

"What are you working on?" he asks.

I wouldn't answer that question from anyone else, but he's got the right.

"Domestics, mostly. Some guy shot his wife because she kicked the family cat. Stuff like that. Slam dunks. Nothing that would interest a super sleuth."

"It's all right. It's mostly what the job is. You have to speak for the dead. Nobody else will, most of the time."

He takes a bite out of his pizza. Then looks over at me with this laser-sharp hazel eyes. My eyes are the same color.

"You ever miss your mom?"

"Always. I think about her all the time."

My eyes begin to fill, suddenly.

"You're more like her than me," he smiles sadly.

"I like to think I've got a healthy dose of you in my DNA, Pa."

He smiles again.

"*Tu familia,*" he grins.

"Sta bono," I counter.

"You know more Italian than I do," he says.

I'm actually fluent in Italian, took three years in college and took to it like a native, my professor told me, long ago.

We finish the pie, and I have to get back to the job. He knows all about lunch breaks and the CPD. My father lectures at the Academy, from time to time.

"Red wants to see you. The twins ask about you all the time. Mary tells me you talk on the phone frequently. Stay in touch with the other half of the clan, too, Michael."

"I will, Pa. I'll call the twins tonight."

"Good. And try to make a Sunday dinner at the house sometime soon when your schedule allows. How's your love life, buster?"

"Kinda slow, at the moment."

"And that means?"

"Kinda slow, at the moment, Pa."

He laughs.

"Nothing new on that Kim lady?"

He knows we're apart. He doesn't know how fresh the pain is.

"None of my business, Michael. Sorry."

"My life is your business. All of it. But we're separate, right now. That's the whole story."

"Your break is over. No?"

I pick up the check before he can. He always tries to pay the tab. Not today.

I walk over to him and give him a full embrace.

"Go do your job," he tells me.

His eyes are filling, but nothing leaks out. Stoic is what my father is. Like a rock. Tougher than any salty Ranger I ever encountered.

We walk out of Sal's together.

We receive a call to a downtown hotel. It's not one of the luxury venues in the city. Mostly it's used by hookers and the homeless. It's on the periphery of the Loop.

My partner is Lavon Martin. He's been in Homicide for five years, and he's considered a comer to rise to the top in our division. Guys are saying Lavon is destined to become Chief of Police in the not too distant future. He's got his eyes on Lieutenant, and he'll probably get there very soon. Right now, he's a sergeant on his way up. His color isn't a determent on the CPD any longer. There are several black men and women in the upper echelons, these days. And Hispanics are on the rise within the force, as well. It's not my old man's Buick here, lately. I rather like the new CPD. My father had his own issues with the force, back in his day.

The body is on the eleventh floor. The hotel is so old that they don't have a thirteenth floor—it used to be bad luck.

She's on the mattress face down. The blood has almost covered the surface beneath her.

She's a Latina, it appears when we turn her over.

When she's on her back we see that she's cut wide open. On closer inspection we see that there are missing pieces of her. Her middle cavity is torn wide open, like an autopsy.

Her ears have been severed and her tongue has been stuffed into her vagina. The tip has been left protruding at the vaginal lips. Lavon doesn't react, visibly.

"Leave her be until the ME arrives," the Sergeant says.

I try to figure the extent of the carnage, but it'll take an MD to determine all that. This young woman—she can't be much older than mid-twenties—has been attacked with severe prejudice, as the legal lingo goes. More precisely, she's been mutilated and tortured. There are remnants of duct tape on the four bedposts. He turned her over on her face when he was finished with her. Her mouth has been duct-taped shut. The tape still remains on her lips.

"There was a similar murder. Manny Conway and his partner took one like this a week ago. He told me about it two days ago."

"You think it might be the same guy?" I ask.

He smiles.

"I thought perhaps it could be a two-timer...This your first possible serial number, Michael?" he smiles broadly.

"You know my history, Sergeant."

"I do. Yes. Welcome to the Big Boy Division, Michael."

• • • • •

We conference with Manny Conway and his partner Maria Elizondo. It indeed appears there's a possibility that I caught a serial killing case in my rookie season.

I call my father and tell him the particulars.

"One murder is bad enough. But series guys are a different breed."

I tell him the specifics of this known hooker's demise.

"I remember a guy like this one from a long time back. Sounds like the same type. He almost killed Red."

"I remember your telling me. Some guy they called The Farmer, no?"

"Indeed. But that badman is dead. I saw him. Red and I had to take him out. Guy was evil, Michael."

"This one seems cut from the same cloth."

"Yeah. He sounds like you might want to take him out of play as soon as possible."

CHAPTER TWO

Sean Amjac, Chicago, 2017

The skill of these hands has made me a fortune. A nip and a tuck and we pull back the flesh around the back of the skull and I wipe off ten, may be fifteen, years. All the celebrities in this city are patients of mine. Once they pass thirty, they're all looking for a little work done on them. Some of it is belly fat or glop around the thighs. I try to tell them dieting is easier, along with exercise, but they all want instant gratification.

And what about instant gratification for me?

All those years I struggled with who I am. The pull of genetics was waging war inside me. I know my history, you see. It has been passed down for generations. My father Delbert was an oral surgeon, and he was able to resist temptation. He told me the story about where we came from, about our notorious great grandfather, Francis Amjac.

Francis was a displaced Irishman who landed in London and who was reminded of his Gaelic heritage every day of his life by the Brits around him. They reminded him that the Irish were the UK's version of the great unwashed, of an untouchable class, almost like the caste system in India. Scum, we were, my father explained to me. We were always strangers in a strange land, much like the Jews. Our Holocaust was the Potato Famine.

The old boy told me that Francis was an angry young man, and his anger was vented upon a class of women he considered beneath the Irish poor. Whores. He let his anger seethe upon them, destroying their bodies until they became almost unrecognizable lumps of ravaged flesh.

It was never about sex with Jack the Ripper, my distant progenitor. It was of course about power. It wasn't just from his anger, of course. It was from some seed of evil that coursed through his DNA. It is something passed down inside the semen.

Francis Amjac married shortly after he arrived in Chicago. He never murdered anyone after he arrived. He understood he was out of the luck that could sustain a new series of slayings here in Chicago. And with the large chunk of population who came here from the Emerald Isle, he felt less ostracized in the Heartland. This was a new country in which everyone was welcome—or so the legend went.

In any case, Francis gave up the knife and his human butchery. He was able to secure a physician's license and served at what became Cook County Hospital on the west side of this toddlin' town. He was well respected as an MD until the day he died. He'd turned the page from the beast he was back in Whitechapel.

My grandfather I never knew. He died when my father, Delbert, was a young boy. I know virtually nothing about him.

My father warned me that I was prone to whatever was inside of us through our inheritance. I never thought I would be called to resume Francis's trade. But it has begun, and I have no desire to stop, now.

The count is just two. I've only begun my true career.

When I cut those two I felt a surge of electricity that I have never felt in my role as a surgeon. When I look into their eyes before I begin, I've been tipped over into the abyss, and the free fall is orgasmic, much better than coitus. It makes me tremble with the godlike energy of creation. Except that it's the power of death instead of the power of life.

It's better than any drug I've ever ingested or shot into my veins—and I've tried them all. I've cheated addiction with my new fix, and the effect is beyond expression. It's more than a high. It's a soaring. I become a predatory bird in full swoop upon its prey.

I'm not godlike.

I'm God Himself.

• • • • •

Michael Parisi

Lavon and I have a sitdown with Manny and Maria Elizondo. They caught the other case of the prostitute murder. It's the same MO. The carnage is equally disgusting. The killer didn't just kill this one; he destroyed her, obliterated her, Manny tells us. What those two detectives encountered was a mauling. This guy tore her up as if it were something very personal.

We meet them at the cafeteria in Headquarters downtown by the Lake. My cubicle is up on the eighth floor. I couldn't get my father's old office. Some lieutenant grabbed that when my dad retired. But I got an office with a view of Lake Michigan. The old man never tired of telling me how he loved that sight, regardless of the season.

The café is mostly deserted. We're doing midnights shift, so everyone is out on a call or they're cooping in their cubicles, waiting for the sun to rise over that Lake in the east.

Maria is very attractive. Seems to have a lot of Indian, mestizo, in her. Her eyes are almond brown, and her lips are a sensuous thick. They're not red because she doesn't wear makeup. She doesn't need it. I see that she's not wearing a ring. I've seen her around from time to time, and she gives me warm smiles each time I encounter her in this building. I ought to say something to her, but I've been told not to enter into department romances. But my father married a fellow detective, and Kim isn't coming back, I don't think.

Manny is a swarthy lifer cop who's two years away from retirement. He's known as a workman-like detective who perseveres until he lands the cuffs on them. He's not known as a genius in the trade, but he simply outlasts them until he hears the jail door clink in front of them. Dogged, I guess you'd say. He could be a Greek or an Italian or a Mexican. He fits a lot of categories.

"This is one very evil customer," he tells us.

He's sitting with Maria on one side of the booth. Lavon and I are on the other.

You can hear the clinking of his spoon as he mixes the sugar in his black coffee. The café is like a tomb, about now.

"It's gonna be very low profile, even though the details are for the tabloids," he explains.

Maria shoots a stare my way. I lock onto her, and she smiles. I turn my eyes toward Manny so I'll appear professional, but there's something stirred up inside me.

I take a hit on my Diet Coke, and I glance back at her again. She's still peering over at me.

"We won't be wasting much time on Carrie Tyler," he pronounces. "It was probably her pimp or a very disappointed john. Who the hell knows?" Manny goes on.

He looks like the product of too many years seeking out the causes of unnatural death. Too many corpses. I think of my father. When did his fuse burn down to a stub? This job is a very harsh mistress, all the Homicides like to tell you. I wonder how long my own string will be.

"I think it's a series," I say.

They all peer over at the young Turk.

"You think?" Lavon smiles.

"Yeah. I do. The details tell the tale. He cuts them open like fish. The signature was the tongue in the lower mommy part."

"Yeah, there is that," Manny concedes.

"That's a big detail," Maria adds.

She sounds all Homicide, now. No more teasing glances my way.

"You think he's a series guy, too?" Manny asks his partner.

"Three'll be the charm," she retorts.

Then she hits me with her almond eyes again. There's only a slight grin.

"It'll complicate things if he goes for round three," Manny admits. "I'm literally too old for this crap. Maybe I should ask for the desk. I only got twenty-three months left to go. Then I'm heading for the desert. I got a down payment on a nice condo with a pool and the all the accessories."

"You want to hand us your case, Manny?" Lavon asks.

"I think I do. Maria here will wind up with a younger partner soon enough, and then she can take on crap like this with a fresh set of eyes...I'll ask the captain if he'll transfer this one to you guys."

"It's fine with us. Right, Michael?"

"Sure," I nod.

Manny finishes his cup of coffee. Lavon wasn't partaking of any libation, and neither was Maria. I put down the rest of my drink in a long pull.

Then we get up and head out of the cafeteria. Maria lags behind, and so do I. Lavon tells me he has some paperwork, and then he and Manny head for the elevators.

"So. Are you single?" Maria suddenly asks.

"Yeah. You?"

She smiles. Then she hands me her business card. It's got another number printed on the face.

"Why don't you dial me up sometime soon?" she grins.

"I'll do that," I tell her.

She walks off toward the elevators and leaves me standing in place, staring at her card.

The captain hands us Manny and Maria's case.

I'm fairly convinced it's a serial killing. I think Lavon's thinking that way, too.

A week later the news comes down that Lavon has been promoted to lieutenant and that Manny will be riding a desk, at Manny's request.

I'm on my own until Maria Elizondo gets assigned as my partner. She's got three years' experience, so I'm guessing she's my new mentor. There were no more seasoned vets available, she explains to me when she tells me the news.

"We're chained together," she smiles as she stands in the doorway of my cubicle.

"That mean I shouldn't call?" I ask.

"I can be discrete. How about you?"

"I think I can give it a serious effort."

She glows at me again and then heads for her own office down the hall.

• • • • •

The third call happens one week later. It's at a similar kind of hotel-hovel on the edge of the Loop. It's perhaps a step or two below the venues of the first two murders. The building is greatly dilapidated—it looks ready for the wrecker's ball.

There's a uniform standing, or should I say crouching, outside the door of the crime scene.

"That bad?" I ask him.

He coughs and nods and heads for the nearest john.

"A nice prequel to lunch," Maria says.

I called her last night, and we're hooked up for Saturday since we're both off this weekend.

We walk into a blood splattered scene. It's literally on all four walls, on the floor, everywhere. I see Maria has turned a little pale. White shows on her because she's so deliciously brown.

He's rigged the body to hang from the light fixture in the middle of the single room. The bed is a fold-out, but it hasn't been taken down. For the third time it appears that sex was not part of the equation.

She's slit open like a slaughtered steer. The flaps of skin hang to either side of her torso. I'm less affected by this scene than my partner is because I've been on battlefields where the snapshots were even worse. Mines can do this to a human being. Grenades, too. I've seen men cut open after death for the sport of it, just to terrorize those who find the remains. Psy Ops, the Army calls it. They mess with your head with what they leave behind for you to see.

"*What* does this?" Maria queries. "It can't walk on two legs."

"It can and it does."

"You were in the military?" she asks.

It's her opportunity to look away.

"Yes."

"I was, too. I've seen bad, but not like…not like this."

"He's trying to outdo himself every time. I'd say he's progressing."

"This doesn't disturb you, Michael?" she asks.

There's a tinge of anger in her tone.

"You can't take it personally. That's the lie you tell yourself every time you encounter savagery. You tell yourself no one's capable of being that bad, and then this tells you the truth. A very inconvenient truth."

She looks as if she's about to stagger. I grab hold of her arm and hold her up. I walk her out into the hall.

"Stay out here as long as you need to. I'll write down what we need. The ME will fill in the blanks."

She looks at me.

"What'd your war do to you, Michael?"

I look at her lovely eyes.

"The same thing it does to most everybody who sees what it is. It's no different in civilian life, except the numbers are much smaller…You want me to stay with you a while?"

She nods.

I hold her by the shoulders.

"I'm not as numb or as cold as you think I am. Do you believe me?"

She looks up at me. She straightens up.

"Prove it," she demands.

"Give me the chance."

• • • • •

I'm not a fan of crime novels or even of true crime books. But I've read my share since my profession demands it. I prefer literary fiction, and my tastes run from Joyce to de Balzac to Melville and Twain and Fitzgerald and Hemingway and Tolstoy and Dostoyevsky…And a much longer list. I like the poetry of Billy Collins and Walt Whitman and Emily Dickinson, as well. I guess you could say it's an eclectic list, something oddly inappropriate for a newly-badged Homicide detective.

Kim thought I was somewhat odd, too. Maybe that's why she walked off. I don't know.

I never had a long-term relationship before her. There was college and then there was the military hard upon. I never really had the time, I suppose.

I missed being with someone in a monogamous way. I don't think I want to die without a wife and family. My dad doesn't keep at me about it, but I know he'd like me to be settled. He always enjoyed having a significant other.

The evening with Maria still looms out there—it's Friday, today. I'm a little anxious about it, but I don't feel as if the date is doomed, with her.

As I say, I'm not a fan of crime literature, but I have read a bit on the subject of serial killers, and naturally one name bursts to the top when you think series killers.

Jack the Ripper.

But the notion is silly. Whoever he was is likely long dead. All the evidence points to that conclusion. And this is Chicago, a good chunk of territory distant from London and the murders from 1888 to 1891.

The Ripper seemed to stop or disappear or perhaps to die after '91. There's no real evidence to suggest otherwise.

But the thought enters my head like an earwig in the ear. It's gnawing at me in spite of its remoteness, its unlikeliness.

Jack the Ripper left London when his home turf became too dangerous for him, too hot. He boarded a ship and came to America. He had offspring and that offspring procreated again. Generations passed.

And Jack is here. In Chicago. Maybe with a different name.

Now.

CHAPTER THREE

Sean Amjac

If I made just the slightest false move, I could cut her throat. But I don't make mistakes. Especially not with a nurse and an anesthesiologist in the room with me.

This one's an anchor on the ABC TV affiliate in Chicago. She doesn't need the tuck, naturally, but I'm never one to turn down a very fat fee. She's barely forty, blonde, great, pendulous breasts, and a very dynamic remainder of a frame to go along with the boobs that she'll likely ask me to do a reduction on when they begin to head south to her tummy.

Right now, she's choice meat. But she's not the kind of subject for me to have a lot of fun with. That kind of entertainment is reserved for the lowly sluts that I meet on the internet where most of the hooker trade resides, currently. The whores don't walk the streets as they did in Whitechapel for my illustrious and saucy forbear. Now they trod the ether, the internet. It's not difficult to locate them. They're fairly straightforward in their 'ads'. They are also the discount portion of the menu. I never do business with the downtown variation of prostitute. They prefer servicing their clients in far more swank establishments, in and around the Gold Coast.

I look for the lowliest of the low. Those creatures who will not be missed by any community. They are the rejected, the outcast of the tribe. Easy pickings, in other words.

There has been no mention of my three subjects, to date, in any of the newspapers or other electronic media. It's as if they never existed at all. I can't think of them in terms of being individuals, human beings. They are simply targets for my own gratification. And I'm doing a public service by removing them. They are, after all, carriers of disease. None of them are regulated by any health agency. They carry AIDS and STDs and a host of other maladies. Some of them are likely thieves, as well, relieving their johns of their wallets. Perhaps some are homicidal, too. They might carry knives and razors in order to get even with the humiliation of their existences.

So, I suppose I'm civic minded, in a very indirect way.

You may say that I'm bounding right past the commandment "Thou Shalt Not Kill". We homo sapiens are still the only species on the planet that couples face-to-face and who kills their own kind—not out of self-defense but for *pleasure.*

Shortly I will have bestowed a very tight, seamless visage to this TV celebrity. Her friends won't even have noticed where her slightly slack facial flesh has disappeared to. I'm that good. Every time, that good. And unlike most surgeons in my trade, I have never been sued for malpractice.

That's how good I am.

• • • • •

Michael Parisi

I take Maria to Travani's on the northwest side. She said she enjoys Italian food. She told me her heritage is Mexican, but she's third generation in this country. Maria speaks fluent Spanish. Her parents insisted on handing it down to her, and it's served her well to be bilingual in this city. There is a very large chunk of the population who *hablas* only *Espanol.* I speak fluent Italian and passable English, and Maria says she wants me to teach her Italian. I don't know that I'm a capable teacher, but she's asked me to give it a shot.

"Can't have enough languages. Chicago is a very eclectic town," she says from across our secluded booth in the back of Travani's.

The food is authentic here, and they refuse to do pizza because they say pizza is an American dish. The chicken parmigiana is excellent, and we both ordered it. I've been here before, so she takes my word. The interior is standard. The checkerboard tablecloths are mandatory. But there are no posters of Brando or any other mob movies. The pictures on the walls depict Venice and Rome, and they appear more expensive than the starving artists' stuff you see at lesser joints.

"You ever read any stuff on the Whitechapel murders?" I ask her.

Her eyes widen with the departure of my question.

"You mean Jack the Ripper?"

"Yes," I tell her.

She snorts and laughs loudly.

I have to smile at her response.

"You can't be serious," she says.

"Serious about what?"

"That these three cases have anything to do with...You can't be serious."

I don't reply.

"Michael. The guy's been dead for a hundred years or more. You're joking."

"I'm just sailing it past you. What if. You know that game."

She takes a tug at her red wine.

"You're teasing me," she grins.

"What if he migrated here? They never caught him. What if he married or had children in the United States? It's just a scenario, Maria, but what if he handed down a proclivity to tear women up, if he handed it down the generations?"

"You really are trying to mess with me."

Her eyes are her absolute best features. The windows to her soul, and I like what I see.

"Dinner talk. That's all. I've got an over-active imagination."

"Boy, do you!" she laughs.

"He might just be a copycat, a fanboy. You never know."

"That sounds a lot more plausible, Michael."

The waitress brings our meals to the table. She takes the bread basket for a refill. The bread is genuine. It has a crunchy crust, like my grandmother's, my dad's mom, Eleanor's.

"You like to push buttons?" she asks.

"If you mean do I enjoy messing with minds, not really. I do like to stimulate the conversation when I can. I want to impress you. Guess I'm not doing too well, huh?"

She smiles warmly. That's when I'm convinced there's got to be more than this one encounter.

"You're doing fine."

"Can I call you tomorrow?"

She laughs again. Even her laughter rings true.

"We're working together. Remember?"

"I mean call you socially."

"I can see it. Yes."

We turn to our dinners and we eat in silence.

When the supper is over, we finish off the remainder of the Merlot.

"You weren't really kidding about that Ripper thing, were you," she says.

She reaches across the table and takes hold of my hand.

"I don't know. I just threw it out there."

"I don't think so," she smiles seductively. "I think you think there might just be the most distant possibility."

"I read too much fiction. Makes me imagine all kinds of crazy plots."

"I read journalism. I don't like fiction. I like facts. They're concrete things, facts."

"I was just trying to dazzle you with my romantic mind," I tell her.

"Speaking of romance," she tells me.

"What'd you have in mind?"

• • • • •

I truly never thought this evening would end up in her bed, but there it is. I look at Maria and cannot believe my good fortune. We came back to her apartment by the Lake on the north side, and as soon as the door was shut behind us, we began kissing. I could feel it was intense or heated, but that would be understating the case. Our clothing was discarded, but I don't remember how it happened.

And then we were on her cool cotton sheets together, fully engaged, and it went on in an achingly long and finally explosive way.

We were breathless when it ended, and the sheets were damp even though her air conditioning was functional and even though it was an oppressively hot July night outdoors.

She turned to me and draped her right arm over my shoulder.

"How much recovery time do you need?" she giggled.

I showed her I was resilient if nothing else.

• • • • •

We lay together until very late, talking. But she was hooked on my Ripper scenario.

"How many generations later would this current killer be, if your theory has any cred?"

I roll over and kiss her and start things up again. She doesn't rebuff my attempt, and it's a while later that our collective breaths have returned to normal.

"We can't keep this up," she says.

"No. We have to sleep sometime," I agree.

"It wouldn't be healthy if we kept this up."

Then she climbs atop me and begins again.

• • • • •

Sunday morning arrives when I open my eyes and see that it's after nine.

Maria is not in bed with me. I rise and head to her bathroom, and I see the fog on the window of her shower door. Then it opens and I am summoned within.

• • • • •

We eat breakfast at her table, and afterward we walk out by the beach at Lake Michigan. It's only a few blocks from her apartment building. She holds my hand all the way until we reach the sand. I didn't bring a change of clothes, but we're not going to be swimming today anyway.

It's already sweltering, probably in the lower eighties even though it's only just before ten.

We sit on a park bench that overlooks the sand and the cobalt blue water. The sky is cloudless, and it's tinged with a white mist that has not yet burned off.

"We'll have to be discrete, like I said," she says as she looks directly ahead at the water.

"I don't want to be discrete. I want to be blatant."

She squeezes my hand tightly.

"The intelligent thing to do would be for me to get a new partner."

"I want to be with you all day. All night…I'm going to frighten you off."

"God help me. I feel the same way."

We get off the bench and walk south toward the city's skyline. I can see what used to be the Sears Tower, now owned by some Brit outfit, I think. Lake Shore drive is off to our right, to the west.

I love this city. It's brutal and unforgiving, but that's not all it is. When I returned home from my three tours, I wanted to *swallow* the whole thing. Take it all in. Even the ugliness of the west side and the south side and some other gray and hostile 'hoods the city contains. The Loop and the Gold Coast are easily palatable, but I love the entirety of this sprawling metropolis, this brawny, terrifying burg. You can't call Chicago charming, but it has some kind of magnificent brute-like appeal.

"Let me know when I should propose," I say as I glance at her.

She slugs me playfully on my arm.

"Don't say that unless you mean it. Don't joke about stuff like that, Michael. I'm more vulnerable than you suppose."

"I'm vulnerable, too."

"What's that mean?" she asks.

"I was involved in something serious before I left on the third tour. It didn't work out very well."

"I was kicked in the heart, too, back in the day."

I touch her cheek and she leans into my hand. I can feel her body heat.

"I don't want to go there again, and neither do you," I tell her.

She laughs suddenly.

"Christ, we talk like two old married people remembering their high school breakups."

"I didn't get it in high school. Just the once."

"Do you feel like the accelerator's stuck to the floor, here, Michael?"

"I'll calm down. I promise."

"That's funny. I don't want you to."

She grips my hand tightly, once more.

• • • • •

At work it's all I can do to keep my hands off her.

When we're out in traffic, on the way to interview the employees of the three hotels where the murders took place, and when we're halted at a red light, she slides over to me in the driver's seat and she kisses me hard and intensely, and a guy behind us, we in our unmarked ride, honks at us when we miss the green light.

"We have to behave," she says in a mock stern voice.

Nobody remembers anything. We hear the same chorus from each choir at each scummy hotel. When I pull out a stock threat that my dad taught me, they loosen up a little.

"I can have the Health Department out here today if you don't get a lot more cooperative in about ten seconds," I tell the day manager at our third stop.

"Well...Come to think of it, I do remember a guy coming in with the woman you described. He was tall, maybe six-two. He might have had dark blond hair. Maybe short of 180 pounds or so."

"Can you describe him to a sketch artist?" Maria asks the late-twenties, balding man behind the front desk.

"I think I might be able to," he replies.

This is the location where we found Kirsten Maniates hanging from the light fixture.

"That would be very cooperative of you," I tell him.

Their air conditioning is ineffective. It's balmy and humid in here. There's an overhead fan that creaks and rotates too slowly to help alleviate the bayou effect.

"You're being very cooperative lately," I smile at the young man whose appearance probably belies his true age.

"I always like to help out the police when I can," he smirks.

We walk out to the unmarked ride. I turn the air on full blast when we get in.

"I don't think he bathes very regularly," Maria chirps.

"I think the odor is part of the establishment. Years of crud'll do that."

We're off afternoon shift by the time we return to Headquarters. Maria sets up the artist for the chrome-domed hotel manager for tomorrow afternoon. She calls the hotel and tells him what time we'll be there, and she gets no argument from him.

• • • • •

We've been together a week. I'm living at her place. It's just easier. I've moved my clothes and my sparse belongings to her apartment, and it seems a natural move that we're both comfortable with. I'll continue to keep my studio on Clark Street until we see if this is going to work out. As far as I'm concerned, it is working out, but I've been down that road with Kim, and I don't want to ask Maria for any commitment until we see we're a fit for one another.

"I want a future for us, Michael. And I'm frightened that I'll frighten you by saying it, but there it is. We're not kids, anymore. We're in our thirties...Do you want kids, some day?"

"Yeah. I do."

"I do, too. It's something to think about. I know it's been a rush. What is it? Eight or nine days of living together? But I feel it right where the truth lives in me. You know what I mean?"

"I'm thinking the same thing. And I'm not afraid at all. How about you?"

CHAPTER FOUR

We use the artist's rendering and send it through the database. And surprising to neither of us, nothing pops. No criminal profile matches up.

Until we send it through Interpol. The results match a likeness to a very unexpected face. The Brits at Scotland Yard have a close match to the sketch. The problem is that the drawing it resembles is that of a suspect in the Jack the Ripper files back from 1891. The other issue is that it's not an exact likeness. The Brits claim our sketch has only an 80% chance of matching the rendering of a man named Francis Amjac.

Amjac disappeared in that same year, so Scotland Yard was never able to apprehend him for questioning. He was considered likely dead. There were no remains to be found, either.

I immediately go to the phone book—high tech, I know—but there are no listings for that name. So my half-baked theory about Jack's ancestors popping up in Chicago seem to wither on a very tender-to-begin-with vine. There's not a single Amjac listed in any of the lists online, on Google or any other search engine I employ.

But the fact that there's an 80% likelihood of a match bites into me like a tick. I can't get it off me, no matter how much the evidence suggests the hunch was meritless.

Maria says she's a bit spooked by the near match, though.

"I don't like that percentage," she tells me.

We're in our unmarked car on the way to interviewing some associates of the three women who were murdered. Carrie Tyler's partners are first. The neighborhood is one of the worst on the west side. It's mostly an industrial 'hood, but there are neighborhoods adjunct to the sprawling factories. It's a mix of black and Hispanic. Mostly it's gangland. We've been here on homicide calls frequently.

Felicia Hernandez is a known associate of Carrie Tyler's, according to the information we received from Vice. There's a crew of about a half-dozen prostitutes who call this badlands home. They work with the help of the internet. No one walks these streets alone, especially at night, unless you're ganged-up.

We pull up to the three-flat where Felicia was last known to live. Maria may be very useful on this call because Carrie Tyler didn't use her real name. Her real moniker was Helena Ortez. Vice tells us they frequently employ Anglo surnames in order to widen their markets.

The bell out front says Felicia resides in the middle apartment. I ring the bell and we wait. A few minutes pass and there's no reply. Then I step back from the entrance and see the curtains flapping on the second floor living room.

"Let's try the back," I tell Maria.

There are dilapidated wooden stairs leading up to three back doors.

"You really want to try our luck on these things?" she says.

We head up the stairs, and I expect to feel a sway, but there's no motion from side to side.

When we arrive at the second floor, I bang on the broken aluminum door. The screen is missing.

The door bursts open, inward.

She's holding a ball bat.

"Felicia?"

I show her the badge and so does my partner.

"Yeah?" she says with an obvious tone of suspicion.

"You knew Helena Ortez?"

"Never heard the name."

"Carrie Tyler, then," Maria says.

"Same answer. Go away. I got a dog in here."

She's a deep brown, like Maria. Her eyes match her facial color.

"You want Vice to come over and have a talk with you, *chica?*" Maria threatens.

She eyes us again.

"Come on in, then."

The place is shabby but clean. This is what west side poverty looks like. The furniture is worn and there are holes in her drapes. I can see the pinholes of light darting inside her living room, if that's what this space is.

She tells us to sit on a sad looking couch by the window.

"Where's the dog?" I ask her.

We're still standing.

"Ain't got one. Sorry."

She sits on a recliner across from us. She's a little heavy-set, maybe 170 pounds, I guess. Her face is thin, however, and the head doesn't match the body. She's big-breasted and wide at the hips, and her blue jeans are way too tight. The top is a tee shirt, but she doesn't seem to be wearing a bra.

"We're not here to give you a problem. We're here about Carrie's murder," Maria tells her.

Felicia seems shocked when she hears 'murder.'

"What murder?" she asks.

"Carrie—Helena—was killed a week ago. You didn't know?" I ask her.

Her eyes begin to well up.

"I been out of town. Went to St. Louis on a...party. Helena's dead?"

"We need to know if she said anything about a hookup in the Loop about a week ago. Were you in town, back then?" Maria asks.

"Yeah. I was only gone a couple days, but I ain't heard that she was..."

"The newspapers haven't given out the information yet," I tell her. "We asked them not to. There've been three killings. We think they might be related."

She looks at me incredulously.

"Why'd anyone want to kill her? She never hurt anybody."

"Do you know anything about that hookup? It would've been on a week ago Friday."

"She never said...Wait. She did say something about a date with some rich prick. I remember. She was all fired up. Said he was some kind of bigshot professional. Lawyer. Doctor. Something...But that's all I remember. Like I said, I was out of town, so she never got back to me.

"Why'd anyone want to kill Helena? She was sweet. She never hurt nobody."

• • • • •

We try friends or co-workers of Teresa Problano and Kirsten Maniates, but we come up empty. They didn't know anything or they weren't going to tell us anything, but I figured the former was the truth.

I buy Maria lunch at the White Castle on 95th and Cicero, here in Oak Lawn. It was a favorite haunt of my father's when he was working with Doc Gibron. It's amazing my dad never had stomach problems.

But we both look at the Castle as a guilty pleasure. I don't come often, but I feel the need, about now. I'm not a coffee drinker. Like the old man I'm addicted to Diet Coke. I drink a lot of water, too, but the belly fat hasn't started to form on me yet. Running two miles every morning helps keep the glop off. And I never was a big eater. The Rangers preferred lean to bulky. That was another reason I never allowed myself to bulge.

"We don't have much. Professional guy, says Felicia. What kind of west side hooker lands that kind of client?" I ask Maria.

She sits across me in our booth. White Castle is rocking. The place is jammed. It's the lunch hour, so it would be.

"The kind of slick who doesn't want to run into anyone he knows in the daylight. This guy is a night flyer, Michael."

"Meaning?"

"That's what they call vampire bats in Mexico. Night flyers."

"We already tried to make a ghost of him. Now he's the undead. Like Lugosi in *Dracula*...'Listen to the children of the night.'"

I try to do my best Lugosi, and she laughs. I love the notion that I make her laugh. I don't think I ever made Kim giggle very often, and it might be the reason she left me. Women like to laugh. It's the only thing I know about them.

"It still makes my skin creep to recall that sketch and the near match from UK. I can't shake it, Michael."

"You'd better. It's probably just a coincidence. Or else both of us are just projecting that image so it'll match. The fact is that we don't have anything that can help find him. Three times he's left a clean crime scene. No prints, no body fluids. He's not having sex with them. He's not touching them with his bare hands, not licking them or biting them."

"It's lunch, Michael. Please. A little help, okay?" she smiles.

I reach across and take her hand.

"Will I scare you if I tell you I love you?"

"Not anymore than it'll scare you when I say the same thing."

"I don't remember you saying it," I reply.

"I do love you. You've known it from night one."

We begin to do damage on our cheese sliders, onion rings, and Diet Cokes. I think I've got her hooked on the pop, lately. She used to drink iced tea every time we went out to eat.

She wipes her lovely, non-cosmetic lips with her napkin. She eats very daintily, very lady-like. It makes me want to jump over the table and do something unhinged, here at the crowded White Castle. Naturally, I refrain from my base impulse.

"They're the hardest to catch. Everybody in the copper trade knows that," she grins at me.

There's some kind of light that darts out of those eyes at me. She has a way to lock in on me, and the next thing I know I cannot look elsewhere but right at Maria.

"Ted Bundy. The cannibal in Milwaukee. Yeah, I know. And all the others who never got caught. Great way to start off my rookie season."

"They gave us this case on purpose."

"I suppose," I tell her.

"No, I mean it. They gave it to us because nobody wants a non-slam dunk. None of the vets wants a red-letter case lingering on their white boards. They can all smell 'cold case', Michael."

"They can't all be that way. There are good guys in Homicide."

"Legends like your dad are history. The bulldogs have given way to more pragmatic detectives, my love," she grins.

"Pragmatic?"

"You gotta know when to fold them...You know the song."

"Maybe things have changed."

"You're old school, Michael. You're my beloved throwback. It's in your genetic makeup and you can't help yourself. The world, however, keeps evolving."

"Into what?"

"A great question," she says.

Then she leans across the booth and lays one on me.

• • • • •

I cut the grass for my father on Sundays when I'm off shift. It's not much of a yard, but I like to keep my hand in on the house, the home where I grew up.

We played catch in front, on the sidewalk. He encouraged me to play baseball, and I did until I found out that I couldn't hit the curve. But I played in high school at St. Rita, over on 63rd Street, and we were Catholic League champs, back in the day. I played two years at Loyola, in college, but I was hurt my junior year and that was the end of my career in sports.

He came to every game he could, and so did my mother Erin, until she became ill with cancer. And then she died, and Jimmy Parisi became a single parent for me and Mary.

But then he found Natalie, and the old man was restored to life. My father took Erin's death very hard. You couldn't necessarily see it in his everyday presence, but he was simply sadder after she left. Then he got it back, when Natalie showed up.

"You know I can do this myself," he tells me as I pass him in his chair on the patio in the backyard.

I'm pushing the power mower over the salad of weeds. It takes maybe forty minutes to do the front and the back. When I make my final pass, I turn off the mower and walk over to him on the concrete. There's an umbrella that gives sufficient shade to the chairs and the metal table.

I sit down and he hands me a can of pop. It's ice to the touch, and I pop it open and guzzle it down.

He pops open another for me after removing it from the ice chest at our feet.

"How's it going with the triple homicide?" he asks.

I bring him up to date.

"That bad?" he asks.

"That bad."

Then I launch into my barely baked theory about the ancestor of the infamous killer from Whitechapel.

"It is a little out there."

He's being kind. I can always tell when he's softening the blow.

"The pictures did look a little similar," I remind him.

"A stretch, Michael. A real, true stretch."

"Just a passing fancy," I smile.

Then he begins to look off into the yard as if he's trying to locate something or someone.

"It was nuts. Just nuts," I laugh.

"Did you believe it in your gut?" he asks suddenly.

I try to remember what I felt when the notion hit me the first time.

"Maybe for a minute."

"You remember what I taught you back when you were a little leaguer?"

"You mean not to over-think?" I ask.

He nods.

"Don't disrespect the gut. It's part of the tool kit, Michael. Don't disrespect the gut."

"But the facts are against it, Pa."

"Seems that way, doesn't it. Stranger things have happened, kid. Believe me. There's always the unlikely element. Keeps it from becoming pedestrian, mundane. Maybe that's why I hung around as long as I did. The unexpected is the world's most deadly hook, sonny. Just when you think a thing's impossible, suddenly it's a fact."

We take a long swig at our Diet Cokes.

"How's your love life, buster?"

"Much improved," I tell him.

"Really? When did all this happen?"

I tell him the tale of Maria Elizondo.

"Workplace romance. Where'd I hear that one before?"

"Where is Natalie, by the way?"

"Out buying us some New York strip steaks. She's in love with this new, trendy butcher shop just opened. It's only a half mile away from the house. She ought to be back soon. Then we'll light the grill...Why didn't you bring Maria along with you?"

"She's a little wary about meeting you."

"Come on. I had all my shots. Invite her over some day soon. Tell her I don't bite."

"I will. I promise."

"How serious is it, Michael? Serious like Kim was?"

I look over at my father and I smile.

CHAPTER FIVE

A psychiatrist would call it an obsession. Dostoyevsky would call it monomania. Whitechapel is like a siren urging me to the rocks, and she's winning. Somehow, I have to get it out of my system.

I don't tell Maria about this hang-up I'm having over a man who likely died in Chicago some hundred years ago. It's not healthy to linger on this ground, but I'm compelled to keep going. I don't want Maria to think she's hitched up to a Section Eight, so I do it on my own.

I consult a genealogist at the University of Chicago. His name is Robert O'Leary. I lie to Maria and say that I'm going to the mall to buy a new pair of running shoes. It's a good fabrication because my current pair has cracks in the soles from all the two-mile runs. Maria runs with me, now, and she has no problem keeping up. I really think she could run me to death. She hardly breaks a sweat.

She wants to know if I'd like company to the mall, but I tell her I'm just going there to make the buy and then come right back here to the apartment.

She seems a little suspicious, but I don't want her to know what I'm up to unless the trip to the university bears some fruit. I leave the flat at two and tell her I'll be back in a couple of hours because the traffic will be heavy, back and forth.

She kisses me and tells me to take my time. She doesn't want me to think I'm on a leash, it appears.

Robert O'Leary is an eminent scholar in history. He won a Pulitzer Prize a few years ago for his book on John Quincy Adams. Genealogy is something he writes on frequently for academic periodicals. He's won awards on the essays, I found out in my research online.

He's a full professor and has some 'chair' with a title, as well.

I could've tried an online service that traces families for $69, but I figured I'd go academic. O'Leary's the man, according to the reading I did.

I find his office at the University of Chicago, here on the south side. It's not a great neighborhood where it's located. The university grounds are beautiful, but the surrounding areas are not prime real estate any more. A long time ago it was a fashionable neighborhood. But the university still thrives and their teachers cop Nobels all the time.

I knock, and he tells me to come in. It's a small cubicle, not much bigger than my cramped space downtown.

He fits the bill. White, full head of hair. Those reading glasses you wear low on the nose. A perfectly manicured white beard to match his top knot.

I show him my badge. He smiles.

"Is this an official visit, Detective Parisi?...I've heard that name somewhere before."

"My father was also a homicide detective."

"A pretty famous one, too. No?"

"He was in the papers, back in the day."

"Yes...What can I do for Parisi the younger?"

"I'd like to look into the family history of someone. I'd be willing to pay you for your time."

"Absolutely not. This has to do with your professional capacity?"

"Yes. I want to tell you up front that it's likely going to sound strange if not insane."

"I'm already intrigued."

The reading glasses are removed. He has violet colored eyes. They're a bit remarkable, and I'm taken back by the unusual color.

"I'm looking into the murders of three prostitutes, and for some reason the unhinged notion has occurred to me that there might be a connection to the Whitechapel murders in London in 1888 through 1891."

"Jack the Ripper."

"Yeah. I'm a little embarrassed by the idea, but there it is."

"You were in the military?"

"Yes. How'd you know?" I ask.

"'There it is.' I was in Vietnam. Tet Offensive. 1968."

"My dad was in the war, too. I did three tours in Afghanistan."

"Then we were both in the shit."

"Yeah. Looks like."

"Anyway, Whitechapel."

I look at the great number of books on his shelves. They barely leave room for his desk and chair and the two of us.

"Yes. We had an artist's rendering done of a possible suspect, and the picture matched, an 80% match, a man named Francis Amjac. Amjac came under Scotland Yard's radar, but this man took off for parts unknown. There was a theory that he came to America, to Chicago, in fact, but I can find no listings for anyone by that name in the city or the suburbs."

"Do you speak Gaelic? Of course you don't. It's an Italian surname, Parisi...The word 'amjac' means 'devil' or 'demon' in the Gaelic."

I don't have a retort.

"Sort of puts a chill on this suddenly, doesn't it?"

He smiles sadly.

"A strange name indeed," he says. "If anyone was running around Chicago in the 1890s with a moniker like that, he'd draw some attention to himself. But there would have to be a record here in the city if he legally changed his name. I suppose that's a point of departure, anyway.

"This might take weeks or longer."

"I couldn't put you out like that," I apologize.

"I'll be happy to give it a try. It's what I do, you see. It's my hobby as well as my profession. You could ask my two ex-wives."

He smiles.

"So you think Francis Amjac might have been The Ripper."

"I think it's worse. I think someone down his biological line might be taking up where Francis left off, back in London."

"That's one hell of a theory. You ought to write a book."

"That's your racket, I'm afraid."

He laughs heartily.

"You have piqued my interest, Detective Parisi. The entertainment factor will more than pay me for my time. It's too bad there are three real victims, as you say, to ruin the fun. As I said, it might take several weeks or months to find anything if there is anything to find. I wish I could promise you that anything I find will be of any help to you in your investigation...Parisi...Are you Sicilian descent?"

I nod.

"So you must suffer Mafia jokes all the time."

"My father had family on the wrong side of the line. Outfit types. He used to use them for information. Once in a while they were helpful. Me, I have no use for them. I don't trust them enough to use them as a source."

He nods solemnly.

"Maybe I'll write the book about Amjac if he turns out to be connected. Would you mind, Detective—"

"My name's Michael. No, I wouldn't mind. If we catch a killer, you would be well worth the fee."

I rise and then I shake his hand as he gets up from his chair.

"You read all this stuff?" I say as I point to the multiple volumes.

He smiles, and then I depart.

• • • • •

I lie in bed that same night listening to the soft breath of Maria next to me. The bed is pleasantly warm and moist from our very recent coupling. She uses birth control, she tells me. I'm glad she informed me because if we ever do have kids I want them legitimate from conception. I know it sounds very old fashioned, but I inherited the notion from my father. He wasn't the strictest Catholic, but he was of the faith. I went to mass with him enough in my youth to know.

But there was an issue with the church that strained his faith and my own. It wasn't so much with the Church as it was with a priest, back when I was very young.

I was molested by a parish padre, and I finally told my dad about it. He reacted the way you might expect. He went and found that reverend and told him that he either left the priesthood or that he would shoot this pedophile in the head as they spoke.

The priest did leave the Church, but I always wondered if my father really would have blown him up, right there in the confessional. I like to think he wouldn't, but the molester must have believed Jimmy Parisi. He wasn't one to make idle threats. It's the Sicilian in him. He can't help it.

The blood ties. It makes me feel surer that Francis Amjac is the biological path to the murders of the three women. I know Maria was right when she said that we caught these cases because we're on the low end of the totem pole. The killings of whores don't get much space on the pages of the tabloids and the newspapers. High profile whacks occupy the columns of the papers and they get air time on TV. A lot of people look upon them as unworthy of sympathy. If they show up dead floating in the Lake or in the Chicago River it's no big deal, no cause of serious concern. They're just whores, after all.

The Catholic in me arrives when I hear that spew. All lives matter, and not just the lives of the unborn. I'm not a politician. I'm not a fanatic right-to-lifer. *All* lives count. If that makes me a romantic or not pragmatic, then there it is.

I don't care how they make a living if it doesn't involve taking advantage of others. I think they ought to be legitimized and regulated. But I don't think these women, and men, should be cast aside like trash.

I'm done pontificating, for the moment. I won't bore Maria with any rants. She's Catholic, too, but she doesn't practice, she told me. I haven't been to mass in a while, either.

I want to ask Maria to marry me, but I don't want to break up our partnership at work. She's a great associate. Very bright, very insightful. Maybe I'm being selfish. There are other detectives who are very adept at homicide solving. But I would miss not being with her all the time. If we were broken up, which most likely would occur, it would cut into our time together. And I never tire of her. It's almost frightening. Most couples need time apart. They need 'their space'. It doesn't work that way with me and Maria.

We seem closer every day, if that's possible. Boredom is a relationship killer, but every moment I spend with her feeds the fire. It's only getting more intense. We're probably more married than legitimate couples who've co-habited for twenty years.

And I don't see it changing. I can tell in her eyes that it's getting hotter instead of colder. When we are apart, I literally ache for her. I cannot get her out of my head. I have a strong impression that it's the same for Maria. She always wants to be with me. It's the same way for me. I almost changed my mind about taking her with me to see O'Leary, but I still want to be certain that this Amjac business is not my own, personal psychosis. I don't want her to think this crazy theory is the way I normally operate with casework.

She rolls over to me. Her eyes are open.

"Hey, you."

"Hey, you," I whisper back.

"I love you," she murmurs. "Let's get married."

"Okay," I tell her. "When?"

We're off today, Thursday. It's mid-August and it's steamy outdoors.

"Today soon enough?" she replies.

"They'll break us up at work."

"I was thinking a civil ceremony. We can keep it to ourselves, can't we?"

"Can I tell my father and Natalie?"

"I guess they can be trusted."

Her mother and father are dead. There were no siblings. Her relatives are scattered throughout the Pacific Northwest and they're not close to Maria.

"Let's do it, then. Our secret. For now. But I want us in the church, some day. How about you?"

"I can live without Mother Church. But I know your dad and Natalie don't want to be cheated out of showtime."

She smiles and pulls me to her. I kiss her, and then things progress as usual.

"You'll never get tired of me?" she grins.

"It's not possible."

"For real, Michael?"

"For real, Maria."

"We'll have the same initials," she giggles.

"Makes it easier for the bath towels. Interchangeable."

"Oh, I love you scary much."

"I'm pretty fond of you, too."

"How did this happen so fast? Are you sure it's not infatuation?"

"No. It's the genuine article, Maria. The real deal. Always will be."

"Is it different from Kim?"

"I thought she was the one, but now I know it's you, only you. I'm lucky I wound up with you, and no one else. Truly. It's just you. There will never be anyone else, Maria. If you believe in anything, believe those words. They're not just words. It's the only truth I know."

Tears seep out of the corners of her eyes.

"You are the strangest man I've ever known. You know that?"

"Is that good? Or creepy?"

"It isn't the latter."

I kiss her again.

"How long until we can go downtown and see the man?" she asks.

"It's five-thirty," I say as I read the digital clock behind her.

Her hair is thick and brown-black. I pierce her thick locks and grab gentle hold of them.

"Sun's already up in the east. We won't have to wait long. I think the JP opens at nine. I'll look it up on the laptop."

"I won't want to keep it secret, but I will. Nobody except your dad and Natalie. She made me feel so damned comfortable at that dinner last week. Your father was not nearly the Grizzly Bear I thought he'd be."

"He just seems non-human in legend."

"I want the church thing someday, too, but not now. Not for a while. I'm very possessive of our time, Michael. I can't have you spending it with anyone else. Not just yet."

"We should go back to sleep."

"Not likely," she laughs.

She takes hold of me and I feel her warmth from my torso to my lower extremities. She is all heat. There is no space between our bodies.

I will not allow it.

• • • • •

The JP's name is Hannigan. He puts out his smoke as he enters the room. A woman who works for him is our witness. The paperwork took only a few minutes, outside here. We don't have rings, yet, but I'll buy them when this ceremony ends. I'll let Maria pick them out.

He throws on his official robe, and the next thing we know we're joined in holy matrimony.

CHAPTER SIX

My mother had issues. You can imagine she must have if she married into our bloodline. The story was passed down from generation to generation, so it's obvious that there was something off, about her. She knew what she was marrying into. But there are cases of women marrying serial killers behind bars, so why is it incredible that someone would commit to the offspring of the most terrible killer in modern British history?

The heart knows what it wants. And so do the deeper, more insidious innards of the human creature. I'm not saying me dear old mum would like to join in on the fun of carving prosties up, but there are those who crave living in danger. There are those who become aroused by the proximity of evil. Even if that evil shares their beds.

Not everyone is a candidate for sainthood, and most of us fall far short of that ridiculous notion that man, and woman, are by nature 'good'. Eve relented to the serpent, did she not? And Adam joined right in with her stupidity. It was so much more enticing to taste the forbidden fruit.

What is more *verboten* than the slaughter of our own kind? Nothing. Thou shalt not kill tops the list of territories foreign to human approach.

I meet them online, and then I tell them how wealthy I am. I even tell them that I'm a doctor in an unhappy relationship—even though I'm single and always have been. The money always makes them take the bait. I offer them a thousand for an overnighter and a chance to make a bonus of another five hundred if they show me an especially good time.

Case in point is tonight's sidewalk princess. I especially like blacks and Latinas. They seem to offer more of a challenge. My single Anglo choice was rather passive. She went down far too easily. I enjoy a bit of conflict before they succumb to my 'charms'. I like them to attempt to fight back, at least.

But their aggressions are all calmed when I stick the needle in them. I do it when they bend over to service me. I jab them in the neck with a dose of curare that quickly paralyzes them. They can make no sound after the venom *quite o'ertakes their souls.* And then I am free to commence upon them. I don't make mortal cuts until I've done what I planned on doing to them.

The eviscerations are merely a show for whomever finds the bodies, inevitably the police.

I keep looking for accounts of my work in the media, but I have yet to see anything. It's quite disappointing. You cannot spread terror unless the public is aware of that terror. Fear is the operative word, of course. It doesn't seem to matter that I select only the flotsam and jetsam of society. They are the fecal matter of a degenerate culture. America has never been at a lower point when it comes to corruption and depravity. Unending mass shootings, primarily of children, but of adults, too, as in Las Vegas—"Sin City".

They were the slaughter of innocents, the adults not being quite so innocent.

From the top of the spectrum to the bottom, America is the new Rome, and Caligula is back in business making artful deals.

Maybe my adventures aren't pithy enough to whet the interests of journalists in any of the media, but I will persist until I have their full attention.

My father broke the tradition, as far as I know. If he butchered anyone, we never knew about it. If he did them in secret, I would find it surprising. I have no such wish for anonymity. I plan on contacting both the police and the newspapers with a notice that *Jack is back.* I can hardly tell them that Sean Amjac is back.

Besides, I use my mother's name, these days—it's Tracy. Too many Irish might know the Gaelic word, although modern Micks rarely speak the ancient tongue. I have no idea where the surname came from. I, too, find it remarkable that Francis didn't change it to something a lot more benevolent sounding.

But Francis was a very twisted pretzel, indeed. I don't think I've ascended to his heights quite yet.

Who knows? Tonight's encounter might approach great grandfather's pinnacle.

I meet her in a motel on the southwest side. It's one of those four-hour nap hovels. Only fifty bucks. It's downtrodden, probably about ready to close. It's about one step up from the Bates' Motel.

I cannot continue using hotels near the Loop. They will soon be watching them carefully. By they I mean the police. The Chicago Police Department has more than its share of problems with gun violence, currently, but their homicide division is a bit apart from the rest of their policemen. They are widely known as state of the art, and they seem to be far less on the take, compared to other of their brethren in blue. They actually do apprehend a great percentage of those suspects that they seek. In other words, I can't make it too easy on them.

The assignation is for 9:00 PM. I arrive twenty minutes early and pay the manager for the four-hour 'nap'. I'm wearing a hat and darkly tinted glasses to make an identification difficult. I've used this method of disguise before, and so far, so good. I don't feel any hot breath on my neck.

She arrives twelve minutes late. As soon as she enters the room, I lock and chair the door behind me. I don't have the hat or the tinted glasses on because there's no need.

"For a guy who says he has money, you pick cheap motels."

"That's why I'm a guy with money."

"This place looks like it's got bugs."

She has African features. No mixed race. Her face is deeply black, almost with a tinge of blue. She's attractive, attractive for the kind of whore you find online.

"You ready to party?" she smiles.

Her teeth are so white they almost gleam at me.

"Ready? Yes. I'm ready. Hope you are."

"I'm always ready to do some hot lovin'."

She starts to disrobe.

"You gonna get naked, or do you like to wait?"

"I like to wait," I tell her.

"What's your first name?"

"It's Sean."

"Irish, huh?" she smiles.

Again, the light-show of those perfect teeth.

Her breasts are small but erect. The nipples are taut and the color of black plums.

"They do anything for you, Sean?"

"Of course. But I like to go slow."

"We got all night, baby."

I don't tell her it's more like four hours.

She walks closer to me. I can see the black bush beneath her waistline. She doesn't trim, obviously. She lets it spread naturally. I find myself becoming more aroused, but it's not for the reason she'd think.

"You can take off something, can't you honey?" she smiles again.

She kneels in front of me without being cued. Then she starts to work on my zipper.

I have the syringe behind my back in my right hand. Then I stab in her in the cheek as she loosens my zipper. She flings herself back on her backside, and clutches at her cheek. There is only one small droplet of blood oozing from my puncture.

She tries to get to her feet to get at me, but her legs give way almost immediately. The curare works right away. Denizens of the Amazon use it with their blowguns. It staggers the prey and freezes it in its steps.

Her eyes widen and her breath softens, but she's still very much alive. And from my research on the drug, she'll be able to feel everything I do to her, but she will have no voice to scream nor any ability to move. The best part of this drug is its difficulty in being discovered in the blood. This is such a rare serum that it's not widely known. Most Medical Examiners have likely never heard of it because it is so ancient and arcane.

I lift her off the floor and prop up on the bed, on her back. She's like a black statue of herself.

"Are you ready to party, Demetra?"

That's her name. Almost sounds Greek.

Her eyes are unblinking and wide, wide as if she'd just met the horror of her life.

My bag is under the bed. I take it out and open it on the mattress next to her.

As I look down on her ebony body, I have a very strange sensation. I'm erect, now, inside my pants, but I don't think it's for the usual reason, the thrill of the kill. I think it's sexual. I have had sex with a number of women, a lot of them being clients, but I've never had this kind of urge with my targets.

It hurts, it's so erect. So, I remove my pants, my underwear, and my shirt. I know I'm taking a chance of leaving hairs and DNA and body fluid, but I have a small bottle of bleach that I'll spread over her when I finish, before I commence with the cutting.

I mount her and pull her buttocks off the mattress. Her eyes are frozen as they have been, and then I'm erupting on her belly. The semen is concentrated in a small area next to her bellybutton. I rise and then retrieve tissues from the bathroom. I clean off the climax, and then I open the pint of bleach and spread it all over her torso.

I'm still erect, but now it's for the usual reason.

I remain nude, and I reach into my bag and pick up a scalpel.

Her eyes seem to be focused on the blade, but it's probably an optical illusion on my own part.

I make the first incision just above her navel, and I begin.

• • • • •

My first patient is Sherry. She works for the local NBC affiliate. Her ratings are sliding downward, and she's just turned forty-five. I know she wants me, but I always have a nurse attendant upon these surgeries as well as the required anesthesiologist. It's a bit too crowded to give her the poke I know she dearly desires. That'll come later, when I see her in my office for the results of this face-job.

She doesn't need much work, really. Just a tightening and a tuck. It won't change her appearance drastically, but that's the point. She'll look a bit more taut and smooth, up front. It might take a few years off her visage, but plastic surgeons can't turn back time. They can only slow the clock down, a little.

The cutting takes only forty-five minutes, and then we're finished. She'll come out of her sleep in a little over a half hour or forty-five minutes. I'm done here, until she comes in for her consultation and free poke, in a few weeks.

• • • • •

Dr. Sean Tracy, it says on the door. I've made a pretty good income, so far. It took long enough to get through medical school and all the other hoops I had to leap through. And those baser instincts I inherited took equally as long to emerge, as well. I knew the stories, as I said. My mother wasn't hesitant to warn me about where I came from and what I came from. She was almost obvious in her joy about keeping the line going. I knew she was mentally ill, but she never behaved erratically enough to have her committed to some place like Elgin. She never took up the knife, never poisoned anyone that I know about. She had a talent for appearing normal, whatever normal means.

Perhaps she went around killing small animals in order to satiate her sickness, but she seemed gentle enough inside her insanity to be able to operate in society. She worked for many years as a receptionist, and then she became a legal secretary for a prominent lawyer in the Loop. Her pay was enough to pay the bills and to keep us fed. We were never without a roof or food or for tuition for school.

I had to take loans, of course. My prestigious university on the East Coast cost me dearly, but I'm paying my loans regularly and will have settled my account very soon. Tucks and tightening are very lucrative, almost as well recompensed as orthopedic surgeons are. The ortho guys can afford golf *twice* a week instead of just Wednesdays. It's an old joke.

I get laid as a sort of bonus for the work, but I have to be discrete. Some of them are married, and some are divorced or widowed cougars just looking for a casual pop. When they start hinting about relationships, I end it right there and then. Too many middle-aged, hungry women, too little time, as they say. Why have one when I can have them all?

But this black girl, this Demetra, was a quirk, an aberration. I can't allow it to happen again. The bleach I used is not guaranteed to clean her body as I intended to sanitize it. All it takes is a tiny cell of my DNA and they'll have a starting point for my demise.

I'm wondering if I fall into that category of series killers who have an unconscious desire to be caught. That death wish seems to be present in some killers like dear old great grandfather, Francis, but he seemed to escape detection. They quit searching for him after his escape to the United States. I can find no history of the police coming after him here in Chicago.

Then he gave up the call. He stopped hunting and got married as if he'd somehow satiated his lust for carnage. It seems all very unlikely to me, but my own father somehow curbed his obsession with the kill. He lived something of an invisible life, at least invisible to crime, to murder most foul.

I don't find anything revolting about my deeds at all. I feel no twinges of remorse nor any pity for my 'victims'. None. I sleep soundly after each excursion into the so-called abyss. I have no pangs of conscience, no stabs of guilt. Surely, I am missing pieces of something that everyone else has, but I can feel no great pain in being without those missing parts.

Who can apologize for their own nature? We are all accidents of birth. I never asked to be thrown from a mother's womb onto this vile rock, this planet of disease. Whatever God there may be is certainly more like Blake's Creator in his poem about the 'tyger'. He put the lamb on the same earth as the 'tyger'. What kind of evil intelligence creates a chain of edibles as the God of Moses and Abraham supposedly did? He's forgiving and kind, is He? Show me the money! Show me the evidence.

When the NBC cougar shows for her consultation, the nurse isn't present. I'm just here to have a look. But she opens her blouse and shows me her tits. I'm supposed to be looking at the results of my surgical handiwork, but I'm looking at her creamy melons, instead.

When I've finished with her aboard the top of my desk, it's my last appointment, and I'm done for the day.

• • • • •

Still no mention of the adventure in the four-hour motel. Nothing in the papers or on television. It's as if these creatures have been overlooked by humanity in its entirety.

Perhaps I'm working too slowly, but I dare not get sloppy the way I did with the black target. I still don't understand why I took that chance. Up until Demetra I refrained from making contact with anything other than my scalpels. I was diligent about not getting fluids or hairs on any of the previous bodies.

And then I stumbled badly.

I don't think I'm feeling remorse or guilt over the African. I knew her not at all except as an experiment. I watched her eyes seem to glaze over when I was finally finished with her. She was still frozen in place, of course, but you can tell when the light leaves their eyes. There's a kind of dullness in the orbs that tells you death has replaced what was there before.

It is a mystery, as priests are wont to tell you. They call it a Divine Mystery, but there's nothing of God in this puzzle. I was an accident just like everyone else, and there is nothing mystical about anyone's demise. Life simply ceases. That's all. And then there's nothing more, no heaven, no hell.

Nihil. Nada. Nothing.

Just silence, as Hamlet suggested:

All the rest is silence.

CHAPTER SEVEN

The homicide in a motel in Orland Park shows that he's building in ferocity. The mutilation is horrible, and the body looks hardly human. This time it's a black female, and this time the manager at the four-hour nap joint identifies the customer who paid him as a close match to our drawing by the department artist. There doesn't seem to be any doubt he's the man identified in at least two of the four killings.

The night managers at two of the four said the drawing seemed close to the man they checked in, but they weren't certain. The Orland desk man seems to think it's a pretty good likeness. So, we're going with the series killing classification. Maria is as sure as I am.

No one knows we're espoused, yet. I haven't told my father or Natalie or my sister Mary or Natalie's twins. I don't know when we'll announce it, but we both want to remain partnered, at least until we catch this guy.

It's well known that serial killers can be the most difficult homicides to solve. And we've kept it out of the papers and media for fear that there'll be a copycat or two out in the weeds to complicate the case. But we cannot keep them out of the news for much longer.

• • • • •

The 'much longer' winds up being the afternoon that we discovered the black woman, Demetra Jackson. I'm guessing the night guy at the motel contacted a stringer, those night crawlers who work on tips. The news got out to the *Tribune* and the *Sun Times*, and now the killings find themselves on the second page of both papers the day after we found Demetra. And then the floodgate opens, and they write articles about the demise of the three other hookers, as well. Television wants to talk to Maria and me, and our captain tells us to cooperate. All good security comes to an end, the captain says, and we don't want to appear uncooperative.

Maria takes the grilling from Channel 2, 5, and 7. I get the spotlight on Channel 9. Maria looks a lot better on the tube than I do. I have the feeling she'll become the darling of the TV media. She's got superstar looks, a lot like the models pretending to be cops on the hour-long television series. Me? I'm just another olive oil, swarthy Italian American. I'm not remarkable in physical appearance. I'm five-ten, about 185. I have the required brown eyes that most of my Sicilian forbears supposedly had, according to the patriarch, my father. But I don't stand out in a crowd, and I've always been rather thankful that I don't.

I don't get recognized as a cop, out on the street. Which works well when I want to come up from behind a suspect. I look like the guy who works the pizza ovens, Maria teases me. She tells me she really loves pizza, though.

So we move from low profile to page 1 in just under a week.

A reporter from Channel 7 asks if Maria and I are a couple.

"We're partners," I tell her with a straight face.

Maria nods at her.

The reporter smiles as if she knows something we don't.

• • • • •

I get a call from a lieutenant in Vice. His name is Carlson, Forrest Carlson. Everyone calls him Frosty, he tells me over the phone. He says he might have something for us on the quartet of murders.

We meet him at White Castle at just after 2:00 AM. The selection of places to meet for a drink shrinks after 1:00 AM in the city. We're not looking for an adult beverage, anyway.

Frosty Carlson looks like someone who might have served with me in the Rangers. He's lean and stringy, maybe just under six feet tall. I can see why they call him Frosty. His hair is platinum blond, and I can see no dark roots. It's either a great dye job or it's a freak of nature. He's only maybe forty, so I can't see his hair going white this soon.

We sit in a booth at the Castle. The place is deserted. This one's at 63rd and Cicero. Maria is next to me, and Carlson sits opposite us.

I wait for him to take a sip of his black coffee. Maria has a coffee, too, and I have my usual diet drink.

"That shit'll kill you," he smiles at me.

I can't help but like the guy and I have no idea why.

"What do you have for us?"

It's too late to mess around with small talk.

"Direct. I like direct...I heard about your old man. The legend."

"He's not a legend. A legend is a lie," I say to him.

"There you have me."

Maria sips at her coffee. Her eyes look very tired. This case has lately become a drain on both of us, especially with all the media attention.

"I think I have a guy who fits your description. I mean the suspect's description."

"Yeah? How's that?" Maria asks.

"We had a sexual molestation beef, a few days ago. Some media babe says her doctor made unwanted advances toward her. We brought the guy in for questioning, but it appears very much a 'he said she said' thing."

"Who are you backing on this one?" I ask.

"She struck me as the rejected victim. From what we found out, she tried to get serious with this man, a relationship, you understand?"

"So you think he angered her because she wanted a commitment and he was into hit and run," Maria suggests.

"Yeah, I like that, hit and run. Yeah."

He takes out a piece of paper and lays it in front of us.

"This is the person of interest you seek, no?"

It's the police artist's rendering of our only suspect.

"Who is he?"

"His name is Sean Tracy. A professional man. He makes the old young. A plastic surgeon, and very big time. We asked some of his clients, females all, and we found he's quite the player. But nothing sticks to him. He's pure Teflon."

"Do you think he might be the answer to our prayers?" Maria smiles.

Frosty takes another go at his black coffee.

"He looks a lot like that drawing. You never know."

"The man in that picture has an 80% likelihood of matching someone you might have heard about."

"Yeah? Who?"

"Some guy in London who disappeared around 1891."

"Bullshit," Frosty laughs.

"Probably," I offer.

"You can't be serious," he protests.

"It doesn't matter. You do think Sean Tracy looks like the subject in this sketch."

"Oh, man, you can't be...You're pulling my yash. Joking, right?"

"This look like Tracy or not?" I ask.

"Yeah. It's an exact match. Take off the tints and the hat, it's this plastic surgeon who loves the ladies. It's him, all right."

He finishes his drink and he wishes us luck. He lays an index card in front of us as he departs with Sean Tracy's information, his office address and his home location and phone number.

• • • • •

We drive over to Tracy's office on Michigan Avenue the next morning after three hours sleep. Maria thinks it can't wait until later, and I'm with my more-than-a-partner.

The receptionist asks us if we've got an appointment, and I show her the badge and ID. She goes into the back and closes the door behind her. She emerges after about a minute or two.

"He'll see you in his office."

The receptionist is nearing retirement, maybe just this side of her mid-sixties. Her hair appears to have been colored to make her look younger, but the striations on her face can't be covered by cosmetics.

She accompanies us to Tracy's private office.

He stands behind his desk and beckons us to be seated in two large leather chairs. It smells and feels like genuine leather.

"What can I do for you, detectives?"

He matches the drawing.

"We're interested in your whereabouts on these four dates, and these particular hours," Maria tells him. She hands him an index card.

He's a handsome male, like the portrait we had made of him. He resembles the Interpol picture of Francis Amjac more than he does this current rendering.

"I'm not sure I can recall any of these dates...Except this one." He points to a night in August.

"Do you know where you were at this hour?" Maria asks.

"I know I was with someone on that particular evening. We went to a play downtown. I think it was a revival of *Hair*."

"Can you give us the name and phone number of the person who accompanied you there?" I ask.

He smiles. I don't like the smile. It's more like a leer. Calculated. It's as if he made a brilliant move on a chessboard against me.

He takes out a pen and writes a name and a phone number for us. It's a woman's name. The phone is a Chicago area listing—773.

"You can't account for the other three times?" Maria queries.

"Offhand, I'm afraid not."

He's leering again.

"You might want to think some more about those three dates. It's very important," I tell him.

The smile-leer vanishes. I think I might have struck something tender in him.

"I'll do that, and I'll get back to you...Can I ask why you're directing these questions at me?" he says with a solemn face.

"We're homicide detectives and we're checking things out regarding some multiple homicides," Maria answers.

"You mean I'm a suspect?" he asks with a weak smile. The leer is still absent.

"No. We're just gathering information, as she said," I tell him. "But we would like to know where you were on those three other dates. We'll call this number to verify it."

He looks at me with a gathering blush on his cheeks.

"We'll be getting back to you soon."

"I hope so. This is all a bit upsetting."

"I'm sorry. But it's just part of the usual investigation of any homicide," Maria says to him. "We'll be leaving, now," she concludes.

We get up and walk out of his office. He never rose from his chair.

• • • • •

"If his alibi comes through," she tells me in my cubicle by the Lake, "we're screwed."

I dial the number. Area 312 is for the Loop and its close vicinity. Area 773 is for surrounding areas, including some of the suburbs.

Her name is Angela Komensky, and she picks up after the third ring. I identify myself and tell her the reason for the call, and when I ask, she immediately tells me that she and Tracy attended the play.

"The nudity thing seemed kind of old," she laughs.

I thank her for her time, and I hang up.

"Screwed?" she asks me.

"Feels like strike one," I tell her.

• • • • •

There is the possibility that Tracy rang her up before I did and that he told her to back up his story. So, we show up at Angela Komensky's address in a western suburb an hour and a half later.

She answers the door of her ranch house on a spacious lot. The back is fenced in, and I hear a dog barking. We show her the ID and she asks us in.

We sit on her sectional sofa, and Angela plants herself in a straight-backed chair across from us.

"We just talked a little while ago," she smiles hazily.

"We needed to see you face to face," Maria explains.

"Why?"

"You didn't talk to Sean Tracy a little while before I called, did you, Angela?" I prod.

"No. Of course not. What is this?"

"We can go to your phone records, but it'd be simpler if you just told us here and now if he talked to you before I called."

"This is absolutely ridiculous...Do I need a lawyer?"

"Not if you're straight up with us," Maria says.

"I did not talk to Sean today or in the last two weeks. We're not seeing each other at the moment."

I see the large wedding band on her ring finger, and it's accompanied by a very large diamond engagement ring.

"I think you should leave now, if there's nothing else."

The dog is barking in the backyard.

Angela is a very striking looking middle-aged woman with thick auburn hair and a tightly knit, luscious body packaged in a tight sweater and shorts that display a dancer's legs.

"You're positive you haven't spoken with him today," Maria says as we rise off the sofa.

"What is this all about?" she demands.

"We're investigating a series of murders," I tell her.

The color evacuates her cheeks. She becomes pale.

But she gathers herself, and now her face flushes in anger.

"I have nothing else to tell you."

We make our way out her door and head the unmarked squad toward the east, toward the Lake.

We check out her incoming calls, and we come up empty. The only call she received was from what turned out to be her husband, a corporate attorney who has an office on the Gold Coast.

• • • • •

"It appears Sean Tracy has an alibi," Maria laments as we lie in bed together, late that night.

We're both exhausted, and we haven't been on this mattress very long in the last couple days. But tomorrow is our day off, and we intend to catch up on the sleep and on other things far more pleasurable.

"When are you going to tell your father that we're married?"

"I thought maybe we'd do it today. We're supposed to come over for a barbeque, remember?"

She flashes me a smile of recognition.

"I wish I had someone to tell it to."

"My little orphan," I say as I brush her hair from her face with my hand.

"It's no good when you have no one else to tell."

"Everyone's going to know soon enough."

"I want everyone to know. I don't like them not knowing, even if it means they break up the partnership. I want them all to know."

"The two most important people are already aware that we are husband and wife."

She smiles wearily and kisses me, and then we both turn over and close our eyes.

CHAPTER EIGHT

We follow Sean Tracy when he leaves his office. He makes a direct line to his apartment about a half mile away on the Gold Coast, the swankiest district in Chicago. The man must be a fair surgeon if he's able to afford this address. I think Oprah used to live in the neighborhood. It's where the swells call home. They are they celebrities, the big shots, the *pezzanovante,* in my father's era with the CPD. When I think how much it must cost merely to rent around here, although I'm sure most of them own their condos, it sends a chill of destitution through me.

"We'll never live here," I tell Maria, riding shotgun.

"I can live with that," she smiles. "I'll settle for a ranch on the northwest side."

"You handled it well with the old man, last night," I tell her.

We informed my father and Natalie that we were married at our small grill-out. Natalie broke into tears, and I think Jimmy Parisi had a few damp spots on his cheeks, too. I never saw my father cry, that I can remember. I've seen him angry, but he never became physical with me. He let me know when he wasn't happy, but he never struck me or Mary, and I'm certain he never abused their twins, Natalie's and his kids. He was a gentle man around our home, but there are stories about some of his methods from the past, professionally, that'd get him fired from the force today. With body cameras and so on, it's difficult to strong arm anybody even when force is required. It's always a tough call.

"He's a teddy bear," she grins.

"It's nice to be confident," I reply.

Tracy stays at home for an hour, and then he's on his way again. This time he's headed for the Loop, and when he arrives, he leaves off his Lexus, it's blood red and new-looking, with a valet at Maggio's, a downtown upscale Italian restaurant.

We pull up on the street and park. It's sultry, and it's early September. I remember we haven't heard from the genealogist yet, and I'm thinking about giving him a call, in case he's forgotten me.

I could have found a long list of Tracys in the phonebook. This is still an Irish town. And Italian and African American and Polish and German and Hispanic and Asian. And there are plenty more ethnicities I left off.

I still want to know about this surgeon's background. The tie with him and Francis Amjac won't go away, at least in my own mind. I'm not talking about it to anyone in Headquarters because I don't much care to be ridiculed. The Vice cop, Carlson, didn't laugh in my face, at least. But he knew the likelihood of a relationship to Jack the Ripper sounded like a tabloid column or a conspiracy theory whack-job notion. So, I've been quiet about it. Even with Maria. I wouldn't be hurt if she were dubious about my theory, anyway.

Sean Tracy is real; that much is certain.

He's got the skills. Good with a knife. Adept at getting close to women, even though it might be through social media. Internet is how it's done, now. You don't hook up in bars unless you're someone who likes to go to bars. And the dating sites are far more private. It's easier to remain anonymous—until it's too late for the victim. Prostitutes work the ether because it beats pounding the pavement, and even though it's as least as dangerous as working the streets, the hookers know their territories. They never know what they're getting from the electronic streets.

"He's been in there for ninety minutes," she says.

She sounds tired. We got a better sleep last night, but you can't make up for lost slumbers, the shrinks say. We both need a vacation and a honeymoon, but it's not likely to happen any time soon. These kinds of cases tend to go on for long periods of time. At least they do when the killers are clever and not sloppy.

At the Orland Park scene where Demetra was cut to pieces, he tossed bleach on most of what was left of her. The bleach means he was trying to hide and destroy evidence, which means he left remnants of his DNA. Body hairs, semen. Something from his clothing. The results from the lab are not in yet, but we should be hearing soon. If he did leave a calling card, we'll have Dr. Tracy. But the bleach thing suggests he was trying to be careful. I figure he had sex with her before he started cutting her. The way he left Demetra, I doubt it was post-mortem.

"How long are we going to wait? Shift's almost over," she says.

She must be wasted. She usually doesn't complain about going home.

"You're not pregnant, are you?" I smile.

"Not unless the pills don't work...Why? You want to be a daddy?"

"Not just yet...Are you burned, baby?"

"Yeah. We haven't caught up with our REM patterns."

"We could cut down on the horizontal boogie."

"Where'd you get that?" she laughs. "That one's new."

"From some mystery novel I read. It rather struck my fancy."

"I'd like to continue striking your fancy, if you don't mind," she grins nastily.

"You ain't getting an argument from me."

I bring along my dad's old CDs of jazz. I play them when we have to surveil or stake out suspects. Jazz was a habit that Jimmy Parisi inherited from Doc Gibron, his long-time partner. Doc's been dead for quite a while. But I learned to like Dave Brubeck, Ahmad Jamal, Ramsey Lewis, Duke Ellington, Count Basie, and a lot of others. I have quite a large collection of my own CDs now, too. And I think I've hooked my wife on the bee-bop. At least she doesn't complain when I take out my battery-operated CD player. I bring my own because I don't want to kill the car battery. And the exhaust with the motor running is a dead giveaway that we're cops waiting on someone.

Out he comes with a drop-dead babe on his arm. She's tall and statuesque, and I can make out her long black tresses from my rear-view mirror.

Tracy and his 'date' await the valet. When the Lexus pulls up, Tracy lays a bill on the valet, and then he and the model-type take off. He's headed back to his place, we find out, and when they arrive and another valet relieves him of his ride, we stop at the curb a half-block from his luxury crib.

"We'll put him to bed," I tell her. "He's not going to defecate where he eats."

She doesn't argue the point. It's closing time in the cop shop, anyway. The end of our shift.

• • • • •

I wake up around three. Maria is soundly oblivious, but I can't go back to sleep. I go into what used to be Maria's kitchen, and I take out my usual diet pop from the 'fridge. I have to have something to occupy me, so I grab hold of her AT&T phone book and I peruse the listings of Tracys. There are dozens, and there are three other Tracys who list MDs after their names. I wish O'Leary would get back to me about Sean's family tree. I'd like to interview others in his family and hear what they have to say about him. It's surprising what truth you can gather from siblings and cousins and blood kin, sometimes.

I can't use the Italians, as my dad did, because they wouldn't know about a lone wolf like Sean Tracy.

His great grandfather Francis must have been a loner, too. You can't share the fact that you're a serial killer and a blood lusting maniac with your family—unless your clan is filled with cutters.

"What're you doing out here?"

I jump, a little out of surprise.

"You startled me. Not a good thing, Maria."

"Were you back in Afghanistan for a moment, my love?"

"No, you just surprised me. I don't react very well when I get surprised."

"I'll keep that in mind...What's going on?"

"Couldn't sleep. That's all," I tell her.

She's not buying. She's a cop, too, after all.

"Leave work for the morning. You can't operate on no sleep, lover."

She takes me by the hand and leads me back to the bedroom. We promptly become amorous, as is usually the case when we're both awake, and after a bout that lasts about twenty minutes, we both give it up and let sleep take us both away.

• • • • •

The captain is unhappy. His name is Gregory Jaworski, and he's a lifer on the force. Thirty years' service, and no end in sight, he's told me.

Captain Jaworski knew my dad, naturally, but that doesn't cut any favors for me, and I respect the captain for his integrity. I never asked for favors, and I got my shield by putting in the time and the work. The captain understands all that, and he's always been fair with me. He seems to like Maria, too, but I'm hoping this interview does not concern our marital status. I'm hoping he thinks we don't have any marital status.

"You know the direction that shit flows, you two?" he demands.

"Quite well," I answer for us. "Sir."

"Cut the military happy horseshit," he says.

"Yes."

I refrain from the 'sir', this time.

He tells us to be seated. He's the king and we're his devoted court.

Jaworski is just over six feet with no paunch and no waste on him. He appears combat-ready, and I know he served in Vietnam at the tail end of that unfortunate war. Two bronze stars and a silver, all for valor in the shit. He came out of Vietnam as a well-decorated colonel with the Green Berets. The Chicago Police Department is well-stocked with ex-military.

"The media has created a cluster coitus, and I'm already sick of it. Have you anything to update me on these four murders of the prostitutes?"

I fill him in on our surveillance of Tracy.

"The guy's a surgeon? You think an MD did all that?"

"He fits the description," Maria adds.

"And do you think he's a likely candidate, Detective Elizondo?"

"I do."

"And you are of a like mind, Detective Parisi?" he demands.

"I am. He's the best lead we have, at the moment. He's got the surgical skill to pull off what happened to them."

"Couldn't a very nice butcher have done the same?"

"It'd take skill to remove the organs the way they were removed. I think the brutality was an afterthought, Captain. He's a very skilled cutter. Too skilled to just be cutting pork chops and prime rib."

Maria looks over at me and coughs out a laugh.

"Something amusing?" he asks her.

"No. Sorry. It's just my partner's choice of words," she replies.

"He does have an interesting vocabulary, does he not."

"I'm just saying I think the killer's got skills beyond those of a layman."

"I read you, Detective Parisi. The fact remains that since this shit has hit the media fan that there's all kinds of interest in solving these heinous deeds. Especially since three of the vics were women of color, we have voices saying that we have not paid sufficient attention to these four black deeds. You both follow me?"

We nod in unison.

"I have had some powerful individuals suggest that I put more experienced investigators in charge of these homicide cases. You know to whom I refer?"

"I can guess," I tell him.

"Well, I replied that I have every confidence in the two of you. They also inferred that I was allowing you, Detective Parisi, to continue your investigation only because of your father's shirttails, which a few of these illuminati insist you're taking advantage of."

I feel my face begin to redden as much as a fairly brown complexion will allow.

"I replied that I'm running this goddamned circus and that they could goddam well relieve me and retire me if they had lost faith in my ability to run this goddam outfit. So, Detectives, if you smell the scent of crap emanating from where I sit, you'll understand why."

"I think I grasp your meaning, Captain."

"Michael, Maria,I know you can handle this case or I never would have assigned it to either of you. Maria, you're as good as they come. I've read your jackets, both of them. You have years of the street on those sheets, and I know you're both straight. I don't allow pad cops in this division. But the sad fact is that results *do* pay the bulldog. I want you to put aside everything else on your board and work on these slayings exclusively. I'll direct other detectives to cover your other outstanding cases. All right?"

"Yes," she says.

"Yes," I repeat.

Then our audience with the Pope of Homicide is finished and we are dismissed.

• • • • •

We tail Tracy for the next two weeks. Nothing. Just more trophy dates to exclusive, expensive bistros.

The molestation beef with his ex-patient is settled out of court, and Dr. Sean Tracy is free and clear of one rap.

"We're looking in the wrong chicken coop," I tell her as we wait outside Tracy's condo yet one more night.

"And that means what, exactly?"

"We'll never get him while we're watching him party with this kind of woman. If he's finding them, I'm convinced he's doing it through social media. He won't allow himself to be seen in public with the kind of victim he's looking for, so he finds them online."

"Then we find him by setting up a honey pot—isn't that what they call it?" she grins.

"*Honey-pot?*" I grin back.

"You're suggesting we set a trap on the internet. We make him think he's hooked up with another prostitute. Do either of us have the expertise to get this thing done?"

"We know who does, of course."

We have a room full of techno-geeks in computer services. They help us hunt online, and they're all gameboys—except for Lisa Taylor. She's the lone female on this crew. But I figure her voice would sound more inviting than one of our male geeks.

I tell her what we're up to, and she's very enthusiastic to help.

She's got strawberry colored hair and a few pieces of metal implanted in a nostril and an earlobe. The uniform code is much laxer in computer services, of course.

"You want me to make him think I'm a working girl looking for a date, right?" she asks me.

Lisa looks over at Maria to see if she's got us right.

"Exactly," Maria tells her.

"I should be able to get it up and running by tonight. But I'm not sure what the odds are that I'll contact your suspect. There are legions of these whackers online."

"Give it your best shot, Lisa," I tell her.

"Of course I will. I'll be in touch if I get any hits."

We thank her and we leave their geek den.

• • • • •

We watch Tracy come and go, even though I have a bad feeling about stalking him. I'm sure he's doing it electronically, but I'm also wondering if he's backed off for a while now that we've confronted him. You always hope they'll make mistakes when you get in their faces, but it sometimes makes them overly wary. He might stop altogether.

But I don't think he will cease and desist. It's not in their MO, not with series killers. The pressure builds in them and they can't say no. It's like an addiction, like opiates, like meth. Once you've gone on the ride, you have to have another buzz, and then another. Cold turkey stops are unbearable.

No, I think Dr. Tracy doesn't get his nuts off doing legitimate surgery. He craves his other kind of cutting much, much more.

CHAPTER NINE

Francis Amjac, Chicago, 1892

It's a wide-open town, this. You can have anything you like for the right amount of American dollars. It buys me a license to practice. Having fallen in with some very well-connected politicians and fixers, a few bucks to the right local chieftain—they call them aldermen, here—and you've got what your heart desires.

I throw out my shingle and I do family medicine. The abortions are done at night, naturally, since they're quite illegal, over here. You would be amazed at the names of the quality personages who require my services. Businessmen's wives who dallied with a lover come here all the time. Some politician's spouses darken my already-darkened door, as well. I charge too dear a price for the lowly and downtrodden who are always getting themselves 'in trouble'.

I'm able to furnish my home on the south side very well with the proceeds. I came to America with a generous stash of English pounds, and now I live in an elegant home in a solid neighborhood.

I've met a woman of substance through my daytime practice. She came in with a case of gout that I have helped her with by telling her to cut down on red meat. She seems a bit taken with me. She's single, even though she's thirty years old. And eligible, apparently. We've been seeing each other, lately, and I think it would be beneficial to my practice to have a wife with a clean reputation.

It's not that I don't get the old urges, anymore. I do. But I know I cannot continue to escape the consequences if I keep going to that well repeatedly. I want to try the legitimate life. I had enough near escapes back in London. The thought of carving up more dregs of society still flames up from time to time, but I'd like to try respectability for a while. Who knows? I might become accustomed to living in style. And every time I refrain from traveling out into the night to forage for a new salty piece, I remember the last few near-encounters I had with Scotland Yard. The coppers weren't stupid, and I was very much out-numbered. Inevitably I would have been snared and hung on the gallows.

Here, I am a respected member of the community. I'm a propertied man. I might want to have a wife and children. This new young woman might suit my needs and further propel me into local politics. I can see myself as an alderman, perhaps even the mayor. What a laugh that would be! Saucy Jack, the Ripper himself, Mayor of Chicago. I might even wind up in the Governor's mansion! Consider the irony of it all. I was the most wanted man of my century, back in England. And I'm an Irishman, to boot. What kind of dark, evil humor is all that?

Chicago is a growing city. It has sprung up from an onion patch by the Lake Michigan. The downtown was a swamp, I am told, and they drained it to kill off the mosquitoes and the stench. It is now on the road to the twentieth century, and progress is its motto. There will be buildings to compete with the skyscrapers in New York.

I only passed through New York via Ellis Island. I was impressed with neither. This is a burly, brawling burg. Filled with energy and lust. There is a future for me here. I will have passed from my darkness into the light. I'm nearly there now.

People talk about Jack the Ripper, over here. It fills the penny-dreadfuls and the tabloids. I'm quite the rage on these shores.

They had the wrong suspects in mind, back across the Atlantic. They thought I might be the Prince, himself. They thought I might be a butcher or a Jew immigrant. They had a plethora of theories, but they never chose me. There was a rumor that some copper had cast his glance my way, but the closest they ever came to nabbing me was the last time I cut a woman to pieces. I barely escaped them in my policeman's disguise. They were within a block of catching me before I transformed into a copper.

It was becoming all a bit too exciting. Too much for my heart. I might have had a stroke, previously.

I want to try a leisurely existence. I want to be well-respected and admired. And to do all that I need to refuse that inner demon that forces me out into the streets to seek another fallen creature.

I don't want their stench on me again. It would not wash off after every killing. There was no purge for my flesh, no cleansing for my soul. I was searching in the wrong place for fulfillment. Perhaps I can find it on these shores. And I needn't seek out satisfaction with tarts in the alleyways. No, I can be complete with a wife and a practice (and one on the side).

I'm a citizen of a rising metropolis. I can find fame of another kind, here. I don't want to be notorious any longer. I reject infamy. I'm going to try the other side of the coin.

I'm going to become a gentleman. No, I won't be knighted by any queen, here, but there are other rewards just as valuable as some title in my new life.

I have been resurrected. I have been reborn.

• • • • •

Sean (Amjac) Tracy, Chicago, 2017

I finally made the papers and the electronic media. The stories have emerged from the back pages to the cover stories in the major tabloids. I'm on all the TV newscasts. The unsolved murders of four prostitutes.

And two of the local channels have even made reference to the Whitechapel murders. I wonder if my great grandfather would be proud. He was able to insinuate himself into this city by choosing not to continue the slayings he perpetrated back in London. He seemingly was able to refuse to continue his inglorious activities in England, and he became a reputable doctor and citizen, as did my own father.

Free will, they say, dictates that we all have a choice over our deeds, foul and otherwise. Science claims we have tendencies to fall prey to our inherited instincts because of the ubiquitous presence of DNA at our cores. The call of the blood is strong, but not necessarily overwhelming. We have choices.

I choose to go with my instincts, bloody as they may be. But I'm not one to blunt what I was born to do. It's too much like abstinence, for my desires. I'm not going to thwart all that energy that demands to be loosed on those sluts who're mired in a depravity that begs to be purged. Evil burns out evil.

But now the reins are pulled back on my bit. I can't operate with the freedom I once had. This new publicity has its adverse effects on my 'choices'. The two detectives were sure it was I who did all the women, and they were almost correct. I've seen them in their unmarked vehicle following me. Following me to my own home here on the most exclusive strip of property in this city. They weren't subtle about their pursuit. They wanted me to know they were there.

I can move about freely, otherwise. I can go out with any number of beautiful women, married and unmarried, and I can take them to the most expensive eateries in town and escort them to concerts and plays and any other sort of public place I desire.

But I'm not altogether free to hunt, now.

I've perused the internet and found a few possibilities online, but I haven't engaged with anyone, the last few weeks. It's to my advantage to lay back and wait. Eventually the public will tire of the stories of all those grisly murders and they'll look for other amusement. There's plenty to entertain them with coming out of Washington, D.C., lately. Our uncrowned clown prince never ceases to fall into his own shit, almost on a daily basis. But even he can be tiresome in large doses.

Sometimes I awaken in a sweat, a cold kind of fever. I have to struggle to control my own impulses to indeed make a new contact on the ether and to act upon it. My blood does not rest easy when I continually frustrate my compulsions to see ruined bodies beneath my blade. The godlike urge to kill comes over me in waves, and I struggle not to let myself to submit to the blood lust.

I want to see their eyes when they pass from life into darkness. It is an act of a god, the killing is. No simple morality can deny me what I was meant to do. The Church *is* the opium of the poor. It controls the instincts of the herd. Nietzsche was correct. Government now takes the place of the Church. They control our natural inclinations, and then we are possessed of needs and desires that can never be fulfilled.

It is difficult to hold back, then. My grandfather and father were able to, but the price must have been very high.

I'm thankful that my father let me know who I really am, and I'm equally thankful that my great grandfather, who was far more unhinged, passed on the history to his own son, Robert.

How many men can say they really know who they are and what they genuinely feel? I think the number is far smaller than anyone might suppose.

I'm able to alleviate some of my pain by engaging in unusual sex with several of the women I'm now seeing. Some of them are in favor of forbidden acts, like anal sex and masochistic intercourse. Some are into three-ways and some are all right with performing lesbian sex with another woman while I watch and then engage with both of them. I've tried it all, but there are only a finite number of 'perverse' acts one can engage in before you've tried them all.

It's not the same as cutting denizens of alleys. It's not the same as destroying human flesh and having the power of death over them. It simply doesn't satisfy. I've found nothing that completes me the way the killings do.

There is, however, a practical side of me. It allows me to function, so far, without returning to my previous vocation.

So, I try to lessen my agony through the subjugation and humiliation I rain down on the women who find my behavior acceptable if not appealing to them.

Tonight, it's bondage. I tie her down to the mattress just as I did my previous homicidal victims. I'll have to forego the homicide, of course.

She's a beautiful woman. Luscious, ripe. Something which almost diverts my attentions from my knife. Her name is Jean. She's married and bored, the usual recipe for such an evening like this one.

I tie her down, face down, each arm and leg secured to the mattress here in my condo. I do not lubricate her because it would eliminate a lot of the pain. But I take her as most animals do, from the backside, and she cries out.

There is some blood, as I withdraw, and it excites me. I know I have my medical bag in the closet, and I am aroused into retrieving it and into taking this gorgeous woman apart on my own bed, but the sensation subsides when I climax.

She's whimpering.

So, I go to the chair and remove my belt from my trousers, and I commence to beating her buttocks and back.

She cries out loudly, but my condo is well-insulated, so no one can hear her. Her cheeks are reddened but I am careful not to beat her so severely that it will leave lasting marks.

I'm aroused again, suddenly, and I enter her. There is a bit more blood when I withdraw, but it doesn't seem to be too copious. I finish quickly, once more.

While she's moaning in either pain or sexual exhaustion, I get some lotion from the bathroom and I apply it to her backside. I clean her inside with a dose of peroxide, and she cries out again, but the pain doesn't seem to linger.

I let her loose from her bonds, and surprisingly she tells me she wants me to take her in the standard form of coitus. It takes her ten minutes to convince my member to stand up by fellating me, and then I'm on top of her for at least twenty minutes before I let loose. She's climaxed at least five times in that interval.

When we finally conclude, I warn her to keep her rear clean and to use some mild antiseptic where I may have slightly torn her, inside.

She tells me she loved every minute of it and wants to do it again very soon.

• • • • •

My father abstained from his natural inclinations. It must have taken great strength or great cowardice, on his part. I'm not sure which. But he apparently was able to withstand the fever in the blood that Francis had. And who knows about Francis's ancestors? Perhaps they were predators, as well. Maybe they couldn't hold back from the butchery that I and my forefather practiced. It is entirely possible that this so-called 'evil' was present long before Francis sprang into the light. And did Francis's father pass the story on to my grandfather?

I wonder if my mother and grandmother knew. I suppose they did not, because what conventional woman could live with the 'horror' of that kind of knowledge? It's not likely. Francis was not married in London, that I know of. So, he had no one to be accountable to for his nocturnal forays into the alleys of Whitechapel. There was no one to suspect him of his 'heinous' crimes. It was more convenient for him to be alone, back in the Old Country.

He was always the stranger in a strange land, at any rate. His Irish background could not have made it easy to fit in with the general population of London in his era. The Micks were the niggers, back in jolly old Britannia. But there was no work and less food on the Isle of Saints and Scholars. Just dirt and rocks. My ancestors were always the lowliest of the low. The untouchable caste, in the UK.

And is it any wonder that anger was elevated to rage and that Francis sought an even lower class than himself to vent that fury upon?

• • • • •

Wherever I go, they're there behind me. When I head to work, they are behind me in traffic. They make no pretense; they don't hide by shifting lanes to stay out of my rearview mirrors.

Now when I get home and I have no appointments for the evening, I entertain the thought that I should be chained up inside my condo as the Wolfman straps himself inside of a locked room.

Monsters *are* aware, after all, that they are monsters. It's not as if I don't understand that most people would think I'm depraved, I'm a lunatic. It feels *sane*, inside me. I am all that, I know. I'm not an empath who feels what others feel. I know only myself. I experience only my own desires. I can intellectually understand what others think, believe, and feel, but it's all foreign to me.

I'm thinking about filing a complaint through my lawyer about harassment. It'll keep my counselor busy, and I haven't given him much work since the sexual abuse complaint. When my attorney threatened to go public and sue her for defamation and slander, she backed off. I know the complaint was what pointed Parisi and his partner toward me in the murders. Somehow, I know that was what triggered them in my direction. I'm just not sure what they were told by some other cop about me. They had to come up with my name somehow, and it had to be that woman's complaint.

I feel as though I may have to settle with her on my own terms, sometime soon. It would be a precarious adventure, but it would be worth the obvious danger to myself.

Wasn't it Faulkner who said history never dies and that it is alive and involved in the present?

I don't know, but whoever said it or wrote it was correct. I'm the product of those who came before me, as we all are. No one truly comes into the world as a lone individual. All those cells and nerves and human pieces are inherited.

Free will is a myth. It gives us a false conscience. It burdens us with man-made morality.

In the end, we revert to whomever we really are.

CHAPTER TEN

Doris Kenyon is the tethered goat. She's the policewoman who has volunteered to meet up with a 'date' at the same Orland Park motel for a four-hour 'nap.'

"Is he that bold?" Maria asks as we head out to the southwest side to surveil Doris.

"We don't have much choice but to find out."

She's driving, tonight, and it's a lousy evening for a stakeout. It's thundering and lightning as if it were a scene from Edgar Poe. Visibility is bad, and the wipers can't keep up with the driving rain that washes away most of our vision.

Doris is wired. We'll hear everything that's happening, if the weather doesn't get in the way. We'll be close enough to her that the electricity in the air shouldn't pose a problem. But the best laid plans and all that. There will be another pair of homicide detectives meeting us out at the nap joint. Bill Carrigan and Tom Joseph will meet us out there on Southwest Highway.

You never know if the mark is strapped, and if it's Tracy, the odds are pretty good he'll be carrying.

The pounding of the rain continues on the windshield as we arrive. I see Joseph and Carrigan parked in another cop ride at the far end of the lot. Maria puts us down three doors from where Doris awaits her 'date.'

"Can you hear me?" Doris asks via her wire.

Maria flashes the headlights once.

"I saw that," Doris confirms. "He's late. Ten minutes."

Then there's silence. The appointment was for eight o'clock. He's a quarter hour late.

I can't play my CDs because they make too much racket.

We can hardly make out in the front seat of an unmarked police vehicle. It would be highly unprofessional, although it might make nice cover for the two of us. But neither of us is in the mood.

I'm thinking Tracy can't be this bold, to come back to the scene of the fourth murder, but you never know with series killers. He might be trying to taunt us, especially after we've been tailing Tracy for weeks. Maybe this'll be his way of taunting us. The guy might have more balls than brains. We can only hope.

"Can't be Tracy. He'd be nuts," she remarks.

"Maybe we could get romantic. Might fool him," I smile.

"You can't be real," she grins.

"I can wait until we get home, whenever that might be."

A half hour passes.

"How long should we wait?" Doris asks from the room three doors down.

We can't communicate with her. We can only hear her.

She knows this deal might be dangerous, but she's trying to move up to a detective's shield. It doesn't hurt her chances to put herself in the line of fire. I think she'd like to wind up working with our crew. Homicide is the elite division in the CPD, and this might get her more street cred.

I don't know what our time limit really is, but forty-five minutes have gone by.

When an hour elapses, headlights pierce the rain that has only slightly eased up. The driver parks in front of Doris's room, but he doesn't get out of the car. It's some kind of dark Toyota, not the vehicle we've seen Dr. Tracy driving.

"Who is this guy?" Maria whispers.

"We'll find out, in a minute."

Five minutes go by, and he just sits inside his car.

"We're going to roust this guy now," I tell Joseph and Carrigan over our radio.

"We're coming," Joseph replies.

But before I can open the passenger's door on my side, the Toyota shrieks into reverse and spits up gravel as it flies into forward gear and tears toward the entrance of the parking lot.

Maria puts the strobes on inside our windshield, and she fires our Ford into reverse. We slide on the wet gravel, but she gets us going after the Toyota. The other guy's got some distance between us, and our brother homicides are tailing behind us at 80. The mark must be going in triple digits as he continues to outdistance us, but the old adage is still true: You can't outrun a radio.

There are two County Coppers waiting for him at 112th Street on Southwest Highway. They block either lane, and there's nowhere for the Toyota to go unless he wants to ram one of them. He screeches to a stop, and then he tries to bolt out of his vehicle.

There is a forest preserve parking lot on our left, and the mark heads for it at full gallop. Maria pulls into the lot, and I'm the first one out of our ride. He's headed out toward a lagoon where people fish for whatever guppies inhabit that murky-looking water. It's more like a slough than a pond.

I've bolted away from Maria, and I can see the strobes of the County cops in the parking lot as their lights twirl round and round and cast their colors toward the slough.

Our man slips and falls on the wet grass in this downpour, and I'm on him, just ten feet from the water. He tries to struggle with me, but I yank his arm behind him and he cries out in pain.

"I'll break it if you don't lie down on your face!" I command.

He doesn't cease and follow my order, and I twist that arm more, and he bellows out again. This guy isn't big, but he isn't weak, either.

So I grasp my cuffs and rap them against the back of his head and he flops prone on the saturated ground. I think he's out like a light.

Police brutality is his battle cry, I'll bet.

We take him down to Headquarters, and of course it's not Sean Tracy. Tracy is obviously smarter than we thought he might be, a few hours ago.

But this man had an athletic bag in the navy-blue Toyota that the County police impounded, and inside the bag was a six-inch surgical knife.

We have him in an interview room in our Headquarters, and Joseph and Carrigan are on the other side of the mirror that allows them to witness our conversation.

His ID reads Franklin Pierce.

"You related to the president by that name?" I ask.

He doesn't appreciate my sense of humor, or he's ignorant of the US Presidents.

"Why the knife, Franklin?" Maria queries.

He remains mute.

"You want a lawyer? Is that it?" I ask him.

"I have the knife for self-defense," he says softly.

"Hookers beat you up frequently?" I pose.

He doesn't respond.

"You need to try harder to be cooperative, Franklin," Maria informs him.

Franklin Pierce, if that is his real name, has pale facial flesh. His eyes are reddened as if he's a weeper or as if he's got really bad allergies. He's clamming up, indeed. But he still hasn't requested an attorney despite my offers for him to make a call.

"Why'd you take off? Been in that situation before, Franklin?" Maria asks.

His face is pocked with the remnants of a bad acne condition. I don't know whether to pity this man or suspect him. The knife is not a good sign. Unless he's a surgeon like Tracy, that blade can't be legal.

"Give us some help," I plead with him. "We want to get some sleep tonight."

He's not budging. The door to the keep is still firmly shut.

"You're making it hard for us to have any faith in you, Franklin," my wife adds. "Tell us why you had the knife."

"I told you," he finally replies. "They can be dangerous. They carry knives and razors, sometimes. I got cut once."

"She have a reason?" I ask him.

"The price. She said it was higher than what she told me the first time."

He was the kid who got picked on in gym class back in high school. They must have been merciless in teasing him about his first name. He should have gone by 'Frank', maybe. High school males can be pricks. Perhaps Franklin couldn't fight back. I'm not sure why I'm rousing pity in myself for a possible suspect, but he's just not our guy. He's a pathetic young man who uses the internet to get laid because he has no other means to find intimacy in the usual social fashion. He has no skills, and his general appearance has been of no help to him.

"The knife is what bothers me, Franklin," I tell him. "I know you're a lonely guy. You've got lots of company, there. But I have to worry about someone who carries an illegal and lethal blade in a gym bag. I know these kinds of women live in a dangerous world and that's why they carry equalizers, but if you're not aware of their world I have trouble walking in your shoes.

"You resisted arrest, also. Not a good idea, either. I'm going to have to book you on that one, my man. I've got no choice...You ever hurt any of them, Franklin, ever cut one of them?"

"I never did anything to any woman. I never hurt anyone."

"You want to call for a lawyer?" Maria asks. "You have rights. Remember? We read them to you."

He remains silent.

"You're not giving us much choice, then. You're going to jail for resisting, Franklin," I tell him again.

He's got nothing else to say, then. So, we walk him down to booking.

• • • • •

"Are we disappointed?" she smiles at me when we sit in the cafeteria downstairs at HQ. It's far past midnight, and the rain hasn't relented yet.

We hear continual rumbles, but the thunder seems to be headed elsewhere, off to the east in Indiana.

"No. I didn't feel it, this time. Tracy's too slick, he's too sly. Don't you think?"

"I wish it had been him. Then we could've gone on our belated honeymoon."

"I want us to go soon, too. But it doesn't look likely, now does it."

She sips her diet drink, and then she chews on some ice.

"You ready to give up the ghost and go home?" she grins.

I love her brown face and her almond-colored eyes. I love her high, Native American cheekbones and everything else about her countenance. I adore her sleek, brown body and every one of her parts. I know I can find no fault with her, and it frightens me because I know I have a legion of flaws in me. She'll find them, eventually, I fear, and then what'll happen to us? There must be imperfections in her somewhere, but I don't want to discover them.

"He was a sad young man. Franklin, I mean. How long do you think he'll be in jail?" she asks.

"Not too long. He didn't have any prior beefs. He should be ready in a day or two."

"And what if he gets cut by one of them or if he slices them, instead?"

"Are you adopting Franklin, Maria?" I laugh.

"Maybe I'm not tough enough for Homicide," she says with a frown.

"You're tough enough. You were in the shit, just like me, except it was in lovely, sunny Iraq."

"I was never in intense combat, the way you were."

"Yeah. I'm kinda happy you weren't, too."

"I was strictly rear echelon, Michael."

"Thank God for tender mercies, my love."

She reaches out for my hand.

"What happens when we want kids?" she asks. "I might want to back off. Kids need a full-time mother."

"We'll figure it out when we get there. You're very good at what you do, Maria. Don't ever sell yourself short. And Natalie still worked after she had the twins. We can afford baby sitters or nursery school...Like I said, wait until we get there."

"I wish Tracy had shown up tonight. I want to get you alone, all to myself."

"We better leave, Maria, before I do something very foolish, right here and right now."

"Does Afghanistan still bother you, at night?" she says.

"Do I talk in my sleep?"

"Once in a while."

"What do I say?" I ask her.

"Nothing that I can figure. It seems like you're in pain, now and then."

"I don't think I've got PTSS, baby."

"No, but I think you're still carrying it around. I can't let go of the faces of the children we saw in Iraq, Michael. I still see the faces."

I don't know what to tell her. We both saw things that no one ought to. It's part of the deal, with war.

"You can tell me things, Michael."

"I want to, but it's hard to get it out."

"I know...God, I want to get Tracy and get us away from this, just for a little while."

"We will. We will, I promise. Tracy's not nearly as important as you are, Maria."

She smiles sadly, grips my hand tightly, and we get up and head home.

• • • • •

"I always hated high speed chases, avoided them whenever I could, and when I couldn't avoid them, Doc took the wheel."

I sit in the backyard with my father on an unusually hot and humid late-September afternoon. I related the scene with Franklin. Maria is inside with Natalie, and they're preparing the food that'll accompany the cookout in my dad's yard, what used to be my and Mary's backyard. We grew up in this house, on this property. Our neighbors have remained the same since I was very young. My dad is civil to them. He says hello. But he's always been pretty much remote except to his own blood family. After Doc died, he was friendless, at least as far as male companionship goes. He's got Natalie, and now that they're both retired, they do everything and go everywhere together.

I think he's making up for time lost with the death of my mother, Erin. He could never be with her as often as he would have liked to. The cancer denied him the time with my mom. Mary and I watched him suffer in silence. Yes, there were a few women before Natalie, but nothing lasted very long, and he was always alone no matter how many other people surrounded him at work and elsewhere.

I don't think he sees himself as a loner, but it was his lot in life, once my mother left. Natalie brought him back, and I'll always love her, almost like a mother, for that. Mary, my sister, feels the same way about Red. She was a God-send at my father's lowest point.

Working homicide can level you and bury you while you're still breathing. Too many deaths, too many murders. They never cease. It's the job. The burnout rate is very high in Homicide. You're not human if it doesn't touch you. Jimmy Parisi is a tough guy, as tough as they get. As tough as any of the operators I knew in the Army Rangers in Afghanistan. Bone hard, he is. But everyone has the soft spot somewhere. You can only hide that point of frailty for so long, and then you're going to be exposed.

It's already got to Maria. I don't know how long she can endure the work.

But I'm a lot like my old man. Someone's got to speak for the dead because no one else will. Maybe the courts and the system of justice might, in the long run, but Homicide is the first line of defense. Or maybe we're really the last line.

"So what do you think about the job, *now*?" my dad asks me.

PART TWO

CHAPTER ELEVEN

The genealogist calls me in early October, so Maria and I take the ride to the University of Chicago together, this time. Robert O'Leary awaits at his doorway.

I told him over the phone that we knew Sean Amjac's name was changed to his maternal side—Tracy, but O'Leary said he wanted to talk to me in person, so we drove to see him.

We sit opposite him at his desk in his cramped quarters. Maria and I are seated on folding chairs.

"I'm sorry it took this long to find anything out, but this family tried to cover its trail, courtesy of Francis Amjac. It's no wonder his great grandchildren took the name of Tracy, their mother."

"*Their* mother?" I ask.

"Sean Tracy has an identical twin. Padraic. But he goes by Patrick. He, also, is an M.D. And Patrick is an oral surgeon. He operates in Oak Park, Hemingway territory," O'Leary grins.

"Twins?" Maria says.

O'Leary nods at my wife.

"Two of them. The identical variety."

We thank him after he shows us the tree he's constructed from Francis Amjac's family. Francis's grandson had two boys, and both of them are very good with knives.

We look up Patrick's address and drive over to Oak Park, which is a western suburb. The drive takes about forty minutes from the University of Chicago in very light, early afternoon traffic.

The receptionist turns solemn when she sees our IDs. She goes back into the innards of the office and tells her boss we're here.

When she returns, she tells us to take a seat, that he's finishing with a patient. Her demeanor has now gone sullen as she re-occupies her chair at the front.

Fifteen minutes later, she tells us to follow her to the doctor's private office.

She leaves us as she opens the door.

Patrick Tracy is a duplicate of his brother Sean. He looks like the first guy we interviewed for the four killings.

He motions for us to sit on two faux-leather, plush chairs.

I hear the slough sound as Maria and I sink into the seats.

"What can I do for you, Detectives?" he says with a serious face.

"We're here about the murders of four women," Maria explains.

"And how in the world can I help you?" he smiles.

"We already talked to your brother Sean," I inform him.

"Then you're one up on me. I haven't spoken to Sean in six years. We're not exactly close."

His eyes stray toward the top of his table. His mood has decidedly turned grim.

"You don't get along?" Maria asks.

"That's a rather personal question, don't you think?" he snaps.

"Murder is a rather personal offense," I counter.

"Yes. I'm sorry," he proffers to Maria.

He taps his fingers absently on the desk top.

"How can I help you?" he asks.

I show him the paper with the dates of the slaughters.

"Recall where you were on these four nights?" I ask.

"Not offhand," he snorts.

"Take your time."

After a few minutes, he responds. He tells us where he was on three of the four homicides, but he can't account for the fourth. The one he doesn't remember is the date on which his twin brother had an alibi.

"I'll need more time to figure out where the hell I was on this one. These times are weeks ago."

"I understand. If you'll tell us who you were with on the three you recall, we'll verify them. When you figure out the fourth, give us a call."

I hand him my business card. Then we get up and leave him sitting there. He's drumming his fingertips again as we leave.

• • • • •

We take our lunch break at a White Castle in Berwyn. Berwyn was Capone territory, my dad told me long ago. So was Cicero. They're both blue collar 'burbs.

"You think they have similar habits?" Maria asks.

Her face has gone stony, now.

"Genetics tells the tale, sometimes," I reply.

"But not always," she adds.

"No, not always."

We start in on our cheese sliders and Diet Cokes. I'm having the onion rings, as well. Might as well go whole hog on the indigestion. We'll both be gassing up the bedroom, tonight. It's the price you pay for these greasy delights.

The onions make you burp deliciously for days afterward, too.

"No, not always, but the tendencies are usually there. It doesn't mean he's doing the same heinous deeds as Sean is, but he might be, and that'd take care of the homicide that Sean has the cast iron alibi for," I remind her.

She sips at her soda. We're in a booth, and the Castle is jammed because it's around noon. The worst time you can eat here. It's much more intimate during the early hours of the morning, but all the attendant chatter in here acts as white noise, so no one is likely listening to our conversation.

"I think it's all rather terrifying."

"Two of them plying the same trade, you mean?" I ask.

She nods in affirmation.

"He might come up with an alibi for the one he couldn't recall," I remind her.

"It's still scary."

"They're both surgeons, love. Both really good with a blade."

"That's what scares me the most."

• • • • •

"Jesus Christ," the Captain murmurs. "Jesus Christ. Two of them?"

"Maybe," I tell him.

I'm in his office, and Maria is chasing down anything she can find on Padraic, Patrick Tracy.

Then I relate to him my half-baked or fully-baked theory on Sean Amjac's likely connection to Jack the Ripper.

"That's nuts. Absolutely whack-a-mole."

"I know how it sounds, but there it is," I tell him.

I'm looking him right in the eye, unapologetically.

"You haven't said a word of this to the media, have you?" he demands.

I shake my head.

"Then *don't,*" he commands. "I can just imagine the fallout on that idea."

"They won't hear it from me. But you know how they like to research homicides. If I found out about that family's bony closet, then they can."

"Then let them, but it's not coming from us, Parisi."

I nod in agreement.

I tell him how Francis Amjac migrated here just after the Whitechapel murders ceased, and he already knows, as everyone does, that Jack the Ripper was never apprehended. It might just have tickled his copper's fancy, however. I don't know how a policeman could not be fascinated by such an unlikely possibility, but there it is.

"You think this guy Patrick might have done one of the women," he repeats.

"Yeah. Or maybe it's Patrick that did all of them. Anything's possible now that the twin showed up on the radar. They both fell out of the same family tree. The rotten fruit of a rotten tree. Or whatever."

"Just make sure you and your partner keep all this to yourselves."

"It was never going to go any other way, Captain."

• • • • •

Maria has a doctor's appointment on that following Friday. I call the old man and ask to take him to lunch. I tell him to invite Natalie, too. We meet at Alonzo's Pizza on 83rd and Pulaski. They've got the best thin crust in the city.

They're in the booth when I arrive at a little after noon. I explain that Maria's at the doctor's.

"Any big surprises?" Natalie smiles.

She's younger than my father by almost twenty years, and she looks remarkably youthful for a woman in her early fifties. Natalie has that gorgeous auburn hair, my favorite hue.

"I don't think so," I blush.

"It's what happens when you're in close quarters," my dad jokes.

"Not yet," I say.

"So," Jimmy Parisi poses. "What's up?"

I tell him the tale of the murderous twins. I include the hypothesis about The Ripper.

"Christ," he says.

"Wow," Natalie enjoins.

"I know. It's batshit crazy."

"It is at the lip of the envelope," Jimmy Parisi concurs.

"I love it. Again, wow!" Natalie blurts.

"Didn't you have a thing with a cutter?" I ask him.

"We both did," he answers.

"There was a scene at the house," Natalie tells me.

Her face goes dark.

"A shooting?" I ask.

"We both were involved in it," she says. "Your dad backed me up and we had to employ force. In other words, we shot the son of a bitch before he shot the both of us."

She doesn't appear happy about her statement.

"I never used a gun in the line of duty again."

Then the pizza and soft drinks arrive and we engage in the lunch. When we're finished, my father looks directly at me.

"They called our guy 'The Farmer'. He harvested the internal organs of the women he butchered."

"I remember, now," I tell them. "But this guy doesn't sell the spare parts. He leaves them around the bodies. Seems like he has a kind of ritual about it."

"I've read the literature about the savage in London," my dad tells me. "I read a lot of true crime stuff. But a lot of the material on this Ripper was half-assed fabrication. A lot of it was lies spread by the local tabloids. Which is the wont of tabloids, to spread the sensational."

"But there was *someone* killing hookers in Whitechapel, and he was never caught, and I came up with Sean Amjac's face because someone at Scotland Yard thought he might be their man. It's strange how he boogied to America and *then* the slayings ceased."

"I've got goosebumps, dammit!" Natalie laughs. "I know. There's nothing humorous, here."

"It's okay," I tell her. "I've received the horse laugh previously when I expressed my 'hunch.'"

"Can you imagine if it were true?" she says.

"Yeah, I've imagined," I tell them both. "It scares me, also."

I tell them how we tried to set up a sting at the motel in Orland Park. I recount all our surveillance on Sean.

"And now you have to look at Patrick, the other one."

I nod at my father.

"I sort of wish I was still around for this one," he says.

"Don't you dare. Don't you even think it," Red tells him.

We all three laugh, aloud.

"I would like to consult you both, from time to time, if that's all right," I ask.

"Of course you can!" Natalie answers.

She covers my hand with hers.

She saved my father's life. I can't forget what she did for him and Mary and me.

"We're sworn to secrecy. The Captain would blow a rod if he found out I told you."

"He ain't going to hear it from us. We're mum on the deal," he affirms.

"You sure Maria isn't at the gynee's?" Natalie teases.

• • • • •

I embrace her when she walks into the apartment around five-thirty.

"What's all that about?" she smiles.

Then she kisses me again.

"Are you pregnant?"

"*What?"* she laughs loudly.

"I thought maybe..."

"It's my six months checkup. Sorry. No surprise inside, yet."

She showers, and then I take her out to dinner at an expensive steakhouse.

"What's the occasion?" she asks as we're seated at Frederick's on Mannheim, way out in the southernmost sticks.

"Nothing extraordinary. I just wanted to take you out for something better than pizza or burgers," I explain.

"There's something beneath the surface, here," she grins slyly.

"That's the Native American in you."

"Yeah, sure. You going to tell me?"

The waiter takes our drink orders and we peruse the menus. The place is swank and the prices are obscene, but I think she deserves it. I wish I could take her to places like this regularly, but I know what our paychecks look like.

"I want to have a kid. How about you?" I blurt.

She chokes on her cocktail, briefly. Some of the drink dribbles out of her nostrils.

She laughs when the quick gagging ceases.

"Don't do that to me."

Then she sees that I'm serious.

"You want us to have a baby."

"I can hardly get someone else to do it for me."

She eyeballs me even more intensely.

"We could live on one paycheck?" she asks.

There, she's got me.

"Don't you suppose we ought to save up a few years for all this?" Maria queries.

"That'd be the pragmatic thing to do. Yeah."

"No, that'd be the sane thing to do," she corrects.

"I won't bring it up again."

I feel the blush gather on my cheeks.

"Stop it. I want a baby, too. But my child-rearing years haven't evaporated just yet, Michael. Don't you want to enjoy us all by ourselves for a little while longer?"

CHAPTER TWELVE

Patrick Amjac Tracy, Chicago, 2017

We are identical twins in only a physical way. And we are similar in our tendency to commit murder. In every other way that I can conceive, we are alien to one another. We are, however, both in the medical profession, I must admit. But our personalities were never a match except in that one peculiar way that we inherited from the perhaps the greatest monster in the annals of 19th Century Great Britain.

I suppose the Brits would blame our inherited trait on our Irish background, but the English have a long history of predators and homicidal lunatics. They invented drawing and quartering. They put heads on pikes in the Tower of London. Richard III had little boys murdered, so the legend goes.

My lone matching tendency to use a knife for non-legitimate reasons has brought these homicide detectives to my door. And I think it happened because my brother committed those other three slayings. Our methods must be remarkably alike if the police looked at Sean first.

But I have only the one killing on my soul, at the moment. It wasn't supposed to happen. I felt I had my inner demons at bay until I could no longer hold back. Why we both seem to have the same penchant for whores is due to our ties to Francis, our beloved great grandfather who escaped Scotland Yard and the Hangman, back in 1891. It seems strange that the police never listed Francis as a prime suspect since it was only after his escape to America that the Ripper murders ceased. I'm sure someone at the Yard must have made the connection, but it never made the newspapers. There were physicians under suspicion, as well as the Prince of Wales, but Francis Amjac never made the most wanted poster.

He escaped justice, as has Sean, and now me, up until the present moment. Somehow the two of us have been framed in the spotlight. I have to be careful.

I live a quiet life. When I heard the story from our father of our real roots, I vowed never to bring a child of my own into the world. I have maintained that promise. I have certainly not lived the celibate life, but any sexual encounter I've had will not produce offspring since I've had a vasectomy. To doubly insure my promise to remain childless, I've made certain all my romantic partners have used proper birth control. They could have lied to me, but I don't think so. Vasectomies are fairly reliable.

There have been women in my life, yes, but if they begin talking about commitment and family, I'm on my way out the door. Monogamy is not something I'm suited for, anyway.

I was doing well on the other abstinence, too, until recently. I've had the urge to go out on the same hunt that Francis and my brother were compelled to do, but I never gave into the impulse until this singular event.

You find them online, currently. 'Dating services' and outright prostitution notices. I don't know how much the vice police are monitoring the internet, but there seems to be an overwhelming amount of choices, if you're looking for something illicit. And if I'm using the ether, I figure that's how my brother stalks the women he wants to obliterate.

There is an anger in us both. I'm sure a psychiatrist would see it as misogyny. He'd likely be correct. I don't see women as the equals of men, and I don't have much respect for the male of the species, either. Mark Twain looked at humanity as creatures climbing out of the mud and the primordial slime, and he wasn't wrong.

There is evil in us all, depending upon the dosage, and the way we're wired in our DNA determines how big a helping of barbarism each of us is allotted to. My forbears must have received more than the usual share, and hence I have Stevenson's Mr. Hyde in my personal makeup. I have struggled against my inclinations, but I've had the same luck in overcoming it as most drug addicts do at kicking their habits.

Free will, after all, is the little fiction we delude ourselves with. We cannot say no, Nancy. Not forever, at least. We can go to therapy, take the cure, head to Betty Ford, and it all comes to the same conclusion, inevitably. We are slaves to our natural inclinations. We are as predictable as automatons. If we somehow break the mold, we return to form, at the end of the day. It's just a matter of time as to when we'll resign ourselves to what is called fate. Some called it determinism. Call it what you will. We're all a non-cartoon version of Popeye—"*I am what I am.*"

The two detectives have been following me to work and also when I go out socially with the woman I'm now seeing. They are not secretive about their pursuit, either. They appear in plain sight in their police vehicle directly behind me in traffic. They've shown up repeatedly in the last few days.

I still cannot come up with an excuse for the date I met the woman at the motel. There's no adequate lie I can create. I will not involve anyone I know as an alibi because asking them to back me up would cause them to become suspicious of my motive, and after all the recent publicity about the four murders of the whores, they might be inclined to tell these two cops about my plea for help.

I have to be careful. It's not a good time to go on the hunt, obviously. Who knows? Maybe they're attempting to set me or my brother up with a ruse online. They're not stupid, although they can be inept quite often.

• • • • •

Andrea is a slut. Perhaps the word 'cunt' would apply. She's twice divorced and I'm with her because she has no intention of trying to ring up divorce number three. She's a general surgeon. I met her at a hospital where I operated. She's got a wonderful reputation as a cutter, as well. Her more deserved recognition should emanate from her sexual behavior. Andrea doesn't require standard sex. She likes it rough and strange.

Tonight, she wants to try the near-strangulation fad which supposedly enhances orgasm. She is still seeing me because she knows neither of us seeks entanglements.

Her body is wonderful and lithe. She's childless, which is also a perk.

"Are you all right with it?" she smiles.

I'm not sure I should put myself in a situation like nearly choking her lifeless so she can achieve a maximum come. But I'm drawn to her because there are no ties, and I know I won't cross over and submit to my desire to tear her all up because she is white, she is prominent, and because I won't get away with it because she will be missed. She's not the trash that gets discarded without notice or care.

"I'm good."

She smiles at me, here atop her bed in her near north apartment. Andrea lives in a trendy neighborhood not far from the Loop, and I'm not in command of the environment here. This isn't a grimy motel on a grimy back road. This is in the heart of the fashionable element in the city, and she does have neighbors who are aware of her.

Otherwise, I might have thought seriously about slicing her apart. She *is* a cunt, after all. Andrea is a very unsavory sort of woman. She cannot connect with a mate, and it's obvious why she hasn't stayed with a single man she's attached herself to. She's ruthless and unkind and untrustworthy. Which is why I want her as badly as I do. I know it's all just temporary with Andrea, and the brevity of it all is what arouses me most. Evil does come in attractive shapes.

We begin with a more mundane sort of coitus. The choking will come in the finale after all the usual foreplay. Her body should belong to a much younger woman, even though Andrea is only in her late thirties. The breasts are erect and I'm certain they haven't been surgically altered. I think I would recognize an enhancement if I saw one.

Her pubic hair is shaped and manicured. Her flesh is creamy and flawless. Her hips are voluptuous but not overly large and her ass is a work worthy of the French Impressionists. She makes me erect simply taking her all in.

I mount her and begin slowly. Her blue eyes seem to wander off away from me. Her lips are full and lush, and she uses them to put me in pure pain when she feels fit to do it. I've never had better oral sex performed upon me, but she does it only when she is so inclined. Not tonight. Not yet, at least.

I'm atop her for an extended time, and then she starts to rock and grind against me more intensely. Her black hair is spread across the pillows, and her eyes are still somewhere else. Then she begins talking to me, and it almost sounds like biblical 'tongues'. It certainly isn't English. It's the tone, the passion, that communicates and resonates with me.

She tells me to take her throat, finally.

I place both hands on her white, elegant neck.

I squeeze gently, at first.

"Harder," she demands.

I make my grip firmer.

"Oh, I'm coming. Harder!"

She's almost pleading.

I tighten my fingers about her throat, and Andrea's eyes widen. I know I'm cutting off her air, now.

She begins to lift me off the mattress as if we're being levitated.

I make it a clench. Her face reddens. I'm beginning to feel the attendant tingle that signals my own orgasm. It's building like a crescendo in a Wagnerian opera.

She cannot breathe. I see it in her distressed eyes, but she doesn't urge me to stop. We're still lifted above her sheets as if by some form of sorcery. We seem to be floating, weightless.

Her face contorts and begins to turn darker, now. I cannot stop choking her. I want to go all the way, kill her, and then come back at her with one of her kitchen knives and butcher her the way I did my only kill.

I'm beyond being able to stop. I'm going to do it in spite of anything reasonable. I know I'll get caught if I continue, but I can't hold back. She shakes her head violently from side to side and she's fallen back to the bed and taken me with her but I don't cease, I don't let go, and then she makes a gargling, choking noise with her mouth wide open, and she thrusts a knee to my genitals and lightning flashes across my eyes and I release her and fall away to her side.

I'm balled up in agony, and even though the pain is searing through my groin, I want to clamp hold of her throat once more and this time finish what I began.

But when I get my breath back and when the agony finally withdraws, I feel her fingers on my back. And then she turns me over and begins to soothe my sagging member with those incredible lips.

• • • • •

My father was a cold-blooded bastard, and it's fairly obvious that his grandfather was the same. Which makes Sean and me cold-blooded bastards, as well, but the illegitimate term does not really apply since we were both duly registered as the result of a fruitful marriage.

I don't remember my father ever telling either of us that he loved us or cared a damn about us. My mother was aloof, as well. I don't know if she was aware of Francis's history, but if she was, she never told us anything about it. My father was the one who warned us what was lurking inside us.

As far as either Sean or I know, he never continued the family tradition. Somehow, he was able to withstand the call of the knife. He, too, was a surgeon, but the only cutting he employed was legitimate. He took his oath a bit more seriously than Sean or I have.

It would somehow be ironic if I were the one caught by the police since Francis and Sean are guilty of multiple murders. My brother and my great grandfather share status I have not yet achieved.

• • • • •

Andrea wants to see me tonight. I know I'll give in and see her again and find out what kind of perversity she requires this time. But I'll have to control myself better. I almost gave in to my nature, last time.

After it was over, she told me how satisfying it was.

"Was it good for you, too?" she asked.

"Couldn't you tell?" I replied.

"You did become just a bit overly enthusiastic," she smiled.

The conversation followed her incredible blow job.

"I'm sorry."

"Never apologize. It's a sign of weakness," she smiled triumphantly.

"Then I suppose I'm weak."

"I don't think so. I think you're very strong. Only you haven't allowed yourself to find out who you really are, what you really want."

"I think I know what I really want."

Then I yanked her hair and forced her on her back and slammed at her for another fifteen minutes before we both went airborne again—but this time without the near-death experience for her.

We were lathered up pretty well, so we went into her generously-sized shower and proceded yet again against her wet, tiled wall.

"What do you really want?" she said, her black tresses streaming down against her back.

"I really want to destroy you."

She smiled.

"You really have a way with words," she laughed.

"I try to be honest."

She looked at me quizzically, and then we walked out of her shower.

• • • • •

They're behind me again, so I stop the car on Michigan Avenue and I pull off to the curb.

But they cruise right past me.

When I'm headed home, they're following me yet again.

• • • • •

I call Sean on the telephone. He actually picks up, which he never does when he sees it's my number.

"They know," I tell my brother.

• • • • •

We meet at a Starbuck's on Michigan Avenue. This time I didn't see the two homicide detectives behind me.

"Was anyone following you?" I ask my brother as we sit in a secluded booth toward the back.

"Not that I'm aware of," he replies.

"They know."

"Who's they?" he smiles.

"You know or you wouldn't be here."

He is indeed my mirror image.

"You mean the police?"

"You know who I mean," I tell him.

"Are you trying to warn me?" he laughs.

"How very cavalier of you, Sean."

"How long did you think you'd be able to hold out, brother of mine?"

I feel my face begin to blush. I feel the heat.

"You feel no guilt?" I ask him.

"Guilt? For what?"

"You honestly have no sense of remorse?" I inquire.

"Don't talk like an idiot. It doesn't trouble you, either."

"How do you know that?" I demand.

"You and I sprang from the same loins. We are both our father's sons. And our Francis's, before him. You know what you are. Don't come simpering to me, bleating about your heavy conscience."

"It doesn't bother me, Sean. I'm just like you. But I'd prefer not to go to prison or to my execution."

"Then why are we here?"

"I'm suggesting we need to work together."

"How?"

"Perhaps we can come up with reasons for the police to seek someone else in these terrible murders," I tell him.

"How does that occur?" he smiles.

"Maybe we should make two detectives a bit less inclined to be aggressive in our apprehension," I explain.

CHAPTER THIRTEEN

We explore the usual sights in Chicago because we've never seen them together. We stroll Navy Pier. We walk the Magnificent Mile. We wander the Loop. Our days off are infrequent. Even though the murders of the prostitutes have halted, the pressure has been increased on us to find the killer or killers. Maria and I have a good idea who they are, but bringing them before the prosecutor takes evidence.

The body he wiped with bleach comes up negative. He left us nothing, no fibers, no semen, no DNA. It was washed away with the bleach. Apparently, he was very thorough in his purge.

I can't escape the twins even when it's my wife and I alone. They won't vanish upon command. They linger like stench in the air, like roadkill. Their handiwork leaves an odor that won't float off into the wind.

We walk into the Art Institute on Michigan. It's my favorite spot because my father took me here many times. I cannot draw or render, but I like to look at what's here. It'd take a good chunk of my lifetime to see everything they have, but I am always particularly drawn to the French Impressionists. I'm certainly not well-read on Gaugin and Renoir and Matisse and Lautrec and Manet and Monet, but I'm always fascinated by their art. My favorite, however, remains Van Gogh. His pain and passion are literally palpable. The smudges that are the black crows in a blazing sky with an unforgiving sun. The haystacks and the weary farm workers. And there is 'Sunny Midi Arles'. I can spend an hour just boring into that canvas.

Maria has to drag me away.

The Institute is crowded because it's a Saturday. There are swarms of onlookers.

My wife is jostled by a man passing her on the way to the Renoirs. It's nothing more than a bump, so I just let it go. I did not see his face, but he staggered her slightly as he passed her.

"Are you okay?" I ask.

The herd continues to stream by us.

"I'm all right...But it felt like I was stuck by something, here on the back of my arm."

I see a red mark on her flesh, and now I want to catch up with the culprit. I begin to lead Maria in the direction he was headed. It's slow going because of the crowd.

"It's all right, Michael. He's gone, anyway."

But by the time we stop at the Institute's café, Maria has become ill. A rash breaks out on her cheeks, and her breathing is labored.

I summon a security guard and tell him my wife needs immediate medical attention. She's still seated upright at a café table with me, but her breathing becomes even more impaired, and her breath is more pronouncedly labored.

The EMTs arrive within eight minutes. I clock them on the timepiece on the wall. The security guys have cleared us a generous space in the café and have moved any bystanders from our vicinity.

They take her to the ambulance out front by the Michigan Avenue curb, out by the lions that stand sentinel to the Art Institute.

They have her on oxygen as soon as they've got her aboard the ambulance. We speed off to Rush Hospital because it's close.

At Emergency, she's wheeled into an exam room immediately. I'm with her in the room. Her breathing seems less laborious, now, but she still looks pale and ill. Her brown flesh has turned into a sickly kind of yellow, and the facial rash remains.

The ER doctor appears in short order.

He asks her if she's allergic to anything, and she shakes her head feebly.

"Did she eat anything there?" the thirty-something, balding MD asks me.

"No. But she has a puncture on her arm. Someone bumped into her," I remember.

He examines the prick mark.

"Looks like a needle hole," he says. "We'll need to take a sample of her blood."

He orders a blood sample from the female ER nurse who's attending him. She takes the sample and brings it off to the lab.

"It'll be a little bit, but it looks like a severe reaction to something that was injected into her. Did you see who did this?"

"Just the back of him. He got away in the crowd. It was jammed, and then I asked her what happened and he was gone."

I show him my ID.

"My wife is a detective, too."

I'm not expecting special treatment, but I figure it can't hurt, and now is no time to play humble.

• • • • •

It takes about an hour for them to figure out what she was given, but they treat it with some drug I've never heard of, and the swelling and the rash subsides, and Maria's breathing returns to normal. Her skin tone also reverts to itself, and she looks a lot better.

But the ER doctor, his name is Ben Manion, wants to keep her overnight so they can keep an eye on her.

I'm in her private room with her, and the TV is on, on the far wall, but the sound is muted. Her nurse has been in to see her twice in the last half hour, but Maria seems to improve quickly.

Now my anger mounts just as fast as her color is returning to her.

I want to hunt for this bastard. I want him immediately.

It occurs to me that I know the perpetrator. At least I have two choices as to whom he is.

The twins, of course.

The investigation has been placed on a new plane. It's become personal. But I don't say anything to Maria. She needs to get out of the hospital. She's likely made the connection to the Tracys all by herself anyhow, by now.

"How are you?" I ask.

I grip her hand.

"This is what we get for behaving like a normal couple," she grins sadly.

"We were never a normal couple."

"And neither are they. I know it was one of them, Michael. They're reacting aggressively. What have they got to lose? They know we'll get them, sooner or later."

I should remember she's a homicide detective and not just my wife. It didn't take her long to figure it out.

• • • • •

She's released the next afternoon, Sunday. I bring the sawed-off shotgun I carry in the squad and leave it in our bedroom. Maria drops her jaw.

"I don't like that thing in our house. We have sidearms."

She's referring to the 9 millimeters we each carry in our holsters. I carry a .38 bulldog strapped to my ankle. Another inheritance from my father. It has stopping power that the millimeter does not. Maria was in the military, so she was conversant with weapons before I ever knew her, but she wasn't required to use them in her tours of duty in Iraq.

"It's an equalizer. Aim it at his middle, and when he goes down, aim it where his ankles would be."

"I never heard you talk like this. I mean you don't talk about Afghanistan at all, and now we have a canon in the bedroom."

"They never came at us directly until now. The doctor said you might've died, Maria."

"I heard him. I was there."

"I want to protect you, us."

"You think they'll come here?"

I don't answer her, at first.

"It's more likely they want to intimidate us. Coming after cops is decidedly unhinged. I don't think they're that kind of crazy. They're both cowards. That's why they attack women. He did a drive-by on you. He didn't show his face. Not just because he didn't want you to make him. They're both gutless, Maria. But I don't want us to find out the hard way that I've misjudged them."

She accepts the shotgun in our room.

"I don't want either of us going out alone when we can help it."

"I supposed I'm duly frightened, now," she shoots at me.

"Fear's a good thing. A very good quality to have when there's reason to be afraid. I was never without it in my tours, not for a second. I still carry it around now."

I stroke her cheek gently with my fingers. She grabs hold of my hand.

"This is a rotten way to start a life," she tells me softly.

• • • • •

"Tell him I want to see him," I tell Sean Tracy's receptionist.

"But he's got a patient—"

I walk past her and proceed to his clinic. There's a patient, a woman, in his operating chair, and his surgical nurse is with him.

"You can't be here!" the nurse chirps.

"I'll see you now," I tell Tracy with a controlled, even tone.

The woman is sedated and is not aware of me. There's also an anesthesiologist in the room. He doesn't speak.

"You come with me or I'll take you out of here," I say. The words are emotionless.

He lowers his mask and follows me to his private office.

He sits down at his desk and is about to remonstrate when I take him by the throat. He tries to grab hold of my arms, but I clamp tighter and he lets his arms go limp.

"You ever come close to my wife again and I'll pay you a final visit. Do you understand?"

I let go of his throat. He gulps in air.

"I'm going to report this!" he says hoarsely.

"Are we being filmed?" I ask.

He looks at me blankly.

"I didn't think so. And next time I'll show up where you live. Locks won't do you any good. Bars on the windows won't help, even though you live way up high. You can get to anyone if you want to, Doctor, and I'll be waiting for you, security guards or whatever. And since you didn't take the precaution to install video, it's a he-said, he-said scenario. You follow, Tracy?"

He nods, massaging his throat.

"You're going to jail if they don't execute you. You and your twin brother. I know who you are. I know where you came from. Let's see how well you learn to adapt. It won't make any difference. It's going to end badly for both of you.

"Don't ever come within a mile of my wife again. Pass it on to your brother."

I close his door quietly behind me.

• • • • •

I'm not leaving it to word of mouth.

I replay the scene at brother Patrick's place of employment. He struggles when I surprise him with a choking grip in his private office, as well, and his arms go limp as I watch the light in his hazel eyes go dim before I allow him to breathe again.

My father's way of doing the job went the way of all the species that couldn't adapt to change. You can't rough up suspects. It's simply not done, anymore. I suppose I wasn't thinking rationally. I could lose my livelihood because of my actions.

But it never occurred to me that my methodology was unacceptable to current standards. I'm open to litigation, but I really don't care. I could always make a living doing wet work for the CIA or some similar outfit. I've had my share of offers. The money is far better than my pay scale as a homicide detective. I wouldn't have to worry about paying taxes.

I really don't want to go there. By nature, I'm one who likes to please. I like to follow the rules and avoid the consequences of bad behavior. I've never killed in any situation other than self-defense, and I don't want to go south there, either.

But when I saw Maria struggling for air, it cut all ties. These killers have no rules, and if that's the way they're going to play it, all right. I'm not cut out to become an outlaw. But my father visited a priest when he found out that I was being abused, and I'm not about to tolerate either of them, or anyone else, harming Maria.

She's all I've got. I have a sister and a father and two half-sisters, but Maria's all I've got of a family of my own. I was never in this situation before, and the Tracys aren't going to take her away from me.

• • • • •

"You did *what?*"

He looks almost amused.

"You can't do that, Michael. You know better...Any splashback, yet?"

I shake my head in the negative.

"I wouldn't try it again."

"They're not allowed to touch her. All rules are off."

He watches me carefully. It's October, and the chill has arrived. The Hawk is blowing out of the northeast, off the Lake, and the temperature is in the mid-forties. Maybe an early winter is on the way. Global warming, and everything. The weather's gone nuts, just like the country.

"I recall the same attitude when that Farmer decided to put the touch on Natalie."

"You took it personally."

"In a very prejudicial way, Michael. Still, things have changed. You know that. This is not a battlefield, even though it feels like it, sometimes. I haven't got any other conventional wisdom for you, son. You got to protect the family.

"Maybe you should have a talk with your captain. Get some security assigned to you."

"Then he'll know we're married and we'll lose the partnership."

"I had to accept it when I married Natalie. And it's probably a good idea to work with other partners. It didn't hurt Red and me."

I take a sip out of the cold can of Old Style. It's the only beer he drinks, and it's not so bad. I prefer micro-brews, but this is the old man's standby beer.

"She could've died, Pa."

"Yes, she could have. It's not that I don't empathize with you, Michael. I've got sins of my own. Plenty of them."

He's referring to that pedophile priest.

"Are you prepared to kill them both, Michael?"

I don't answer.

"You prepared to live in their world?"

"I won't let them hurt her. They've already killed at least four women that we know about."

"It's your sworn duty and all that to bring them to justice. You're not a hired hangman. Just a policeman, and murder is not part of the job description."

I take another sip of my father's beer and I look into his brown, Italian-American eyes.

CHAPTER FOURTEEN

Maria Elizondo Parisi, Chicago, 2017

I asked him not to go to the Captain, but he insisted, saying it was the only way they could give us security. By 'us' he means me. I tried to explain that I'm almost as good a shot as he is (probably an exaggeration since he was a trained sniper in the Rangers) but it didn't dissuade him.

I know he's thinking about keeping me safe, but it's going to separate us as partners. We both went to the Captain because he again insisted that we agree on the separation.

It doesn't take long for our boss to hand down judgment.

"You're officially un-partnered, right now. I know it probably pisses you both off, but it's not good policy to have married detectives working as duos. It takes away your perspective on shit. At least that's what I'm supposed to tell you.

"Did you get a look at this guy who stuck you?" he asks.

His office as spartan as you'd expect. Like most of the rest of us, the Captain's ex-military. Multiple decorations and all that.

"No. Just the back of him."

Michael concurs that that's all he saw of him, too.

"I don't like this personal shit. It might be better if we assigned someone else to these two assholes. The case is still suffering from lack of evidence, as I understand it. No?"

"We don't have anything to bring to the prosecutor," I explain.

Michael nods in agreement.

"Give me a good reason to leave either of you on this case," he tells us.

Michael insists we are doing everything anyone can do. I stand mute.

The Captain scratches the little bit of hair he has left on his head. Then he appears resolute.

"Michael, you'll stay on them. I'll assign you a new partner as soon as I can. Maria, you're going to work with Ned Diamond. He's got a shitload of outstanding cases and his regular partner is in the hospital with a stroke. The guy's in bad shape and won't be available for a long time, if ever."

We knew this was coming, but I wasn't sure he'd allow either of us to continue after the twins.

"A little birdy told me you paid each of the Tracys a personal visit, Michael."

Michael looks at the carpet beneath his feet. I can hear him breathing out in a huff.

"They've each filed a complaint. But their shit sounds weak. I asked them for proof of extracurricular behavior on your part, Michael, but it shut them up. For the time being, anyway.

"There cannot be a repeat performance."

"Yessir," my husband replies.

"Your dad's day is over. You know that, right?"

"Yes," Michael tells him.

"We can't have that. Not in this social climate. We've already become the bad guys in certain circles, as you know. I talked with Internal Affairs, and they also tell me the Tracys' shit is weak. But don't do it again, or you'll force me to intercede.

"You two are on leave for one week. Get the hell out of town. We'll deal with those twins while you're gone...And I'll try and find you a suitable partner, Michael, who'll keep you on a tighter leash. You've been a bad boy, son. This ain't Afghanistan."

He dismisses us curtly.

• • • • •

A week doesn't give us much time for a honeymoon, but we're going to make the best of it, I tell him. I know he likes southern Wisconsin. He's told me about the trips to Delavan and William's Bay and Lake Geneva.

And he knows Geneva is a basic tourist trap, but he always loved going there when his father could afford the time and the money.

So, we stay in a hotel in Fontana, a resort town which lies on the shores of Lake Geneva. The lake, not the town.

It is scenic, here. It's just across the border from northern Illinois, maybe a drive of ninety minutes. Time is not working with us, on our brief honeymoon, so the driving distance helps.

We buy rings in a jewelry store on the main drag of the town of Lake Geneva. The street isn't too crowded because this is late October, and the tourist season is over. Mostly it's just the locals who live here year-round. The traffic is sparse, and it's easy to find parking, but the meters are a pain because you've got to have quarters to load into them. Michael was aware of the meters, so he brought sufficient change.

The jewelry store has exorbitant prices, but he's buying the rings with some of his 'stash' from his days in the Army. Michael tells me that he never went on R and R and he kept every nickel of his combat pay while he was in-country. I saved my own, so we have a decent savings account back in the city. We share our account just as we share everything else. There's no 'his' or 'hers' when it comes to our belongings, and my husband insisted on the arrangement. I'm terrible at simple arithmetic, so he takes care of the checkbook. I can spend as I like, but I have to present him the bills so he can handle the check ledger. He's a lot better at adding and subtracting than I am.

The rings are the usual gold bands. He gave me his mother Erin's engagement ring when we first decided to make a commitment. It isn't a large diamond, but I know it's priceless to Michael. And to me.

We walk down by the lake shore and amble out on one of the piers. The water is blue-green, and there's some algae popping up by the edges. There are numerous boats tethered to this dock, and there are multiple vessels hitched up to all the other many piers, as well. It is a tourist trap, of course, but it's growing on me, too.

I grew up in South Dakota. My mother was Lakota Sioux, and my father was Mexican-American. They had a small farm of two hundred acres, and my dad farmed and worked a side job at a factory. He died when he was sixty of a heart attack, and she passed two years later of breast cancer. By that time, I was old enough to enter the military. I was eighteen and had no desire for college. I wanted to fight terrorism and serve my country.

I'm glad I was in the Army before the current Commander in Chief. Things are strange, now, and I have to wonder who exactly I would be fighting for if I was in, now.

When my hitches were over, I became a police officer. I took some junior college courses and received an associates' degree. Maybe I'll finish my bachelor's, but I rose to homicide without a BA or a BS with the help of my split heritage. Being a minority didn't hurt my ascent to Homicide, and I'm aware of it. But I think the bachelor's might be some insurance that things don't go south on me.

Michael Parisi was sort of a fast-moving storm that swept me up. I had no intention of settling down with one man. I've dated frequently, but it wasn't even close, with all the other young men. Anglos didn't seem to be put off with the hue of my skin and with my personal ancestry, but I think some of them looked at me as sort of a novelty. Like 'let's try that flavor!'

Michael sees only me, and I don't mean the crust on the outside of the bread. He sees only *me*. I don't mean just the soul or the spirit or the personality. I mean the complete self that is Maria Elizondo Parisi. The whole package. I think I've been compartmentalized before with other men. Not this time. I could sense it almost immediately with Michael. We *were* kindred spirits, soulmates. As cliched as that may sound, it remains true.

I don't know what else I could've done except to marry him. You have an intuition, a voice, that tells you 'he's the one, don't let him walk on you'. I really didn't have any other choice but to tell him yes when he asked.

It was abrupt. It happened like a thunderbolt. There should have been a period for our engagement, maybe the usual six months. The wedding plans should have taken at least another half year. But I wasn't about to lose any time with him. I'm in my thirties and my baby years are burning behind me like a California wildfire. There was no waiting. It had to be immediately.

It was all very existentialist. We had to do it *now*.

Michael has killed men. He's told me so when I asked. He said he'd never lie to me. He also told me he didn't feel proud of the shootings, even though they were in combat, in self-defense. He never found joy in taking life, he said, and he was glad his tours were over when they came to an end. Patriotism was never an issue with him, as it was for me. 'Obligation' was the word he used when he told me why he'd signed up for service overseas with an elite outfit like the Rangers. Letting someone else bleed for him wasn't an option. The politics didn't motivate him.

I was much more gung ho. I believed in the American Dream because my parents passed it down to me, even though my mother's Sioux heritage didn't seem to fit my mother's love for this country. She told me all great countries do great good and great evil, both, and that it was our job to make certain the country shed its evil and aimed toward the positive in life. All that came from a high school dropout. My dad wasn't well-educated, either. He dropped out after the tenth grade.

The wedding bands are plain gold. Sturdy and thick. Not the most expensive rings in the jeweler's case, but they weren't cut-rate. We both agreed on them. It didn't take much time to decide. It's been that way for Michael and me since the day we first spent time together. The only overly dear item in our lives seems to be time. Nothing material seems to come close.

• • • • •

We make love on a king-sized bed for the first time.

"I didn't take my pill," I tell him.

"You sure you don't want to?" he asks.

He hasn't finished yet, but he stops in mid-thrust. He's on top, the best position for baby-making.

"I'm absolutely dead-on certain," I tell him.

He looks down into my eyes.

"We're going to struggle with one paycheck."

"I'll work until I deliver. And then there's maternity leave, and when the baby's old enough we'll put them with a good sitter or a daycare. I've done some research on daycare."

"This is a helluva time to let me know we're walking the wire without a net," he smiles.

"I'm sure, Michael. I'm absolutely positive...Can we continue, please?"

He laughs, but then his face changes to serious, intense.

He begins again, but this time is different from all the others. This time we're making a new life, or at least we're making the attempt. We're extending ourselves by one. Another member of the tribe. I'm betting it's a boy and that he'll be as brown as I am, just a shade darker than his future father. He'll have our brown eyes.

Or it'll be a dark little girl. Not delicate, not frail, but strong. An individual, no one's little princess. She'll be tough on the outside, but tender when she needs to be. She'll have the best of both of us.

He begins coming at me stronger. His thrusts are deeper, as deep as they can get. He throws two pillows beneath me to increase the angle of entry.

Then I'm urging him upward, meeting him off the bed.

It's done. We're done. The surge inside both of us lingers in waves, strong and stronger.

Then he collapses on top of me. He doesn't disengage. We're still connected. We're still one.

• • • • •

"You pregnant yet?" he teases on our final day at the hotel.

We're headed back to the apartment tomorrow morning. They kick us out of here by eleven AM. We have to get every penny's worth. The mattress and the sheets haven't been torn asunder quite yet.

"Do you think you might be?" he grins as we lie next to each other on this gigantic piece of foam and fabric.

"I think I might be. It takes a while to take, you know."

"No more pills?"

"No more pills, no more holding back on anything. I know it'll work," I assure him.

"Don't feel bad if it doesn't happen right away. I don't want to put pressure on you, Maria."

"Yeah? Who's the one who's got to get knocked up, around here?"

"I just don't want you to get nuts about all this, think it's all on you. I could be the one who might be holding up the show."

"Italians are notoriously fertile, men and women both."

"Where'd you get that?" he demands.

"I just made it up."

Then I climb on top of him and work my way down on him.

"You're supposed to be below," he reminds me.

"We don't have to make a kid every time we do this. One time does it, dummy."

"I just want to increase the odds," he smiles.

• • • • •

We pack up before they come roust us out of this four-hundred-dollar-a-day suite. We were lucky enough to get the bridal room, probably because we began our stay on a Monday.

The drive home takes less than ninety minutes. We beat the rush hour traffic.

• • • • •

Ned Diamond is in his late forties. He's been with the CPD for twenty-five years, and his retirement is coming soon. He's been married only once, and they're still together with three teenaged sons, two in college. I'm fortunate he's not a player. You can see the weariness in his eyes. I don't think he's got the energy to be sexually abusive toward me, in word or action.

Besides all that, he's a nice man who treats me more like a daughter, in our first full week together as partners, than like a potential pop. I'm only a decade or so younger than he is, but it feels as if he's somehow protective of me.

He's also a very good policeman. We have a full slate of homicides to investigate, so there's not all that much time to fraternize. He's put me at ease, at least.

Ned insists on picking me up from the apartment and delivering me home after every shift. I told him that Michael can do the delivering, but he says the Captain told him it was part of the job for him, seeing that the twins were still on the loose.

I don't argue with him.

But I still watch who's coming up on me wherever I am. In the street. On the scene of a homicide. At the grocery store, even when Michael's with me. When he's not on duty, he's with me when I'm not doing a tour with Ned. He never lets me out of his sight. I think he'd come into the can with me if I asked him to.

It's still early in the baby watch. I don't feel nausea in the mornings, but the doctor told me when I saw her, two days ago, that I might not get the typical heaves that a lot of women do. She told me every pregnancy was different, and she told me not to listen to other women or to read books on the subject of babies.

The gynee did tell me about the home pregnancy tests that I can buy at the drug store, but Michael comes in this very night with a bag from Walgreen's. It's got a kit inside.

We wear our bands to work, now, and we changed our personnel files to indicate we're married and cohabiting. It feels somehow freer, now that it's no secret.

Michael wants us to get married in the church, even though I was raised a Baptist. I was never devout, and neither was Michael, but he says his father would be pleased if we did the ceremony with a priest. In spite of an incident that happened to my husband long ago, he and his father still seem connected to that Church of Rome.

I wouldn't mind wearing the white bridal gown.

But I'd like to do it before I'm carrying baggage in front of me.

CHAPTER FIFTEEN

My brother Patrick sits across from me at Starbuck's. We both have a taste for expensive espresso. With lots of extra caffeine. It makes our blood race, although neither of us has a problem with high blood pressure. It's the next best thing to popping uppers, but as far as I know neither of us is addicted to anything.

Except for that one thing we share in common. I'm not referring to our being twins, either. It's the blood lust, of course.

"You're sure you weren't followed," I say.

"Who can be sure? But I didn't see that Parisi cop behind me, anyway."

"He's proving to be a very sore point for us both," I tell my brother.

"He's a bit frightening, don't you think?" Patrick admits.

"He's more of an annoyance."

"He assaulted me," Patrick complains.

"Me, too. And the lawyer didn't seem to help us, either."

"We need to put cameras in our offices. We shouldn't let him talk to us alone again," he says.

"I don't plan on it," I reply.

"Perhaps we should simply stop while we're ahead. He hasn't got anything on us or we'd be in jail."

"We can't stop, and you know it, Patrick."

He lowers his eyes and then takes his cup of caffeine in his right hand. But then he returns the mug to the table. The Starbuck's is virtually empty. It's close to closing time. Except for the help, we have the place to ourselves.

"Have you ever considered that our father lied to us about our great grandfather?" he asks abruptly.

"Why would he do an insane thing like that? It was a warning, that's all. You don't fabricate a tale about your old man being London's most notorious killer. You don't believe that version, Patrick. You know he was telling the truth."

"We might try psychotherapy."

"And tell a shrink what's really going on? You know he's bound to report a murder, Patrick."

"Just trying to think out loud."

I take a sip at my own triple shot drink.

"We might try a different tactic."

He looks up at me.

"And that is?"

"We might try working in concert," I explain.

"What does that mean?" he demands.

"One of us can draw Parisi in the wrong direction. I mean when he follows us, we communicate the information to the other."

"Don't you suppose they've got more than one policeman assigned to follow us?" he points out.

"With the number of cops trying to keep up with the shootings in this city, I can't imagine they have enough cops to go 'round, just now. Don't you read the papers or watch television? Chicago is the murder capital of the country. We're headlines, Patrick. But the headlines have come and gone about those four...creatures. No one cares about those cunts. Don't you understand? They're old news, and old news means no news."

"But that means we can't continue. If we do, it'll open everything up, again. We'll be in the headlights."

"Not as long as the gangs keep those lights on them. Who do you suppose seems to be more of a threat to the average boob? We don't hang over their heads, not over the skulls of the middle class unwashed. We only kill non-descript throwaways, Patrick. We provide a service the police cannot. This isn't Victorian England. No one thinks anyone like Francis

Amjac exists in their streets. The serial killer fable is old news, too. The urban terrorist is the story, these days.

"We're not mad Islamic bombers. We don't pose a threat to society. We're Chicago's vultures, we're its scavengers, cleaning up roadkill."

He drinks his brew down.

"It's late, they're getting ready to close," he says.

"We can't stop, Patrick. You know it as well as I. You've only done it once. Believe me, it gets better as you go along. You're getting smarter about it. The compensation multiplies, every time. It's not a kickable habit, brother."

"You really think we can keep on together?"

"I'm certain of it."

"Maybe we both really want to get caught," he tells me.

"Of all the lies, that's the stupidest. Cops would like the public to believe it. They teach them that farce at Quantico where the FBI has its profilers."

"They have done research, Sean."

"Did they ever ask you if you want to go to prison for the rest of your life?"

He doesn't answer.

"You want to feel it again, don't you, Patrick?"

"I guess I'm not as passionate as you. I never was."

"You're a liar!"

"Keep your voice down," he whispers.

"Do you want to work together or not?" I ask.

He sits mute. Then he looks up at me across the booth.

"I suppose we might try it."

I smile at him, but he doesn't return the gesture.

• • • • •

I go back to the internet, and there are several ladies of leisure online.

I ask 'Myra' if she likes it strange.

She asks me what I mean by strange, and when I reply, she says she can do that.

I make the 'date' for tomorrow night. We're to meet at the Holiday Inn in Oak Lawn. I know I'm taking chances by trying this in a highly-populated area, but I can't try the other places of assignation again. We used the spot out in Orland Park twice, and the heat got a little too high.

I call Patrick and tell him about my 'date'. He says he'll go for a drive when I leave the condo. He'll have his cell with him and he'll let me know if he thinks anyone is following him. If Parisi decides to tail me, I back off and I'll try again some other time.

• • • • •

When I leave the condo, I keep my eyes on the traffic behind me. I wait ten minutes before I dial my brother.

"No one that I can see. Just cars and drivers, and no one's stayed behind me. I think I'm clear."

"It looks the same here. Let's stay on the line for five more minutes, though."

"All right."

I can hear the sounds of traffic from Patrick's end. But no one shows up in the rear-view mirror that I recognize, and no one looks suspiciously like a gendarme.

After the five minutes pass, I tell him to head back home. He hangs up, and I put the cell back into the console.

I make it to Oak Lawn in thirty minutes. Traffic has unsnarled because it is long after six PM. It's almost nine.

I convinced 'Myra' to check in to the motel. She took some cajoling because she was afraid I'd stiff her on the money for the room, but I offered her an extra two hundred and said I'd reimburse her for the suite, as well. She liked the sound of the offer, and it sounds like she might be willing to risk it for the extra cash. She's likely not all that well-to-do if she took this chance, so perhaps she's desperate.

She calls me from the room at the time we agreed upon—9:20 PM. I take the elevator up to the fourth floor and seek out 425. It's in the middle of the hall. Noise won't be a problem because I have my medical bag inside a gym bag.

She opens the door when I knock. She's white, about five-seven, a bit overweight, and has only a passable body and face. 'Myra' has long white hair and she's wearing a lot of unhealthy white looking makeup.

"You're right on time," she smiles. "I was afraid you weren't going to show up."

"You'll find out I keep my word."

There is a single lamp lit next to the queen-sized bed. She's already withdrawn the covers. She's in a hurry, I suppose. She's only booked for two hours.

She'll be here a lot longer than that.

"You like foreplay?" she asks.

She might be forty, not much older.

"You do this full time?" I ask.

"No. I have another job. This is like supplemental."

I smile warmly at her.

"You'll be rich when we're done."

"What's in the bag?" she wants to know.

"I have another engagement, later on."

"Oh. Another 'date'?"

"No. Nothing like that. I'm sure you're here to satisfy."

"That'd be a safe bet," she grins with a leer.

"You're that good?"

"I'm better than good."

"Why's that?"

"I put pride in my workmanship."

"You've been to school?"

She sits on the bed.

I remain standing after I place the gym bag next to her.

"Looks heavy," she gestures to the bag.

"Just a few necessaries."

"Are you really a doctor?"

"I'm really a doctor. Plastic surgeon."

Her eyes light up.

"No fooling? You think I need a touchup?"

"You ought to make an appointment. I think I could tighten you up a bit. I'll loosen you up tonight, though."

"Really? You're that good on the sheets?"

"I'm like nothing you've ever had before, Myra."

"That's not my real name."

"What's your real name?"

"Diane. But that's all you'll get. You know how it works."

"Should I call you Diane, or Myra?"

"It's your money, Doc."

"Don't call me Doc."

"I'm sorry."

I feel the flush at my cheeks.

"I didn't mean to piss you off."

"It's all right...Where were we?"

She begins to unbutton her white cotton blouse. She's wearing black jeans, and flats on her feet.

She undoes the bra and exposes two perfectly shaped white breasts with red, small, erect nipples. The perfect breasts don't seem to fit with an otherwise slightly overweight body, but I'm aroused now.

"Take it in your mouth...But don't swallow."

She complies. She's on the edge of the bed, seated, and she takes me inside her lips. Myra seems very adept at what she does, and it's over in a hurry. I catch the semen in my own hand.

Then I go into the bathroom and wash as thoroughly as I can.

"That's gonna cost you extra," Diane informs me.

"How much extra?"

"A hundred."

"How about five?"

"Hundred?"

"Yes."

"Sure!" she beams.

"But you need to top that. Think you can handle that?"

She smiles.

"You're a strange guy. A doctor, and looking like you, I can't figure out why you gotta pay for it."

"No ties. No entanglements."

"But a handsome guy like you...You could get anyone you like."

"Are you flattering me, Diane?"

"You don't know how handsome you are?"

"I don't pay much attention to my own looks."

"Not vain, eh?"

"I might have other flaws."

"You married? Forgive me for asking anything personal."

"No. Never. You?"

"I was engaged when I was seventeen. That was forever ago. He went into the Army and got killed in Iraq. One of those IEDs, you know? Blew him all up. So bad they couldn't have open casket. I went to the funeral and the Army guys gave him a nice send-off. Uniforms and all. It was real impressive.

"We were gonna get married when he came back from his tour, but he came back in pieces."

Her eyes glisten. I suppose I'm supposed to offer her my sympathy.

She's just a whore, just like the others. The story is probably a lie to boost the price, tonight.

"No other offers?" I ask.

"Just the ones like this. I gotta pay bills. Apartments are expensive, and so is everything else."

"You have family?"

"No. They're dead. Dead or moved away. I don't have anybody, really."

"Neither do I. Mine are all dead...You believe in ghosts, Diane?"

"I don't know. You mean like the ones on those TV reality shows where they're plumbers by day and spook chasers by night?"

"I mean real ghosts, the kind that stay with you and don't vanish. They live in your head and they're real. They tell you to do things. Terrible things. And you can't stop from doing what they tell you."

Her already white visage turns somehow more bloodless.

"You know the kind of ghosts I'm talking about? Like someone in your past who did horrible things, and he won't go away and leave you alone, he keeps pestering you, pushing you to do the same awful things he did when he was alive."

She rises off the bed, but I've already got the bag opened.

CHAPTER SIXTEEN

Everyone seems to insist that you come home changed when you've fought in combat. I'm not sure if I agree, but it does at least sober you about the human condition. I don't know if I'm more cynical or more pessimistic, but optimistic doesn't come into play.

I watched all those years weigh on my father, and tough as he is, homicides are like lead weights attached to your body as well as to your soul. By nature, I'm not really a spiritual person, and the only reason I infrequently attend mass is that I'm still seeking what it is that troubles me, bites into me, about the mythos of Jesus Christ. It looks like he was indeed a mortal man, an historical figure, but if he transcends his humanity into something very different, I'm just not certain.

A lot of what the church teaches seems false, to me. The departure from reason centers around sex. I don't have any issues with 'thou shalt not kill' and the rest. But there are moral dilemmas with the human sexuality dogma. I rather enjoy reading Thomas Aquinas, and he said that when *'it's between my church and my conscience, I chose my conscience'*. It was a rather heroic stance for a man of the church, then or now.

Which leads up to why I joined the military and then the Chicago Police Department. One thing I'm sure of is the presence of evil. I'm not certain if there are literal demons or the devil, but there is plenty of human evil evident on this planet, and I can't in good conscience try to run from it.

Afghanistan did nothing to alleviate horrific behavior. What I did, what we all did, was try to stanch what some despicable people do to innocents. I thought that was why I did the tours. To strike out at merchants of pain like the Taliban and Al Qaeda. I'm not so sure I even made a dent in their thorny armor.

So, I came home with the romantic notion I could do something positive in a more local setting. My dad says that he speaks for the voiceless, for the prematurely dead. It's a good enough reason for me. I won't wipe out crime in Gotham. I'm no Dark Knight. I'm just frail and frustrated, like a lot of other men and women who toil at a basically thankless job.

Anyone who thinks he's constructing a brave new world will be detached from his or her high idealism in short order.

But you have to try to do what you can, as miniscule as that might be.

The evil incarnate, right now, is the Tracy twins. There are hundreds of other murderers loose in this city, but those two are in front of me at the moment, and I am focused solely on them.

I'm standing in a hotel room looking down at something which must have been human. I know it must have been a woman because I see her various parts spread all over a very blood splattered carpet. I've had to put plastic booties over my feet so I wouldn't drag blood out of the room when I leave.

He has dispatched this woman all over the suite. Pieces of her are on every square foot. The sight has driven two other experienced homicides out of the room, gagging and running for the john. My gorge has also risen, but I'm not sick enough to retreat out into the hall.

Here is the work of one, or both, of the Tracys, I'm certain. It's got their signatures all over this room.

When the ME enters, he almost staggers. His name is Dr. Quillan. I've worked with him before. He's in his fifties, nearing retirement, and I think what he's witnessing along with me and the police photographers is pushing him away from this job faster than he might have intended.

But he straightens up and looks over at me.

"You're the only one still here," he tells me.

He's tall and is graying on the sides of his black hair. He wears glasses, and they perpetually slide down on his aquiline nose.

I nod because I'm afraid if I say anything, I'll be joining the other cops down the hall in the can.

"I knew your father. Did you know that?"

"Yes, he mentioned you," I'm finally able to say.

"He had an iron-clad stomach, too. Never saw him run for cover," he smiles.

"Welcome to homicide, as the old cliché goes."

"It's one of the Tracys," I utter.

"Pardon me?"

"Nothing. Let's get this over with so they can clean up the mess and gather her in bags."

"It's going to take a lot of bags," he smiles grimly.

"You ever wonder what kind of two-legged thing does this to another person?" I ask.

"I don't wonder. In this profession we deal with monsters all the time. That's why your brethren burn out as fast as they do. The desk begins to look better and better after a while."

I scan the carnage once more.

I was a rookie when I saw one of these. The coppers present said it was nearly as bad as the Richard Speck slaughters of the nurses. There was an old-timer present who was there on scene on the west side near Cook County Hospital.

Her name was Diane Reiser. I put a call into Vice, and they knew her name. Apparently, she was a veteran. Worked as a waitress and did this to help pay the bills. The Vice guys had pinched her several times, but she stayed in the life.

Until now.

• • • • •

One of them pulled this job when Maria and I were in Wisconsin. It's the Monday back at work when I get the call from the hotel.

The maid who found the body is at the psych ward at Rush Hospital. They had to give her a shot to tranquillize her. I don't think she'll be talking to me for a while.

The guy at reception at the hotel said the woman, Diane Reiser, paid for the room. He never saw her 'guest.' No one at the hotel recalls anyone other than Diane entering the suite. He got in and out without a witness spotting him.

I knock on the Captain's door. I called first.

He motions for me to sit, but I stand.

"No one was tailing either of them?" I ask.

"Guess not. There was some miscommunication, Detective Parisi. My mistake."

"Can't we get a full rotation to follow the two of them?"

"You have any idea what the stats are for shootings in this goddam city?"

"Yes, I've seen them."

"Then you've answered your own question."

"I don't mean to lay this at your door. I feel personally responsible."

"Cut the crap, Michael. One of those twins is responsible. Maybe they're playing tag team and working in tandem."

"The thought crossed my mind, too."

"You can ditch the guilt trip. You don't have the luxury of self-pity. Not on this tour. The Tracys would be what they are with or without any of us. You read me?"

I nod.

"Detective, you have a life. You have a young wife. Maybe you want to start a family, some time. You know because of your dad how much personal fuse gets burned in this line of work, so I needn't give you the lecture. Is that correct?"

"It is, Captain."

"Would you like to be relieved of this case?"

"I would not."

"Good. I'm still trying to fix you up with a new partner, but you heard the tale about manpower. We're slightly overtaxed in Homicide, at the moment."

"I'll get on them immediately."

"Michael, how bad was this one? I mean really?"

I look into his gaze, and then I walk out his door.

• • • • •

I don't like Maria being alone in the apartment or anywhere else. I don't have the luxury of being at her side twenty-four-seven. There is the sawed off in the bedroom. I've had a security system installed in the apartment with the permission of the landlord who responded positively when he saw my badge. I check in with her every hour or two via cellphone. But I can't bother her on the job because it isn't fair to Maria. I know she can take care of herself. She is a marksman with her 9 mil. She can hit her target, dead center. I've been with her on the shooting range. She really is almost as lethal as I am with a sidearm and a long gun. She's certainly not helpless. Maria's a black belt in karate—I forget which degree, but she can most definitely handle herself mano a mano.

As it is, she finds it mildly insulting when I express my concerns for her safety. I'll learn to keep my mouth shut, but I won't stop fretting. It won't stop until we put them both in adjoining cells at Joliet or somewhere equally as forbidding.

I worry about her getting pregnant at this time because we've got enough on our minds while I'm pursuing the twins. It is still my sole case. My whiteboard has only the two names written in red upon it. The surnames look almost lonely when I see them there when I enter my office.

I will have to alternate surveillance on the two of them. I can hardly bi-locate, and it doesn't appear I'll have any reinforcements any time soon. The problem is that the media has gone silent, once more. The stories cease, and even the murder of Diane Reiser rates page six in both of the major newspapers.

They're no longer high profile, the five of them, now. They're back to being just prostitutes. They're back on the lowest rungs.

• • • • •

I wait for Sean Tracy at the entrance to his office on Michigan Avenue.

"Hello, Detective," he smiles wanly.

"Let's take a walk," I proffer.

"A walk where?"

His smile vanishes.

"Don't worry. My superior already informed me of your complaints."

We're standing out in the chill of the northeast breeze off Lake Michigan, which is infamously known as The Hawk, in this city.

"Then why are you here?" he demands.

"You know why. I've got the date, here in my pocket. Her name was Diane Reiser. Were you aware?"

"I don't know what you're talking about."

We walk slowly north on the sidewalk. The temperature is bottoming out, getting more frigid by the moment. Winter is arriving early.

"You tore her all up…Or maybe it was your brother. It's possible, but I don't think so. I think you're the one who did four of them. I think Brother Patrick is the novice. He's just a beginner, isn't he."

"Are we finished? It's cold out here."

"You show me those teeth again, you even grin, you're going to need your brother's professional services."

"Is there anything else?" he says with his best cold stare.

"Either of you comes near my partner, you're dead. If you want to survive until your trial, I hope you'll remember that."

He again tries to penetrate my eyes with his.

"I'll be around," I tell him.

Then I walk away in the opposite direction.

• • • • •

I alternate following each of them, and I make myself obvious. I'm camping out in front of Sean's Gold Coast condo. It's a gray building that looms in the equally gray sky just before sundown. I'll spend the first half of my tour sitting in the ride here, and then I'll drive over to Patrick's address. I'll have to get as close to splitting myself in two as I can.

The Captain has still not come up with a partner for me, and I prefer it that way. I do wish that he had the numbers to help me keep tabs on the twins, but this has been one of the most murderous years for homicides, specifically gun killings, that Chicago has ever known. The clown in the oval office talks about sending in the troops, but it is all palaver. Elect a conman and that's what you get. I'm not a political animal, but I would like to see someone competent in that White House. And the carnage continues. We can't keep up, presently.

I play the jazz CDs, and then I sit in silence. I see a light up at Sean Tracy's condo. The yellow light spills out at me when the darkness takes over.

I'll take a dinner break before I visit his brother. There's a Starbuck's not far down the street when I need to take a leak.

I brought a large Diet Coke from McDonald's along with me. The ice has almost melted away, but the pop is still cold because I'm not running the motor. Waste of gas. I'm big on conservation and going green, and it's another reason Orange Man in D.C. irritates me.

After ninety minutes passes by uneventfully, I pull away from the curb and head to the coffee place. I don't usually drink this kind of brew, but I feel bad using their facilities without making a purchase. I buy a small black coffee and take it with me after I visit the head.

I sit in a booth and call Maria. She's off shift, now.

"Everything good?" I ask.

"Of course. I'm sitting at the kitchen table with the shotgun aimed at the door. Make sure you identify yourself before you walk in."

She laughs.

"I'm all right, Michael."

"I won't call again if it bothers you," I apologize.

"Don't be an idiot. I want you to call when I'm not working."

"Anything on TV?"

"I like television as little as you do...Anything happening where you're at?"

"Quiet."

"Well at least we know where one of them is...It was pretty bad, the latest one?"

"It was the worst of the five, and the other four were bad enough. Now you know why I keep calling you."

"I'll be all right. I can handle it, Michael. You know I can."

"I'll be home as soon as the tour is finished, probably after two or so. I'll knock three times before I open the door."

She laughs. I love to hear her.

"Not necessary. I'll be in bed with both barrels cocked, locked and loaded."

"You know I love you, right?"

"I've heard the rumor."

We hang up because I've got to get back to Sean's den.

• • • • •

The hours go even slower as I'm parked at Patrick's swank residence. I play my tunes to keep awake. Even the coffee doesn't help. The caffeine from the Coke and the brew has worn off.

I suppose I could circumvent the law and take the both of them out. I could plant myself across from their homes on top of a roof and explode their melons with a sniper rifle I snuck back home from my various tours of beautiful Afghanistan.

But the likelihood that I'll actually follow through is highly remote. We are supposed to arrest them, not liquidate them. I don't see myself as an assassin. But it all depends on whether or not they stay their distance away from Maria.

I have enough motivation to blow them both up after being on scene of their five previous grisly homicides. But it wouldn't be legal or moral to dispatch either of them.

Conscience really does make a coward of me, after all.

CHAPTER SEVENTEEN

I can't bear it much longer. I have night tremors and cold sweats. I know the police are coming for me. Just when things seemed to cool off, Sean went out again. But this time it was worse, much worse. I read about it in the papers. They were rather restrained in their depictions of the woman's murder, but the details suggest that he's becoming more enraged and more violent with this killing. They quoted veteran policemen who were unable to stay in the room.

I only fell into the abyss one time, and I'm quite certain that I'm not going to allow it to happen again. I'd been strong, until that happened. We were told by our father what great grandfather was like. He was quite graphic in recounting the tales Francis told him as a warning. He let our father know what was coursing inside us. He had not succumbed to the demons that were handed down to him, but he was stronger than Sean or I.

I don't know why I let myself go out that night and why I allowed myself to go berserk on that prostitute. For years I had denied the instinct, and then I weakened.

But it will not matter to the police or the courts that I fought as hard as I did and failed only once. One murder is sufficient to lock me in a cage for the rest of my life.

I never married because I refuse to pass his genes to another. I won't put them through the agony that I've endured. If only I had held off just one time, I would be free. Even if I had no children, I could've had a wife.

Sean will get us both imprisoned if not executed. Capital punishment comes in and out of vogue in Illinois. With my bad fortune, this state will again feature the lust for justice.

I have to stop him. But he is my brother, finally. If I turn him in, he'll do the same to me. I'm trapped on the inside and out in the world, as well.

I could try to reason with him. Try to insist that he stop while the trail behind us is still cold. They have no witnesses, no evidence. Just the gut instinct of one lone policeman. This detective, Parisi.

He also has a tie to the past. His father and grandfather were both homicide police. I did some research on them online. The grandfather Jake was a famous old-school investigator who used some rather old-fashioned methods to track killers down, and his son, James, Jimmy, held onto some of the patriarch's techniques.

I can't find much about the youngest member of the line, Michael. He's only in his thirties, but he's a well-decorated veteran of the elite Army Rangers, having participated in the Afghanistan conflict. I've found nothing at all about his partner, Maria Elizondo. Except that she also served in the Army in Iraq, twice.

Inheritance deals a heavy hand, no matter which direction of the road you take. Something like the Frost poem about the road not taken. It's the avenue we're on that has been chosen for us. The past lingers and never releases us from its icy grip.

I can't sleep. I can't eat. I have trouble concentrating on my work, and it might prove dangerous to me and my patients. It doesn't take much for the knife to slip. I could be ruined professionally by a single mistake.

Suicide has entered my mind. But I fear death. Even though I have taken a life, I can't imagine ending my own. Perhaps it's the fear of hell, of retribution by something far more terrible than anything human can invoke on me. Great grandfather penned a 'letter from hell' that was published in the London newspapers, back in the day. Maybe Francis already knew what awaited him when the darkness came over him for the final time. Certainly, he didn't fear religion and what it preached. He was baptized Catholic, but Sean and I have never had the holy water sprinkled on our infant faces, and neither had our father. Francis came from the Old Sod, and it was customary to bring a child into the faith soon after birth.

I don't believe in God and neither does Sean. If we really did, it'd be a bit difficult to engage in what we both have done.

But Sean is getting crazier as time goes by. He will indeed get us caught if he doesn't stop. There are too many policemen, too much technology. It's not like it was in London in 1891. The people at Scotland Yard were not nearly as sophisticated as modern investigators. The odds are very poor that either of us can continue getting away with murder.

It's making me exhausted, wondering if Parisi or his brethren will be behind me when I go out of the house. Sean was fortunate neither of us were followed when he slaughtered this Diane Reiser woman. Christ, what a risk he took! Just because we didn't see anyone behind us doesn't mean we weren't followed. I'm sure the police know about drones. They have all kinds of electronic devices they employ. Sooner or later, my brother will be caught on a surveillance camera.

Maybe I'll be compelled to do it again, and my face will turn up on the video. We are doomed, after all, regardless of whether we're apprehended by the police or whether it winds up there is a God and vengeance really is His.

• • • • •

He calls and I'm summoned to the downtown Headquarters. He informs me that I can have an attorney present. I tell him I'm very busy with patients, but Detective Parisi tells me he can come to my office when those said patients are there to see him flash his badge to me in front of them.

So, I'm there at the appointed hour of 3:30 P.M.

His office is a minute cubicle, and its only redeeming virtue is a rather beautiful view of Lake Michigan. The water is tinged with white because of recent snow flurries. It's not yet Thanksgiving, and it feels more like January outside.

"Thank you for coming," he says. "You're sure you don't require a lawyer?"

I shake my head. There's nothing on his face that I can read.

He asks me where I was on the date of the latest murder. The one Sean did.

"I don't recall."

I sit across from him. There are no papers on his desk. There is a white board on the wall to my left, and it has our names, in red, on it.

"I've made your whiteboard," I smile weakly.

"It was Sean, wasn't it. I make only one of the five that you did on your own. I can't prove it, but I will. Why haven't you tried to keep up? I realize it's only a guess on my part, but I know you have it in you. I know where you're from, all those years ago. I know who your great grandfather was. Francis, right?"

I remain mute.

"It's in the blood the way you inherit your hair and your looks and your IQ and your tendencies. As a physician, you'd know that better than I would. I'm not a medical doctor and I'm not an anthropologist or sociologist or genealogist. But I've done my homework on you two, Patrick. Like the brothers say, *I know where you live.* Did you ever read *Crime and Punishment?*"

"Where is all this headed? I'm very busy, and I really don't have to be here, unless you charge me, Detective."

"Really, have you ever read it?"

"No."

"You ought to. Dostoyevsky knew, he understood. A young man named Raskolnikov axe murdered two old women and got away with it. No evidence, no witnesses. But there was a bulldog of a cop named Porfiry Petrovitch who just wouldn't leave Raskolnikov alone. He was on this poor guy day and night, showing up all the time, always on this killer's peripheral vision. Are you following this, Patrick?"

"I think I am."

"Great. Because I know you two are dirty. I know you're both guilty of the worst offense there is. And I'm going to grab hold of your pants legs, like a bulldog would, and I'm not going to let go.

"So, the best thing for you to do is tell me what you did. I already know you did it. It's just a matter of your scoreboard and Sean's personal tally. You killed at least one of them, but I don't think it was Diane. That was a virtuoso performance. You should've seen what Sean did to her.

"You don't have that level of viciousness, I don't think. What you did was bad enough for any killer, but I think you just slipped into character the one time. I'm right, no?"

I look over at his whiteboard.

"I killed no one," I whisper.

"You don't believe that any more than I do, *Padraic*."

"Are we finished? Because I have two surgeries this afternoon, and they can't wait."

"Go right ahead. Now we both know where we stand, don't we. I'll be around. I'll always be around. Tell Sean, too, please. I want him to know."

I get up and leave his tiny office hurriedly.

This time we go out to dinner at Le Bistro in the Loop. I haven't seen Parisi in my rear- view mirror, but I'm sure someone has been following me or Sean. They're obviously not showing themselves because they've gone to war against us.

Le Bistro is an exclusive eatery. One of my clients has money in this place. Otherwise we'd be on a waiting list for six months.

The inner part of the restaurant fits the notion of exclusive, as well. The taste is very apparent in all its trappings.

My brother is already seated.

"Well? What's the occasion?" he smiles.

It is literally like looking into the mirror when I peruse his face.

I wait until the waiter takes our orders for drinks. I have a vodka tonic and Sean has a very dry martini.

"He knows," I tell him.

"He who?"

"Parisi, of course."

"Yes, I'm aware."

"You sound very cavalier about the idea, Sean."

"Are you frightened by all the bluff and huff? He's just trying to mess with our minds. You know that, don't you?"

"He reads Dostoyevsky, apparently."

"What are you talking about, Patrick?"

"He brought me to his office. He said he'd embarrass me in front of my patients if I didn't go."

"Get a lawyer and sue him for harassment."

"We had an enlightening discussion of *Crime and Punishment*."

"Jesus Christ, Patrick."

"He said he wouldn't let go of either of us, that he'd always be there behind us or right on our heels."

"So, what did you say to him?"

"I said I was busy, and I left."

"Great. Good. Let's enjoy this obscenely expensive meal."

"He isn't going to go away, Sean."

My brother stares into my eyes, our identical eyes.

"Is he frightening you, Patrick?"

"You shouldn't have gone after his partner. You made it personal," I tell him.

"Oh, it is personal, brother. It can't get any more personal. You cannot be any more intimate with someone than try to lock them away into a prison in this state, something like Joliet or Menard or some equally hideous dungeons."

"You need to stop. Stop while he hasn't a way to get you. Or get me."

"So, you're saying you will never go out on the hunt again. Is that it, Patrick?"

"I'm not going to do it again. No."

"Because you're afraid of this policeman."

"Because I am terrified of *myself*, Sean."

He smiles wildly.

"You cannot be serious. You know what you are, what I am."

"I deny it. I won't let it have me again. I'm serious."

This time he laughs aloud. People at nearby tables look over at us.

The waiter comes and takes our order, but he has a sullen look on his face.

"Is there a problem?" Sean demands of the server.

"Oh no, sir," he blushes.

He takes our orders and departs.

"What are you going to do, Patrick? Confess? Is that what you're saying?"

"I would never drag you down with me if I did."

"How comforting. It's because you were always the weak half of us. I've known it for a very long time."

"I would never betray you, Sean. Why do you hurt me?"

"Don't be a fool. He has nothing on you or me or we would've been arrested long ago."

"You went out and began it again. It was going away, but you wouldn't have it."

"You're very tiresome. Did you know that, Patrick?"

"You're right. You're the strong one. You're the *uberman*. I'm not. I gave in to it just once, but I'll never give in to it again."

I rise from my seat.

"Where the hell are you going?"

"It's already on my credit card. Take my dinner home in a doggy bag. I won't be seeing you again, and don't communicate with me. I won't answer the phone and I won't text."

I walk away from the table, and I hear him laughing loudly again.

• • • • •

Insomnia is not cured with medication. What passes for sleep is merely an aroused coma. I don't know how else to describe it.

He calls me and leaves messages. I wonder if the phones are tapped? All those policemen, all that technology. And I'm sure they have secret ways to watch me. Maybe the doorman is an undercover policeman. Maybe our maintenance man is a police plant.

I've been watching too many movies, too much television. It's all in my mind.

I am the weaker one. He was right. I had a faint voice inside me when I killed that whore. I know it was a semblance of a conscience.

Sean has no such inner voice. No angel that whispers to him about his better nature and who warns him about the demon who urges him to turn his back on the light.

I am burning inside me. It's a cold fire that I feel mainly at night when I fail to fall off to sleep. No pill helps. There is no remedy for my omni-wakefulness. My eyes want to close, but my mind continues as if it's attached to a runaway locomotive. I'm headed for a crash, I know.

My blood pressure is rising. I've checked it, lately. I may have to use medication to lower it. It's at a dangerously high number, top and bottom.

It occurs to me I might be in the throes of hypertension because I'm not doing what Sean does. If I tried to do it again, maybe I could quiet that damned voice and perhaps I could sleep at night.

Because it does resemble a sexual climax. The cutting, I mean. It does release everything and anything pent up inside me. I literally leave this world in a way no drug can set me free. I know it is my nature, my brother's nature, but I am afraid, truly horrified what will occur if I continue as Sean has continued.

I want to sleep for centuries. I want my life to be finished. Dreamless sleep is what I crave, what I desire.

I go to my medical bag in the closet. I retrieve a scalpel from inside. I walk over to the window and stand in the moonlight, waiting to be transformed into something that has no feeling. Into a predator whose business it is to kill its prey.

I see the blade gleam in the light of the full moon.

Then I slice my left thumb open with the most minute of cuts. And I watch the blood seep out of my skin. It seems black, not red, in the muted illumination of the lunar glow.

CHAPTER EIGHTEEN

Francis Amjac, Chicago, 1911

Robert, my son, is a grown man, now. Nineteen years old. He says he wants to be a surgeon, like his father. I want to send him to Harvard University Medical School, but he wants to stay here at home. Robert tells me he plans on going to the University of Chicago Medical School. He tells me it's an up and coming university, there on the southside, not far from Lake Michigan.

He is the reason I stopped. He and his mother. His mother doesn't know about my past, but I'll have to tell my son. He must never give in to the impulses which controlled me, back in London. It will be difficult for him, but he must be warned that it's in his blood.

The rage seemed to cool when I came here from New York and Ellis Island. Things came to me, here, and I was determined not to jeopardize any future I might find in America. The sight of the Statue was indeed impressive, and it gave me hope that whatever it is that made me do terrible things in Whitechapel might not follow me to this New World.

I have troubled nights, sometimes. I cannot sleep and I break out into cold sweats and I want to begin it all over again. The thrill was the hunt and the escape from the police. It haunts me occasionally, but the desire to go out and repeat the murderous acts I committed has not overwhelmed me yet, and I feel I'm becoming stronger all the time in my resistance. Will can overcome natural inclination. Drug addicts can escape their chains as alcoholics can free themselves from drink. It's all very hard to do, but it can and has been done.

To think how I taunted the investigators from Scotland Yard. It was a wish for capture, a wish for death. But something made me take the chance of boarding that ship and sailing westward, to the center of dreams. Many come and many fail—that is also true. No one guarantees success by merely stepping on these shores. But there is a chance, an opportunity, to right yourself from your previous life.

Who would have ever dreamed that Jack the Ripper could arrive here and flourish? Yet it has happened.

But the journey is hardly finished. I have to tell my son who I really am. I have to risk his disgust and revulsion at what his father once was. I have to face his rejection, perhaps his hatred and betrayal to the local police.

But there is no evidence anywhere that I am the one *from hell.* I'm quite certain, if the papists are correct, I will be headed to that netherworld of Dante's. There is, I'm sure, a concentric ring awaiting me, perhaps a step above Judas Iscariot.

I'm not letting Robert go unprepared into this new country. He's an American. I became a citizen, and his mother was born here, in Chicago.

Gretchen is of Dutch stock. Her beliefs are very much Puritanical, perhaps Calvinistic. Hell is literal for her and her fellow believers. Hades is no myth to frighten children into obedience. There was no way for me to relate to her what I must pass on to Robert. He's all I've got, my only son. He needs to know what he has to fight against all his days. This insidious thing that lurks in me, that made me do mad things. That impelled me to tear flesh asunder and rip out the very inner works of human beings. Even though they were whores, useless incarnations of something close to human.

I try not to let my mind wander to them. Because they gave me great pleasure, and the memory of that satisfaction has not fled from me. I remember the terror in their eyes, the three of them, when they knew they were looking at death in the flesh standing before them in those squalid, putrid alleys and hovels that they inhabited. I took my time killing them after I severed their throats and removed their ability to scream out and summon the constables.

It makes me sweat coldly as I recall it all. I can see it as clearly as if I were in Whitechapel this moment.

I was almost moved to kill my wife just after we first met. Although she was pure, a virgin, I still wanted to rip her from her genitals to her throat. I lusted to tear her inner organs away from a savaged shell of a body, and I wanted to feel the rush of making another escape from the local police.

I denied myself, obviously, but it was very strenuous to do so.

Then we were married, and shortly thereafter she was with child. He proved to be our only offspring. There was difficulty in the birth, and the surgeon tied her tubes after the birthing.

There is only one. I cannot let him forfeit his life the way I almost did. I cannot be certain that he's inherited more from his mother than he did from me. I can take no chances that he received his mother's better maternal half.

He looks more like me, after all. His face is a duplicate of my own visage. We could almost pass as twins but for the difference of age. He's a handsome young man, and very bright, as well. He'll make an excellent doctor, better than I.

The talk we're going to have is far different from the usual sex lecture most sons are victim to when they reach an age of maturity.

He sits by the hearth in front of a furious fire I've built. The flames reach up the chimney as if they're bent on escaping.

His mother has gone to bible study at her church. The building is only a half mile from where we live on the southside.

"Are you a forgiving man?" I ask my boy.

He laughs, surprised by the question.

"Are you forgiving, son?"

"I don't understand why you're asking me."

He is a striking young man. He'll be very popular with the young ladies, but he's shown no inclination of his interest in them, to date.

"How forgiving might you be?"

"What are you asking, father? You're frightening me. Have you done something wrong?"

"My sins are grievous and many, Robert."

"Perhaps you need a priest. Why are you asking me?"

"Can you forgive the unforgiveable?"

He watches me warily. The fire flickers lower, now.

"Have you had an affair? Is that it?"

"It's far worse, I'm afraid."

"I can't bear this. Tell me what it is you've done."

I watch as the flames grow weaker at the hearth.

"I've killed people, Robert."

"You've killed people? Who?"

"I murdered three harlots back in London, before you were born and before I came here."

He cannot speak.

"They were wanton, worthless women, but they were human beings, and I slaughtered them like cattle."

He stands up.

"Why are you telling me this? Why are you tearing me apart?"

"I'm not attempting to hurt you, son. I'm trying to save you."

"How in God's name is this story going to save me? My Christ!"

"You wish to become a physician. You know anything of inherited traits handed down from father to heir?"

"I've read about it, but it's nothing science has yet proven by fact. It's simply theory."

"Not according to some researchers. I'm telling you you have some of me, and perhaps it's not the better part of me, either."

"And you waited until now to speak of it."

"Yes."

"Who is it you've slain?"

I tell him their names.

"No…It can't be. You can't mean…"

I look directly into his eyes.

"You don't have to become what I once was, son. That's what I'm desperately trying to say to you. You must be aware of the chance that it's inside you, like a latent disease, like heart disease or cancer. If I never told you, who knows what might happen.

"You can hate me all you like, and I'll understand. But you're a Christian, at least in name, and Christians believe in redemption, no matter how grievous the sin or sins. No, I do not want your forgiveness, really. I want redemption to be yours, because what I have done is indeed unforgiveable."

He slumps into his chair and the tears well in his eyes. I want to say more to him, but he raises his right hand and halts me.

Then Robert rises and leaves the room.

In the morning he has left our home. Forever.

• • • • •

The house is empty. Gretchen blames me for its abandonment, and she is correct in her reasoning. I have forced our son away from this house. No one but I. There is punishment for unsolved crimes, it appears.

I have only my practice. Gretchen sleeps in a separate room, currently. She locks the door at night so I am kept away from her bed. I don't know if Robert talked to her before his departure, but she knows we talked the night before he left.

She receives letters from him. I've read them when she leaves the house. He is living in an apartment on the near north side and he has a job at a pharmacy. He is attending school at a public college downtown, and he tells her he has hopes of going to the medical school at the University of Chicago.

I mail him money at the address on the envelopes, and at least he hasn't returned the cash. I'm hoping he's saving it for tuition.

What would I have done if I were he? I would have bolted. Anyone with a sense of decency would have run away from me.

I've found out where the pharmacy is, and sometimes I stand outside the window to catch brief glimpses of him. I'm careful not to let him see me standing outside peering in, and I flee down the street after I catch sight of him.

If suffering is what I deserve, then justice has been fulfilled to a small degree. I know I've got worse coming, far worse, but this pain suffices. I suppose I thought I was being noble by telling him what I did, but it would have been far less excruciating for both of us had I remained mute.

The blood lust comes back to me at night, but I somehow refrain from acting on it. If I were to return to my old habits, both Gretchen and Robert would pay for my sins if I were apprehended. I've done enough to my son and my wife. I took him away from her prematurely. Now she has to see him away from our property for he will not enter my door. He told her he would never come back unless I were dead. It was in one of his missives that I procured from her bed table.

• • • • •

"Father, I have sinned."

"When was your last confession?"

"More than twenty years ago."

"That's a very long time, my son."

"It is."

"Do I detect an Irish accent?"

"I was born in County Cork. Yes."

"Well, then, so was I...What are your sins, my son."

"I have broken the most important of the commandments."

"Was it war time, my son?"

"It was not."

"We have several parishioners who were in the Army, you know which one I mean, and they have confessed to killing those who they thought were their enemies. I am aware of the troubles, back home."

"It wasn't like that, Father."

"Then what was it like?"

"I have done evil. I have done the work of the devil, and now I have lost my son because of what I have perpetrated."

"You need to explain to me a bit more clearly, I'm afraid."

"I have taken life. I have taken everything from more than one person."

"Perhaps you should confess this to someone else. Maybe you need to pay for your sins in a different venue."

"Can I be forgiven?"

"Christ commands it."

"But Christ can't help me, and neither can you."

I leave the confessional before the old Irish priest can remonstrate with me.

• • • • •

We don't eat meals together, either. She dines alone in the kitchen. All we share is a roof. My only consolation is my work. I labor twelve hours and more at my practice six days a week. I have not entered a church since the confession, and I have no plans to go back. The old priest did nothing to relieve my agony, and the Pope himself couldn't alleviate my pain.

I want to kill. It is my nature. I have denied it too long, but the two of them stand in my way. I think the unthinkable, about murdering Robert and Gretchen, my wife and my only blood kin, my only son.

Into what depravity have I fallen?

The time crawls away. Every day is infinite in my self-torture. I tell myself I have earned this existence. I brought everything on myself. But my self-knowledge doesn't ease anything. It was easier when I was a minister of darkness, spreading my violence all over Whitechapel.

I was never caught. I wasn't even on a list of possible suspects. My name may have crossed someone's desk at Scotland Yard, but my likeness was never released to the papers. Perhaps someone thought I might be worth looking at, but I was far gone from England if anyone became aware of me.

Saucy Jack from hell. The devil's spawn. The terror of Whitechapel and the bane of the whores who infected the streets there. I was feared. I spread horror even into the homes of the aristocracy, even into the castle where the Queen lived.

They all knew my name, my reputation. I rose from the underworld, from the stench of the sewers, from the offal below.

No, they never caught me. I was too swift, too elusive, too sly. And I made it all the way to the New World. And I had a son, an only son, who spurned me as did his mother, my wife.

I am the darker side of the coin. I can only wonder about the seed I sprang from. Did my father's father have to tell his son that father was a murderous beast from the bowels of hell? Did he, too, lose that son when the words fell from his lips? Did his heir flee him like some kind of modern black plague?

So, this is my lot in life. I am to be free. I can roam the streets of this city as I did London, a decade ago. If I give in to my primal instincts, I can kill again, I can rampage through these very mean streets and I can further eliminate some fallen women who are the feces of the alleys and broken tenements.

I can begin again.

CHAPTER NINETEEN

The winter brings on a halt to the drastic number of homicides. It's mid-December, and I've been assigned a regular caseload. The 'Ripper reruns', as they are now being referred to in Homicide, have stopped cold. There are only the usual number of butcheries, and I'm at a dead end with the twins as far as being any closer to snapping the cuffs on them both.

The inroad at getting them might lie with Patrick. Last time I saw him coming out of his office, he looked pale and twitchy. I let him see me, and I suppose that's like the 'white coat syndrome' for medical doctors and dentists as far as their patients are concerned.

But he appeared frightened. He looked as if he didn't know whether to run up and get down on his knees or if he were going to bolt away from me like a spooked rabbit.

If he killed one or more of the girls, I think his personal career has terminated. I have no solid reason or evidence to think so, but it's my gut instinct, nevertheless. He looks ready to go over the top, way past the edge of the envelope.

Our best shot at them was when one of them dumped bleach on the victim. It was fortunate for either of them that nothing remained on the corpse that we could use.

And we continue to try and lure them on the internet. Our nerds have had no luck, so far.

Sean is more likely to go out looking for prey again. As I say, Patrick looks like he's headed for his own little basket to go hide in. That's why I'm ramping up the surveillance on him alone. I have other cases to attend to, but every free minute I have I'm right near him or right behind him. I told him about bulldogs. My father had that reputation. He'd simply outlast the perpetrator. Whether there was a case based on tangible proof or not, Jimmy Parisi grabbed hold and did not let go. His list of unsolved cases is the shortest in the history of the CPD.

There's no sympathy for Patrick or his brother, naturally. Not from where I stand. Patrick is becoming more pathetic than anything. He looks haggard and exhausted, and if that's where I have to take him, he's there. I'll break him. I can feel him crumbling right now.

• • • • •

My wife has a full load of cases, herself. But Maria tells me none are as hideous as the Tracy twins'. Hers are the standard shootings and strangle jobs and beatings with tire irons and cast-iron fry pans—the garden variety of murders. They're usually done for the most pedestrian of motives, nothing that Dick Tracy or Sherlock Holmes or Columbo would be interested in. Most are no-brainers and are solved in forty-eight hours or less.

"It must be very fulfilling," I smirk when she rattles off the list of brain-deads she and Ned Diamond have collared in the last few weeks.

"Very adroit, very cutting."

"I'm glad you're successful, is all."

I take her tightly to me and kiss her. We're standing in the middle of our miniature living room. This place was designed for single occupancy.

"Let's go looking at houses," I tell her.

"We can't afford a place of our own...Can we?"

"I have a few bucks saved."

"A few bucks? What does that mean, Michael?"

"You may have noticed I'm quite frugal."

"You mean cheap?" she grins.

"Have it your way."

"Like McDonald's," she jabs back.

"I've got some money from my combat tours that I put into a few investments while I was gone. One of my high school buddies became a pretty successful broker, and he made some outstanding investments for me while I was gone."

"How successful?"

I kiss her again, but she pulls back from me.

"Six figures successful."

"How high in that bracket? Remember, we share everything, now."

"I should've nailed you with a pre-nup," I retort.

"You nailed me well enough in other ways...C'mon. What're we talking, here?"

I wait and smile at her.

"Just south of five hundred K."

Her mouth drops open.

"Why didn't you tell me before?"

"I just talked to Danny Maloy. He's the broker. He's been trying to get a hold of me for a long time, but I haven't made it easy on him. The pot's been building for the last two years. But he told me to stick what I've got in savings and play with about ten thousand to re-start my earnings. He's nervous about the knucklehead in Washington and thinks another recession's coming soon."

"So you have all that in savings?" she says with a still-opened pair of jaws.

"Except for the ten K. I gave it to Danny to play with."

"You're rich, and you never told me?"

"I wasn't aware of it until recently. I kept changing my phone number and address, and he finally found me at work."

"I don't know what to say."

"I do. Your name is going onto that savings account. We've already got joint checking."

"You don't have to do that. I was just kidding about..."

"Everything I have *is* yours. You know that. You've always known that."

"I guess we have a down payment, then," she smiles.

"We do. Shall we go celebrate?"

I take her by the hand and lead her toward the bedroom.

"The new house is going to have a master bedroom for you and me and three big bedrooms for the rest of us."

"Not just yet," she says.

She sounds a bit disappointed.

"Then we'd better get back to work," I tell her as we land atop the bed.

• • • • •

He walks out of the entrance to his office at 6:30 PM. He's very predictable when it comes to time, Patrick is. I'm still staying away from his nastier brother, for the moment. I'm certain that Patrick is the road toward getting them both. He's the weaker half of their brotherhood.

"Can I walk you to your car?" I tell him as I catch up with him.

"This is harassment, pure and simple," he answers.

It's already dark, but the street lamp overhead is casting dim illumination over us. Snow showers have commenced, and his hair looks like it's covered in dandruff. I never see him wearing a hat. I never wear one, either.

"It's just that I want you to be safe. This neighborhood draws flies."

"It's winter," he says.

"Not that kind of fly. The human kind. You know what I'm saying. The muggers go where the money is, just like that guy who was a famous bank robber when he explained why he robbed banks."

"This is not at all amusing, Detective Parisi, and I'm asking you to leave me alone."

"You look all beleaguered, Patrick. Is anything wrong?"

"Please."

"Don't beg. It's a sign of weakness. You got to keep up with the times. This is an age for wolves, not sheep. But then you and your bro are more like vampires, aren't you. Ever read that Bram Stoker book?"

The snow is falling more heavily when we approach his new, black Mercedes.

"Can I go now?" he asks as he clicks the door of his ride open with his key. "This is really becoming intolerable."

"I'm just doing my duty, walking you to your car."

"I'm sure you have more pressing matters."

"You and your brother are my most pressing matters, Patrick. I told you I'd be around…You might want to seek some medical attention. You look a little anemic. Those children of the night need to hunt. No hunt, no blood. Isn't that how it goes?"

He starts up his motor, and the tires slip on the snow-covered blacktop of the lot, and then he's out into the street.

• • • • •

"He's filed a complaint," the Captain asserts.

"I knew he probably would."

We're sitting in his far more spacious office with an equally appealing view of Lake Michigan with its frosted surface.

"Christ, and I'm trying to get my goddam Christmas shopping finished, Parisi. Why do you task me so?"

"My apologies, Captain."

"Lies don't sit well on you, Parisi."

"No. I guess not."

"You'd better lay off the little prick."

"He's the way to landing both of them."

"How?"

I tell him what I see in Patrick Tracy, his down-spiral looks.

"You can't harass him anyway. You know how it works."

"He's ready to pop, like a crowning boil."

"That's what I needed to hear. Thank you very much. Jesus Christ."

"I can get his brother if I get Patrick first."

"You can get yourself de-horned, my man. Look, Michael, this is not some field of fire."

"I'm well aware, Captain."

"The rules of engagement differ diametrically."

"Yes."

"You can't keep getting in his face unless you're ready to read him his rights and charge him. Can I become any more basic than that, Detective?"

"No, you probably cannot."

"I had trouble losing my military life, Michael. They change the rules on you. When someone pissed you off, you had the double-oh-seven attitude, license to kill."

"I don't want to kill them, Captain. That would involve far too little suffering on their parts. I want them locked in a cell until they've seen the sun for the last time from some window in their cell blocks."

He looks at me with amusement or bemusement; I can't tell which.

"Your father was old-school, but he wasn't an executioner, so I'm glad you're not into 'vengeance is mine'."

"I'm a Catholic, sort of. I'm pretty much New Testament, but I'm only forgiving to an extent."

"Don't get carried away. Cases go cold all the time, even when you goddam know who did the crime. You're a little early into this tour to burn your candle from both ends, Michael."

I don't answer.

"Back off on him, trooper. Got it?"

• • • • •

I don't approach him as I did before. I don't need to make my boss's life more miserable than it already is. He's got pressure from the Commandant and the Mayor, and that tub of guts in the White House is calling us out publicly for the homicide rate in Chicago.

So, I stay back a little. I let him pick me up on the periphery of his vision. That kind of image is more frightening than a straight on sighting. You're never really sure if anyone's there or not.

• • • • •

Tonight, I do a drive-by at Sean's office. The king of the nip and tuck, he's known in these parts. He and I and Patrick all know that his knife has been doing jobs on the off hours. They've been moonlighting in murder.

Does evil come in degrees? I suppose it must. Some crimes are far more inhuman than others. You steal a guy's ride, you piss him off and inconvenience him a little. Murder is The Show, however. It's the thievery of all thefts. You take away everything he's got.

Yeah, I think Sean's the worse of the two. I can't shake the notion that Patrick is more of a novice. I'm pretty certain, from the gut perspective, he's done maybe one of the murders, and I feel pretty sure it was Sean who became literally sexual with Demetra, the black victim.

I'm keeping my promise, so I'm not getting in Sean's face. He's the more aggressive of the two, and I don't think he wants to lay back passively and make a mild protest about 'harassment' the way Patrick did.

No, this guy would lawyer up, and I don't want to get bounced from this pursuit. I want to be there at the end with these two slapdicks.

He meanders out of his office building at 7:47—he's not as punctual as his sibling. He walks toward the parking lot. This time the sky is clear and the temperatures have plummeted into the low twenties. It's unnaturally frigid for this early in the winter. The snow that we had has melted, but the warming has turned to polar.

I cruise slowly toward him as he approaches his red Lexus. He pulls out of the lot slowly, deliberately, as if he knows that I'm out here behind him, but I don't see him looking in the rear- view mirror, and he takes off down the street at the speed limit, 35.

I follow him all the way to an apartment building that's not his own. A valet takes the Lexus from him and drives around the block. Toward a private lot, I assume.

I wait until he goes inside the complex.

Then I get out into the chill and approach the doorman. He's wearing the full regalia, with little gold braids on his shoulders and a doorman's lid on his pate.

I flash the shield at the guy.

"Officer, can I help you?"

He's way past the retirement age. In his seventies, I'd guess. I'm certain he'd rather have been in his bed by nine, tonight, but it doesn't look like it's happening for him.

"The man who just entered. Where was he headed?"

"I'm afraid I can't talk about our people, Detective. I'd get fired."

I show him a twenty. He grabs it.

"Her name is Barbara. He's been here a few times previously, but I'm afraid that's all your twenty can buy you."

"What's your name?" I ask.

"Charlie, the residents call me."

"Would you rather take a ride downtown with me right now? We can make this official. I guess I can't play Mr. Nice Guy with you anymore, Charlie."

"Her name is Barbara Ryan. Suite 1012. That's really all I know."

"See how easy it is to keep it simple? And I better not hear that you said anything about me to Barbara or her gentleman friend. You read me, Charlie?"

He nods.

I go back to the unmarked ride and I turn on my tunes. It's Charlie Parker, tonight. I have a feeling I'll be here a while.

I don't run the motor, and it gets very cold in here very quickly.

CHAPTER TWENTY

I'm beginning to drink. I never did before, perhaps an occasional glass of wine at dinner. But now I sit in a bar on Michigan Avenue, not far from my office. No one seemed to be following me, and I watched to see that no one came into this knockoff of an English pub behind me. Maybe Parisi took heed to my warning about a harassment claim, but there could be other policemen I'm not aware of following me. No one looks like an archetypical cop in here, however.

It's not crowded, perhaps twenty or thirty patrons. There are tables and booths, but I sit at the slab close to where the bartender operates. I order a manhattan and it's a stiff one.

A woman decides to sit three stools away from me. We're the only ones at the bar. She orders the same cocktail I did. But she never looks my way. She's very attractive and isn't wearing a wedding band. This is hardly the time for me to notice such things since my last chat with Parisi has been tearing at me for a week. I'm sure Sean would laugh his threats off, but I can't seem to.

She has shoulder length auburn hair and she's wearing a tight, ribbed periwinkle sweater that accentuates her prominent breasts. I haven't had a sexual urge in quite some time. The single encounter with the prostitute was as close as I've come to anything sexual at all.

"You ordered the same drink I did," I hear myself saying aloud.

The spoken words shock me awake.

"Pardon me?" she chirps.

She's smiling, however.

"I said we're having manhattans," I reply.

"We are indeed."

"Kind of dead in here, tonight," I tell her.

"I usually don't come to bars...Why don't you move over here?" she suggests.

I find myself obeying her.

After we finish our drinks in silence, I order us another round.

She asks my name, and I tell her.

"My name's Aurora," she grins.

"Like the borealis?"

"Just Aurora. No, I wasn't born there, either."

"I like it."

"Patrick's a nice, solid name, too...What do you do, Patrick?"

"I'm an oral surgeon. My office is just a few blocks away."

"I have perfect teeth. Sorry."

I find myself smiling at her.

"Are you single?" she queries.

"Yes, I am."

"Ever been married?"

"No."

"Me neither," she grins.

"I find that hard to believe."

"Are you saying that men don't think I'm suitable?" she laughs.

"No, I mean you're very attractive, and by now I would've thought someone might've noticed."

"They've noticed. Nothing ever took. How about you?"

"I suppose it's my work."

I'm thinking about the whore I cut. I'm thinking about the bad blood coursing in my veins and in my brother's veins. I'm remembering the curse laid on us both by Francis.

But then my attention returns to this beautiful woman. What would it be like to tear her apart? Would it be the same as the whore, or would it be even more exciting? Imagine the sight of this body beneath my blade.

I become aroused in an embarrassingly painful way. It's dim enough in here to mask my budding erection, the projectile rising beneath the fabric of my slacks. I try to shift myself so it'll go away, but it grows in spite of the move.

"What do you do?" I ask her.

I have to distract myself before she sees my folly.

"I'm an attorney. I guess my work has kept me out of anything long-lasting, as far as relationships go."

I can't stop my member from betraying me, and I can't remember wanting a woman as much as I want this stranger right now. But I'm not certain if I want to bed her or cut her to bits. I've been denying the depravity I gave in to just one time. I keep telling myself it must never happen again. They haven't caught either of us, but they're watching me. That homicide detective, Parisi, is always somewhere close by.

"Hello? Still there?" Aurora interrupts.

"I'm sorry. My mind was just wandering."

"Can't I hold you under my spell?" she sighs.

She leans closer to me.

"Next round's on me," she says with a whispery allure.

She summons the barman.

I'm feeling a bit woozy, but I like the sensation. As I said, I've never been a drinker.

Mount her or cut her?

Why not both?

"Would you...Would you like to come over to my condo? It's not far."

She lays her hand on mine. I can smell the liquor on both our breaths.

"I thought you'd never ask."

• • • • •

I should not have brought her here. I have no idea what's going to happen next.

My surgical bag is, as always, in the closet in the bedroom. She leads me to that bedroom as soon as I tell her where it is. Aurora is very liberated.

There's nothing coy or subtle about her. Perhaps it's because she's an aggressive litigator who's lived alone too long. I'm simply guessing.

There's something to hate about her, then. She's certainly not a virgin, not the type of woman you'd think could mother your children. Maybe she's a ball breaker. That might be the kind of aggressive she is. Likes to command, likes to demand. Enjoys making men subordinate to her because she plays sex as a card in a game, and she always has to win.

She kisses me hard on the lips and goes for my penis without foreplay. I'm still very stiff, the way I was at the pub. It cooperated with me and deflated just in time to take Aurora out to my car, but now it has risen back with a vengeance.

Her sex is furious. She wants to get on top, she wants to set the pace, the rhythm, and I allow her to take control of our joining.

She is as beautiful as I imagined. Her body is porcelain and perfect. The dimensions are geometrically flawless—it's prime symmetry. There is not a flaw on her lovely, smooth skin. I trace my fingers up and down her flanks as she rises and then lowers herself onto me. When she erupts, I do, and the current flows between us for an extended moment.

She rolls off me and lies next to me, breathing like a runner who's finished a long- distance race. We are perspiring profusely, and then I feel her hand on me again. There seems to be no down time for me with her. She has me primed and ready, but this time I force her on her back.

"You want it rough, Patrick? You want to dominate?"

The leer on her lips and face makes me enraged. I want to slap her, punch her, beat her, turn her gorgeous visage into a blood-covered pulp.

Now her eyes sense what is to happen. I pierce her to her deepest depths and her mouth forms an oval. Her breath is sucked inside herself.

Then I put both hands on her throat and I squeeze.

She must think I'm engaging in a form of coitus that involves deprivation of oxygen. It is supposed to enhance her orgasm.

But she senses that this is no rough sex. She understands that I'm not out to enhance her climax.

I'm going to strangle her.

To death.

Awareness enters her eyes and face. Fear encompasses that beautiful visage. Her cheeks redden and then turn a darker color. She tries to flail away at me with her hands and legs, but her air's been cut too low, and she begins to fade.

When I ease up, she suddenly rebounds and comes back to life and we're struggling on the mattress. She's desperately trying to find my loins with her knees, but I've got hold of her neck again and I ram her back onto her backside. This time I grip her throat until I can literally feel her windpipe.

I hear it crack as I take even tighter hold.

The light begins to dim in her emerald-colored orbs. And then she's gone.

Panic hits me.

Christ, what'll I do with her?

I can't cut her. I can't do what I wanted to. After all that inner talk about controlling myself I took her up here, to my own apartment, and I really thought I was going to open my medical bag and take out a knife and starting making incisions that would cut her from her breastbone to her pubis? Was I mad?

Haven't I always been insane?

I have to put her somewhere where they'll never find her. I have to put her in water, somewhere where the smell won't betray her location. Water erodes, water removes things from sight, it conceals.

Yes, I'll put her in a blanket. I'll bind her up and I'll weigh down her ankles. It's very late. I know where I can dispose of her. I'll put all of her clothes and her purse in a trash bag and I'll tie it to her body in the blanket, and I'll throw her in the drink and watch her go down where no one will find her.

• • • • •

Getting her out to the car is going to be dangerous. If I get stuck on the elevator with a body draped over my shoulder...I could take the stairs, but they're usually vacant. However, there is her weight as I descend. She's not at all heavy, but I have the dumbbells in a bag to haul, as well.

I settle on the stairs. It's only a few flights, and I won't feel as entrapped. It's late enough that there's no one around.

Outside is another issue, but I have no choice. I couldn't have left her on the bed upstairs. When I venture out into the street, there's no one, and at the moment there's no traffic going by. My car is close by in the lot, and it, too, is deserted. Fortune is backing my play. Then I put her on the pavement, drop the heavy bag with the weights, and I pop the trunk.

There is no one to witness the body in the blanket. I have her hidden.

• • • • •

There is a slough out in the southwestern suburbs that will suit my needs. I've brought along a roll of duct tape and I've bound her inside a blanket. A body bag would have been better, but I don't have access to one, and I don't have time to get a hold of one, either. She has to go now, now while it's still dark.

But what if the slough is frozen over in ice?

It's been in the mid-thirties, currently, right before Christmas. Perhaps there's enough thaw that I can throw her into the murk.

There are rowboats at this slough. They're tethered to the single dock, but apparently the park rangers don't fear theft.

There are no cars in the parking lot. It's too cold for this lot to be used as a lover's lane, so the rangers aren't around as often as they would be in spring or summer or early fall. It seems as if everything's cooperating with my plight.

I take her out of my trunk. I lay her on the frozen grass, and then I shut the trunk and begin to drag her to the dock. I haul her up and lower her into the rowboat, and then I remove the rope that ties the boat to the stanchion. I get onboard, and I row out to the center of the slough.

It hasn't iced over. When I'm well away from the dock, somewhere near the middle of the slough, I duct tape dumbbells to her with the weights I use at home to exercise. I pull out her ankles from the bound blanket and I strap the weights to her feet.

I roll her to the side of the boat, and then I lift her over the side.

She makes a flapping noise as her body hits the surface of the slough.

The body in the blanket lingers on the surface and I can't breathe. It remains in place, and the panic returns to me.

I peer back at the parking lot, looking for the headlights of a park ranger that will signal my doom. I'll be arrested and then Parisi will have me. They'll find Aurora and my semen will be my downfall.

I lean over the edge of the rowboat once more and I try to urge the body to submerge. It doesn't sink.

I look again at the lot where my car is parked, and there are still no lights. It's well after one AM. This preserve is far away from the glow of the city or any neighboring suburbs. It's isolated, on the periphery of Cook County.

I look over at the floating mass. Why aren't the weights dragging her down?

Again, I reach over and try to push her below.

This time she begins to lower in the water. Slowly, slowly, the body disappears. I wait five minutes to see if it'll bob back up, but I've been out here too long. Eventually someone will pass the parking lot. The rangers do still make rounds of the preserves. It's their goddam jobs, I remind myself.

I can't see anything but the black surface of the slough. There is no moon, tonight.

I begin rowing back to the dock.

Then I see a pair of headlights enter the parking area. I stop dead and watch and wait.

He'll see my car. He'll come looking, out by that dock. I have nowhere to hide from him. I'll be locked in a cage for the rest of my life because they will search the slough and find Aurora sodden in her burial blanket with my weights attached to her ankles and feet. Christ, I'm lost. I'm finished.

I didn't even have the opportunity to rip this bitch into fleshy fragments.

Then the car circles the parking lot and heads back out onto the highway again, and it's black, once more.

I row to the dock, slip the rope over the stanchion, and climb onto the short pier.

I waste no time getting into my vehicle and heading back east toward Lake Michigan.

• • • •

I made certain to retrieve Aurora's car key before I dragged her out to the slough. I couldn't very well leave her Camry sitting on the curb outside my building. They will of course look for her.

Then there's the barman. He got a very good look at the both of us and he'll be able to identify both of us. But no one saw her follow me the eight blocks to my condo. As far as anyone knows, we left separately. I'm covered, I think. We have no doorman at our building, and it was late enough that no one saw us as we rode the elevator to my floor. I think I'm all right, so far.

I drive Aurora's Camry out by Navy Pier and I leave it parked by a meter that still has time left on it. It's still late. The sun won't be up for a few hours, and no one sees me as I walk away from her ride.

I catch a bus and make it back to my building. I didn't want to take a taxi and have a driver with a long memory remember his fare. Bus drivers don't study faces. They just haul bodies.

I can't sleep when I get back to bed. I call my receptionist at eight and tell her to cancel all my appointments and tell her to reschedule all of them.

What a stupid man I am. I didn't have to throttle Aurora. I could have just had her all night and then have let her go.

But she showed me what a haughty cunt she thought she was, and I was hardly aware of my hands on that delicate neck and then I was gripping her harder and harder and what had to happen happened. I cannot deny who I am. I'm the descendant of the most heartless killer who ever roamed the alleys and tenements of Whitechapel. I am my great grandfather's legacy, and whatever he had coursing through his veins runs the same through mine.

I belong to him. I always have.

CHAPTER TWENTY-ONE

They don't walk the streets much when it's cold, in the heart of December. The internet is no longer safe because I've used it too often and a smart cop like Parisi will figure out how I've located my marks, eventually. Stupid, he is not. They have their young Turks of technology and they will try to nab me with some kind of sting setup.

So, I have to try a different hunting ground. The trouble, as I say, is finding a whore hearty enough to be walking the avenues and boulevards in twenty-degree weather. There is no snow, tonight, but the wind is slicing its path out of the northeast, off the lake. The inhabitants of this city call it 'The Hawk.'

I'm cruising the Old Town district since it has a reputation for prostitution and for vice in general.

I'm bothered that I haven't heard from Patrick, of late. He won't answer my emails or my phone calls. I suppose I'll have to visit him at his home or at his office. I'm worried that he might fall apart and turn himself in to Parisi or some other policeman. He has a weakness, my brother. It's called a temporary conscience. It plagues him, it tasks him, from time to time.

I, on the other hand, have no such frailty. I suppose a psychiatrist might lump me into that vague classification called 'sociopath.' They don't seem to have any other designation for people like me. Except for the notion that we're very difficult to apprehend. We're plotters, what they call 'organized killers'. Most murderers do what they do out of undisciplined passion. They strike out, but they never plan their bloody deeds in advance. And they are snared quite quickly and easily.

That's why I've changed venues. It might be very difficult to find a mark roaming about two days before Christmas on a frigid night, but you never know. It helps to be unpredictable. I intend to keep going this way, also. I'd like to do someone in broad daylight, in a public place, in plain sight, but that'll take some serious thought. Just because it's never been done doesn't mean it can't be accomplished. I understand the logistics seem impossible, but if a President can be assassinated on a crowded street, a murder such as is my wont might be possible. It's the mess that complicates matters.

I see a lone figure standing outside a sex club on Kelly Avenue, here in Old Town. The bars stay open until 4:00 AM, and this sex club goes under the name of a 'gentleman's' bar. They have strippers, totally nude, and they have sex for cash in the back rooms. I've never been inside, but Cal's Gentleman's Club is notorious.

I pull over. I roll down the window on the passenger's side.

She flicks her lit cigarette onto the curb and walks toward me. Three drunken males stagger out of Cal's front door. One of them makes a lascivious remark to the woman approaching me.

"Go home and fuck your fat cow of a wife!" she yells at the trio.

The drunk who insulted her walks toward her and my car.

"Get in," I tell her.

She wastes no time in boarding. She slams the passenger's door and I squeal away from the curb, leaving her vocal attacker and friends behind us as I lurch away from them.

"Thanks," she tells me.

I can only see her dimly in the sparse glow of the outside street lights. Her hair is dark, brown or black, I can't tell which. She looks young, but there's already mileage there. She's not unattractive. She's lean. I can tell, even beneath her heavy winter coat.

"You looking for a party?" she asks.

"Could be."

"You don't sound very sure of yourself."

"I thought I was saving you from the fiery dragon."

She peers over at me. The lights from those street lamps cast brief and sporadic illumination over the side of her face. It's almost like a surreal, garish profile, as I drive along.

"It's too cold to do it in a car."

"We haven't discussed a price," I tell her.

"Get us some place warm and I'll give you a pre-Christmas discount," she laughs.

"Where would you like to go? It'd have to be discrete."

"You married?" she asks.

"No."

"Then what the hell do you care about 'discrete'?"

"You're right. What do I care?"

"You look like you can afford something downtown."

"It'd have to be a little more distant than that. I have a professional reputation to protect, not a wife."

"You're a lawyer, I bet."

"Why do you say that?"

"The fancy ride, here."

"I'm a doctor, as a matter of fact."

"No."

"Yes. Why? Don't I look like a physician?"

"You're not old enough. You're too good looking."

I have to laugh at this dumb cunt.

"I'm a plastic surgeon."

She looks at me warily.

"Then why can't you get non-pros? Like I said, you're handsome."

"I seek women who know what they're doing. You're part of the world's oldest profession, yes?"

"I suppose. I don't spend a lot of time thinking about it. You gotta eat, right?"

"There are all kinds of appetites in the world...What's your name?"

"All you get is my street label. Jeanine."

"Good name. It'll do...I know a place that's not too far away."

I haven't used it before, and it's not too close to the other hotels I've used for such assignations.

"You gotta be careful, lately," she continues. "There's been all those murders. You read about them, didn't you?"

"You mean the murders of your sisters on the street?"

"Yeah—very funny, 'sisters on the street'."

The hotel is five minutes away. My bag with my equipment is in the trunk. I'll have to tell her I take it wherever I go. If she bought my profession, she'll let it slide. I'll remind her how expensive my tools of the trade are and how I never leave them in the car. She'll believe it or she won't. There are other whores if she puts up a protest and turns rabbit on me.

We make it to the hotel on McMullin. It's on the periphery of downtown, where I do all my best work. I pull into their parking lot. There's no attendant working. This is a discount venue, and they're never crowded. Talk is that they're going to fold, here, and redevelopment is going to tear the building down and replace it with upscale condos in the next year or two.

"You get us a room," I tell her as we get out of the car. "Here."

I hand her a hundred-dollar bill.

Then I go to the trunk and retrieve the bag.

"The stuff in here is worth a lot of money...That ought to take care of it," I say.

Our breaths make small clouds in front of us.

"We ain't settled on a price for your party."

"What do you think it should be?"

She looks me over.

"You look even better in the light, out here. Two hundred for two hours. How's that?"

"All right."

"Half now," she demands.

"Quite the entrepreneur, you are."

I hand her another hundred.

"You better earn your wages of sin."

"Was that a crack? You don't have to be a bastard and be mean."

"I was only joking, Jeanine. Believe me...Can we get out of the cold? Call me on your cell and let me know the room number. And don't think about skipping out with the money. I'll have an eye on you."

Her face goes taut.

"You're not that guy who's been knifing everybody, are you?" she grins suspiciously.

"Do I look like that kind of a guy, Jeanine?"

"What do those kind of guys look like?" she snaps back.

"Great comeback. Are you going to get the room or not? If you don't, hand back the money and I'll give you cab fare."

She peers at the two hundreds in her right hand.

"I have to eat, you know."

"Or be eaten," I smile back.

"You're a player, huh? A diver, huh?"

"You'll find out."

She looks one more time at the two bills, and then she heads inside.

I wait about thirty seconds and then I follow her in. I make sure the man at the desk is pre-occupied with Jeanine, and then I head to the bathroom and wait for her call. I brought the bag, and I have it firmly in my right hand. I take the cell phone out of my pocket with my free hand.

It takes about five minutes until the buzzing sounds.

"Three-sixteen," she says.

"I'll be right behind you."

"I don't do Greek," she giggles.

"Neither do I. But you'll really like what I'm going to do to you, Jeanine."

Then I turn off the phone and head out of the john. I make certain that the night clerk isn't looking my way, and then I head toward the elevators. She's already on her way, and it takes a moment for the doors to open for me. I punch in for three, and I'm headed up alone in the elevator.

The doors open again, and I walk out and down the hall to our room. She's left the entry opened. Then I close it behind me.

I don't see her. But then I hear water running from what must be the toilet.

Her coat is draped on the middle of the queen-sized bed.

Then Jeanine appears.

She's got a gun in her hand. A .38 snub-nose, it appears.

"Hand it over," she demands.

"What a disappointment," I mutter.

"Hand it over. No one will think much of a pop sound in this flea-infested shithole, *Doc*."

I take my wallet from my back pocket.

"You really suppose you're going to get away with this?" I tell her.

"Watch me. Now hand over that bag, too."

I throw the wallet and the bag onto the bed.

"You know what you're going to do, Doc? You're going to count to a hundred and twenty before you leave this flea trap. Then you can leave. If you pop up before then, I'll shoot you in the head. And I'm an excellent shot. Trying me wouldn't be a good move. You understand?"

I nod. The rage is boiling up inside me.

"You give me that full one twenty, hear?"

"I will, Jeanine. I'll be seeing you soon, sometime."

"Not likely. At least I left you your ride."

She walks toward the door. The .38 is pointed at my head. I'm trying to think if I have a chance to rush her, but this is no goddam movie and I'm no hero. She holds the piece as if it's not her first time.

Then she rushes out and shuts the door.

I don't count to one twenty. I don't count at all. I wait inside here for around twenty minutes, and then I get up and depart.

• • • • •

There's no sign of her outside.

But I find my bag sitting on the concrete behind my car. She probably thought the insides of the valise weren't worth her time to drag it with her.

I open the trunk and toss the bag inside.

I drive off and go home. I call Barbara up at this very late hour on my cell. Surprisingly, she agrees to meet me at the condo.

"I've been thinking about you," she says in a husky voice.

• • • • •

I fling her on the bed, but there's no fear in her eyes.

Perhaps she might be a suitable substitute for Jeanine, but Barbara is far more beautiful, and I can't shit where I eat. I can't very well undertake what I'd like to do to her here in my home. The logistics are ridiculous. Getting her body out of her would be a lunatic move, and I'm not stupid. I have no death wish, no desire to be cuffed and carted to prison by Parisi or any of his friends.

"I like it angry. I love it rough. Just don't leave any bruises."

I put my hands on her throat, again. We're naked on the middle of my sheets.

"Don't get carried away," she gurgles.

I turn her over suddenly and I get up and remove my belt from my trousers.

I bring the belt down on her buttocks, careful not to use the buckle.

A welt springs up to the surface, but it doesn't look like it'll turn black or purple. She bleats a little when I strike her, but she doesn't try to stop me. So this time I lay a lash across her shoulder blades, and a red stripe appears. She cries out quickly, but she still doesn't move.

I turn her onto her back and I lash her across the stomach. And then I do her thighs, and I see the tears streaming down her cheeks.

It makes me crazy aroused, and I mount her and enter her and she cries out again, this time more loudly. I batter her again and again, and then she rises toward me as if she were levitating, and finally we finish, almost together.

I check her front and back, and the blows have left only red marks that are turning lighter by the moment.

"You like pain, Barbara?"

"Within reason," she replies. "As long as you don't leave anything permanent and ugly."

"You really think I could do anything to ruin that beautiful flesh of yours?"

I peer over at my medical bag, resting upon a plush bedroom chair. It would take no effort to go over to that bag and to remove my six-inch scalpel and then to cut her throat so that she could not scream. There would be copious blood, of course, and the aftermath would be extremely difficult to clean up. All it takes is for them to find a trace of her blood, a particle of my semen inside her remains, and then I would be lost.

"You don't really suppose I could harm you in any way, do you, Barbara?"

She rakes her fingernails across my wet chest, and then she finds me, she finds me as she always does just when I think I cannot come back at her again.

I look down at her face and I superimpose the visage of that tawdry, dirty, diseased whore who stole my wallet, and I can see my scalpel ripping downward into her perfect blue left eye.

CHAPTER TWENTY-TWO

I get a call from Frosty the Vice cop. He says he has something I'll be interested in. So I take the elevator down to their floor and I find him waiting for me.

"How's Jack the Ripper hangin'?" he smiles.

He offers me his hand and I shake it.

"Still dead, like the fascist in the Spanish Civil War."

"Too cerebral for me. Too early in the morning."

"Franco. Chevy Chase on *Saturday Night Live.* You weren't a fan?"

"I don't watch TV, not when there's all that porn on the net," he grins.

I sit down opposite him.

He places a wallet on my side of the table.

I open it, and then I see a driver's license: Sean Tracy. His photograph tells me he's one of my favorite twins.

"Isn't this the guy you were looking at?" Frosty asks.

I nod.

"How'd you get a hold of this?"

He smiles again.

"We busted a hooker for soliciting, and the silly bitch still had it in her purse. Along with a .38 snub-nosed piece. She mugged your buddy, it looks like."

"You contact Tracy, yet?"

"No, I thought you might want to have the pleasure of hauling his ass into your domain upstairs."

"I don't want to intrude on your territory."

"Let's say the wallet will just be a loner. I'll need it back for evidence, but I trust you, Michael."

He beams at me again.

"What about the hooker?"

"She goes by the street name of Jeanine, but her real moniker is Darlene Fitzgerald. She's downstairs in holding. We just grabbed her late last night."

It's Christmas Day and I'm working. Maria has New Year's Eve and New Year's Day off, and so do I, so we'll celebrate the holidays later. She's on shift with Ned, right now.

"You ask her about Tracy?" I query.

"Yeah, but just in passing. That's your ball park."

I stand up and thank him.

"You still think he's that descendant of whatsisname?"

His face is dead serious, but I don't answer and I leave his cubicle.

• • • • •

She sits opposite me at a blond, rectangular table.

"There anyone behind the mirror?" she asks.

She sits erect on her straight-backed wooden chair. As if someone taught her about posture when she was younger. She's not unattractive, but the wear and tear are already showing on her face. It might've been pretty, back in the day, but now it looks simply worn out, and she appears ten or fifteen years older than the age listed on her sheet in front of me.

"Why'm I talking to a homicide detective?" she wants to know.

"Because I'm interested in talking to you about a homicide, Darlene."

"What homicide?"

"It's actually a multiple."

"Whoa!! I haven't done anyone that way."

"Why're you toting a canon, then?" I ask.

She shifts nervously in her seat.

"The Vice detective said you're being uncooperative. That's not a good move when you have no license to carry firearms, Darlene."

"I gotta protect myself."

I have to laugh.

I set the wallet on the table between us.

"What's that?"

"You ought to know. It was in your purse when they arrested you."

"They planted that. I never..."

"It's got your prints all over it."

She sits still, now.

"You were with a man in a room when you pulled the piece and robbed him of that wallet."

She remains mute.

"Come on, Darlene. Don't be stupid. I just want to know about that man."

She waits a beat.

"Is it gonna help me out if I talk to you?"

"Nah, you're still going to jail for armed robbery."

"Then why should I help you?"

"Because the judge is going to know you wouldn't help *me*. I'll make it my business to make sure he knows."

Darlene looks at the wall behind me.

"They have you cold, Darlene, but the judge might be a little lenient if you helped in a homicide case."

"What do you want to know?"

"Tell me exactly what happened. How he solicited you, for starters."

She relates the tale to me. And then she tells me one last fact about her evening with Dr. Sean Tracy.

"I took this bag he had, too."

"What was in the bag, do you know? Did you look inside?"

"Yeah. I thought maybe there was something I could sell in there, but all he had was a bunch of doctor shit, you know?"

"Like what, exactly?"

"I don't know. Bottles. There was a syringe and some knives. Scalpels, I think. One of them was long and nasty looking."

"That it?"

"Yeah. I didn't think I could get away with pawning or fencing anything. I stuck with the cash in his wallet. He was carrying, large."

"Why'd you hold onto the wallet?"

"I thought maybe I could get a reward out of him, you know? For the credit cards and his IDs and all that shit. Like ransom. Get it?"

"You should've dumped it. You shouldn't have gotten caught with it, Darlene. You made a couple bogus moves on this one."

She reddens a bit, and it makes her look a little more youthful.

"What's all this got to do with a murder?" she asks.

"He's a person of interest."

"The hell's that mean?"

"Remember that big knife in the bag?"

She reddens deeper.

"You mean..."

"Like I said, he's a person of interest...Did he make any moves on you like he might mean you harm?"

"I didn't give him the chance. He walked in the room and I met him with the gun in my hand and then I made him wait a few minutes while I got the hell out of there."

"You're going to jail, Darlene, but it could've been a lot worse."

"You mean he was gonna cut me up, like all those other girls?"

"You lie down with dogs and you get the itchy crawly things. And sometimes you just get dead."

Her eyes redden, and then the tears arrive.

"How long you think I'll be put away?"

"A few years, at least. I'll do what I can."

"You mean it?"

"I said I'd have a word with the prosecutor and the judge, Darlene, but you're going to do time for an armed robbery no matter how you cut it."

"I shoulda dumped that goddam wallet."

"You really ought to find another line of work. You'll have some time to think about some other options."

I get up. I knock on the door here in holding, and the policewoman comes for her.

• • • •

I still have the wallet when he walks into my office. He has an attorney with him.

"My name is Donald Pearson," the lawyer says as he introduces himself.

They sit opposite me on the other side of my desk. The room seems crowded with the three of us.

I place the wallet on my table.

"We found that in the possession of a prostitute. She says she relieved you of it, not too long ago."

Tracy stares at his billfold, but he doesn't reach out to take it.

"It's evidence, so it won't be returned to you, just yet," I tell Tracy.

"Why are we here, Detective?" Pearson demands.

"I just have a few questions."

"My client wishes to remain silent."

"You sure you want to take his advice, Dr. Tracy?"

Tracy keeps his mouth shut, but they don't get up and walk out.

"It's your business how you spend your money, Doctor, but I'm interested to know why you took your medical bag into that room with her."

"I don't like to leave it in the car."

Pearson looks at him with a scowl on his mug.

"She said she looked inside and you were carrying the tools of your trade. Do you always carry surgical knives with you?"

"That's the end of this conversation, Detective," the mouthpiece insists.

"You don't want to explain all that, Doctor?"

They rise from their chairs.

"You generally have to pay for it, Doctor?"

He moves toward me, and I rise. The lawyer has him by the back of Tracy's suede jacket.

"I'd have thought you'd be able to get it free. I've seen some of the beautiful women you take out on the town. I just happened to be in the same neighborhood."

He wants at me, but the attorney is about six two and looks powerfully built, and he holds his client back.

"You can let go of him, Mr. Pearson. Any time."

"This constitutes harassment. We've already made one complaint against you, Detective."

"Feel free. Good afternoon, gentlemen. I'll be seeing you soon, *Doctor*."

Pearson escorts his client out of my office.

• • • • •

He was mugged by a hooker. That doesn't connect him to anyone on my board. He had weapons in his bag and he saw fit to take them into the room with Darlene, but it hardly establishes his intent to cut her to hell the way the others were mutilated.

But I got inside his noggin, this time. He lost his temper, and maybe it'll lead him to make a mistake.

"*I'll be there.*" That's what Tom Joad told his mother in *The Grapes of Wrath.* Tracy knows I won't let go of him.

• • • • •

They find a body in the slough out in the forest preserves on the southwestern edge of the city. I get the case because I'm back to carrying a full load. The corpse has been in the water for a week or so, the ME explained to me, and the small fish in that slough had taken nibbles out of her after the blanket she was wrapped in came apart after the duct tape was soaked enough to lose its hold on her covering. Her ankles had weights bound to them by that same duct tape.

The ID is made by her dental work, and she was an attorney who worked with very select clientele. In other words, she worked the rich. She'd gone missing when she didn't show for work for five days.

The only reason her remains were found is because part of the blanket came free and drifted to the surface. When one of the park district rangers caught sight of it, he tried to raise it to the surface. And then he felt a lot of weight on the submerged end. When they hauled it up, the lawyer was attached.

It'll be a while until the autopsy and the forensic details are finished. All I know now is her name and her previous profession.

I need a partner if I'm going to keep up with my caseload, but manpower is still at a premium. The homicides, mostly gun-related, continue, and every swinging dick is overloaded with cases to be dealt with and solved. I don't mind working alone, but I've had six new murders dumped on my desk in the last ten days.

• • • • •

New Year's Eve we spend at home. Tomorrow we're invited to eat with Red, the twins, Mary, and my father.

I bought some decent champagne, although I'm not a fan. It's our first New Year's together, and the bubbly just felt right.

I pop it open at precisely midnight, January 1, 2018. We're watching Anderson Cooper and somebody I don't know ringing in the New Year at Time's Square. The ball does its thing, and 2017 is history. The embarrassment still sits in the oval office. North Korea is going nuts. He's welched on the deal with Iran. He's pissed off most everyone in Europe and throughout the world who used to be our allies. And he's raking in the cash because of the office he won by losing the popular vote by a couple million ballots.

My life goes well in spite of this international humiliation. I'm glad I'm not in uniform any longer because this jackass is likely to get a lot of good people killed. Some of my friends are still in harm's way in Afghanistan and Iraq. Some of Maria's pals are in the same predicament.

Lifers. They're not political people. They just do the serving and the bleeding.

I feel mostly impotent—not in the sexual way. 2020 seems a long time away, and sometimes I wonder if there'll be anything left of a world before that day in November finally arrives.

Then I look over at Maria. I remember we're trying to have a baby. Her gynecologist tells her not to be worried. Sometimes it takes a while for the right sperm cell to fertilize the right egg. I don't mind it being just she and I, but I really do want a son or a daughter. I want it as badly as I do because Maria wants it equally badly.

It does occur to me that something might be wrong on my end, but it's still too early to tell.

"Happy New Year," I tell her.

I embrace her tightly and I feel her arms pulling me against her in a fierce embrace.

"It's got to be better than last year. It's got to. You're all I've got, Michael. You're all I've got."

I look into her eyes.

"But that's a whole lot," she tells me.

CHAPTER TWENTY-THREE

There is an article in the *Tribune* about the death of Aurora Teller. They suspect foul play. Very amusing. How else does her body wind up in the water wrapped in a blanket and weighted down with dumbbells?

I was careful to use latex when I wiped down the weights, and I cleaned her body as best I could to remove any chance of leaving fingerprints, but there's no way to be certain I didn't leave them something. And that something would be semen. I tried to clean her vaginally, but it takes only a trace of sperm. DNA can be minute, but it'll send them after me if they can match it to mine.

Perhaps I should have burned her remains, but that would have been far too dangerous. There might have been bone particles, even in a crematorium.

Now I have more to eat at me. There was the first murder. I suffered over that one, not so much for the killing but for the chance I'd be caught. If it weren't for the punishment the crime wouldn't bring on nearly as much anxiety. You're only truly sorry when you are caught at it. Sometimes I think I really do have a conscience, but it keeps turning into something else.

Aurora was supposed to satisfy my hunger, but it seems to have whetted it, instead. I thought I was getting it out of my system, like a purge, but it has only increased my appetite.

But now that they've found her, I have to wait on the edge of a razor until I see Parisi in my office or at my front door again. Except that this killing didn't involve mutilation, cutting. My first was a lot like my brother's deeds and a lot like those of great grandfather's in Whitechapel. Grisly and bloody and angry and vicious and nauseating to behold. This was simply a strangling, and if they find any residue of the sex, it'll lead them to think that it was a rape and murder.

Rape! Murder! It's just a shot away! That was the chorus in the Rolling Stones "Gimme Shelter".

It's a different modus operandi from the initial killing. It might throw them off. I cannot be certain that this Detective Parisi will investigate Aurora's demise, but it might be just my luck.

I won't be able to sleep or eat until I know they're looking at someone else.

Sean would have no problem since I think he never feels anxiety or remorse. I must have inherited those two emotions from my mother. It could've been my father, Delbert, however. He never followed in great grandfather's homicidal footsteps that we know about.

I have to bury myself in my work. I can't be distracted by Aurora's discovery because if I make a slip of the knife I'll be buried instead in a malpractice suit. I still have to pay the bills.

• • • • •

He's behind me again. He must have been sniffing at my twin brother for the last couple of weeks. He may not have linked me to Aurora Teller, yet, but there's still my first killing. He's never let go of that one, obviously.

He never stops. Sean warned me about him. He has a reputation of relentlessness, supposedly inherited from his own father, a homicide detective who was the son of yet another homicide investigator. Your fate lies in the blood.

He stays away at a decent interval, but he must be aware that I'm aware of him. He's behind me on the way to work and he's right there on my way home. I'm afraid to go out at night to find him attached to me yet again.

There is nothing quite as deliciously excruciating as unrelieved anxiety. It stretches you out like a taut wire until there has to be a snapping. The mind is a powerful piece of equipment, but it has limits like any other organ in the body. You test it to the extreme, and it shuts down. It was called a nervous breakdown in the beginning of modern psychiatry. And it certainly is a breakdown.

I think I'm halfway there already.

• • • • •

What're you wearing? It's the gateway to sexual encounters on the sites online. Some women turn you off immediately when you type in the words, but some are enticed by them. Needy women, lonely women, desperate women. It's incredible how many there are. Dating sites abound. They are legion. Some are expensive and are picky about whom they allow on their services. I tend to go on the free sites and on general chat sites. You're more likely to locate professionals on the public spots.

I'm wearing nothing.

Her name is 'Ella'. I'm sure it's false.

She asks me if I want to party, and I tell her she'd have to come to me because I say my ex-wife is having a private investigator follow me. Messy divorce and all that.

She's up for it, Ella replies. I watch her words appear magically on the ether. But she says nothing good in life comes free, and I respond that money's not a problem. Ella likes the way I think. I tell her it'll have to take place in the wee hours because the private investigator doesn't leave my curb until well after midnight.

Ella doesn't mind. She's a night owl. She likes to sleep all day and party all night. She's a big fan of vampires and zombies and creatures who only come out after the witching hour. She digs witchcraft and the black arts and wants to know if I do, too.

I tell her I'm up for something out of the ordinary, and she says let's do it. I ask her if she can make it out here tonight, and she says why not? We make the 'date' for three AM, and she confirms. I ask her for her email address and say I'll give her my address there because I'm wary about who's looking at our conversation. Ella says she understands. She'll be there at three, and she gives me her email address.

• • • • •

I go outside my building for a walk around 2:30. I'm not here for the exercise. I'm looking up and down the block for Parisi or for a car with someone or two someones who're watching me. But all the vehicles are unoccupied on both sides of my street, and I come back in out of the January chill and reenter the warmth of my home.

The buzzer goes off at 3:06. I ask who it is.

"Ella. Anybody else nuts enough to be out this late?" she giggles over the intercom.

I buzz her in. It takes a few minutes for her to arrive at my floor.

I open the door and I see her standing before me in a black leather jacket that extends to her hips and she's wearing black leather pants to go with the jacket. Her hair is long and raven dark, as well, and she wears an ample dose of white pancake on her cheeks. Her lips are crimson. They almost appear as if they're dripping from some night kill. Ella's face belies all the makeup, however. There's a pretty, young woman somewhere behind all the cosmetics.

"Come in."

I shut the door behind her.

She walks right up and kisses me with an opened mouth and a probing tongue.

"Well hello," I smile at her.

"Two hundred fifty. An extra fifty for a blow job. And another fifty for anal."

It sounds like she's rehearsed the line.

"Would you like to sit down and warm up a while? The price is fine."

I remember I'll have to dispose of the body. Maybe this time I'll take her out onto the pier at Lake Michigan. It's late enough that I could cut her up there and toss in the body. This time I'll use a condom, and I'll make her take a shower, even if I have to accompany her in there and scrub her down myself. She'll think it's just part of the 'party'. I can give her something in coffee or a soft drink that'll put her to sleep about the time we arrive at that jetty. If I time it right, there'll be no struggle. There's no moon tonight, and it isn't too cold to work on her out there. It's only in the mid-thirties.

"How kinky you want it?" she smiles with those garish red lips.

"What do you want to do?" I grin.

"How naughty do you want to get?"

"You have a whole lot of clothes on."

She begins to disrobe.

"Can't you at least dim the lights, light a candle?"

I find matches and three candles and I light them and place them on the coffee table in front of the sofa.

She's wearing nothing but a thong.

I turned off the lamps, but I can see her clearly enough.

"How old are you, Ella?"

"What brought that on?" she huffs.

"Just want to make sure I'm not hooked up with jail bait, that's all."

"Twenty-one. Just turned."

"That makes me feel more at ease, Ella. After all, I'm not a pedophile. I may be a crooked man in a crooked house, but I'm not into children."

"That's a relief."

We sit on the couch and she begins to unbutton me.

"You want to go the extra fifty?" she asks.

"I told you money wasn't an issue."

"What do you do? I know this is a primo neighborhood."

"I'm a doctor."

"What kind?"

"The oral surgeon kind."

"How appropriate. Oral."

She bends down and begins.

• • • • •

She is more experienced than her age would indicate. We couple twice, and then I think it's getting too close to dawn for what I have in mind.

"You want to take a ride out by the lake, Ella?"

"It's a little cold, isn't it?"

"It's an extra hundred."

"I suppose you could keep me warm, Doc."

"Don't call me Doc."

"Jesus, sorry."

"I just don't like that term. Doc."

"I won't say it again."

"Call me by my name. It's Patrick."

"I like Patrick."

She was enthusiastic in the bedroom and on the couch.

"Let's take a shower, first. It'll warm you up."

"It should cost you extra, but all right. Why not?"

We enter the stall and wait for the water to warm. When we get under the spray, I take the soap and I lather her from top to bottom. She isn't concerned about getting her hair wet. She bends down and starts up on me again.

"No charge, Patrick. This is gratis."

But when I climax, I withdraw and finish on her stomach. I wash away the semen under the warm flow.

"You don't like me to swallow?"

"I like to see it on your belly."

She smiles, and then I finish lathering her as carefully as I can.

Ella has a good, lean body. Small breasts and narrow hips. Not good for child-bearing. But then she'll bear me no child, tonight or any other night. There should be no traces of me on her or in her. And I've washed her so that no other traces of me remain. When we finish in here, I hand her a clean towel that I've not used so there won't be any of me rubbed onto her. I'll burn the towel in the incinerator in the basement.

We dress hurriedly. The sun will rise in four hours.

We walk to the elevators.

"Did anyone see you come in?" I ask her.

"No. There was no one in the lobby, out front, or anywhere else. Don't worry about the private investigator...Aren't you divorced yet?"

"Separated. The divorce is imminent."

The elevator opens its maw. My scalpels are in the trunk of my car. I brought them down when I took a walk, in search of Parisi or any other surveillance outside.

We arrive at the lobby. When the doors open, I'm relieved to see that there's no one around. We walk to the lot and get into my car and pull out onto the street.

I look in the rear view and there's nothing behind us. The streets are deserted.

"How long have you been doing this?" I ask her.

Her makeup is washed away and she hasn't replenished it. Her lips are pinker, now, and she looks like a child.

"Why do you care?" she snaps.

"How old are you really?"

"Eighteen. Does that make you hard, Patrick? I'm still the age of consent."

"Do you want to keep doing this?"

"Again, Christ, why do you *care*?"

"Don't become angry, Ella. I'm just interested in you."

"I know why you're interested, so please don't begin the sermon."

"I wasn't preaching, believe me. That's the last thing I want to do. I told you I'd pay for everything, including now and at the lake. You still want the money, right?"

"I left my mother because she liked to talk down at me, and I don't like anyone to tell me their personal bullshit about morality and proper behavior and all that shit. So don't start with me, okay?"

"Never crossed my mind. I have other things I want to do to you, Ella."

She smiles coyly. I can see her teeth in the light cast into the car by the street lights as we pass them.

I forgot to give her a drink with a sedative in it. But it can't be all that difficult to snap her thin neck. I'll embrace her from behind and then I'll grip either side of her head as if I were stroking her hair, and then I'll yank her head to the side and finish her. I can't have her alive while I'm working on her. Even in a remote place like the pier this late at night, I can't chance the noise of her screams.

When we're three blocks from the beach where the pier is located, I glance back in the rear-view mirror and I see a pair of headlights. We arrive at a stoplight and I look again behind me. I stare at the glass, and in the light of the overhead street lamp I can make out clearly the face of Detective Michael Parisi.

And then I see his hand raised.

He's waving at me.

I look over at Ella.

"I changed my mind. It's late and I'm very tired. But I'll pay you extra anyway."

She looks curiously at me.

"I thought you wanted to party a little more out in the great outdoors?"

I smile at her as the light changes.

"You're a very lucky young woman. You know that?"

"Why?"

"You just are, Ella."

I point the car west at the next intersection after she gives me her address.

The headlights follow us all the way to Ella's apartment building.

Then he stays behind me all the way back to my condo.

CHAPTER TWENTY-FOUR

It's a cold ride following Patrick Tracy northbound on Lakeshore Drive. He finally came out of his building around 5:00 AM, and there was someone in the car with him. By the puff of hair I could make out in the dim lighting of the street, it looked like a female from behind. Or a very short male.

He doesn't make the tail until we're close to Oak Street Beach. Whoever she is must live on the near north side. I have a feeling Patrick is not taking her home—not at least until he sees me behind him. When we reach the stoplight, I can't resist waving at him. Then he turns left and goes west until he reaches a neighborhood on the periphery of the Loop on the near north. The dwellings have become progressively drearier and more worn down, and he lets her off near a building with trash littered all over its postage stamp sized front lawn.

He gets himself turned around and heads back to the more fashionable barrio near the Gold Coast. Then I put him to bed, close to dawn, and I head back to Headquarters.

• • • • •

I have a sheet lying on the middle of my desk. It's from the ME. He says they've found traces of someone's DNA on the remains of Aurora Teller, and he wants me to see him late this afternoon. I don't go on until midnight tonight, but I'll stop in early and see what he's got.

The DNA was found in the vaginal area, and it doesn't belong to Aurora Teller, that much the ME knows. He says it's up to me to come up with a match, and he smiles at me tiredly.

• • • • •

I circulate around the area where Aurora was known to frequent. From what her associates informed me, she was highly social, single, and hit some of the local clubs near her office in the Loop near Michigan Avenue. There are at least twenty joints in the near vicinity, and I'm going to show her photograph in all of them.

It's ten-thirty, and I'm on pub number eighteen. No one had seen her on the date she disappeared.

But on number nineteen I strike ore. The bartender named Frank says he remembers her. Frank is a rugged-looking, burly man over six feet three, it appears, and I'd guess he weighs in at 245 or so. Looks ex-military. He has the stare that only comes from one place. Combat.

He recognizes the photo, as I said. I ask him why he recalls her.

"You look that good and she's the only female in the place, and you remember her. And she was sitting with a guy who I guess picked her up. At least they walked out together."

"You remember what he looked like?"

"Only vaguely. Blond, good build...But I heard her call him by name. I guess he introduced himself."

My adrenalin begins to kick in, late as it is and tired as I am.

"What was his name, Frank?"

"Just heard the first name. At least I figure it's his calling card...Patrick, it was. Didn't hear another name. They seemed to hit it off."

I can feel my blood racing a little faster. I have Tracy's photo in my jacket.

"This him?"

"Could be...Yeah, it looks like him, anyway. Like I said, the woman was far more interesting."

"Frank, are you allergic to taking big tips for services rendered?"

"How much we talking?"

"Fifty. I'm just a low-grade rookie, you understand?"

"Fifty sounds all right, depending on what you want."

So, I explain what I'm thinking.

• • • • •

I have Patrick's phone number, and I don't much care how late it is.

"What do you want?" he snaps.

"I want to buy you a drink."

"Talk to my lawyer," he barks.

"I could do that, yeah, but then I'd have to drag both of you downtown during the middle of your busy workday, no? That's lost income, right?"

"Call my lawyer."

"He can come have a drink now, too, if you like."

He mulls it over. Maybe he's thinking someone might photograph him at Headquarters. Perhaps he's thinking about all those fat fees he'll miss from slicing out rotten teeth.

"How long's this going to take?" he asks.

"Maybe twenty minutes of your time."

"It better not go any longer."

"Hey, Patrick, I want to get home at a reasonable hour, too. I won't hang you up."

"I saw you following me."

"What can I say? It's my job."

"What's this about?"

"I don't want to discuss it over the phone. I'm more of a face-time guy, Patrick."

There's silence for an extended moment.

"Patrick? You there?"

"I'll be there in a few minutes."

I tell him where I am.

There's another lull.

"All right."

Then he hangs up.

• • • • •

He walks in around midnight. This club doesn't close until two. This time I take a booth, but Frank comes over for our orders.

"What'll it be?" the big man asks Patrick Tracy.

"A manhattan."

"For you?" he asks me.

"Just a Diet Coke. I'm watching my waistline."

Frank stalks off to the bar.

"I shouldn't have agreed to this."

"Why not, Patrick?"

"I should've called my attorney."

"Why give him any more money? All this'll cost is your time."

He waits and watches me. It looks as though he thinks I've cornered him in this swank watering hole.

"I don't appreciate being followed," he says.

"As I said, it's part of the job description."

"You have no reason to be stalking me."

"Stalking? Christ, you're hardly my type, Patrick. I'm married, remember? You or your brother made my wife very ill. I won't forget you for it, either. I told you what would happen if there were a rerun."

"Did you bring me here to threaten me?"

His face has colored a little darker, now.

"No no. Nothing like that."

I take out Aurora's picture.

"You recall this woman, Patrick?"

He pauses. It's either to concoct a lie or it's because I've surprised him.

"Yes. I had a drink with her. In fact, it was right here, in this bar."

"She's dead, you know."

He looks at me intensely. I'm not expecting him to appear guilty. I'm not expecting him to display remorse.

"I didn't know."

"You didn't see the story in the papers? It came out a few days ago."

"I don't read the papers...I met her here for a drink and then we left. Separately. She was a lawyer, and she said she had to get home because she had a big day the next morning. A trial or something. We had the drink. We left, and I never saw her again."

"She must have met someone after she left you here, then. She wound up in a slough, wrapped in a blanket with some weights tied to her ankles. She 'd been strangled, Patrick. Somebody murdered her."

"I'm done talking, right now."

"That's fine. I just wanted to find out where the two of you went after you left this tavern."

He picks up his manhattan, finally, and he drains it in a long slug.

"You don't want to waste a free drink, Patrick. You want another?"

He bolts upright and walks away.

"I'll be in touch," I call out to him.

When he's out the door, I look over to Frank. He comes over and I hand him a fifty. He hands it back to me.

"But I'm taking the glass," I explain.

"I didn't see a damn thing," he grins and he walks away with my empty Diet Coke glass. I wrap a paper napkin around Patrick's glass, and I get up and walk toward the exit.

• • • • •

DNA can be a slow process, sometimes a couple of weeks, sometimes longer.

But the good news is that Patrick knows I've made him. He also knows, being an MD himself, that I haven't got him unless I can match his body fluid with the trace they took off Aurora's body. And all he knows is that he might have left a little piece of himself on her remains. No one saw him dump her in the slough after he throttled her.

All I've got going for me is that he understands I'm right behind him.

I wrote down the address of the building where he dropped the live one he was with the other night. I never saw her face, just a clump of dark, bushy hair. So, I have to stake out her residence until I find her. I don't think Patrick Tracy would be helpful enough to give me her name.

Late the next midnights shift I see someone with a black mop of hair leaving the building in this near-north, squalid neighborhood. I get out of the unmarked car and I approach her on the sidewalk. It's about 11:30 PM.

"I've got a knife!" she warns me.

"All I've got is this badge," I tell her with a smile. "Can we talk? I'll buy you a coffee. It'll only take a few minutes, I promise."

"Let me see your ID," she demands.

Her voice is still quivering a bit.

I extend my hand close to her face and she reads it.

"Detective Parisi, Homicide. What's your name?"

She tells me.

"Is that a real ID?" she demands.

"Use your cell and call 911. Tell them my name and find out."

She appears to be thinking about it.

"You hungry? I'll throw in some sliders, too."

This is becoming a cash drain on me. Fifty for Frank and now another couple bucks for her.

"You drop me where I'm headed, after?" she asks.

"Why not?"

We head to the car and she gets in on the front passenger's side.

"This car isn't marked."

"Detectives drive unmarked rides. You watch TV, no?"

I head us to a near north White Castle that's only about a mile from her building. There's no traffic, so it only takes a few minutes.

We walk into the white glare of yet another White Castle and we have our choice of booths. We sit close to the entrance. The middle-aged waitress with snow white hair takes our order. I go for four cheese sliders and the diet pop, and she takes four without cheese and a full octane Coke.

"You a working girl?" I ask.

"Thought you were a homicide."

"I am. Just asking."

"What is it that you want? I gotta be somewhere soon."

"Eat, and then I'll drop you, like I said."

• • • • •

I slap the photo of Patrick Tracy in front of her. I see instant recognition on her.

"What's this?"

"You know him?"

"No."

"Aw, after I'm feeding you and shuttling you to your 'date'...C'mon, give me some help."

She looks down at Tracy's likeness.

"I followed you home with him."

"So? I thought you weren't Vice."

"I want to know what happened with you and this guy."

"Are you kidding? You already know the answer."

"I don't want all the juicy details. I want to know what he said to you, how he behaved."

"Are you nuts? He was a john. He paid well, and then he took me home."

"That's it?"

"Yeah...He wanted to head out and do it in nature, you know? Out in the cold."

"Out in the cold where?" I ask.

"Out on that pier, near the beach on 22nd Street, you know? That dock, like, or whatever."

"Why didn't you go?"

"He said he was tired. The usual bullshit."

"Out of nowhere he cancelled the last bit?"

"He said he was tired...We stopped at a light and he kept looking back in the rear view. Like there was somebody following us. He got all twitchy, nervous. There was a car behind us, but I don't know if the guy was following us."

"I was the guy."

The waitress deposits our order in front of us.

Her face has gone a whiter shade of pale, like the lyrics in the song.

"Why do you want to know about him? What's going on?"

"You remember my line of work?" I smile.

"Jesus. Shit. You mean..."

"I'm looking at him, that's all."

"You think he killed someone?"

She bites into her hamburger. The fragrance of the fried onions wafts across the booth at me.

"You never know...How old are you?" I ask.

"Jesus, I'm getting that question a lot, lately."

"You lie down with dogs," I tell her.

"You get fuckin' fleas," she replies.

A patch of red appears on either side of her face, and she puts down the slider and looks right at me.

CHAPTER TWENTY-FIVE

I don't like it when he's on a different shift from the one I'm on. Sometimes we can't even sleep together. 'Sleep' includes making love. Michael makes up for it when we share a day off, but it's not the same as when we were working as partners.

The twins aren't his only case, but they might as well be. He works overtime trailing them both at all hours of the day. He especially likes to keep them in his sights during the night time. It's when they hunt, he says. Lately, they've been non-homicidal, though he tells me he likes Patrick Tracy for what some of the other homicide detectives are calling 'The Lady of the Lake'. Even though it was really an over-sized bog or slough.

This one was strangled, not cut, and it's what gave him pause to connect Patrick to the case. Then the DNA thing came up, and he's waiting on the results.

My cases with Ned are more run of the mill. You couldn't write a decent thriller out of any of them. They're just the usual mayhem. These perps cut, but they don't dismantle their vics and leave body parts all over the crime scene. There's plenty of blood splatter, but not like what we saw with the Tracys' handiwork.

He won't talk about his Jack the Ripper theory anymore. I think Michael thinks it sounds farfetched even in his own head. The romantic in me likes the notion, though. It'd be a helluva thing if he were right and Francis Amjac was the notorious monster of Whitechapel. I've done some reading about the Ripper cases online, and it curdles your blood a little bit. I suppose it was the ghost-like presence of whoever it was that fascinates everyone who reads about the murders. He was like some kind of intangible mist that no one could grab hold of.

Anyway, when I'm in the apartment alone I get the creeps, now and then, even with the sawed off and my service weapon in close reach of the bed. With guns you have to hope you're awake enough to blow them up before they cut your throat while you're asleep. I never tell Michael any of that because then he'd want to become my personal bodyguard twenty-four- seven, and that dog don't hunt.

Even with his down payment money sitting in our bank account, we can't afford to fly on one salary. And if I do get pregnant, then we'd be living on our savings. So, I keep my mouth shut about my personal fears. The Tracys aren't ghosts. There's nothing spiritual about them. They're made of flesh and the other assorted fluids and bones and so on, but it's from the neck up that they're different from most of us.

Today is my day off, and I have shopping to do. I never really got used to being armed whenever I go out, but I should be all right with it since I carried a rifle when I was in the military. Slept with my GI soulmate, also. My rifle was my only true friend, they taught us.

The 9 millimeter is less obvious than a long gun, but I keep it strapped to my waist and I wear a jacket even when I don't need one to conceal it. It feels odd being strapped when you're pushing a grocery cart anyway.

I do Walmart because we're both particular about letting go of a dollar bill. I know it's not fashionable to shop here, and I have to drive out to the western burbs to find Sam's pride. But the prices really are a cut below the others, and I like saving money. I tell myself it's for the baby, for the family.

I breeze through the aisles in thirty minutes. There's a strip mall next to the Walmart, so I lock up the groceries and figure I have time to get some exercise. There are a couple of shoe outlets I like in this mini-mall, so I head to one first.

When I'm looking in the store window, I see the reflection of a man leaning against the hood of his car. He's wearing sunglasses even though it's overcast, but I know the face immediately. It's one of the twins; I'm sure of it. I ought to call 911 and get some backup, but he might just claim it's a coincidence that we're in the same place at the same time.

Screw him. I'm not going to let him intimidate me. I walk inside the shoe outlet, and I look out their window.

But he's gone.

It couldn't be a trick of the mind, and I've got twenty-twenty vision. Perfect. Never needed or wore glasses or contacts. Michael thinks it's the Indian in me. I scolded him for his cliché-blurred version of Native Americans. 'Eyes like hawk', he teased me.

I wander the store, but I can't get the twin out of my head.

That's exactly what he wants, to get in my skull.

I walk back outside, hoping he'll be out there so I can confront him.

I don't see anyone who looks remotely like him. I'm not certain if it's Sean or Patrick. Patrick seems to walk in a slight stoop, but I didn't see the guy in the parking lot walking.

It's cold and it's the third week in January. It's a Monday, and the mall is nearly empty at 9:30 in the morning. I'm an early riser, mostly. I like to get going and I'm no fan of sleeping in. Michael is the same. It's probably the military in our veins.

I figure I'll walk around, anyway. The urge to look for shoes has gone. I'm looking for that twin. There are remnants of the snow on the sidewalk beneath me. I hear the crunch as I tread down the concrete.

Then I hear an additional crunching noise coming up from behind me, but when I whirl around, there's no one there.

He's here, I tell myself. It's him. He's trying to screw with my brain.

Or I'm just a little too wired up about them both. They're not my cases, but it seems like I'm connected because of my husband.

I turn and keep walking. If this strip is this empty, even though it's Monday morning, I don't see how they can stay in business much longer. I look into the windows of the shops as I pass.

I see his reflection in the window of the sporting goods store. I stop and wait. He's off behind me to my right, standing by a black Lexus.

I'm not going to play his game, so I walk into the sporting goods outlet. I walk directly to the back of the store and I'm standing in front of an aisle full of fishing rods. I never went fishing in my life. My line of vision gives me a straight-on view of the entrance.

No one has followed me inside. Tactically I understand that he doesn't want to get caught in an enclosed space. There's no place to retreat. And he's broken no law by merely being here. But following me is a deal breaker when it comes to his rights.

I wait a few minutes. An employee approaches me.

"Can I help you, ma'am?" he smiles.

He's a middle-aged, portly sort, but he looks amicable enough.

"No, thank you. Just browsing."

"You a fisher-person?" he grins.

"I don't even like to eat them," I grin back.

"Let me know if I can be of help," he concludes, and then he walks away from me.

I meander back to the front. I peer out the window, but I see no one but a young woman and her three very young kids out there.

I open the door and walk out, headed toward my car. It's parked back by the Walmart.

When I arrive at the car, both my doors are wide open and so is the trunk. The bags of groceries are spread all over the black top, and all of the bags are torn apart.

I feel the anger mount inside me. The heat has risen to my temples.

Then I feel a tap on my back, and I spin around, reaching for the piece inside my leather jacket.

I've got the barrel aimed at Michael's nose.

"Jesus," he laughs, his hands raised.

I lower the 9.

"Oh my God, I'm sorry."

"What the hell happened here?" he asks, pointing at the goods on the blacktop.

I holster the gun, and then I cling tightly to him.

• • • • •

"Can't have this," he says to me at home in the living room on the couch.

"I never saw him do it," I admit.

"Anyone else with a motive, you think?"

"You can't go after him."

"I already am."

"You can't roust him anymore, and I'm not sure which one it was."

"Then I can try both of them."

"No, you can't. He just tossed our groceries around like some kind of demented child."

"Can't have it, Maria. I won't."

"We're buying a house, remember? Just catch them for the murders. Isn't that good enough?"

He pulls me toward him and holds me tightly.

"You don't shop alone again."

I pull back.

"I can take care of myself."

"Yeah, I know, but—"

"But nothing! I can handle it. You don't need to save me, Michael. I'm capable of doing it all by myself."

Then he goes silent, which is worse than having him express his anger out loud.

"Don't do this. Don't."

I rise from the sofa.

"It's our first fight," he says, matter-of-factly.

I have to laugh.

"And we have those two pukes to thank for it."

"Just one of them, this time," he says.

"Yeah? Which one?"

"I'd wager on Sean. I think Patrick is a little less confrontational. At least when it's not a victim."

He becomes all contemplative and silent again. I'm glad he's not pissed at me.

"Don't you even think it," I warn him.

"Think what?"

"About telling Jaworski and having someone follow me around."

"He doesn't have the manpower to send out a watcher for us."

"Tracy can't get into my head, Michael. I won't let him."

"He's got into me already. Both of them have. It's got to stop. Can't have it."

"Stop saying that."

Then his mood seems to soften.

"Any news on the home test?"

"Negative," I say.

"It'll happen. Just wait. It will, baby."

"Stop calling me baby, too."

He laughs.

"Rather have me call you 'woman of the house'?"

"I don't think so."

"You're right. I'll behave. I won't shoot either of them in the face. Are we good again, Maria?"

"You can't take care of things the way you used to, in country."

"I understand. I got my mind right, boss."

"Don't call me boss, either."

"I'm full of wrong turns, ain't I," he laments.

"Just don't do anything stupid, Michael. I really can take care of myself."

He raises his hands in surrender.

"Isn't this one of those prime baby nights?" he asks.

My doctor has consulted with me about my most opportune days in the cycle.

"Yeah, it is. But I don't know if you're worthy."

"I'm not worthy, but it'll take a full measure from me if we're going to have a kid, right?"

I sit down next to him.

"You better not be a great actor, Michael. You better not go after these two animals in spite of what you just told me."

"I'll never lie to you. Never."

I look at his brown, Sicilian eyes, and I just have to believe him.

"I don't disappoint well," I inform him.

He pulls me up as he rises, and we head to the bedroom.

We look at a house on the far northwest side. Its only downside is that the lot is too narrow, maybe eighty feet wide. The depth is much larger and there's a good-sized yard behind the brick dwelling. They're asking $225,000, which is reasonable for this neighborhood, Bob the realtor informs us. We like Bob. He was recommended by Michael's father.

We peruse the inside and we like what we see. Four bedrooms and three baths. A fully paneled basement with a wet bar, even though neither of us is a drinker. The living room and the dining room are comfortably spacious, and I fall in love with the place.

I think Michael is in love with it, also. It has to remind him of his father's house. It's centrally located—good schools and shopping nearby. We walk away from Bob the realtor and we conference together in hushed tones.

"Let's make an offer," he tells me.

I hug him and kiss him. This looks like a place we can come home to.

We walk over to Bob and tell him. He says he'll contact the owner and he'll let us know as soon as he hears anything.

• • • • •

Looking at a home felt so normal, so every-day. It was natural and good. Then we go off to work and deal with bloodshed every single workday. And I had a lunatic fling our groceries all over the parking lot and I wonder how madness can so easily co-exist with the mundane.

It's the business Michael and I are in. Just as it was the daily function we were part of on the other side of the world. The military wasn't so long ago for either of us. I know Michael's tours were vastly different than mine. There was no trigger time for me. I was just a cog in the machine. I'm pretty happy I didn't have to squeeze one off on anyone. We had a few hairy encounters in my time in Iraq, but I never had to do wet work, personally. I caught a break.

With Michael, as I say, it was much different. He was trained to hit what he shot at. I was, too, but his line of duty was a lot more dangerous than mine.

I'm thinking about all of this because I'm still not convinced he won't go off and do something to either or both of the Tracys. His thing in Afghanistan was dictated by taking direct action. His outfit was not known for its passivity. I want to believe him, and he's never lied to me yet. But the look on his face when I told him about the parking lot and the scattered groceries was stone cold frightening. His jaws tightened slightly. There was no slack in his cheeks. I could see the pulse at his temples.

I know that a marriage is based on trust. I'm going to put my faith in him. I can't see me doing anything else. I love him crazy. I'll never leave him, and I don't think he'll boogie on me. It's not in him.

But when I told him what happened in that strip mall, I thought there might just be murder in his eyes. For him it wouldn't be murder. It would simply be reaction. It's what he did in the shit. He reacted. There was no thought about pondering what to do.

You shot back. You shot back with only one intent.

To kill.

CHAPTER TWENTY-SIX

My father used his family ties in the Outfit for information. I don't and I never will, but the thought crosses my mind to get in touch with someone who does wet work to kill the Tracys. That would be the fastest way to eliminate them from our life, but it also means that I'd be an accessory to murder. It isn't very palatable.

I'm convinced it was Sean who stalked Maria at the strip mall. If I lean on him, it's harassment, and I have no proof that it was either of them. I can't have any face-to-faces with either of them again unless I have something dead-to-rights.

The ME wants to see me. It has to do with the DNA sample.

"It's a match to Patrick Tracy," I say to Dr. Cohen.

"Yes. It is. That's good news. Right?"

"Best thing I've heard in a long time...You're certain?"

"As good as it gets as far as certainty goes. You can use it in court."

I thank Cohen, and I head back to Headquarters to see about a warrant for Patrick's arrest.

• • • • •

When I arrive at Patrick Tracy's apartment with three other Homicides and three uniforms, no one answers. We try the door and it's locked. I bang on the entry again and announce we're the police, but there's no sound from inside.

John Terrian, a homicide detective, takes a pick out of his pocket and pops the lock.

"From my time in Robbery," he grins.

He opens the door carefully, our weapons are raised and pointed inside the condo. We rush in and search the place, but we come up empty.

I leave two uniforms outside the door after we lock it again behind us.

• • • • •

The other three detectives and I head to his office, but it's past office hours and the place is locked up and dark—it's after seven PM.

"Where to, now?" Terrian asks.

The other investigators are Marc Blanc and Susie Gidalpho. Veterans all. I'm the junior member of the quartet.

"Let's try his brother's."

• • • • •

Sean opens the door for us.

"It's a little late for any interviews. You have a warrant?" he smirks.

"Where's your brother?" I ask.

He lets us inside. He's got an expensive place of his own. Luxury toys—TVs, stereo, the works. A wet bar, too.

"How would I know?"

"We need to talk to him right away," I tell him.

"Then you'd better look elsewhere. He doesn't make a habit of coming to visit."

A woman walks out of the bedroom wearing a white robe.

"Excuse me," she says.

But she's not apologizing.

"The officers here are looking for my brother, Barbara. They'll be leaving soon."

She looks at Sean with a pout on her lips.

"If you don't mind, then," he tells us.

"You guys take a walk," I tell the other three cops.

They turn and walk out. Barbara has retreated to the bedroom.

"What is it?"

"I told you once to stay away from her. There won't be another warning."

"Is that a threat, Detective?"

I clutch him by the throat.

"It only takes a little bit of pressure to crack your windpipe."

He's coloring deeply and his arms are waving as if I'm shaking a child's ragdoll.

I release my hold and he clutches his throat. He's wheezing, trying to regain his breath.

"No witnesses, Sean. That's your thing, isn't it?"

He's still gasping for air.

"It's interesting to note how little it takes to kill a human being. You only have to know where to go on the body. You're a doctor. You should appreciate that fact...No more warnings, Tracy. If there's a next time, you'll never see what hit you."

I walk to his door and leave him struggling to breathe.

• • • • •

I anticipate the Captain reaming me for the last encounter with Sean, but the command visit to his office doesn't happen.

We put out an all points for Patrick. I revisit his office, and his receptionist informs me that the doctor is away on vacation and she has no idea where and he won't be back for three weeks to resume his practice.

"What's his emergency contact number?" I demand.

She doesn't hesitate to tell me the phone number. She remembers I'm a homicide detective because she saw me here before, and she looks a little bit disturbed that her boss has been visited twice by the likes of me.

"You might want to seek new employment," I tell her.

She blushes brightly, and I leave the office.

He doesn't answer the cell.

We might be able to trace the phone if he still has it in his possession. There's no way he could've known about the DNA test. He must have simply developed paranoia about Aurora's body being located. He must have thought we'd find something on him if the body were located. Patrick anticipated our arrival, unfortunately for us, and now he's a runner.

The all points doesn't turn anything up. We check O'Hare airport to see if he's booked a flight out, recently, and nothing pops up from them or Midway Airport. We try bus stations and railroads—also a blank.

His car is missing from his parking lot at his building, and the all points has his make and plates, but we hear nothing on that front, either. He's disappeared for the moment.

Until we find his car on a used dealer's lot. A patrolman sighted his fancy ride and licenses while checking out a call for an auto theft at the lot. I drive over to the dealers and talk to the owner.

"Yeah, I did the deal with him, myself. He traded that sweet ride in for an old Chevette. Can you believe it?"

The owner's name is Dan Charles. He's pushing sixty, and he's bald and overweight by about fifty pounds of belly blubber.

I get the new plates number from Charles, and then I call the license in.

• • • • •

We find the Chevette on the street in Joliet. The keys are still in the ignition, but there's no trace of Patrick. There's nothing in the trunk.

The only way out of Joliet is the Amtrak and Greyhound Bus. I try Greyhound first, but no one answering his description has bought a ticket out of town. It's too soon for Tracy to have bought and procured new ID, I'm thinking. He's not accustomed to running. He's never had the need, until now.

But I come up luckier at Amtrak. He's booked a ticket for St. Louis. He left just four hours ago. You have to give him credit for being elusive.

I go back to Headquarters and make a call to St. Louis PD. They take down his description, and I FAX them a photo we come up with of Patrick. They check Amtrak, but that train arrived two hours ago. St. Louis is a little out of my territory, so I'll have to leave it to the locals.

I talk to a homicide detective named Steven Loy, and he says they'll keep me informed. They'll check the airport and the bus stations, but he says Amtrak has no record of Tracy purchasing another passage out of St. Louis. Loy says he'll call me immediately if he finds anything out.

He's loose. But his brother Sean carries on with his life as if nothing important has occurred. I tail him wherever he goes. I follow him to his office and back home again. I watch him bring that babe Barbara over to his condo. She doesn't leave until dawn, and then she drives her Lincoln back wherever she lives.

Sean is quiet. We're picking up nothing from him on the internet traps we've set with the tech people. He's made no rounds of the districts where the working girls still make their rounds.

I feel weary. I have other cases, but this is the only one that matters—the Tracy twins, I mean. They overshadow all the other killings I'm investigating. It's becoming fatiguing to chase them all without a partner.

Then the Captain calls me in. I'm thinking Sean has filed another complaint.

"This is Molly McGuin," the boss tells me.

She's got red hair, sort of auburn, and green eyes. She's a little over five and a half feet tall, and she appears lean, but not thin.

She shakes hands with me. Her palm is warm and her grip is strong.

"She just arose from Robbery-Auto Theft," Jaworski tells me.

She blushes, and the hue almost matches her top knot.

"Glad to meet you," she smiles.

The smile is as warm as her grip was.

She stares down at the ring on my finger.

But she doesn't say anything.

"You're partners, bub," the Captain pronounces.

"I heard about your dad," she tells me on lunch break at Sal's Pizza on 87th and Damen.

"Everyone seems to," I grin weakly.

"You must be proud of him."

"I am...What about you? What's your story?"

"Well I'm not sure how to answer that."

I look at her and see a little tightness in her face.

"I didn't mean that the way it sounded. My apologies."

"Not necessary...Can I call you Michael?"

"The other options are pretty limited," I try to smile.

Sal's is a traditional pizza joint that also serves the best Italian beef on the south side.

The waiter takes our orders, and he comes back with my standard soft drink, and Molly chooses ice water. Might be why she's as lean as she is.

I'm wondering how Maria will take the news, here. I have to tell her before she finds out from someone else. It's not going to go down easy that I've been paired with an attractive female partner.

"My story is that I was on patrol for three years and with Robbery for three more years...And I'm engaged to be married to a guy named Robert who's a lawyer with a practice in criminal law...Will that work for you, Michael?"

She smiles widely and takes a plug out of her ice water.

"I'm hooked on this," I tell her about the diet pop.

"It builds belly fat," she grins.

"So I've been informed...Were you in the military?"

"Who hasn't, in this business. I was in the Marines."

"Combat?"

"Yeah. Two tours in Afghanistan."

"Funny, I never saw you over there."

She laughs. She seems genuinely amused.

"There were quite a few of us over there."

"I'm sorry if I seem overly inquisitive."

"If we're going to be partners. Michael, it's only natural to want to know."

I tell her the tale about the Tracy twins, and she listens intently. The pizza is placed between us, and we eat because our time is limited on break, and we've got all those red names on the white board back in my office. The Captain gave Molly a cubicle just down the hall from me.

"No sightings on Patrick?" she asks when we've finished and are emptying our drinks.

I shake my head.

"Why do you suppose he dropped his MO and strangled this Aurora?"

"He's a twin, identical in appearance, but he's not exactly like Sean. Sean is absolutely ruthless, but his brother is conflicted. He's got the instinct to kill just like Sean, but I think there's just a seed of conscience in this prick. I think Sean's done the majority of the mutilations. Maybe Patrick tried it and didn't quite have the stomach for all the cutting. But he's still connected to his brother when it comes to the urge to murder women. I just think Patrick's the weaker of the two. But he was smart enough to know I'd place him with Aurora's death."

"Someone has to spot him."

"You'd think."

"So we're on Sean until the brother surfaces."

"There it is."

We finish the dregs of our drinks, and we walk out into the street.

She gives me the stare when I tell her.

"Her name is *Molly*?"

"Yeah. Why?"

"*Molly*?"

"So?"

"It's so...smarmy."

"What the hell's that mean?"

"It's so...cute. So dear."

"She's engaged. To a lawyer with a criminal practice."

She's cutting up an onion by the sink. I watch her just a bit warily.

There's ground beef frying in the pan on the stove. I'm hungry, even after the pizza at lunch. And the onions make my mouth water. Maria makes great spaghetti. She even made the sauce with her own fresh tomatoes. I can smell the garlic in the sauce that's simmering next to the ground beef.

Maria turns and points the butcher blade at me.

I raise my hands in surrender.

"I assume she's good looking, too."

"What can I say?"

"You can lower your hands, Michael."

I lower my hands to my sides.

"I haven't got any of that kind of blood in my system. You can relax," she says.

"I'm telling you before you hear it from Ned or from someone else."

She turns back to me.

"You can set the table. That's what you can do."

I behave obediently and take the plates out of the cupboard on the other side of the kitchen.

"Do I have anything to worry about, Michael?"

"Yeah, you do."

"Say again?" she demands.

"You have to worry about the garlic breath that's going to be all over you when we get in the bedroom tonight."

She turns and faces me again.

"I'm blind to everyone on this planet but you," I tell her.

Her face softens for a moment, and then she resumes chopping up the rest of the onion.

CHAPTER TWENTY-SEVEN

I can't call my brother. They might have tapped his phone. Sean would be the most likely person to hear from me. Isn't that the way the police would think? I'm not a professional spy. All I know about fleeing from the police is what I've read in thrillers or seen in movies. I just have to make certain I don't give myself away by making phone calls or using credit cards.

I withdrew fifty thousand from my savings account before I left. As soon as I saw that they'd recovered Aurora's body, I knew it wouldn't be long before Parisi found something on her body. I didn't have any choice but to risk being seen taking her out to my car in the blanket and then dumping her in that slough. It was insane to have killed her at my place, but the compulsion was overwhelming. And just after I'd nearly convinced myself never to give in to the impulse again.

It's worthless to mull it over and over, but what can I do?

St. Louis is not as large or as sprawling as Chicago, and its size poses new problems. I can't disappear here, and I cannot linger very long before the St. Louis police find me. I'm certain they're looking for me here, too, and when I awake and go down to the lobby of this Best Western motel, I pick up a paper, and on page eight I see my face and an article about 'man wanted' for questioning. They say they suspect I'm in this very city.

I have to get out now, but I can't fly or use the train or the bus because I'm pretty sure they'll be covering all three.

The only thing to do is buy a car. I can find some beater for a few hundred and leave today.

• • • • •

I go back to my room, shower, and put my things together in the one suitcase I was able to bring. It was too much of a rush to leave Chicago for me to be all-inclusive. I took what clothes I could jam into the bag along with the fifty thousand I took out of my account. I don't know how far I can go with that amount, but it should tide me over until I can figure a way to withdraw more cash. My credit cards are worthless now. I'm sure they'll be watching for purchases.

I walk out of the motel. I paid my bill in advance in cash. I hail a taxi, and then I ask the driver if he knows about any used car lots close by. He says he does, that his brother-in-law owns one not far from here. He takes a good look at my face, but I don't see any recognition in his eyes. Maybe he hasn't seen the papers yet.

He drives me out of the downtown district, and we wind up in some outlying area of St. Louis. I give him a generous tip when he leaves me off at his brother-in-law's car lot. It's Del's Used Cars, the sign says.

Del himself greets me. I don't think this is a very large operation because Del's the only salesman visible. I tell him my needs, and he shows me a Ford Taurus that's only four years old. He says it's only got 9,000 miles on it. He's probably messed with the odometer, but I don't have time to argue. He wants four thousand for the Ford.

He wants to see my driver's license, and I tell him I lost my wallet and I have to get new ID. I tell him I've got the four thousand in cash, and he lets me fill in a bogus name on the sheet. I can see he's convinced when I peel off the money for him. It's not exactly a prosperous-looking car lot. I think he might not be too scrupulous about bookkeeping, either.

It takes him a few minutes to put new plates on the Taurus. The plates were included in the price along with the tax and all the rest. I figure this vehicle is probably worth half what I paid Del. I don't have time to negotiate.

Once I throw my bag in the trunk, I make my way to south 55, headed for Memphis. I've never been south before, so it seems like a likely direction to take. Florida seems like a proper place to head to. It's far away enough from the city to be safe. Perhaps I can find a way to get to the islands, maybe even Cuba, now that travel restrictions are less stringent. It might be possible to disappear forever in Havana.

After several hours on 55 I arrive on the outskirts on Memphis. There's a Holiday Inn just off the highway, and I exit and head to it. They don't ask me for ID, strangely. They're happy with the cash and the false name I enter on their sheet. I take my lone suitcase up to room 323.

I crank the air conditioner up because it's unseasonably warm for February. The room seemed stuffy when I entered. I don't even take off my shirt or slacks. I peel off my shoes and flop on the bed. I fall asleep almost immediately.

• • • • •

My great grandfather sits across me at the dinner table. It must be his because I don't recognize it. It's rectangular and has a mahogany finish on its top. The dishes and silverware seem expensive. It's only Francis and me. He's cutting into a rare piece of prime rib, but I have no food on my plate, and he doesn't seem to notice there's nothing for me to eat.

"Fine boys, you are. Fine boys."

He looks up at me with a dripping piece of barely cooked beef on the tip of his fork, and then he puts the food in his mouth and chews vigorously.

"What's the matter, Patrick? Lost your appetite? My slaughters all made me incredibly ravenous. Isn't that strange?"

I can't answer him. I've gone mute, unable to open my lips.

"Were the stories true?" I finally manage to mutter.

"Stories? What stories?"

He drops his fork and knife loudly on his plate.

"You know. The killings. The murders in Whitechapel."

"You already know the answer, my fine boy. Of course they're true. Why would I make such things up?"

"Were you...Did you ever feel remorse for killing those women?"

"How about you, my fine boy? Has your conscience pricked your soul? Is it bleeding in there?"

He begins to laugh uproariously. The table shakes as if there were an earth tremor below us. I grab hold of the edge in front of me.

"Don't let that disturb you, Patrick. It's nothing but a chimera. That little voice you think you hear inside yourself that tells you you've done something awful, something unthinkable and obscene. The mind of the beholder, my fine boy. Your brother's more like me than you are. There's too much of your mother in you. It's weakness. All those laws they make, all that bilious spew about morality—it's all an invention to keep us in line for not doing what we really desire to do. Sean understands. That's why he is what he is. But you, my fine boy, are conflicted.

"You meander from your tasks in life. And now here you are. Where will you run? Is there a safe place for you anywhere? Given up so easily, have you?"

He goes back to sawing on his meal. I can see a pool of blood on his expensive china.

"I like my meat rare, barely seared. It contains the flavor. There's a sweet fragrance to blood. You must have noticed, certainly. It's the attraction for all predators. The smell of the kill. And when I commence upon them, I rip and tear so that no one can ever put them back together again. It is god-like, isn't it, Patrick? Certainly you felt that way when you cut her, didn't you?"

I know I'm in a dream and I'm commanding myself to awake, but I can't escape him.

"Run, young man. It's all that remains. I had to do just the same thing when I could sense the end coming. But it wasn't the conclusion, after all. It was the beginning of a new life, instead. I found sanctuary in this country, but I knew I could never return to my former deeds. No, I made a proper living, here, even if it was by illegal means...The abortions, I'm saying. Very profitable. The money was better than anything I accrued in my general practice.

"You must not let them capture you, good son. Perhaps you can start again, just as I did...Ah, your plate is empty. Let me get you something."

He comes back out of the kitchen, and he's holding something in his right hand.

It's my mother's severed head. I jerk up from the table and my chair tumbles behind me. He begins to laugh and the sound builds into a crescendo.

Then I wake up, swathed in sweat. I rise and take my clothes off and then head into the shower.

• • • • •

I continue south on 55. I'm not stopping in Memphis. Too many police, too much exposure. Even though the car is new and so are the plates, there's always the chance that the car dealer might have glanced at my photograph in the newspaper and then he might have reported it to the police. So I'll have to dump the Taurus soon and buy a new car. But that will mean a quick drain on my stash of money, and I'm not sure I can replace it any time soon.

I drive through Tennessee. The landscape is hilly and full of color.

I'm headed to Atlanta before I attempt to make it to the Florida border. This time I choose a more modest motel off the road. They'll be less likely to demand identification, and cash is more acceptable than it is at larger chains. They want credit cards, primarily.

The Friendly Inn is just outside Atlanta, and it has cabins instead of a single building. There are two fast food restaurants adjacent, so it seems convenient. The manager accepts cash as if it's the only way he does business, and he doesn't bother with identification. There's only a brief form to fill out.

After I've locked my suitcase in the cabin, the third from the left by the office, I walk over to the burger place and I order a cheeseburger and french-fries and a chocolate milkshake. The place is almost empty because it's 8:30 PM. They're closing at ten.

A young woman walks in just as I'm about to finish. She's probably in her early twenties, has strawberry blonde hair that descends onto her shoulders. She's wearing a tank top and shorts, and no bra. She comes up to me since there are no other patrons.

"I'm sorry to ask, mister, but could you afford to let me have a few bucks? I'm trying to hitch my way south, and I ran out of money, this morning."

She has gray-blue eyes. Her breasts hang slightly slung against her orange tank top.

"How much do you need?" I hear myself answering.

"Twenty'll do," she smiles. "If that's all right."

I go into my wallet, take out a bill, and I see it's a fifty.

"Here. It's the smallest bill I have."

"Jesus, mister, are you sure?"

I extend my hand to her.

"Really?" she asks.

"Take it. Why don't you join me?"

She smiles, and then she goes to the counter and orders food. When she comes back to my table, I see she's ordered the value meal, the cheapest item on their menu.

"I have to be tight with a dollar," she says. "I got a long way to go."

"I'm heading south myself, in the morning. Would you like a ride?"

She eyes me warily.

"I got no place to stay, tonight."

"There are two beds in my cabin. No strings. Really. I'm harmless."

She eyes me again.

Then she bites into her burger.

"I couldn't put you out," she says after she swallows.

"I understand. You don't even know me."

"It ain't that. It's just that hitching is dangerous enough as it is. I've had issues with a few guys already."

She nibbles on her french-fries.

"I understand completely, but the offer still stands. I wouldn't harm a fly...What's your name?"

"Carrie."

"I'm Jack," I smile.

I extend my hand to her. She thinks about it, and then she shakes.

"Where exactly are you headed, Jack? That's short for John, ain't it?"

"No. It's just Jack. Always been just that. Nothing else."

"You just have to be careful. The cops roust me off the road, too. And some of them offer me rides. I ain't stupid. I know what they want."

"You're very attractive, Carrie. You can understand why they're trying to lure you into their cars."

"Sure. I've had those kinda issues since I got outta grade school. I matured pretty quick."

She goes back to eating.

"You wouldn't be looking for trouble if I stayed in your room and if I rode to Florida with you?"

"Do you think I'm that kind of a guy, Carrie?"

"You're handsome. You could get lots of women, I'll bet."

"That's very kind."

"What do you do?"

"Work, you mean?"

She nods.

"I'm a doctor. An oral surgeon, actually."

I don't feel compelled to lie, this time.

"A good-looking guy, and a doctor, and you got nobody to go south with you?"

"I don't do all that well with women. Nothing seems to last very long."

"Maybe you're too picky. I know you're out of my league."

"Don't sell yourself short."

She smiles coyly. She betrays her youth in that smile. She's not a virgin, surely, but I don't think she's literally sold herself. Yet.

"If it's okay, I'll stay with you and head to Florida with you. But no strings, right?"

"No strings. Yes."

She finishes her bargain meal, and then we head back to my cabin.

She throws her bag in the corner. My suitcase is under the queen bed on the left side. It's out of view. Carrie might be a hustler after all, and I'm not going to make it easy on her. And I'm an extremely light sleeper. If she goes for my bag, I'll kill her.

I might kill her, anyway. It would be a stupid move. There'd be the body to get rid of, but this time the manager got a good look at my face. Carrie might be amusing to take along for the journey—if she isn't a thief and a con artist.

She takes a shower and comes out wrapped in a bath towel.

"Gotta get a change of clothes," she says as she goes for her bag.

She gets out another tank top, green, and another pair of extremely short shorts.

She walks back into the bathroom to change.

When she walks back out she looks prettier than she did at the food place.

"I'll sleep in my clothes. I usually don't wear anything, but you know."

"I understand. I just wear my shorts. I'll turn out the lights when you're ready."

"I'm pooped. We got a long ride ahead," she smiles.

"I'll turn them off now, then."

The only illumination in the cabin comes from the dim light seeping through the cheap curtains covering the window. There's no traffic except up on 55, a block or two from the motel. The white noise seems to calm me.

It'd be crazy to walk over to her bed and to grab hold of her throat and do what I did to Aurora. And I didn't take my surgical bag with me because I was in too much of a hurry to grab it. I won't need my instruments where I'm headed.

"You really a doctor?" she asks.

"I'm really a doctor."

"Seems like you ought to be with your trophy wife and your two blond-headed kids."

"You think so?"

"Doctors are rich, ain't they?"

"Some of them."

"Aren't you rich?"

"I've got some money, yes."

"Strange you're out on the road alone…I'll leave you be, now, Jack."

"Goodnight, Carrie."

She doesn't answer, and soon I hear her feminine snore, something like a cat's purring when it's being gently stroked.

CHAPTER TWENTY-EIGHT

The St. Louis Police calls me to inform us that they've had a sighting of Patrick Tracy at a used car lot. They tell me that he's bought a used Taurus and they pass along his new plate numbers. The owner of the lot didn't know where he was headed, Lieutenant Farrell of the St. Louis homicide division informs me. But their State Police are on the lookout for the auto and they'll let us know if they sight him.

I tell Molly about the call when she comes into my office.

"Where do you suppose he's headed?" she asks.

"As far away as he can get—other than that I have no clue."

"Maybe he's looking for warmer climes," she adds.

"If I were Patrick, I'd get out the country. But that isn't easy to do. Takes money. Far as we know he's only got the fifty K he's taken out of his savings. There are no records of any credit card transactions, yet. So he's living on his savings. That can't last long.

"The Missouri State Police are watching the roads, but this guy is hiding by using up his cash. He'll have to emerge eventually."

"So we're concentrating on his lovely twin brother for the time being."

"We got all those others on the board to keep us busy."

I point up to the white board and all the outstanding cases.

"You ready?" she asks me.

"Whenever you are."

"You really think we'll catch the two of them?"

"Yeah. They're both cowards. That in itself is a character flaw of gigantic dimensions."

I smile at her, and then I get up out of the chair, take one last look at an iced-over Lake Michigan, and then we head out to the streets.

• • • • •

My father has two tickets to the Blackhawks game against the Boston Bruins at the United Center. They're primo seats that some copper he knew back in the day gave him. His buddy couldn't use the tickets, so he gave them to my dad.

"Why didn't you ask Red?" I ask him as he drives us to the stadium.

"She thinks hockey's too violent. She's a baseball fan."

We arrive at the west side location after forty-five minutes of mildly snarled up traffic. You park in their lot, here, or you might wind up losing your ride to a booster. We lock up and walk toward the entrance with the rest of the swelling crowd. These games are all virtually sell-outs, so it's a big deal to get to see a game live. I asked Maria if it was all right to leave her alone, and she told me to get out of her life for a couple of hours. She's not a hockey fan, either. Red called her and told her to come over to my dad's house and they'd spend some time together.

Red still has a piece in the house, and so does the old man. She's as good a shot as my father, the old man let me know. Red and Maria get along very well, but my wife always addresses her as 'Natalie'. She says it's a sign of respect. I've called her Red ever since I heard my dad referring to her that way. Natalie doesn't seem to mind that I use her nickname.

The inside of the United Center is brilliantly lit, and it's noisy already. It'll get more deafening when they do the National Anthem. The roar is excruciating when the Anthem comes to the end.

The teams come out and do their warm-up skate-around. There's a near fight at the center line between two opposing players. The Hawks wear their home red sweaters with the Indian head on the chest and Boston wears their road whites. The referees have to separate the two players before the Anthem forces them to withdraw.

"Confrontations already," my father says.

He orders us two beers from the vendor. I try to give him a twenty because the prices are outrageous, but he won't let me pay.

"It's on me, tonight."

I have to laugh.

The opera-trained baritone rips into the National Anthem, and the chaos ensues. The place literally vibrates from the sound.

The game goes back and forth for eight minutes, and then Boston scores on a power play. The crowd becomes subdued until Kane scores on a break-away, and then it's bedlam. The rest of the period goes by scoreless.

At the break we stay seated, and it's then that I see Sean Tracy and a drop-dead redhead walk up our aisle. My father sees me and Tracy locked in a stare-down as Tracy and his trophy date pass by us. Sean doesn't say anything, but his eyes lock onto mine as he goes by.

"That's the guy, no?" my father asks.

I nod.

"Which one?" he asks.

I tell him.

"You're off duty. Forget about it."

"You're right. I'm off duty."

"You want me to go have a chat with him?"

He's smiling.

"You're retired. Remember?"

"Every morning I wake up and I'm still breathing, I remember it."

In a few minutes the game starts up again, and after another ninety minutes, the Blackhawks pull it out, 2-1.

• • • • •

He insists on taking me to Paulie's Pizza on 63rd and Laramie. It's yet another Italian restaurant with great thin-crust Neapolitan pizza. Classic stuff, the old man tells me.

Red and white checkerboard table cloths. What else? They stay open until one, and it's eleven by the time we drive there.

"Red'll take good care of Maria. You can call her when we're ready to leave and tell her to head home."

We take a booth in the back, as usual. He likes to have a visual on everybody coming and going, he tells me. Old habits die very hard. He's got his back to the wall, and I trust he'll notice anyone unusual coming up on us.

"This guy in your head?" he asks suddenly.

"I try not to let him get there, but you know how it is."

"Don't let either of them in. Stay objective and don't make it personal," he says.

The waiter comes for our order, a large sausage and pepper, and two Diet Cokes. The two beers at the United Center were our limit. Neither of us is a big drinker.

"I know, Pa. I'm aware."

"Okay, I'll cut the lecture. You're a big boy, after all."

"I lost the boy thing back in country, I think."

His eyes sadden. They darken noticeably. You can tell his moods from his eyes.

"What's going on with these two pukes?"

I fill him in.

"Missouri, huh? He'll get caught soon enough. The state police are pretty competent."

I nod, and our drinks arrive.

"How's it going at home?" he asks.

"How do you mean?"

"I mean in general, Michael. I'm not looking for a recap of your love life. I just mean how's it going."

"She's not pregnant, yet, if that's what you're after."

"It'll happen. I have a feeling…I meant I wondered how Maria was holding up after she saw that prick in the parking lot."

"I had a talk with him."

"You can't do those talks anymore, Michael."

"I know. I didn't hurt him. Much."

A slight grin flashes over his face.

"You know about your grandfather, Jake."

"You've told me, dad."

"He was part of a different breed. But he wasn't a violent man, overall. He just had a temper, and back then you could get away with different techniques, let's say."

"Beatings, you mean."

"Yeah. Some guys got carried away, but Jake only used the rough stuff on deserving perps. It was SOP, back then. It was dying out well before I retired. But it just isn't worth it, these days, Michael. You could be sued or worse. Don't let these two pricks make you forget there are new rules back here in the city. I don't want to see you forfeiting your career because of these two animals. Don't play it their way."

The pizza arrives and we eat in silence. When we finish he grabs the bill before I can swipe it away from him.

He drives me back to the apartment. I call Maria and tell her to come home, now. She says she'll meet me there.

The colors of the stop lights reflect on the hood of his car. I'm happy that I'm off, tomorrow. I can sleep a bit longer. Sleep has become a luxury. The two of them have invaded my head there, too.

When I saw Sean Tracy at that game, I wanted to rise up and throttle him with my hands. I didn't want to use a gun on him. I wanted to feel his throat cave under the pressure of my own fingers. I wanted to see his headlights dim manually.

The image recedes in my mind. I can't fight them on their own turf. I can't employ their means to bring them down. My father was right. I have to get them with these new rules I have to play by. The law.

We stop in front of our building, and he looks over at me.

"I know you don't want to hear this," he says. "But I faced the same shit you're looking at when I got back from Vietnam. There's no more free-trigger time on these streets. It's a last resort. I know that you know all that, but you got to keep it in mind before you go vigilante on the Tracys. You can't forfeit your life because of them. You can't take any shortcuts. It's not just you, anymore. It's Maria.

"You're a unique kid, Michael. You were always a little more mature than your age. But you never gave me that blowoff shit when I tried to tell you anything. Even when you were a teenager, I thought you really listened to me. I know what I'm telling you you already understand, but you don't brush me off. I love you for it. I know how smart you are. I've been watching you all along. I hate to say it, but you were always a special kid.

"I know. Everybody's kid is special. But you've got something all your own. I should've told you all this a long time ago."

"It's all right, Pa. Really. I won't let them or anyone else get to me. You're right. There's Maria to think about. And maybe some kids. I can't lose her. And I care what you and Red think, believe me."

He touches my face gently.

"How 'bout those Hawks?" he says.

Then I wave at him and get out of the car.

• • • • •

Maria's already home when I enter the apartment.

"How was the boys' night out?"

"Sean Tracy was there, too."

She doesn't respond, at first.

"You mean at the game?"

"He walked right by us in the aisle. I just saw him the one time."

"Was he there alone?"

I tell her about the redhead.

"Maybe you ought to warn her," she says.

"Not his type to slice up, I don't think."

"You ought to warn her anyway, Michael."

"I've already had too much contact with this piece of shit. Like I said, she's not his typical target. He cuts her and people miss her. He likes what he thinks are disposable women."

"I'm off tomorrow, too. We need to go shopping."

"Let's sleep in a little, first."

"It's one of those gold star nights, you know."

I remember her calendar on the bedroom wall with the peaks of her fertility.

"You heard anything from the realtor?" I ask.

"Not lately."

"I'll call in the morning and find out what's going on."

"How's your father?"

"He doesn't seem to age. It's scary, almost. He just gets a little grayer. That's all."

"Natalie is fine. She asked about you. We have to have them over for dinner."

"Let's wait until we get into a house...Maria."

"Yeah?"

"You're all right, aren't you?"

"What's this?" she asks.

"I mean, you're not frightened to be here by yourself when I'm working, are you?"

"We've had this conversation before, Michael. I can handle it."

"Don't get upset...I just had the talk with the old man about letting them get into my head, but you're the one who's been to the hospital and then the thing at the mall..."

"Stop. I'm fine. One of them is running to parts unknown, and you're going to get his brother soon. I know you are. I can handle it, Michael. You know I can."

She walks toward the bedroom, and I follow her inside.

• • • • •

The day after my day off, I receive a call from the Georgia State Police. A motel manager saw Patrick's picture in the Atlanta papers, and he called the police to tell them that he thought he rented a cabin to the man in the picture.

The manager said, however, that this man and a young woman were gone the following morning, early, but he had no idea where they were headed.

He was still driving the Ford Taurus when he left.

"He's headed south, looks like. First Memphis, then Atlanta," I tell Molly.

"He'll ditch the ride. He's got to."

"I'd guess he's going as far south as he can go."

"Mexico?" she asks.

"Maybe the Keys. Maybe the islands. Who knows?"

"They'll be looking at used car lots," Molly suggests.

"You'd think. You're right. He needs a new vehicle, and the cars are becoming a drain on his stash."

"Maybe he'll weaken and have to try a credit card," she adds.

"It'll take a while to burn through fifty K, but yeah, he'll need funds very soon."

"He might try to get to Cuba. He might think he can disappear there. It wouldn't take too many American dollars to survive a while on the island."

"Let's hope we sight him before he leaves the mainland," I tell my redheaded partner.

I look out on the Lake, watching for the slightest clue that there's a thaw arriving any time soon.

CHAPTER TWENTY-NINE

The car has to be altered. I can't risk trying to buy something new. My photo is everywhere, but the good thing is that Carrie doesn't seem to be interested in reading a newspaper or anything else. I dispose of the newspapers as soon as I scan them, all along the road south.

I'm looking for a cheap paint job, and I find one of those quickie outfits right off the highway in southern Georgia. The man in the overalls with the scruffy ZZ Top beard doesn't seem to recognize me, and I give him three hundred to change the color of the Taurus to black. He never asks why I want the paint job, and he says it'll take a couple of hours.

I'm still trying to think about why I took this girl along for the ride. But she wound up in bed with me that first night, and for some inexplicable reason I had no compulsion to kill her. The image of my hands throttling her never came to me. Carrie aroused something unusual in me—I don't know what it is. Perhaps it's her youth. She seems even younger than the twenty-one she claims to be. Whatever it is, she's still along for the ride.

We don't watch television, either. She seems to simply want to talk, as if she's been alone all her life. Carrie hasn't divulged much about who she is, but that works for me. She's a blank sheet, as far as her history goes.

She is, however, ferocious in bed. Maybe it's because I really wasn't expecting it. I don't know. I suppose the fact that she so willingly accepted my offer to share a room should have been a clue, but sex has not been the dominant issue on my mind, lately.

If I can just make it to Cuba, I might have a chance, but I know it will prove very difficult if not impossible to elude what's coming after me. The story has made the front pages in numerous papers I've looked at all along our route south. Serial killer on the loose! It makes good tabloid reading. I'll be in all the grocery store rags, I'm sure. Every wretch who peruses those trashy pages will be on the lookout—and now there's a $10,000 reward from Aurora's parents that makes the scent of my blood even more attractive.

We sit in the waiting room until the painter covers the Taurus in black.

"Black's the color of hearses," Carrie laughs.

"It might've rusted away with all the salt in the air down by the Gulf," I tell her.

"That makes sense."

She sips at her bottle of Coke and nibbles at the bag of Cheetos I bought her from the vending machine.

"You really want to go to Cuba?" she asks with a mouthful of orange snacks visible.

"Sounds like a plan."

"But why Cuba? Isn't it hard to get there?"

I smile.

"You want to go along? Might be a few grins."

"It might," she smiles.

"Got anything better to do?"

"I can't imagine what...And I'm growing a little bit fond of you."

"I feel exactly the same."

After she swallows another gulp of the Coke, she comes across the waiting room and bends over and kisses me with a full thrust of tongue. She grazes my crotch with a light swipe of her hand.

"You think they'd notice if I got naughty in here?" she grins.

"Doesn't seem to be anyone else in here but the beard, and he's pretty much occupied."

We hear the bluster of the paint sprayer in the beard's booth outside the window of the waiting room.

She opens me up and gets down on her knees in front of me. She pulls the top of her tank top down and exposes her breasts and commences to make me electrically aroused. It doesn't take long for her and me to finish, and then she fixes her tank top and rises and walks back over to her chair. I find myself gasping for air.

"That take care of you for a while?" she laughs.

• • • • •

We stop at a motel not far from the painter's. The finish on the car looks like it was the original color of the car. The beard was more professional than I figured he would be. But the problem of the license plates remains, so I drive over to a nearby hardware store and I buy a screwdriver.

"What do you need a screwdriver for?" she wants to know as we walk out of the place.

"You never know when you might need one."

"It ain't for anything kinky, is it?" she leers.

"No. I like flesh on flesh only. You don't have to worry."

"If you'd picked up a butcher knife, I might've been a little scared."

"I only use knives in surgery, and to spread the butter on toast."

She kisses me as we get back into the newly black car and we head back to the motel.

• • • • •

She wears me out. She is a bit more resilient than I am We're both covered with sweat and I slide my hand from her patch to her throat. She shivers.

"Do it again," she asks.

When I do, I feel her immediate response. I'm a bit more resilient than I thought I was.

After we're thoroughly spent, we go into the shower together, and surprisingly it happens all over again.

• • • • •

Carrie falls asleep quickly after dark. It's after midnight, and we've been at it for hours. We simply let the perspiration dry on its own with the breeze from the window air conditioner. I throw a sheet over her and she moans and turns onto her left side away from me.

I want to know why I haven't gotten rid of her. It wouldn't have been all that difficult to leave her lovely but dead body on this sweat-soaked mattress, but I want her with me. It's as simple as that. I've got two murders on my soul, and you can only die once if you get caught. There just doesn't seem to be a need for the killing any longer.

If I surrendered, if I went back to Illinois, I'd probably get life. They stopped the executions a while ago. If I drag Carrie with me, she might do jail time as an accomplice. I don't know the law that well. If they caught me here or in Florida, they would likely extradite me back anyway. But I don't like the reputation of southern-fried cops. They seem a bit trigger happy, and I might get us both killed staying in the South.

Maybe we can press on, maybe come up with a miracle and get to Castro's domain. It's possible.

My great grandfather got all the way across the Atlantic Ocean, and he was never captured, never prosecuted, never jailed. Maybe his ability to flee might also be in my blood. Or it could be my fate. To get away with murder, I mean. The local police certainly don't have the intensity of motivation to nab me.

Cops do like headlines, though, and my incarceration would make some local's career.

Then there's Carrie. Suddenly I seem to care about the welfare of someone other than myself. Sean and I are twins, but neither of us feels very much sibling loyalty to one another. He's a lone wolf, and I guess it's pretty much my attitude, as well.

If we're going to continue south, I have to do something about the license plates. Hence, the screwdriver.

At about four AM, I carefully rise from the still damp bed without awakening Carrie. I realize that I don't know her last name. She only knows me as Jack.

I'm not naïve enough to think I'm falling in love with her. That would be inconvenient. But there's something that's kept me from disposing of her the way I thought I might after she came to my bed on the first night.

I put on my clothes as quietly as I can, and I walk out the door, shutting it gently behind me.

I walk out into the parking lot and find that there are seven other vehicles here. I walk to the Taurus and with the screwdriver I purchased I remove the plates from my Ford. I walk soundlessly to the car farthest from mine, and I replace his plates with the Ford's. We'll have to leave the motel in a hurry because his plates are from Louisiana. I return to the Taurus and screw on the new licenses.

I walk back into the room and wake Carrie gently.

"We need to get an early start. We have a long trip."

"What time is it?" she asks blearily.

"Early," I tell her. "We don't have time to shower again. We'll stop at another motel in Florida."

"What's wrong? What's the rush?"

"You want to get to Cuba or not?"

She sits up, wipes her eyes, and then bends over and kisses me.

"We got time for another go?" she grins, hazily.

"Christ," I murmur.

Then I drop my pants and climb onto her.

• • • • •

We're out before daybreak, and luckily the man with the Louisiana plates is not an early riser. I won't be able to use his licenses very long, so I'll have to make a switch again very soon. It's taking a chance to keep it up, but we have to hang onto my money, and the cash drain is ongoing.

I might risk using a credit card withdrawal just before leaving the mainland. By the time they see the withdrawal Carrie and I just might be in Cuba.

• • • • •

We drive for ten hours, stopping twice to eat and fill up the tank. I find myself counting my cash after every expenditure.

"I wish I could help out with the money," she says.

She's sitting close to me. I feel like we're both teenagers running away from home.

I think about telling her who I really am. If she's as fond of me as I think she is, she might accept the truth. Some women are even turned on by serial killers—but it usually happens when those men are safely behind bars.

I think I'll withhold that kind of information. Certainly, most women would run for cover, fearing for their own lives. Perhaps it's my vanity that thinks she'd live with the notion that the man she's with has blood on his hands.

"You really don't know anything about me," I tell her as she rubs me deliciously.

She's got the zipper opened, and she pries me loose.

"I know everything I need to know."

"What if I were some bank robber on the lam?" I smile.

"That's make me Bonnie and you'd be Clyde."

"You saw the movie?"

She nods, and then she goes down on me.

"That might be a little dangerous. Haven't you heard about the urban legends? The guy in the story gets a free amputation."

She comes up for air.

"Keep your eyes on the road, then."

She submerges and resumes.

It all ends with another electric jolt.

She sits up and rests her head against the seat, but she still has me firmly in hand.

"What if I were a very bad person?"

She lets go of me and zips me up.

"Why are you trying to scare me?" she asks with a frown.

"I'm just saying you don't know much about me. I could be anyone."

"I know how I feel."

I glance over at her and I caress her cheek quickly with my palm.

"We have a long journey. It might even be dangerous, where we're headed."

"If I want out, I'll let you know."

She's looking into my eyes, but I have to look out onto the road.

"I don't want you to leave," I tell her.

"That's just about the way I feel," she responds.

I hold the steering wheel with my left hand and I clutch Carrie's with the other.

• • • • •

We're in central Florida by early evening. I tell her we're only going to stay here one night because we've got to keep moving.

In bed after yet another round, she lays her head on my chest.

"What'd you do?"

"Pardon me?"

"I know you gotta have the law after you. I'm not stupid, Jack."

"And how do you know that? Maybe I have an ex-wife who wants her alimony."

"I had a boyfriend, a year ago. He got into some shit and he wanted me to go along with him, and like a damn fool I went along. And then he ditched me in Indiana. I've been on the road a long time. He left me a note and said he loved me too much to let me get caught up in his thing."

"Maybe I should let you go, too."

"It's bad, then?"

"It's very bad."

"Why'd you do it, then?" she wants to know.

"You think you did a stupid thing by going along with that boyfriend?"

"Dumb as dirt."

"You might be doing the same thing, with me."

"I know."

"You really want me to tell you?"

She looks over at me with tears drifting down onto her cheeks.

"No. I just want to keep going and going for as long as we can. I got nothing to go back to, Jack. Nothing."

I don't want to feel sympathy for her. I can't afford it. And it's not sympathy. It's something else. I really don't know very much about her. Not even her last name.

"Neither do I," I tell her.

We embrace each other ferociously and the heat overcomes us once more.

• • • • •

I switch plates, and this time they're Florida licenses. We leave again before dawn, and there are no lights in any of the cabins in the motel as we make our way out of the parking lot.

• • • • •

Hours go by, and finally we see signs for Miami—85 miles, it reads.

Another motel awaits and I hope my luck holds out for yet another switch for the plates. It's like playing Russian roulette with too many slugs in the cylinders. Eventually you become unlucky.

This manager gives me the thorough eye, so before we light here for the night, I walk out and tell Carrie we'll try somewhere else.

On the periphery of Miami, we stop at yet another motor hotel. This night manager looks too bored to care who I am. He likes the color of my money, though.

We don't make love after we shower. We're both too weary. We simply hold onto each other as if we're on a life raft.

"I'm going to see about passage to the island."

"You mean Cuba," she smiles.

"We're never going to make it by plane or the usual means."

"So how are we gonna get there?"

"We'll have to see if we can rent a private boat to take us there."

"You think we can?"

I don't answer her. I just hold on to her.

CHAPTER THIRTY

We cross the Card Sound Bridge to North Key Largo. We kept on going south from Miami because it was too large and it was too sprawled out. I want to find someone who is willing to transport us by private boat, illegally, to Cuba. I'm sure cash will do a lot of talking. And Key Largo is smaller and much quieter than Miami.

We find a motel near the beach on North Key Largo. I ask the desk clerk if there's anyone he knows who might be interested in taking me and my 'wife' on an excursion. He looks properly slimy enough to know anyone who might be willing to provide such shady services.

He is dark and has an Afro, and he has a Hispanic accent, maybe Cuban, I'm not certain. His name is Javier. Maybe thirty years old and he has a gleaming gold front tooth.

"Where you want to go?" Javier asks.

Carrie is waiting for me in the room, three doors away from the office.

"Cuba."

Javier smiles widely and shows his gold tooth.

"It's illegal, sir."

I wait.

"You want someone who does out of the ordinary trips, then. It'd be expensive."

"I can handle it."

"And there's my finder's fee."

"How much?" I ask him.

"A hundred."

"All right."

He looks at me as if he's amazed I took his first offer.

"Guy's name is Enrique. Go down to the dock after five o'clock. His boat is the *Diablo*. He takes rich guys on fishing expeditions out on the Gulf. Sometimes he takes people to exotic destinations—for a price."

"What kind of price?" I ask.

"Let's say it begins at four figures. Dangerous work...My hundred?"

I take a bill out of my wallet and hand it to him.

"You can fly into Cuba, now. Obama fixed it. Why you want to do it like this? Could be dangerous."

"Why are you asking me questions?"

"Just interested. No offense. It's an unusual request. They got patrol boats, you know."

"Enrique, the *Diablo*. After five."

"I'll give him a call. He's my cousin," Javier glints again.

I walk out the door and down to our room.

She's lying on the bed naked.

"The air conditioning isn't worth a shit. It's warm in here," she says.

She smiles. It's perfectly crisp in here and the air conditioning is quite functional. But I take off my clothes anyway and lie down next to her.

"We're almost there," I tell her. "Tropical, sunny Cuba. We'll melt right into Havana. I know it," I grin.

She leans into me and kisses me long and hard and searches for my tongue with her own.

"Can you speak Spanish?" I ask her.

"Are you kidding?"

"Neither can I. But we can learn. We'll be *habla*-ing like natives in no time."

She climbs aboard and her eyes open widely when she feels me thrust deep in her.

"We're almost there," she murmurs.

• • • • •

I walk out to the car and drive to the strip mall to buy us some supplies: tooth paste, mouthwash, soap, and the like. I'll have to cash in my dollars for the local currency when we get to the big island, to Havana. It almost seems as if we're really going to make it. Not a single cop in my rear- view mirror, all the way to Key Largo. It's as if we were fated to get there, Carrie and me.

I haven't had another nightmare with my great grandfather in it. He seems to have finally left me, as if he were exorcized, somehow. The old rage in the blood seems gone, as well. I never look at Carrie and wonder if it'll return, if I'll somehow be compelled to put my fingers on her throat and...

I feel released, free. Human beings are supposed to be redeemable. Isn't that what the old, corrupt faith of Rome teaches? We can all be reborn. We can all be renewed. We can all be forgiven, no matter what the crime. I have never embraced the faith. Religion hardly runs in my family, in my genes. It's always been the target of scorn, from my great grandfather to my father to my brother and me. We embraced evil—at least Francis and Sean and I did. God was a myth, but the devil was more likely. Look at all the evidence of his existence.

Can I wash away my sins? I'm not looking to faith to cleanse me. Carrie has. A young hitchhiker with nothing to lose and nowhere to go back to. Just like me. Except I'm a decade older. That's the only difference between us. A decade. She'll stay forever young. I'll never see her wither up and decay.

I'm still having trouble believing this life is possible. I should be chained to my blood, chained to Francis and to my own past horrors, but this young woman has cleansed me. Somehow, she's altered my fate and she's written a new script for us. Nothing is written. Nothing is cast in stone. I've shed my fate like the snake in Eden shed his skin.

I walk into the Seven-Eleven, and the girl at the counter stares at me. She appears to be Hispanic, like Javier. She has an Afro, too, and her lips are painted blood red. She eyes me as I walk down the aisle toward toiletries. I cast my eyes back at her and I lock my gaze on hers. Then she turns away as if she's become suddenly self-conscious.

There was a large rack of newspapers by the entrance, and I'm thinking maybe my photo is on the pages in the rack. Maybe she's seen my face.

I pick out several items and place them in the red basket I'm carrying. I walk back toward the girl and her cash register. I pay my bill, and she keeps her eyes away from mine. I've suddenly got the urge to use my knife on this young woman, but I have no blade. I left it behind on the mainland, a thousand plus miles from here.

She doesn't speak as she hands me my change. I walk quickly back to the car and head toward the Largo Motel.

• • • • •

She wonders why I seem nervous.

"I'm just anxious to get going," I smile.

"You look upset."

"Just anxious. I'm fine."

It's four o'clock. I'm heading out to the dock in forty-five minutes. Even if Enrique isn't punctual, I will be.

"You sure everything's okay?" she asks.

She's wearing her orange top. She's showing me some wonderful cleavage, and I almost forget my qualms about the girl at the Seven-Eleven.

She takes off the top.

"Come here. I know how to calm you down."

I lean into her on the bed. The covers remain on the floor where we threw them when we arrived.

"You think we can keep this up?" I ask her. I try to smile.

"I'm not worried about either of us. Cuba, Jack. Cuba. Beaches and sun and warm. It's tropical. I've seen the pictures. It looks just like heaven."

"And what's heaven look like? All I can see is you."

"Jesus, you feel tense."

"I'll be all right. I'm leaving soon, and everything'll be fine. You'll see."

Now her eyes look taut.

"Don't do that," I tell her.

"I don't like to see you nervous. I want us to be happy, the way we've been happy ever since we hooked up in that burger joint."

"We'll be happier. I promise. Just a few minutes and I'll go make it happen."

"Take your pants off."

I slide them off and she pushes me onto my back and then she makes me think about sunny beaches and palm trees, about learning to speak Spanish like a native.

• • • • •

I leave the room at precisely 4:45. She stands by the door, still nude, and kisses me before I leave.

"I won't be long."

"It'll give you time to refuel," she smiles teasingly.

I look at her and I touch her face with the tips of my ten fingers.

"Listen, in case anything goes wrong..."

"Don't you say that."

I step back inside and shut the door behind me.

"Just to be safe. I'll knock four times. So you'll know it's me. You better get dressed because we might have to leave in a hurry. I don't know what this guy's going to do, when he wants to leave.

"The rest of the money's in my suitcase. If I don't come back in two hours, take it and head back to Florida. Don't come looking for me."

"Jack—"

"Don't come looking for me. You understand?"

"You're scaring me."

"I love you. You know that."

"You never said it before."

"Now I have...Do what I tell you...Please?"

She nods, and then tears pool in her eyes.

"Hey, I'll be back soon, but you always have to have a Plan B, right?" I smile.

She tries to curl her lips upward, but she's struggling.

I turn once more and this time I leave her behind me.

The dock is maybe a half mile from the motel, so I walk it. I left the keys to the car back in the room for her if something does go wrong. It was the way that young woman looked at me at the convenience mart. As if she'd recognized me.

But that was an hour ago and so far so good.

The dock is in sight.

When I'm within a few hundred yards I see the police cruiser parked at the lot next to the pier.

When I get within a few hundred feet, a cop appears and he's walking toward me. I keep going thinking he could be here for any number of reasons.

Then a second man in uniform appears, and then a third. Another cruiser pulls into the lot and I turn and break into a dead full sprint.

I hear someone calling out at me.

"Stop!"

But I don't halt. I turn hard right and I run toward a dilapidated looking block of run-down houses. I hear another command to halt but I keep right on running toward the barrio.

I make it to the first corner and I hear sirens approaching. I've got to find somewhere to hide. They'll be on top of me in seconds.

As I turn the corner I see a copse of pines standing on a sandy lot. The trees are in a thick clump, so I head toward them. I can still hear the sirens getting even louder, and maybe there are more of them coming by now.

I think of Carrie. I see her on the bed beckoning me. Her arms are opened bidding me to embrace her. I can feel her warm flesh against me, her ripeness, her wet and her heat as I join her again and again.

The trees are in front of me and I dart inside the cluster. There's foliage growing wild between the pines and I flop onto the sandy soil.

The squad cars roar down the street. They've lost sight of me. Maybe I've lost them. It's getting darker. It's March and the days haven't become as long as they will in the next few months. I look at my watch and it's 5:30. The sun is headed downward. If I can just stay here until it's dark, I might be able to get away.

But I can't go back to the motel because they'll be waiting there. They'll check out that place because it's the only motel in the direct vicinity. I can't lead them back to Carrie.

She's gone, and I have nowhere to go. I don't know anything about North Key Largo. All I know is the sandy soil beneath my stomach.

They'll be waiting for me back at the room. Maybe they'll figure out the Taurus has been freshly painted. By now the owners of the license plates will have called in the thefts. They'll locate me. They'll find Carrie there, instead. They'll find a suitcase full of my remaining cash, and maybe they can trace the bills, somehow. My mind races feverishly.

I hear the sounds of the sirens, but they're becoming fainter, now.

Maybe I can still escape with Enrique if the police have left the dock. Perhaps he can take me to Cuba alone. I can't retrieve Carrie. She's lost. I have to resign myself to the fact that she's lost. So much for my brief encounter with freedom.

The sun is on the wane. I'll have to risk trying Enrique because I have no other options. He's my only chance to escape.

Freedom? It always was an illusion. Getting to the island with Carrie was part of a fantasy that could never become reality. It was all too sweet a scenario. Now the other thing has set in. I don't know what's going to happen in a few minutes, but whatever it is, I'll have never penned the story. It was written for me a billion years before the tide of the Gulf washed to the shore.

It's still twilight. Just a few more minutes and I'll try to get to that dock where the *Diablo* waits. Just a few more minutes and it'll be completely black. There are no street lights to light my way, just the glow of any lights they have attached to the pier where Enrique awaits.

How could that time with her have flown away this quickly? It seems like a dream. They say dreams only last perhaps a minute or a minute and a half.

My time with her ended very abruptly.

I can't stay here very much longer because it's just short of miraculous that they haven't searched the blocks around me. They'll be coming soon, maybe with dogs.

Maybe they think I'm armed. Maybe they already know exactly where I am and they've gone for reinforcements. Perhaps every cop on the island is headed right toward me. They were just setting me up for capture. Certainly, they wouldn't give up so easily, and how far can one man make it on foot?

They're out there, just a few feet away from me. They're waiting for me to emerge from this clump of pine trees. They must think I'm carrying a weapon, a gun, maybe, and they want me out in the open where they have the advantage.

No matter what's really going on, I can't linger here. That boat is my only escape. I have to chance it that the police have left the dock in search of me.

I stand up slowly and the sand drifts off my clothing. I take a few steps forward out of the bushes and trees, but I can't see anything out there.

I lost them. I'm free, after all. They're scattered elsewhere, seeking me. I keep walking.

Then a bank of headlights appears, and I hear the order to halt, once again. The voice tells me to raise my hands where he can see them.

I leave my arms at my sides.

He barks the command again, and the headlights seem to stab out at me from behind, as well. They have me surrounded, it seems.

"Leave her alone. She didn't do anything. She's innocent. She just went along for the ride," I yell at them.

"Get your hands up and get down on your knees!"

I feel my lips curling into a smile.

It was always in the blood. There was no running away, no escaping him. I'm Francis. *Francis Amjac is me.*

I bolt into a run directly at the headlights.

"Stop!"

He keeps commanding me to halt, but I run right at the lights.

Then I hear the multiple cracks coming directly from the headlights. There are three more popping noises, and suddenly it's nothing but darkness in front of me.

And then nothing more.

PART THREE

CHAPTER THIRTY-ONE

Someone once said, in a classroom where I sat, that the teacher was no longer the smartest guy in the room. He was referring to computers.

He never met Jimmy Parisi, my father. He's got more information tucked in one corner of his brain than there is stored in all of Google. You might say I'm exaggerating, and maybe you have a point, but the wealth of experience he has seems to overcome the bank of facts in the computer's center.

I meet him on my lunch break, and I take Molly McGuin, my new partner along. She tried to beg off saying she'd be intruding, but I convinced her not to be intimidated, that my old man had all his shots and that he hadn't bitten or mauled anybody recently. The 'recently' made her eyes widen a bit.

We meet at his standard choice, another Italian joint that specializes in pasta—no pizza. They have beef sandwiches that make me salivate just thinking about them. They melt provolone on the Italian beef, and you get a clogged artery just thinking about them.

"I'm on a strict diet," Molly protests on the way out of our ride.

"They've got nice salads just for heathen such as you."

We're a lot more relaxed around each other, lately. Now that I haven't slapped any sexist moves on her, she realizes I'm faithful to Maria, and she's loyal to this guy Robert that I've still never met. She keeps saying the four of us should go out for dinner.

My father is waiting inside Rocco's for us. He stands up for Molly. Other detectives don't rise for their female counterparts when we sit down for dinner hours.

He shakes hands and introduces himself to her.

"Your legend precedes you," Molly grins.

"Legends are for dreamers and children," he smiles back. "I'm just flesh and blood with feet of clay. It's the Catholic in me, you understand."

She laughs and sits opposite him in the booth. I sit next to my partner, facing my old man.

"One down, I hear," he says to us.

"We saw him in the morgue. Twelve shots to the torso, legs, and two to the head."

He looks at me grimly.

"They made certain," he says.

"He charged them. They called it a clean shoot," Molly adds.

"You're one of the crew. You look awfully young. You must have been a shooting star," my father says.

"I moved up pretty quick," she throws back.

"Then you must be really good at the job. Congratulations," he smiles.

He's got her under his spell. He has a talent for doing it to males and females.

"So, the other one is still out there," he says.

"Unfortunately, yeah," I join in. "The papers are suggesting that maybe Patrick did all those young women."

"Convenient for the survivor, no?" he tells us.

"Maybe not," I answer. "Maybe he'll become a little too relaxed."

My father smiles warmly at me.

Molly looks as if she's become quizzical.

"Am I missing a signal, here?" she asks both of us.

"It's the Sicilian in us," I answer. "You relax the target before you come up behind him."

"My son likes to deny his genes. I used to use family from the wrong team to come up with intelligence. It was mostly from his grandfather

Jake's side of the clan. They were mobbed up, and I squeezed them from time to time. Michael is too pure to try that side of the *familia*."

He grins slyly and looks right at Molly.

The waiter takes our order. My father tells the waiter he wants the bill, and before either of us can protest, the order has been made and the swarthy wait staff guy trots off. My dad winced slightly when Molly asked for the caesar's salad with chicken.

"When in Rome?" she laughs.

"You don't know what you're missing," he tells her. "The beef is food of the gods. But you gotta do what you gotta do."

"I don't see how the Outfit side can help us with Sean," I say to him.

"Neither do I," he admits. "But street talk can still be valuable. Problem is that assholes like your surviving twin aren't likely to confide in anybody. You always hear from the neighbors how the perp was such a nice man, how quiet he was, how he was such a great neighbor. And then you found the body parts in his meat freezer... Not exactly lunch talk. I apologize, Molly. You Irish heritage?"

"Yes, I am. County Cork."

"His mother was Irish, too. My first wife. Her name was Erin."

"Michael has spoken of her, yes."

A shadow crosses his face. He seems to age a few years, just with the mention of her name.

"She was a school teacher. Great with kids."

I look over at him and he smiles and the thunderheads disappear.

"My current wife is Gaelic, also. She has the temper, too."

Molly laughs, and it makes both of us laugh with her.

The food and drink arrive, and he motions for us to dig in.

"I know your lunch break is short. I've been there, too."

We finish our meals in silence, and then he looks over at us.

"Serial killers are the hardest to deal with. It's a cliché by now, but it's still true. They're organized, they're plotters and planners. They don't become out of control very often. Which makes them difficult to catch."

"Patrick was found with a young woman. She told the police in Key Largo that they were headed for Cuba. They said she was very distraught when she heard he was dead. Looks like there was something serious going on," I add.

"Which is why it's even more certain that the other one did all the heavy carving. Patrick was a novice. He followed the general plan one time. The woman in the water was spur of the moment."

"That's what we think, too."

"Let him see you," my dad tells us. "Be around, let him know you haven't forgotten him even though he's gone dormant. They're like those seven-year locusts. They go on rampages. They can't control the impulse. He'll try to outwait you both, so don't let him. Hang on like one of those gila monsters. They grab hold and nothing makes them let go."

"I guess we'd better take off," I say.

The waiter arrives with the bill.

"I'm paying the tip. Don't give me the look, either."

I grab hold of the bill and see the total.

"He might try to keep it personal, Michael. He already has, with Maria. Keep her close. And look out for this one, too."

He nods at Molly.

"Yeah, I know you can take care of yourself...These guys like to intimidate, sometimes. You have to be prepared. I don't mean to sound like your mom, Molly, but they're dangerous, this kind of killer. They take it personally, someone trying to put them out of business."

"Thanks for the concern, but you were right, Mr. Parisi."

"Jimmy, please."

"Okay, Jimmy. We'll watch out for one another."

He waves at both of us as we leave Rocco's, but he hangs around to finish his soft drink.

• • • • •

"Nice man," she says as we drive over to Tracy's to set up for the night. We're working a double because Patrick's death has stoked up the publicity, and Jaworski, our beloved captain, read us the riot act. We need to pinch the brother, he said, so the shit flow stops. The mayor's gotten in on the fun, what with the shooting homicides beefing up complaints about the expertise of the CPD. And the doofus in Washington likes to spear us every chance he gets, even to the 'fake news' reporters.

I've got my usual selection of jazz for the night, and Molly seems not to mind the music I bring along.

"It's relaxing," she tells me.

"It's not the cure for insomnia," I retort.

She laughs again. I like the sound of it.

I don't think Sean is aware of Molly McGuin, yet. He's used to seeing only me.

The motor is turned off and I tell her I'll run it if she gets cold.

"What makes you think I get cold easy?" she cracks.

I raise my hands in surrender.

"I like it cold, up to a point," she explains.

"It won't matter if Tracy sees the exhaust. He already knows we're out here."

We sit in silence at the curb. The ride hasn't lost all its heat just yet. The music is The Modern Jazz Quartet.

Finally, she turns toward me.

"What was it like, in combat, I mean? I was a desk rider. Only went out a few times, in harm's way."

"You didn't miss a damn thing," I tell her.

"If you don't want to talk about it, I understand. I knew other vets who kept it zipped about their experience."

"I was trained as an operator to eliminate targets, subjects. You know what we were up to. They won't let it go in the movies and in the books."

We sit again in quiet listening to the jazz.

"I like these guys," she says, after a while.

"They're trained, a lot of them Julliard grads."

"Really."

"Yeah, really...It's not pleasant to talk about. Don't take it personally. I'm not clamming up on you, Molly. It's just over with and I like it to be gone, in the past. History, you know?"

She looks over at me.

"You talk about it with Maria?"

"Not much. She's got some things that need to stay buried, too. Not as much as I do, I don't think. But she got her share of ugly. Mine was just more abundant."

It's one when Tracy comes out with the trophy babe he's been seeing for some time. He throws money at her at the downtown clubs and the fancy, exclusive eateries where you wait for months to get reservations. Places Maria and I can't afford. Most of my investments are going into the new house. We move in in mid-April.

"Is Robert doing well with his practice?"

We pull away from the curb and follow Sean and his lady back toward the Loop. Most of the joints are closed, now, and the only light comes from the street lamps. Michigan Avenue looks forlorn and desolate. It's pre-Easter, and the hangover from Christmas and New Year's is long since vanished for another year. Easter seems more subdued, although it really shouldn't.

"We won't hurt, financially. They're going to offer him a partnership, eventually. He's their best litigator and they're aware of it."

"You think you might want to quit and take care of a family?" I ask her.

The low illumination from the overhead lights makes stripes of black and gray cross Molly's face, almost like zebra stripes.

"Not right now. Maybe never. I don't know if I want kids or not."

"If I'm in private territory, don't hesitate," I tell her.

"You can ask. You're my partner," she smiles as a shadow passes her face.

"Maria would like to stay home, but we can't seem to finalize the deal," I grin over at her.

"It'll happen. Italian lovers and all that."

"I'm worried it's me."

She looks over at me. Tracy and his partner are two cars in front of us in the right lane. We're in the left.

"Been to a specialist?" she asks.

"I'm thinking about it. Maybe I don't want to know, you know?"

I feel uncomfortable telling her this personal business, but it seems I can't stop.

"Maybe a doctor could up your chances, Michael. You know you'll have to find out. And guys our age, in their thirties...If you're a woman in her thirties, the clock is running...Now I'll shut up."

"It's all right. Thanks for talking like this. I mean I don't have any friends other than Maria, you know?"

"You're not the most social animal I've ever met," she teases.

"I'm socially handicapped."

"Maybe you're just shy, Michael."

"I don't think that's it. But I always liked to have things to myself. I guess I never took to sharing. Toys, whatever. I liked to be at the beach early when I was a teenager, before it got crowded, you know? Then when it got mobbed up, I felt as if I was in the wrong place. Freud might have had a little fun with me."

"You're very normal, mostly."

She giggles after 'mostly'.

"Thanks," I jab back.

"This reminds me of the military," she says. "Hurry up and wait."

"Ninety percent of the job, yeah."

"Make a pretty crappy two-hour movie."

We arrive at Tracy's destination, Barbara's building. He parks on the street and walks her inside, and he stays inside.

"What would you like to hear next? A little Brubeck or Basie?"

"Did you like jazz when you were in khaki?" she asks.

"There was no music at all, then. I liked it quiet, mostly. Came with the work, you know?"

She doesn't answer.

"I don't think I want kids, but Robert does. Could be a problem."

"If he's such a great litigator, you better be ready."

"We never argue. He's different away from work, he says. He doesn't like to battle and I'm not big on it, either."

Her face has tightened and gone serious.

"You think Tracy'll get overwhelmed to act, like your dad said?"

"I think it's a distinct possibility. But he's off the net, as far as we know. Tech hasn't turned up anything interesting in a long time. The working girls seem hesitant to make dates there. They're not stupid. And the sidewalk types are keeping low profile, too, our friends in Vice have passed along."

"How many kids you want?" she asks.

"I'd settle for one," I tell her straight-faced.

"One would be good," she affirms.

CHAPTER THIRTY-TWO

The police release my brother's body, and I have him cremated. I keep the ashes at my apartment in a closet. I feel no desire to display them, and there are no family members remaining except for me. I'm the sole survivor of the Tracy-Amjac family. Although I never considered us all that familial. My mother was quite insane, but she managed to escape a mental institution since most people simply thought she was quite odd. She never erupted into violence, nor did our father.

Great grandfather was the unique member who proceeded Patrick and me. The rage seemed to jump two generations, but Patrick was a mixed bag when it came to violent tendencies. I inherited the full dosage from Francis, but Patrick's dose was very much watered down. And he had those conflicts with conscience. It was his weakness, not mine. It got him slaughtered, inevitably. He shacked up with some road tramp, and his obsession with her cost him everything.

Perhaps if he hadn't run away from Chicago he'd still be alive today. We both have competent attorneys, and who knows what the verdict might have been for my brother regarding that woman they fished out of a slough. He wanted to fuck her, and then he decided to throttle her. Even his method of killing her was diluted from my modus operandi of dispatching sluts to somewhere they belong. It was a sloppy killing. He took far too many chances—dragging her out of his apartment. Something inevitably had to go wrong. The evidence floated to the surface along with my brother's genetic code.

Sloppy.

I was always the more careful of us. Patrick could be prone to impatience, and it showed with his final handiwork.

Now only I remain, like Ishmael. But they have no evidence to connect me to the killings I own. There are no fingerprints, no swabs of DNA to be removed from the corpses. No hairs, no fibers. I left nothing to entrap me.

Parisi is no doubt waiting for me to go out and do another, but I'll outwait him, I'll outwait all of them. It would be very foolhardy for me to hunt again so soon after my brother made his unfortunate splash on the headlines. I've had several requests for interviews with the media, and each time I've referred them to my lawyer who tells them we have nothing to say about the abrupt end to Patrick Tracy. They've found out we changed our name to Tracy, eliminating Francis's brand to our lives.

Some of the tabloids have tried to link Francis and Patrick and me to Jack the Ripper, but it's only the supermarket trash mags that dare to link me to the killer from Whitechapel. The general media demurs from the salacious connection to the incidents of 1888 to 1891. Francis was never an official suspect, after all.

Barbara has become a bit problematic. She reads the papers, of course, and lately she hasn't returned my phone calls. My only option was to wait for her to emerge from her apartment building. Detective Parisi is parked accompanied by what appears to be a female partner just down the block. He's not really trying to remain invisible. He's been behind me for the last few days.

She comes out of the entry on this fragrant, warm, early spring day in late March. It feels more like May than the actual date.

I wait for her at the sidewalk.

"Can we talk?" I ask.

The sun is setting. It's just after 5:30.

"Can I take you to dinner so we can discuss all this?"

"All what?" she answers.

Her face looks surly.

She stands still and stares into my eyes.

"It was my brother, Barbara, not me."

"I am on my way to an appointment. If you'll excuse me..."

The light has begun to dim drastically.

"You're being extremely unfair," I protest.

"As I said, I have an appointment. If you'll excuse me."

She begins to walk past me, and I grab her arm tightly.

"You have a short memory, Barbara. You were the one who wanted us to move in together. Do you recall?"

"You're hurting my arm."

She shakes the arm as if I've sealed off the flow of blood. I want to take her by the throat, but then the two police are parked just down the street and no doubt they've taken interest in this brief confrontation.

"I apologize. You seemed to enjoy pain, as I recall."

She walks toward her parked car just a few feet behind me.

"I want to get this straightened out, Barbara. You're punishing me for what my brother did."

She keeps walking and then unlocks her car, gets inside, and drives off without looking back at me.

I walk down the street to where Parisi is parked. He's outside his vehicle, standing in front of it while his female partner remains inside.

"Aren't you tired of harassment complaints?" I ask him.

"I find them very satisfactory, thank you."

"My brother was shot fourteen times."

"Yeah, so I've been told."

"I'm sure you visited him at the morgue."

"Yes, I have. He gave them no choice. He ran at them, and it was dark and they couldn't be sure he had no weapon. It was unfortunate."

"They murdered him. We're suing the police who killed him without cause."

"It's already been cleared as a justified shoot, Sean."

"We have very competent attorneys. They'll pay in a civil suit if nowhere else."

He doesn't answer.

"I'm going home, now."

"Was there a problem with the lady? She didn't seem happy to see you."

"Good night, Detective."

"You'll forgive me if I don't return the good cheer."

He smiles at me. I've never seen him smile before. It drips of malicious intent, of course.

I turn and walk back to my car. When I pull away from the curb, I soon notice he's behind me, about fifty feet from my bumper. He's not letting go. It was his reputation, from what my lawyer tells me.

When I get back to my building, I see that he's resumed his previous spot by the curb, just down the block. I walk to the entry and let myself in.

• • • • •

My attorney's contact at the Chicago Police Department tells him that they'll look into why Parisi is stubbornly still out there watching me. He receives no satisfaction from the police, and he tells me there's not much else he can do, at present. I hang up angrily on him. There are other lawyers I can hire.

Barbara continues to ignore my messages and my texts and my emails and my phone calls remain unanswered.

My anger is building. I want to retaliate, and the heat is beginning to rise in my blood. I have to have some release, but I don't dare go over there and act on my rage because the Italian-American detective continues to be wherever I go. I wind up spending my time away from my practice here at home.

There are other women, naturally, so I focus on the available talent I run into in the course of my professional duties. There's a recently divorced blonde who just turned fifty who looks good enough for me to forget our age difference. And being recently divorced from her husband of twenty-five years—he cheated on her countless times, she's told me in confidence as I gave her an estimate for a job on her loose throat flesh—she's ready to get back in play.

Her name is Helen, and she's going to be worth millions after the legal, permanent separation from her construction barren ex-husband. He was involved in a billion- dollar deal to renovate a big chunk of the near-Loop.

And Helen will not likely want anything remotely permanent in the way of a relationship with any man in the near future. She'll want to get back in the game gradually. Women her age are too experienced to be headstrong about getting tied up again any time soon.

She's perfect. I won't be able to do exactly what I'd like to her, but she doesn't fit my type when it comes to cutting and killing. She looks like she might like it rough, however.

And after I take her out for a very expensive dinner at an exclusive bistro in the Loop, she's more than willing to come back to my place.

Parisi and friend are again behind me in traffic, as I expect them to be, but I'm not about to give them a reason to break down my door and catch me in the act.

Helen has a more than workable body. She seems to have kept herself in shape. There's only a slight sag in her pendulous breasts, but she won't require my help there for a little while. Her stomach is flat—she's been working out with weights, likely. Her legs are taut and firm, as is her very desirable ass.

It doesn't take me long after we entered my apartment to get the full appraisal in the bedroom. She doesn't want to spar with me or play the tease. She wants to get laid, and there's no faux drama about her desires.

She handles me like she's been celibate for quite some time. Apparently, the construction baron was fucking everyone but his wife. There must have been a lot of anger and isolation in Helen's household for a very long time. The horns are on her head more than on mine. But if I can't tear her up, I can try to defuse my own blood rage, at least a little bit. It's reached a fairly intolerable level since Barbara shut me off.

There's no foreplay except for her oral attack on my surprised member. But Helen's sincerity goes a long way to get me properly aroused. She wants me to climb atop her in the missionary pose. She says she wants me to stab her as deep as I can.

She actually uses the word 'stab', and now I'm very much engaged in it. I slam her repeatedly and violently and she simply urges me on to do my worst. The climax takes a while for both of us, but when it arrives, I'm slapping my lower half at hers, and there's a fair amount of pain involved.

I see her wince as we meet, but she continues to buck against me until it's over.

We roll away from each other trying to regain our wind. I'm perspiring heavily, and her front from breasts to knees is slick with sweat. I roll back at her and slide my hands from her legs to her pubis to her hardened, erect, red nipples, and then I'm atop her again.

• • • • •

She wants to stay the night. We have a few glasses of wine, and then we attack each other one more time until we've exhausted ourselves. Helen sleeps in the nude, and fortunately she doesn't snore. When I hear her regular breathing, I go into the kitchen for a drink of water.

But I'm compelled instead to open the drawer where I keep the knives. I have only one blade that is suitable for carving meat because I rarely eat at home. Even alone I go out for my evening meals. It isn't like I can't afford it, so I don't prepare my own meals. I'm entrapped enough in this apartment as it is. The least I can do is dine somewhere other than here.

I take out the long carving knife and I walk into the bedroom and look down on Helen's luscious body lying unadorned minus a sheet or blanket. She's lying on her back with her arms along her sides. Those breasts rise and fall with a sure rhythm. She's in deep REM, soundly asleep.

I walk over to her right side. She lies on the left half of my queen mattress.

I raise the knife to my shoulder, and I picture the tip as it pierces the left side of her chest, and then I see that blade rise and fall repeatedly in a series of thrusts and each time the gore literally bursts from her torso and some of it splashes up into my face and I feel the warm stickiness as the blood drips heavily down onto my chest and my stomach and it blinds me a bit in my left eye but I don't cease raising the carving knife and swiftly ramming it down into her, her soft flesh yielding to incision after incision. Helen has an endless supply of blood that leaps from her stomach now and then from her perfect thighs...

I lower the blade and listen to her breathe. The blade is now at my side, impotent, and her body is intact, intact as it was when I rose initially to go into the kitchen.

I turn and walk back and I replace the cutlery where I found it. Then I softly shut the cabinet and I draw a glass of water from the tap. I stand at the sink holding the glass, but I do not drink.

• • • • •

I drive Helen home in the morning. It's a Saturday, so I have no appointments. She invites me in. Her husband has long since vacated her Lake Forest home. It's not a house; it's an estate lying on twelve acres in a secluded area of this wealthy suburb on the north shore. Her house has a view of Lake Michigan, and she owns a private beach. She invites me over breakfast to go swimming with her.

"Nude, of course. We have enough sand that there won't be any gawkers. There are security fences on either end of our property by the water, so it's very private. We can make love on the sand and in the water."

She's showing a bit of her age in the morning light, but nothing too severe. I feel movement at my groin, and she smiles to reinforce the lust.

"Unless you'd like to have me on the breakfast table," she smiles lewdly.

"How long has it been?" I smile.

"Can't you tell?" she returns.

She takes off her blouse and bra and slithers out of her pants and panties. She's made us fried eggs and bacon, and now she clears the plates off the wooden slab of table.

She comes to me and kneels down and undoes my pants.

• • • • •

"It's still a bit too cool to use the beach," she smiles at me, here in her king-sized bed in her king-sized boudoir. There is a full- length mirror above the bed, and I'm wondering why her construction baron left her. Perhaps she exhausted him, too.

The image of my kitchen knife returns to me as I lie next to her. I'm looking at the incredible curves that this fifty- year- old woman has somehow retained after a half century. I'm trying to imagine, also, what it'll look like in just another decade. And I remember the way I conjured that carving blade to tear her to pieces.

Parisi did not follow us beyond the city boundary. Lake Forest is well out of his jurisdiction. So, there were no other followers to Helen's mansion by the lake. We're alone. There are no witnesses, no one followed us to her electronic entry gates. Only Helen knows I'm here. Parisi and his partner disappeared in my rear- view mirror well before we arrived.

Helen Pauley is not my type, she doesn't fit any of the categories that I employed in selecting my targets. She is wealthy. She's older than my victims. She's not a whore, to my knowledge, although she did fuck the baron in the midst of all his money, here in Lake Forest. But she remains an improper fit.

It's Barbara's fault that I'm thinking of hunting while I'm under such close scrutiny by the Chicago Police Department and by Michael Parisi and his female accomplice. She's the one who caused me to find a kitchen knife and to fantasize about using it on Helen Pauley. I should have raised the blade against Barbara, not Helen, but I had to go with whomever was available.

The incredible heat that Helen generated between us just ramped up my rage, it appears. I try to defuse it when I throw myself at and into Helen, but it only affords temporary release.

I know I can't give in to my instincts. Francis could never deny what pulsed in his veins. He gave vent to it.

My poor, dead brother only allowed himself to become free, to soar, just twice, but the second encounter cost him everything.

They blew him apart. Fourteen slugs. One took the top of his head off quite literally. I viewed the body for identification as his only surviving family member.

Parisi didn't pull the trigger, but he might as well have. He forced my brother to run, forced him to wind up as he did.

There will be no further intimidation of his wife. Or of his female partner, yet unknown to me.

No, next time I'll inflict everything on Michael Parisi himself. Then, perhaps, I'll kill the wife and his partner, as well. There will be an accounting for Patrick. It will extend well beyond revenge.

It will be a reckoning.

CHAPTER THIRTY-THREE

The gynecologist tells me it's not me.

"All the parts are functional," she smiles.

It brightens my day until I foresee the response on Michael's face. He'll be happy for me, of course, but he'll know the indicators might be pointing at him. And I don't want him feeling guilty, even if it means he can't have children and even if it means our only option is adoption. I love him too much to let the negative scenario tear us apart. I love him more than I ever have, and I hope child-bearing isn't the center of our relationship.

But I'm still anxious about giving him the report I just heard.

I have another piece of business to attend to. I'm off duty for two days, until Friday. It's one week before we move into our new house, but this thing hangs over me, and the problem is I can't share any of it with my husband. He'll probably become angry at me for doing it, but I'm proceeding anyway. It's something I have to do on my own.

• • • • •

I walk up to Sean Tracy's receptionist and show her my credentials.

"I need to see him immediately."

"He's with a patient," she replies.

"Either you go tell him I'm coming in or I'll just go back there. Which'll it be?"

She frowns and walks to the back. Then she comes and waves me inside his personal office. I am armed even though I'm off duty. The book says we're really never off shift.

He appears surprised at my appearance as the receptionist closes the office door behind me.

"What a pleasure," Sean Tracy grins.

"This won't take long."

"Please, sit."

I remain standing on the opposite side of his desk as he seats himself. I watch his hands. They remain atop the table.

"My husband talked to you before about your visit to me in the parking lot."

"Excuse me?"

"It was you. I know he talked to you about it."

"He threatened me, if that's what you mean."

His eyes are aimed at my nine-millimeter Glock couched at my waist in its holster.

"Is this an official visit?"

He's trying to appear calm and unflapped, but it's playing a bit thin. He keeps looking at my weapon.

"No, it's not. This is personal, just between you and me. I know my husband can come off as a violent man, at times. It's because of his background. He's not used to putting up with bad behavior from others, especially if he feels threatened. Please, don't respond. I know what you're going to say, and this isn't police business.

"Stay away from me. I don't let Michael or anyone else take care of my business. You can take this as a threat or a warning—I don't care how you take it. But if you try intimidating either of us again, I'll end it. I won't wait for anyone else. I'll put a stop to it. You take that any way you like. That's all I came to say."

I wait for him to say anything, but the smile has left his face, so I turn and walk out of his office and I close the door behind me.

I make him his favorite, chicken parmigiana. When we finish our meal, I look over at him.

"Are you excited about the move?" I smile.

"Sure...Aren't you?"

"Of course. Can't wait."

I pick up my plate and go over to the dishwasher and put it inside along with my silverware. Then I head to the sink and begin cleaning the pots and pans.

"That's my deal," he insists.

He's put his own plate and silverware in the washer.

He turns on the hot water in the sink, and he takes out the scrubber from below it.

"Didn't you see the doc today?" he asks.

The water is running, but I hear him clearly.

"Yeah. I meant to tell you about that."

He shuts off the tap.

"It's me, isn't it."

I look at his eyes and I see the hurt already.

"There's no way of knowing that, Michael."

"Unless I go find out for myself."

There's no softening the blow, and there's no lie that'll assuage him.

"Yes. Unless you go find out for yourself."

• • • • •

He walks out of the exam room.

"There's nothing more embarrassing than doing it into a little sample cup."

"Did you think of me, at least?" I try to grin.

"They had magazines, back there. And a couple of videos...Please don't ask."

We walk out to the parking lot, but there's nothing to say.

A week later the fertility doctor calls him back in for the results. We both go into the doctor's office. I insisted on it.

"Your octane's a bit low," the physician tells him. "There are things you can do to up the odds, however."

The doctor seems young, perhaps in his forties. He's rather handsome. The poster boy for dreamy doctors who show up on the soaps.

"What can I do?" Michael asks.

"Make a few changes in your diet. Exercise, although you look like you're in good shape. And then there are the dreaded boxer shorts. The tighty-whiteys have to go, I'm afraid."

"I've been doing briefs since I was a kid," Michael complains.

"They have to go. Your fellas have to go free range."

I have to smile, but Michael's dead serious.

"All right," my husband concedes.

"You get the count up, and I think the results will be very gratifying for you. You're not all that low. A little fine tuning should do it. I want to see you in a month."

"I have to do...that again?"

"Only way we can tell if there's improvement in your aqua-men."

I groan openly. The doctor looks over at me and smiles widely.

"You fall into that kind of talk in this business. I don't want you to think I take your issue lightly," he says to Michael. "But I think you can help yourself if you follow the program. I talk to a lot of young men going through exactly what you are, and believe me, I am empathetic."

He stands up.

"Please make an appointment for next month. Sorry about the little cups. No way around them, I'm afraid."

We walk out of his office, stop at the receptionist's, and he makes the date for May.

• • • • •

The captain appears unhappy. Jaworski called and made the meeting on my first day back after we moved into the new house. It sort of took the glow off our move. He told me to come alone, not to bring Michael.

I sit across from Captain Jaworski in his office. His look is lean if not angry.

"Tracy called," I anticipate.

"Indeed. But it was his lawyer. We have yet another complaint lodged against the two of you, and what concerns me most is that you're not assigned to Sean Tracy—that I know of."

"I am not, sir."

"Don't call me sir, Maria."

"Yes...Captain."

"It has to cease and desist for all time. You follow? I really am too old for this shit. If this man really does attack either of you, then by all means, blow his shit up. But if he simply happens to appear at a strip mall, it hardly condones threats about the use of force. And your husband had better not be laying hands on him again. This shit cannot go on forever. Are you reading me?"

I nod.

"I know Michael thinks Sean's the one who put you in the hospital, but there is simply no evidence to that effect. I'm sorry we didn't hook this sorry son of a bitch to your illness, Maria. I truly am. But you cannot threaten this man again, and neither can Michael. If either of you do, I'll be forced to take severe disciplinary action which will please me not at all.

"That's it. You're free to go."

• • • • •

The house move is exhausting, even with the paltry amount of baggage we both own. We've had to purchase everything new—furniture, appliances. The only thing we took out of the apartment except for our clothes was my bedroom set. Michael cleared out his apartment months ago and gave everything to Goodwill. We certainly didn't need two of everything, and my stuff was a little newer.

It still cost us enough to make a large dent in Michael's investments. I have little and nothing in my savings. I feel like he's taken too much of the load, what with the down payment on the house and all our new expenses.

He tells me not to worry, that the costs have been exactly why he put the money into the funds his buddy advised him to while Michael was overseas.

After everything is finally hooked up, including the cable TV service, the washer and dryer, and all the furniture, we invite his dad and Natalie over for dinner. Actually, we're just having a few pizzas delivered because both of us are literally wiped, but there's beer and soft drinks in the fridge, and we both have one more vacation day remaining after tonight. We figured we had to celebrate.

His father and Red appear precisely on time at 6:30.

"It's lovely," Natalie exclaims after I give her the tour.

"You done yourselves proud," Jimmy Parisi adds. "It reminds me a lot of our place, only this is newer and bigger."

Michael leads us out to the backyard. It's warm for mid-April—in the seventies. Global warming, Michael says.

The grass is thick and plush.

"I'll need to buy a mower," he says.

"It'll be our housewarming gift," his dad tells us.

Michael tries to protest, but Natalie and his father won't have any of it.

We go back inside because it's already dark, and Michael turns off the outdoor light.

"We're getting some lawn furniture," he informs his parents.

It's news to me, I tell him.

"We're not broke, yet," he smiles.

The pizzas arrive at seven. We ordered them from Salerno's, Michael's and Jimmy's favorite because they're Sicilian, the deep pan. When I open the boxes, I see we'll have leftovers for weeks.

"This is so fattening. We'll need to get to the gym for a month to burn all this off," Natalie smirks.

"Food of the gods," his dad chirps.

I can't remember feeling as happy as I do at this moment. I have a new home. *I live somewhere.* I belong to someone. I take hold of his hand, and the confrontation with Tracy and Jaworski seem to melt away. I never really felt the way I do now when I was a kid because we were always moving around. We were nomads, gypsies. It was my lifestyle until the military. I never really believed I'd take roots anywhere. Then I met Michael, and now everything is firm and solid. I know what I want; I know who I want.

"I heard about the captain," Michael says after a gulp of Old Style.

I look over at him, and I'm shocked.

"How'd you hear?"

"People have big mouths," he explains.

"It was supposed to be confidential," I retort.

"I thought you were great. I'm proud of you," my husband declares.

"This is none of our business," Natalie tells us.

I tell her and Jimmy the tale.

His dad laughs out loud.

"You bearded the guy?" he says. "You braced the little prick?"

Then we all laugh together.

"Maybe it's my turn to visit Sean Tracy," Jimmy Parisi declares.

"You will not," his wife scolds.

"No, I guess you're right. I think Maria can handle this little craplet."

We laugh together again. I bend over and kiss my husband.

"I would have preferred to waste him, but you can't have everything."

"She's joking," Michael says to his parents.

He really thinks of Red as his second mother, he's told me.

"I think we know her well enough by now," his dad throws in. "But I understand how you feel. Too bad we're not assassins."

We finish off one huge Sicilian deep dish, but there's no way we'll make a dent on the second.

We sit at the dining room table that just arrived today. Michael had me pick out the table and four chairs, and the price didn't prevent us from buying them.

I have the windows opened because of the balmy early spring weather. Sunday is Easter. It's very late, this year.

"A guy came after Red. But I told you this one before," Jimmy reminisces.

"Marco Karrios. They called him The Farmer," Michael remembers. "He came to the house to kill Natalie, and I had to drive backwards in a blown VW to get home to help her remove Karrios from his shoes the hard way. I don't think I was ever so scared in my life."

"*You* were scared?" Red guffaws.

"Yeah. I thought I lost you."

He reaches over and takes her hand and then gallantly kisses the top. She begins to tear up, slightly, and so do I.

"I know what you're going through," Jimmy tells me. "But you can't let Tracy live here with you. This is where the world leaves off."

He reaches over and squeezes my hand.

"I'll kill him before he gets the chance, if it comes to that."

None of us say anything. The darkness spreads, but here inside our new home, it's warm and light. The darkness does not extend to where the four of us sit.

Michael looks over at me and mouths the three words I want to hear, even if he doesn't say them aloud.

CHAPTER THIRTY-FOUR

I tour the closest thing Chicago has to 'red light' districts, and even as warm as it is in the third week in April, these streets are deserted. No one is peddling their wares. The stories about the whores are being recirculated, now that my brother is dead. A lot of them are convinced Patrick did them all. Then it would follow that I'm innocent.

But Parisi and his new partner don't seem to go with the theory that it was my dead twin who killed them all. He's always seemed to lean on me more than he did my dearly departed brother. It's as if he holds some kind of personal grudge against me. I'm still the one with the bigger bullseye on his back. I suppose he would call it intuition, but I wish he'd follow the herd and place the blame on Patrick.

The hunting grounds in this city are pretty much fouled for me now and I know it. Parisi will always be around hoping that I'll make a mistake that he can pounce on. He fantasizes I'll leave a little piece of me on a body. Any crumb will do.

My options aren't pretty. I can go totally dormant and eventually force him to consider me a cold case. But he's the kind of policeman who latches onto an idea and then never releases himself from it. These kinds of investigators take these 'cold' cases personally. I'm sure most of Parisi's colleagues are pragmatic enough to know when the trail is frozen. I suppose it's simply stubbornness, doggedness, whatever you like to call it. In any case, he's not through with me.

By now my photo has been circulated to every hooker in the Cook County area. The action is not as hot in the richer suburbs, but the vice detectives have undoubtedly made every cunt in their jurisdiction aware of my face—now that Patrick is out of play. I have been isolated without being indicted or prosecuted. It doesn't matter that public opinion has focused on my twin's crimes; they've thrown my killings in with my brother's. My photograph has left the streets nearly empty. I hear that girls are working out of hotels and bars and that they have made certain they've acquired a pimp to keep a very tight rein on them.

How can I be certain that one of these thugs isn't standing outside the room door just waiting to hear the first signs of alarm from within? Then at best I am severely beaten and at worst I'm mauled to the point I can't make a living.

As it is I'm incarcerated with invisible walls and bars. Sex with Barbara and any of the others will prove no outlet for what's building inside me. I don't have my father's self-control, certainly. He withstood his inner demons. I, however, am still prone to them.

• • • • •

She has fallen under to the sedation and I begin.

I feel my hand, the one with the scalpel, quivering.

"Doctor...Are you all right?" Janet, my nurse, asks.

"I'm fine."

The anesthesiologist looks up at me warily.

But the tremor in my hand won't subside.

"Give me a minute," I tell them both.

The brunette on the table will have to wait, but every minute I tarry the anesthesia is burning off.

I try to meditate and get myself together. After a delay of less than five minutes, I see that my right hand is steady once again, and I walk over to the table where the brunette lies. She's sixty and wants to look forty. I can help her compromise and appear to be a decade younger than her age. Ageing always wins, tuck or no tuck.

I make the incisions, and there are no further shakes. We finish with her in forty minutes, and she'll be coming out of her sedation within an hour.

When we're scrubbing up, Janet looks over to me.

"Are you ill, Doctor?"

"I don't know. I might be coming down with something."

"We've got two more surgeries, tomorrow," she reminds me.

"If I'm under the weather, we'll reschedule. All right?"

I hear myself snapping at her sharply.

"I'm sorry, Janet. Maybe I am coming down with something. I'll let you know if I have to put them off."

She eyes me warily, and then she leaves me alone.

• • • • •

I can't use dating services. I never know if they're keeping records that could come back and bite me. I would have to leave traces of myself if I used professional 'escorts'. It's all too dangerous.

I find myself browsing the internet for lone women who will not leave a trail behind me. And with that same publicity regarding Patrick, the net is becoming a vast wasteland. The details of my brother's first murder have appeared in the trashier tabloids. All of which makes hunting very difficult. Perhaps things will improve with time, but I have my doubts.

I ask her what she's wearing. The screen remains blank for a moment.

What would you like me to be wearing? she answers, finally.

I like women in their altogether, I reply.

LOL.

What's so funny? I ask.

Altogether! Who talks like that? she wants to know.

I find her boring and I leave her. I ask the same perfunctory come-ons to several more females, but they're all pretty much the same. They're wasting time on the ether and they have no intentions of meeting anyone in the flesh. This is all a result of *ennui*, boredom.

After another twenty minutes I give it up and turn off the computer.

He's behind me yet again. My protests and complaints have fallen on deaf ears, and it's not worth the costs to pursue litigation. Maybe it is true that you can't fight City Hall. I don't know how much sympathy I can expect from the Chicago Police Department.

I've cancelled my appointments for a week, citing health reasons. My patients are not emergency cases anyway, and they can always seek another plastic surgeon. But it's not likely I'll lose them because of a seven-day delay. My reputation is still strong in my field of medicine.

I know I should simply relax, go slow, but I'm too much of a workaholic to lay off. Day one of my 'vacation' seems interminable. I don't know what to do with myself.

I'm headed to a massage parlor. A Thai massage parlor. I pull into the parking lot here on the northwest side, and I watch as Parisi and company pass by the lot in their police car.

I don't see the cop as I walk toward the entrance, and I scan in front and back of me.

An Asian woman is the receptionist. Who else? She smiles and tells me to be seated. It'll be a few minutes, she says.

I pick up a magazine and I'm thumbing through, but I can't seem to read the words or pay attention to the photographs.

I should be at a shrink's, not a massage parlor.

"Mr. Tracy?" the receptionist utters.

"That's Dr. Tracy," I inform her.

She nods and smiles. Very cliched and Oriental (very un-PC).

"You can go back, now. Li is now available."

I head toward the door she's holding open.

When I enter the massage room, a much younger Asian female awaits. I'm wondering if this place is strictly legitimate. Li looks like someone who has more skills than just with her fingers.

She has me disrobe, and she walks out of the room while I take my clothes off and hang them on a rack. There's a plastic bag for socks and underwear.

She reenters momentarily.

"I'm Li," she smiles warmly.

I lie down on my stomach aboard the table.

Only a towel covers my rear end.

She begins kneading my legs, primarily my calves, and I'm beginning to relax. There's not a twitch in me, at the moment.

"You have anything special you'd like me to do? I mean, sore back, arms? Anything in particular?"

I'm wondering if this parlor offers more exotic therapy, but it doesn't seem quite sleazy enough, inside or out. And Li has no hint of an accent. She sounds totally Chicago, with the accompanying nasal way of sounding like she was born here in the city.

"No. I'm just a little bit tense," I tell her.

"I don't know anything about meditation or Zen. Sorry," she laughs. "But I'll try to loosen your muscles a bit. You're a little tight."

She has a table with an opening for my face so I can lie flat on my belly. She works my lower extremities, and then she works her way up to my neck and shoulders. Finally, she tells me to roll over onto my back.

She works my thighs and my feet while I'm on my back.

I feel the beginnings of an erection, and I try to divert my thoughts. She has the standard black hair that extends to her shoulders. Her face seems to be a mix of Asian-European. The Thai women have the reputation of being the loveliest women on their continent. Li confirms their reputation.

There's a slight rise against my towel.

But then I recall my shaking hand on the surgery table yesterday. What if it happens again? What if it continues to occur?

I'll be ruined.

My erection subsides.

She's wearing a plain white blouse and white pants and white running shoes. Nothing very erotic.

I close my eyes as she kneads my chest and I see myself springing up at her and grabbing her by her long black hair and throwing her down on the massage table. Somehow there's a knife in my right hand and that hand is steady and sure, and I slit her throat from left to right and the blood spurts out onto her pristine blouse and blooms like a scarlet flower. Then I slit open the blouse and I slice off the bra and I see her small black nipples and I slice one off as she clutches her ruined throat and the blood seeps out between her fingers with her black fingernails, and then I tear her open from her belly to her chin and I see her black eyes dimming as her hand falls away from her neck and I pull her wide open and see the organs and the vascular apparatus, and I begin cutting everything loose and then throwing all those human parts onto the floor on either side of the table...

I open my eyes and she's smiling.

"Don't be embarrassed. It happens all the time."

I look down and see the tip of the tent I've erected.

"It'll go away," she grins.

My face turns red, diverting the blood flow elsewhere, and said tent folds.

"You can get dressed now, Dr. Tracy."

I notice for the first time that she's wearing a wedding band on her left hand.

• • • •

I pay my bill to the Thai woman up front. She has the expected accent of someone her race. I wonder if she's related to Li, and then I walk out.

• • • •

Parisi is nowhere to be seen. He can't follow me twenty-four hours daily, naturally. I figure I should start paying attention to when he's behind me. He's got to go home some time, of course.

I feel a bit calmer, now. Her hands were very soothing. I suppose I expected her to do something about my hardon, but it never happened. I feel strangely positive about the fact that she didn't attend to it. It's refreshing to find that some people are still honest. And I left her a twenty-dollar tip to show my appreciation.

I remember my fantasy, however, about cutting Li asunder. The images are still playing in my head. Maybe they won't leave me for a while, yet.

And images seem to be all that is left to me, of late.

• • • • •

Again, there is no cop in my rear- view mirror. I decide to wander the Art Institute, which is no great distance from where I live. I suppose I could have walked there, but I feel tired, again. My hand doesn't tremble, though.

I park in the city lot, underground. There are all kinds of vehicles down inside, but I see no one else walking around.

There are numerous pillars I have to pass as I emerge up to the street, and I find myself worrying that someone will bolt out at me from behind one of them.

It never happens.

I'm coming apart. Unhinged. Paranoid. Name your own favorite psychosis.

The sunlight nearly blinds me. It's as if I emerged from Homer's netherworld, like Ulysses. Odysseus. He was condemned to the bowels of hell before the gods allowed him to rise to the land of the living.

As I walk on the sidewalk in the still-warm heat in late April, I have to shade my eyes from the glare. I left my sunglasses in the car. I have perfect vision and I don't need prescription lenses to be able to see clearly.

It's free admission today but they ask for a donation. I put twenty into the slot as I pass the donation box.

I seek out Titian and Michelangelo. I have no idea why religious artwork fascinates me, but it does. I enjoy seeing God and man touching fingertips. The renderings of hell interest me, as well. Mostly, these artists would rather paint scenes from paradise than recreate visions of the underworld.

Is my brother in hades? Is there really such a destination point after death? Certainly, if religion isn't simply myth, we are both destined to sniff sulphur. We might even be relegated to one of the lowest concentric rings of Dante's version of perpetual damnation. Patrick was not one to desire pain of his own. Inflicting misery is more like what we both sought. I still seek that infliction.

I walk to the cafeteria after meandering for an hour.

I see Parisi by himself sitting at a table at the farthest reaches of the café. But I order a coffee and sit down to drink the brew. I will not allow him to chase me away.

When I finally turn around to search him out, he's gone. I scan the room, but I cannot see him. I sit and finish the coffee. I was going to eat something, but I've lost my appetite.

My hand, my right hand, the hand I employ in surgery, is quivering again.

I will it to stop, to cease, and after a few moments, it appears to be steady and not shaking.

I vowed that I would hurt this policeman, his wife, and his partner, but it looks like my threats were hollow. Now they seem to rise inside me again. I cannot continue to let this man prevent me from living my life and following my profession. Parisi caused this uneasiness in me. He's the root of my unsteady right hand.

I should ignore him, but I cannot. Just when I think I'm free from him he appears magically, like some avenging spirit. He seeks justice for those whores, but he can't come up with anything damning against me.

And yet he tasks me. He heaps me.

I rise from my seat and head back out into the painful glare of the April afternoon.

CHAPTER THIRTY-FIVE

I meant to ask Sean if he was an art lover, but I don't want to push my luck. He's into religious paintings while I'm into the 'heathen' French Impressionists. It warms my heart to know we have such divergent tastes in art. He only saw me when I sat in the café, but I maintained an appropriate distance from him so Captain Jaworski doesn't endure yet another shit slide. I've tested his patience enough.

We're settled into the new house by now. It's May, and the temperatures have soared into the upper eighties. It's been an unnaturally warm spring, and the summer might be the big meltdown. California and the West will likely burn to the ground as they seem to, lately, and more frequently. The world seems bent on self-imploding. I don't have any historical perspective to explain anything other than to say that this globe has gone batshit nuts.

It's time to visit the fertility doctor again. Not my favorite thing to do. I wonder if he'll let me sneak Maria into the little room with the sample cup.

"Yeah, right. Handle your own business on this one, bub," she scoffs.

We're lying in bed, but we have to get up so I can make the appointment.

"You can give me a little help. Remember your vows?"

"I vowed to help you make a sample of your stuff?"

"It doesn't seem like much to ask, Maria."

"Make use of the video. Use your imagination."

"Never had a taste for auto-eroticism, baby."

"You must have done it when you were a kid."

"Nope. I compensated with wet dreams. Did a lot of cleaning up before my mother caught me dirtying the sheets."

"I didn't need that much information."

"Wet dreams bother you but whacking the mole doesn't?"

She slams her pillow in my face.

I lie back down.

"You're not worried about this test, are you?"

I look over at her.

"We'll live through whatever, Michael."

"This is a pretty large whatever."

"You're turning it into Godzilla."

"You're probably right."

"Look, I'm gonna love you no matter what. You know that going in, right?"

I turn and touch her face with my fingertips.

"I don't want you to be disappointed is all."

"Get up and get in the shower. We have to leave soon."

She insists on going with me. Her sign of wifely solidarity.

What always fascinates me is watching us get dressed. The last thing we do when we get ready for the day is strap on our weapons. I have the extra piece on my ankle. I tried to convince her to carry something small like a .32 snub-nosed in her purse, but all she would say is she'd think about it. If there were some way to carry the shotgun in a sling under her arm, I'd try to convince her to do it. But I know better.

We arrive fifteen minutes early to the doctor's. It's a rule, getting there fifteen minutes early, and you don't screw with these guys. It takes months just to get scheduled, normally, and we got lucky by getting an appointment right away, my first time.

The nurse gives me the usual instructions, but I don't know how she can keep a straight face. I go into the small room and I do what I'm required to do. Now I remember why I preferred wet dreams. If masturbation is so popular with men and women, I must have some kind of sex deficiency. I much prefer a partner being involved. I just never saw the attraction in abusing little Michael.

It takes about fifteen minutes of serious coaxing, but it finally happens and I take out the covered sample cup to the nurse. She smiles, and I think I want to run and hide. Maria sits there with a very shit-eaten grin on her lovely brown face.

"Did we have liftoff?"

"Yeah. It went spectacularly well."

I go in and talk to the doctor and he again tells me the results will be in in a few days. The suspense is going to kill me. Afghanistan didn't, but all this seems somehow worse than some Taliban raid.

• • • • •

I see him a week later, and the news is positive.

"Your count's up. It's getting near normal. See what I told you about the boxers? You are still wearing them, right?"

I feel a pinch between my legs. They seem to get balled up between my legs.

"I'm getting used to them, I guess."

"You can go back to the Jockeys when you have enough kids to wish we'd never met," he grins.

• • • • •

"I think it might be taking," she tells me after we exhaust each other again.

When I get my breath back, I roll over to her.

"Say again?"

"I missed my little friend."

"How can you call that your 'little friend'? How long?"

"A week."

"Did you do the at home test?"

"I'm a bit afraid to."

"This is no time for retreat. How 'bout it, Maria."

She grudgingly lifts herself off the sheets and walks into the bedroom bathroom.

She seems to be in there a long time.

Finally, she emerges, but I cannot read her face in this dim lighting.

"Houston, we have ignition," she smiles.

• • • • •

The gynecologist gets her in, two days later. She takes a thorough exam because the at-home thing is not always accurate.

"You done good," her doctor tells me.

She changed gynees because the first one moved to California. This one's name is Dr. Linda Sturgis. She's very young, and Maria likes her absolute bluntness.

"You're about seven weeks along," she says.

Now the cloudburst breaks completely, and Maria is weeping like I've never seen her bawl, and then I join in, and finally Sturgis has damp cheeks, too.

"Not very professional, huh?" the doctor apologizes.

I give her a hug. She responds back at me.

"I still get all crazy when I can tell someone the good news."

"We don't get much good news to spread in our line of work," I tell her.

Maria's told her we're homicide police.

"We're talking mid or late February, 2019," Dr. Sturgis tells us. "Give or take two weeks. Everything looks good. I'll give you a schedule of appointments...Don't listen to war stories from other women, Maria. The other doc told you that, right?"

"Yes."

"And don't read books. Talk to *me*."

We all three mop up our faces with the tissue the doctor shares with us, and then the appointment is over.

• • • • •

"So, what's your big news?" my dad asks after we walk into their house.

Red is in the kitchen, so we walk in to see her.

She takes a single look at Maria, and she starts to bawl.

"Congratulations!" Natalie manages to say before she bearhugs Maria and then me.

"Can I get in on this?" my father pleads.

He embraces me and then Maria.

"You're going to be a grandfather again," Maria gushes.

I haven't seen the likes of all these waterworks in a very long time.

My sister Mary has previously brought life into the world. But this time our children will carry the Parisi name. I'm secretly hoping we'll have a boy. Maria and I agreed on the way over if it was a boy it'd be Jimmy, and if its got indoor plumbing it'll be Natalie. Maria has acquired a new mom in her relationship with Red.

Natalie's prepared food for us. As soon as I called and told my dad we were on the way, he insisted we stay for dinner.

"Can't break out the champagne. You won't be drinking alcohol for a long while," he tells us.

"No great loss," I add.

"You don't need booze for a genuine celebration," he tells us.

We sit down at the kitchen table while Natalie grills some sirloin steaks on her electric grill.

I can still hear her sniffling a little bit.

• • • • •

After dinner, we go sit out in the yard at their new lawn table and chairs. We sit beneath an umbrella, and Red serves us some lemonade. It's so cold that my teeth ache.

I have to reach over and take Maria's hand.

"Don't make me start crying again," she scolds.

I squeeze her hand even tighter.

My father looks over at me from his side of the circular, metal table. Its surface is white, and the chairs have a matching color.

"Every day you were out of country I dreaded getting bad news from some sergeant standing at our door. Those were the longest years of my life," he informs me.

"I'm sorry," is all I can think to say.

"Don't be. I'm not asking for an apology. I'm very proud of you. I don't give a damn about the politics of that engagement in Afghanistan. I was simply relieved and happy you came back in one piece...I'm glad Iraq didn't tear you up, either, Maria."

She smiles at him.

"You are going somewhere with all this, Jimmy?" Natalie cracks.

"I just wanted to tell Michael I was happy when he got home and I didn't know how he could ever make me happier than when we met his flight at the airport...Until now. I don't know what you can do for an encore to top this one."

He raises his glass of lemonade.

"*Salud,* Michael...*Salud,* Maria. Natalie and I both love you very much."

I clink glasses with my father, and Maria does the same with her adopted mom, Natalie.

• • • • •

Going back to work seems to take the edge off a little, at least temporarily. I begin to worry about Maria's safety, again. Now there's a third party involved.

I go in to see Jaworski knowing that manpower is at a premium, but he surprises me and tells me he'll have patrol cars in our neighborhood do a few drive-bys when I'm not at home and when Maria's by herself.

"Tell them to knock real loud if they want in," I tell the Captain. "She's got a shotgun in the bedroom."

He looks up at me wearily from behind his desk.

"You really think this piece of shit'll reach out to you and Maria?"

"I was on scene at his murders. I think I know where he lives."

"You'd think he'd want to back off now that his brother took all the heat, at least in the papers."

"He doesn't think like anybody else."

"Yeah, I know, but you'd think he'd back off since he knows we haven't got a damn thing on him...Do we?"

"No. We do not."

He stares at his desk top.

"We can't surveil this prick endlessly, Michael. You know how it works."

"I know. I have a lot of other cases."

"Sure you do," he smiles.

"Thanks for the drive-bys. I appreciate it very much."

"Just common professional courtesy, kid...Don't go looking for trouble, Michael."

I show him a glimpse of teeth, and then I leave his office.

• • • • •

I have less and less time to follow this thug around. Sean Tracy must be aware that I'm more and more infrequently in his rear-view mirror. I follow him around once or twice a week, but I can't afford to do more.

The anxiety about knowing he's out there free is building inside me. It's like a festering blister that grows larger and larger and the pain from the swelling magnifies every day until it's almost unbearable.

I can't jeopardize the safety of my wife and our baby by bracing Sean Tracy again. Somehow, I simply have to be patient.

But I also have to actively pursue him. I can't just stalk this bastard.

So, I re-interview the desk clerks who worked the nights the murders were committed. I try to pressure them by looking at Tracy's photo. Sean is an identical twin, but he combs his hair differently from the way Patrick did. I notice the dissimilarity in the photos of them both.

And Patrick had a mole on his left cheekbone that is missing on Sean's face. Those subtle distinctions might not work well for a positive ID, but I'm frustrated, and I can't just do nothing. I have to rework it and rework it until something pops up that lands Sean Tracy in court and then in prison.

There has to be something.

There is no perfect crime. There are only missed details.

But what those missing details are, I can't imagine. I've exhausted every investigative move I can make.

Short of shooting Sean Tracy in his brain pan.

I don't need to remind myself that I'm not a criminal. I've killed men, but only in the line of duty, only when they were trying to do the same thing to me. It's the only way I can live with the killings I've done. Maybe I'm in for a surprise when I reach the gates and when the interview goes south on me and when I'm headed into the lower regions.

But I'm neglecting the fact that Sean Tracy knows I'm still out there, so the anxiety factor is working inside him even if he's really a true sociopath. He still has a very well-honed instinct for survival, and he knows I'm a threat to his survival. He can't be lying easy at night. He might just think I might step out of bounds and come right at him outside the sidelines of the law.

When I took him by the throat, he knew I meant what I said. Or at least he thought I *might*.

It might occur to him that I have something he does not.

A conscience.

For now, I'll have to be satisfied that Jaworski will have patrol cars keep an eye on Maria when I'm not around to do it. It'll have to do, I'm afraid.

If I kick open his front door and kill him I won't be any better than he is. And I'm going to be a father early in the New Year, I'm told. Fathers with families don't go around kicking down doors and liquidating people, even if they're very evil people.

I can't call in any favors from my father's Sicilian family in the Outfit. They'd own me if I did, and I'm still convinced that I'll never have anything to do with them. Not information, and certainly not setting up a whack. If anybody's going to pull the trigger on him, it won't be one of them.

And I've resigned myself to the fact that it won't be Michael Parisi.

CHAPTER THIRTY-SIX

I have to go through my brother Patrick's belongings which have been left to me in his will, his lawyer informs me on this late June, torrid afternoon. I drive over to his apartment, and the attorney, Michael Spence, lets me in. My brother never gave me a key, and I didn't give him one of my own, either.

He lets me in and then he shuts the door behind me and tells me to take all the time I need.

I can't see that I want to claim any of it. I have no need for furniture, and his artwork doesn't appeal to me. It's all cheap prints of artists I've never heard of. His music collection is sparse and uninteresting.

I look through his bedroom closet, and when I rummage through the shelves in that closet, I find a loaded .45 automatic handgun. I know it's loaded because I take out the clip, and it's full of bullets. I slap the clip back in, and I make sure the safety's on. I have nowhere to conceal the gun, so I stuff it in my waistband and I go into his bathroom and take out my shirt and hide the .45 with the tuck-in.

It's too hot to wear a jacket, so I'm hoping that the attorney won't spot the bulge at the small of my back.

After spending a dutiful thirty minutes perusing my brother's personal effects, I walk out of the apartment and make certain the lawyer never gets a view of my back. We ride the elevator down to the ground floor, and Spence walks away from me after wishing me well. He heads toward his car on the curb. I wait until he's taken off, and then I walk to my own vehicle, look up and down the street for any witnesses, I remove the heavy automatic from my waistband in back, and then I get into my car and hide the piece in my glove compartment.

• • • • •

I learned to shoot when I was in college. They offered a course in firearms safety, and I took it for the two hours credit as an elective. We spent several hours on the firing range, and I ranked as a marksman at the end of the course which was taught by a former Chicago policeman. I never bothered to buy a gun, and I haven't fired one since that course in college, but I'm still conversant with hand weapons. I know how to use the .45.

When I get the gun safely into my apartment, I place it in the night stand by my bed. I've had a few night sweats imagining that Parisi or some other cop might come bursting in here in the middle of the night and I conjure seeing them take out a pistol and firing it multiple times into my prone body.

I know that kind of thing doesn't happen in this country, but the way things are in the world now, who knows what might happen?

I try to feel sorrow for the loss of my brother, but it turns into rage, instead. Parisi put his hands on me more than once. He grabbed me by the throat and I truly believed he'd snap my windpipe. He has the training to do that kind of thing, I've found out. Big war hero. Elite soldier in the Army. A trained killer, assassin.

With a badge.

I could see the fury in his eyes. It was about his woman, that half breed brown bitch who he's now married to. I'd like to violate her the way he violated me. And he repeated his performance with my brother.

I've never felt much of a sibling-familial tie with Patrick. Now I just want to vent all this latest anger I've pent up because of his assault on both of us, but also because I'm boxed up and cannot release all this blood rage I used to release on the whores. It's literally arriving at the boiling point. There will be an explosion soon, and I'm getting less and less worried about the fallout from my eruption. Damn the consequences. I can't keep it under the lid much longer.

My life is nothing precious, anyway. The cop has taken everything away from me—my work, my vocation. And my profession is hurting, as well. I've had to stop twice in the last few weeks because the trembling in my right hand has made it impossible to operate. The quivering has become obvious to the nurses and the anesthesiologist, too, and I'm afraid they might report my handicap, and then my livelihood would cease for me. I've got money, but the work is the only thing that's prevented me from going nuclear, of late.

• • • • •

Barbara relents and allows me to see her again. But she will only meet me in a public place to see her. We meet at Fontaine's in the Loop. It's exclusive, as always, and obscenely expensive, even for me.

She looks lovely, but the first thing I think of as I sit opposite her in this swank bistro is to grab hold of the butter knife and stab her in the throat and then to start sawing away while all of the other patrons scream as Barbara's blood spurts all over this white, pristine table cloth.

The image evaporates, and I smile over at her as charmingly as I can.

We finish the pricey meal of lobster in silence. All I hear is the clinking of our silverware and the white noise of the nearby chatter from the surrounding tables.

She finally breaks her silence.

"Your brother murdered a woman. Isn't that right?"

Her face is stony and stern.

"My brother had mental issues."

"The paper says you might be related to someone who was suspected of being—"

"It's nonsense!"

My voice is much louder than I intended. It gathers the attention of the tables near us.

"Is it true?"

She remains resolutely calm.

"It's ridiculous. My father was a well-respected physician, and so was my grandfather. I don't know what triggered all that sensational claptrap, but I can guess. Like everything else, it's fake news."

"Can you understand my concern?"

"Not really," I tell her. "I told you my brother had psychiatric issues. They don't run in the family. No one else had his 'problem'."

I make certain my tone is far more subdued.

"You like rough sex."

"As do you," I remind her.

"Can't you understand why I'm anxious?"

"I can imagine your concern, but it doesn't mean it's reasonable, or that I deserve it. You enjoyed my being physical, as I recall."

"Some doctors think behavior is handed down from generation to generation. You might be predisposed to behave as your brother behaved."

I smile as casually as I can.

"Then why are you here, tonight, Barbara? If you fear me, you should never have allowed me to see you."

She stares at her coffee cup. Then she lifts it slowly to her lips and drinks the brew.

"Perhaps I should simply leave," I say.

But I don't rise.

"I suppose the papers tend to be sensationalist. It sells copy."

She smiles vaguely.

"But I need to think about whether or not we can go back to where we were."

I can feel the heat rising to my temples. The quivering begins again, and I find I have the butter knife clutched into my right fist. My knuckles are white, and now she's staring at that very hand, and her face has tightened and blanched.

I release the butter knife and smile at her.

"Why is your hand shaking, Sean?"

"Oh...I've had spasms, lately. Something to do with nerves, I suppose. I'll have to see a neurologist. It's affecting my work. I've had to call off surgeries, and I've been on hiatus for a while."

I try to smile reassuringly, but the fire has enflamed my cheeks.

"Your face is flushed," Barbara observes. "Are you ill?"

"No, no, I'm fine. It's just everything. My hand. Patrick's death and the murder of that woman. I'm a little distraught."

"Anyone would be."

I see an avenue, and I force my temperature to cool and I will my hand to cease trembling. And I succeed in both.

"I had feelings for you, Sean."

Her face softens.

When I don't want to fuck her, I want to tear her to shreds. I can't decide which it is, right now. The impulse vacillates with this woman. It would be very inconvenient to rip her from top to bottom and then dispose of the carnage. She's not a disposable whore. She's well known, has a wealthy family, and Barbara would certainly be missed if I cut her the way I want to.

And Parisi is aware I know her, that I used to see her.

Perhaps the sex, even if it weren't violent, might assuage my burgeoning anger.

The policeman assaulted me. He threatened me. He's preventing me from continuing to hunt. The blood won't let me be. It seethes inside me, it demands me to repeat it all again and again.

"I have feelings for you still," I tell her.

Then I reach across the table and take her hand, and she tightens her fingers upon me.

• • • • •

"I think we should avoid the maso thing," she smiles.

She lies beneath me on her bed. It didn't take very much convincing, I tell myself.

"It's fine with me."

When I thrust into her, her mouth gapes open into a perfect oval.

• • • • •

We lie silently together. Neither of us is asleep, but we're still.

"I have to get a drink," I tell her.

"There's bottled Perrier in the 'fridge," she smiles languidly.

"I'll be right back," I say as I rise.

"Hurry."

I walk into the kitchen and retrieve a bottle of her expensive water, and as soon as I have the cap off, the shaking returns to my hand and the water spills down onto my chin because I can't keep the damn thing in my mouth. The bottle drops onto the floor, but luckily it's plastic.

"What's wrong?" she asks from the bedroom.

"I just dropped the water. I'll clean it up. Be right there."

"Let it sit until morning. I'll take care of it."

"It's all right. My mess, so I'll clean it up."

She doesn't retort.

I leave the bottle and the puddle in place.

Both hands are shaking, now, and I can't stop them. Until I walk over to the counter and open the cutlery drawer. Barbara has some fine, long, sharp kitchen knives in here. Perfect for carving. I remove the longest blade with the serrated blade. I'm sure it would slice through beef as if it were butter.

The quivering has stopped, almost magically. I look toward the bedroom and I see her prone body waiting for me on the sheets. They're lavender colored, and I wonder what blood would look like on top of them. Maybe it'd appear black. I'm not sure.

I walk right through the mess on her tiled floor holding the butcher knife in my right, stilled hand. I proceed into the bedroom, and I see Barbara lying on her right side.

I hear her snoring gently.

Certainly, this is not what I expected to find. I expected to see her lying on her back with her legs spread wide in anticipation. Her arms would be raised, beckoning me to ram myself into her again. She'd be wet and hot and ready to rise up against me.

And she's snoring quietly, like a cat with its mouth opened lying on its back.

I can grab her by her hair and slit her throat and watch her attempt to cry out and see her eyes widen when she realizes her voice has been muted because her larynx is severed and then her light will dim and she will expire and then I can satisfy this insatiable desire to savage her.

I come closer to the bed. I'm standing right next to her.

I raise the kitchen blade with the sharp, serrated edge. It's above my right shoulder and there's a quick glint from the light behind me in the doorway that leads to the kitchen.

She stirs, and I lower the knife quickly and hide it behind me. I drop it, but it makes almost no sound as it hits her plush carpet.

Barbara opens her eyes and sees my blood-bloated member in front of her.

A drowsy smile crosses her face, and she moves more closely and makes my erect member disappear.

• • • • •

She finally falls off about 4:00 AM. When she does, I rise, walk around the king-sized bed and I retrieve the knife from the floor where I dropped it. I walk back into the kitchen and quietly open the drawer and replace it where I found it.

Then I go back into her bedroom, get my clothes on soundlessly, and leave before she reawakens.

• • • • •

The trembling won't stop. I should make an appointment, but when I take the .45 out of the nightstand, the thought occurs that I could turn the barrel toward my head and pull the trigger and end my misery.

I hold the piece against the left side of my head, but then I'm thinking I might pull the trigger and somehow graze my skull. Perhaps I should put the barrel in my mouth and remove all doubt about the outcome.

Parisi wins, then. He will have forced both of us to commit suicide. He'll win, if I pull this trigger and explode the back of my head against the wall behind me. *He'll win.*

My hand is still. I take the barrel out of my mouth and lay the piece on my mattress. The fury, the rage comes roaring back to life. I feel my cheeks burning with it.

He wins. I lose. Patrick loses. This man who battered me and threatened to kill me if I came close to his brown cunt *wins.*

I wait for the tremors to return, but they don't. Not as long as I'm looking at the weapon beside me. Then I know the only way for me to stop Parisi, to stop my palsy, is to kill him. I'll use this .45 on him, and then I'll kill his wife.

When they're not working, I assume they go out together. I'll have to watch them both, learn their schedules, their comings and goings. I have plenty of time now that I've left the practice.

I won't get away with it, certainly. I might kill them both, but I won't run free from the slayings. But I will get a small amount of satisfaction from seeing them both depart. I'll get that much before the rest of them find me and dispose of me.

I will not go to prison. I will not allow them to lock me up.

None of this would have been necessary if Patrick had not strangled that woman and thrown her body in the slough where it promptly arose like Lazarus in the bible. If he hadn't given himself away, I'd be free to prowl and do what I did best.

It's too late to mourn my personal losses. Parisi and his wife will be my final legacy, my small gesture to this filthy life, to this vile existence. I really couldn't cleanse these streets if I had multiple lifetimes to do it.

It comes down to him. He assaulted me, beat me. He stopped me from doing what I was destined to do.

The two of them will become my fond farewell to this bilious life, this putrid planet.

CHAPTER THIRTY-SEVEN

Maria and I get two free tickets for a private celebration of the Fourth of July. It's from the Police Benevolent Association, and it takes place on the 103rd floor of the Willis Tower, which used to be the Sears Tower. The big finale is stepping out onto the glass-enclosed addition that juts out from the building. It's totally see-through, top, bottom, and sides. Maria is a little hesitant to step out onto the clear floor and to look down 1353 feet to the street.

But the view of the fireworks will be spectacular, and there's no other visual experience like it, I'm told by those who've been there—other than looking out the window of a jet.

"I'm not crazy about heights," she tells me as we drive to the Wacker Drive location.

"I'm not crazy about fireworks," I return.

"Very funny, after what you went through not so long ago in that godforsaken hell hole."

"Afghanistan is very beautiful, actually, if you didn't have to walk through the place with a constantly constricted rectum."

"Spare me the details...Iraq, on the other hand, is no summer vacation spectacular. And I'm wondering if this is good for the baby, Michael."

"He won't see a thing, unless he's got a secret periscope."

She gives me the 'duh' look.

"Sean has gone underground," I say.

"Since when?"

"Since three days ago."

"Have you looked for him?"

"Have I ever stopped? There are six detectives trying to locate him. Not a sign. The apartment's vacated. But his clothes are still there. I got the landlord to let me in, illegally and without a warrant."

"Why he'd let you in, then?"

The Tower looms before us.

"Oh my God. Let's go home. I'll have a seizure up there," she warns.

"You won't have a seizure. The baby'll be fine. If it weren't safe, they wouldn't let anyone step out onto it. Stop being silly...The landlord reads the papers, too, and Dr. Tracy has become a persona non grata because of his genetic ties to dear brother and deceased twin, Patrick."

"But we haven't got anything on Sean."

"The landlord doesn't seem to care. He thinks whatever Patrick had runs in the clan."

We park out on the street and then we get out and Maria does her rubber-neck impression, looking straight up. The glass walk-out isn't even at the top of the building.

"Holy shit," she utters.

"Baby's listening. He hears everything we say."

"He might as well get used to it."

"Maybe it's a she. Our little princess in a white confirmation dress, with a veil."

She laughs.

"It's probably only my imagination," she says.

"What's that?"

"I had the feeling someone was following us."

"Did you see something?" I ask her.

"Not really. It's just that creepy feeling you get when you think there's someone following you. The hairs on your neck, and all that. It was just a feeling."

At least she's not peering upward anymore.

"Intuition. Or are you psychic?"

"Sean's still out there, and I'm not going to lose it until he's locked up in a very tight dungeon with a ball and a chain...And maybe one of those iron masks, too."

"Or a hockey mask?"

She slaps my arm, and then we walk inside along with several other cops that we recognize. I greet the ones I know, and they wave back.

There's a reception on the main floor before we go up for the view of the fireworks which don't begin until dark. They have a full bar and snacks, and there are perhaps fifty or sixty policemen and policewomen here in the ballroom. The event is to support the Benevolent Association which looks out for widows and disabled coppers. They do good work, and even if the tickets are free, I throw in fifty bucks for a donation at the jar by the door.

Maria and I stay off by ourselves by the entry to the ballroom. The sun is headed down, and the show will start at 8:30 or so.

"You really scared of heights?" I smile as I sip my beer.

She's nursing a glass of Diet Coke. No booze for nine months, of course.

"Not really. I'm more concerned about that plastic surgeon."

"He is supposedly and officially on vacation, but I heard from a cop who knows one of his nurses that he's having a few physical issues."

"Like what?" she asks.

"He's supposedly become a little unsteady during surgery. Had to back off on a few and could barely finish the job. Something to do with his hand, she said."

"Maybe it's his conscience," she adds.

"He hasn't got one. No problem."

"Maybe he developed one?" she poses.

"Not likely."

"No, but maybe it's like manifesting itself in his grip."

I have to smile at her.

"And you got your MD where?"

She swats my forearm again.

Then someone announces it's time to get to the elevators. The show begins shortly, and we have to walk out onto the glass in small groups, so everyone has to take their turn, ten or twelve at a time.

Maria keeps looking out at the assembled cops.

"We ought to be safe among all our brothers and sisters, no?" I grin at her.

But she's still straight-faced. She keeps looking for someone. Tracy, I'm guessing.

"You brought your pieces, right?" she asks as we move toward the elevators.

"Of course. Top and bottom, I'm heeled."

"I've got mine in my purse."

She carries a bag of considerable size and heft.

"Got any bricks in there, too?"

Another swat with her free hand.

We're in line for the first lifts. There are three, side by side by side. They should accommodate half of the crowd. We walk into the elevator at the far left. The thing moves without that nasty lurch upward. It rises smoothly, and the numbers of the floors fly by. It doesn't take long to arrive at the 103rd floor.

All of us walk out. I feel relieved. I've been semi-claustrophobic all my life, but I've been able to conceal it from the military and everyone else, including my wife. It's not so bad that I can't close the door in the john or in the bedroom, but I especially don't like being sealed up in an elevator. The way I learned to cloak my fear of enclosed spaces is to recite a decade of Hail Marys in my head when I'm stuck on one. I throw in an Our Father and a Glory Be if the ride up takes a while. If it's really long, like this one, I just start over again.

We wait outside the glass addition until the fireworks actually begin. It's not a long wait. Maria and I are with the first group.

"Ready?" I ask.

She nods. I can see the strain in her jaws.

We walk out onto the glass enclosure. I don't look down, at first, but when my eyes head to the street, I feel the rush of adrenalin.

Then Maria grips my hand like a sprung bear trap.

"Oww," I smile.

She loosens up just as the explosions begin over the Lake and we watch as the rockets go up and the colors stream out and fill the sky with light in a myriad of hues. I see her mouth open just a little, and then she turns and looks at me.

"Still scared?" I ask.

"Hell yes!"

Soon it's the turn of the small group behind us.

Maria is obviously relieved when she steps on what appears to be firmer ground—or firmer flooring that isn't transparent.

"I need to use the bathroom," she tells me.

"There's a john by the elevators," I remind her.

She walks toward the lav.

I walk over by the benches provided opposite the enclosure of glass. I can still see outside through the scattered observers.

Then I see him there, in the center of all of the cops, He's in the observation addition, glass beneath him and at his sides. The cops and their wives and husbands are walking out at me, but he stands in place.

I see his hand slowly rise, and I make out the weapon in his hand, and then someone screams "Gun!!"

Everyone scatters, and I roll off the bench and grab for the .38 Bulldog at my ankle and I tear it away from its Velcro enclosed ankle holster, and I hear the boom of the large caliber handgun, and the wall explodes above me, here on the floor. I scramble to my knees and he stands there yet, pointing the big gun at me, this time taking better aim.

The crowd has dispersed toward the elevators. Before some of the other cops can find their own weapons, I'm on my knees with the Bulldog raised and aimed.

I squeeze off one round, and the roar almost deafens me.

Sean Tracy flies backward toward the glass.

I fire another round and I hit him again dead center, but this time the bullet has passed through him and I can hear the shattering noise and the tinkling of shards as they fall, and then the entire plate behind him becomes a spider web of cracks.

But he stands there with two golf ball sized holes in his chest until the glass all descends and I hear the whoosh of suction behind him.

Only at the last do his eyes fall on mine, and he tries to raise the pistol at me one more time. I squeeze off another before he can fire at me, and this round tears into his throat and jerks him backward, out into the air.

There is no scream, only the sound of the air being sucked out of the enclosure.

Tracy disappears. Everyone surrounds me, but no one dares walking anywhere near the gigantic hole in the observation enclosure.

Several of the cops are holding their weapons, now, and they ask me if I'm hit. There's only the grapefruit sized hole in the wall behind me, and they help me to my feet.

"Jesus Christ!" one of them tells me. "Who the hell was *that?*"

I don't answer him, but I strap the .38 snub-nosed back to my ankle, and I walk toward the john that my wife is still using.

• • • • •

When we've finally descended back to the ground floor, she's still shaking. I take hold of her and walk her outside. The body is lying out on the street. A woman who Sean just missed in his free fall is standing at the front of her car and she's got her hands over her mouth in a soundless shriek. One of the cops who walked out with us goes to her and leads her to the sidewalk.

There are sirens screaming and lights swirling in just a few minutes. I take Maria back to our ride, and I drive us toward Headquarters.

Captain Jaworski will be making an unexpected trip downtown, tonight.

Just for me.

• • • • •

I'm riding a desk until the inquiry is completed, but the Captain tells me it's a no-brainer. He says I might get an award for bravery.

"Or some shit," he adds.

• • • • •

August is unbearable. The air conditioner barely keeps up with the sauna bath out of doors. It takes ten minutes to get the fog off the windshield when I drive to work, night or day.

Maria's pooch is gathering in front of her. She won't take maternity leave until the birth is imminent. Women aren't coddled during pregnancy anymore, she informs me.

Her sex drive has surprisingly increased, lately. I keep asking her if it's safe.

"Don't flatter yourself, big boy," she snorts at me when I ask.

We're going to need a new furnace and air conditioner soon. Ours is dated, inefficient.

We'll be flying on one salary soon, but I've got enough left over after the down payment and all the purchases for the new house. We'll be all right. I dread seeing the kid go to pre-care or nursery school or whatever they're calling the babysitter. I dread the separation, and I know it'll be worse for Maria.

But we'll get through it.

My white board lists six outstanding murders, but none of them are multiple homicides. Solo jobs, every one. I doubt it'll take more than a few days to change the red letters over to black. It won't take an arch sleuth to solve them, it doesn't look like. And Maria's got a full load of homicides to contend with and Ned Diamond is ready to retire.

Like Sonny and Cher sang: "The Beat Goes On".

• • • • •

"She was in the john the whole time," Jimmy Parisi laughs.

"A tender mercy."

"Yeah. Indeed...How's the inside of your own head, lately?"

We're sitting in the living room because it's too hot outside. The boil order is still in effect.

"I survived worse, I guess."

"Don't be so sure, tough guy. This is the world. The other wasn't."

"There it is," I murmur.

"So, they gave you a gold star on your report card," he smirks.

"They did. I'm going to take the sergeant's exam next winter."

"That should be easy compared to dealing with the twins."

I look over at my father as he sips his Old Style.

"I'm claustrophobic, Pa."

He watches me.

"I'm not happy in enclosed spaces."

"But you handled it, right?"

"I hide it. Yeah."

"I still have a night light. It drives Red nuts."

We laugh together.

"There's plenty to be frightened of in this world, Michael."

"You're the bravest man I know," I protest.

"I've bleached my share of brown stains in the laundry. Anyone who denies they're afraid most of the time is a certified idiot."

"Except for Audie Murphy," I remind him.

"Yeah, and that's only because he was absolutely nuts."

He raises his Old Style toward me, and then he burps very loudly and abruptly.

CHAPTER THIRTY-EIGHT

Evangeline Murphy, Chicago, 1892

He's a charmer, all right. Tells me I'm the prettiest girl he's seen since he landed here from all the way back in London, England. Tells me he's Irish, just like me, and both of us not long gone from County Cork. He tells me I remind him of the Emerald Isle, the Old Sod, and he makes me laugh.

Then I find out he's got the wrong impression of me. He thinks I'm a girl of the streets. Just because he saw me and three of my girlfriends come out of a saloon on south Halsted Street, he thinks I'm some kind of floozy, easy to be had. He doesn't show me the color of his money because I straighten him out right away. He takes me into a café down the street from that same saloon and tells me how awful lonely he is. And him just setting foot in this town not two weeks ago.

But I suppose his line of gob takes me over, because the next thing I know I'm at his apartment. Says it's just temporary until he can set himself up. A medical doctor, he says he is. I don't believe him until he shows me his bag with all those doctor tools inside it. Then he locates a piece of paper that shows me his degree from Dublin College.

I don't know what to say. He says he has to get 'certified' so he can practice his trade here in Chicago, but he says it's all political, you know. I think he's hiding something from me. I ain't stupid. I went to a little elementary school back in Ireland, but we all had to work, and then there weren't no work to be had, and I wound up here with all the other potato farmers that got rooted out by the famine and the troubles back home.

He don't much like the limeys, he says. He says they look down their noses at you like you was dirt beneath their feet. I don't like the look of anger in his eyes when he says those things, either, but then he turns that charm back on as if his face goes from cloud to sun in a second. It happens that fast.

I didn't mean to let him take advantage of me, but there was the drink and there was his handsome face that reminded me of home, and he had this look of need on him that I just couldn't fight against.

He keeps on inviting me over to his place and I don't mean to keep letting him do what he wants, but I can't seem to tell him no.

He looks at me real strange, from time to time. His eyes go empty and I get scared he might want to hurt me. But he never makes a move at me, that way. It's like he's fighting inside his head, but he never says what the fight's about. When I try to pry it out of him, he gets all lovey and I wind up giving myself away.

I was with no other, and that's the God's truth. I was going to save it up for the man who puts the ring on my finger, and I have gone to confession and told the priest how I've fallen but just to this one man and no one else. The priest scolds me and warns me about the fires of hell, and then I tell him he'll be there before I will and I never been to church since.

• • • • •

I see him for just short of two months. I'm up with him at his little slab of a flat, and then one night when I walk over on south Halsted to meet him again, he don't answer his door. I keep knocking until the landlord comes up behind me and tells me to get the hell out of his building and stop making the disturbance. He's gone, he tells me, and he don't know where to.

• • • • •

I get sick in the mornings and I'm scared and I don't know what to do. I can't afford a doctor, and I don't want to go to them free clinics. Butchers run 'em, my girlfriends tell me.

Then I hear from one of my girls that someone told her that he just threw out a shingle for his medical practice on Damen Avenue, not far from here. So I take the street car over to the address my pal found out for me, and I walk in all bold and ready to tell him off and say look what you done to me, my belly already beginning to sprout. But some nurse he hired tells me to sit and take my turn.

A half hour later, I get in to see him and I rag him proper about taking off on me. Here I am, a seamstress who works to make her daily bread, no whore am I! He tells me to lower my voice. Can you imagine?

He examines me, and it simmers me down. He tells me what I already know.

Then he sidles up to me real friendly and says he can help me.

I ask him how, and then he says it. He'll get rid of my problem. But I can't tell no one that he helped me.

I know it ain't right. It's illegal. And it'd send me to the place the priest said I was headed to.

I spit right in his eye. I swear I do! Then I walk out in a huff, out onto Damen Avenue.

Some charmer, he.

I'm keeping this baby. I don't care what anyone thinks, neither. I can't kill it. And it's not an *it.* It's a human creature, just like all the rest of us, and he or she'll be perfect. Perfect.

I'm betting it's going to be a boy. I can tell by the way he kicks. I take a bloody pounding inside, sometimes. Strong and healthy and fierce he is. And perhaps he'll become a doctor and then go back to him and spit in his charming eye. He'll make that charming Mick sorry he ever ditched the two of us. And my son'll be rich and I can give up the needle and live like a lady in one of those bleeding estates by the Lake.

I'll show you, my *charming* lad. I'll raise your son to be someone. Someone who wouldn't sneak off into the night and leave a girl, a girl who gave you her most precious possession. Me, pure and sweet and never done no sin like that before you came trotting along into my life.

Yes, I'll show you, *Francis Amjac.* I will. You just wait and see.

About the Author

Thomas Laird was born in Kansas City, Missouri, in 1947. He grew up in Chicago, Illinois, and was educated in the public schools. He graduated from Northern Illinois University with a BA in English in 1971.

He moved to Peoria, Illinois in 1973 and has taught English and Creative Writing at Spalding High School and Notre Dame High School for 43 years. Laird finished his Master's in English at Bradley University (December 2010), and taught composition at Bradley University for four years.

His first story was published in the *Pacific Sun Literary Quarterly* in 1976, and he subsequently published several other stories in literary journals around the country. *Blue Color & Other Stories*, a collection of short fiction, was published by the *Dan River Press* in Maine in 1994. The two printings sold out. *Cutter* (2001), his first novel, was published by Constable & Robinson in London, England, and by Carroll & Graf in New York. *Season of the Assassin* (2003) and *Black Dog* (2004) were published by the same houses, and all three were translated into Czech by Domino Publishers in the Czech Republic. *Season of the Assassin* was also published in Dutch in the Netherlands. Domino published *Voices of the Dead* in 2006. *The Underground Detective*, Laird's fifth novel, was published by Parkgate/Dionysus on April 14, 2012. *Desert Storm Heart* was published by Parkgate in 2013, and the ebooks of *Underground* and *Desert* came out in 2013-2014. Recent publications are: *The Ruin of Souls* (Ecanus, April 2015), and from Endeavour Press in London, England, in 2015-2016:

The Long Midnight, *My Brother's Keeper*, *Healer*, *Boats Against the Current* (recently a Number 1 Bestseller on Amazon Kindle), *In the Forests of the Night*, *The Last Sleep*, and *Black Widower*. *Cutter*, *Season of the Assasin*, and *Black Dog* were all reprinted in ebook and in paperback. All the Endeavour Press books are available in paperback and ebook.

Laird lives with his wife, Marsha, and Mick the Australian shepherd, Tar the Amazon yellow nape parrot, and with Jimmy the cat near Germantown Hills, Illinois.

Note from the Author

Word-of-mouth is crucial for any author to succeed. If you enjoyed *Child of the Night*, please leave a review online—anywhere you are able. Even if it's just a sentence or two. It would make all the difference and would be very much appreciated.

Thanks!
Thomas Laird